CLOSE ENCOUNTER

O'Fallon could make out a thin, metallic ring around the UFO's perimeter, and on the edge of this rim, varicolored lights flashed off and on—purple, neon blue-green, electric yellow, the strangest orange he had ever seen. On the underside of the craft, a blue-white beam of light flicked on like lightning striking the ground, and stayed on, bright as a welder's torch. The beam swung until it pointed at the Cadillac, and light flowed into the car.

As the size of the craft dawned on him, O'Fallon's mouth opened in a silent gasp as he squinted against the brightness. He wanted a weapon at this instant—badly. He wanted to get his hands on the director of Air Force Intelligence and the other generals who had given a classified briefing two months ago on the non-existence of UFO's.

BEING

Michael Redfinn

LEISURE BOOKS 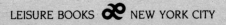 NEW YORK CITY

Dedication to the Reader:
Come in the narrow gate,
Swinging open,
Play in the sun-speckled yard,
Until home we must go.
—The Author

"Let us then take our compass; we
are something, and we are not
everything. The nature of our
existence hides from us the knowledge
of first beginnings which are born
of the Nothing; and the littleness
of our being conceals from us the
sight of the Infinite.
—from Pensées No. 72
Blaise Pascal

A LEISURE BOOK

Published by

Dorchester Publishing Co., Inc.
6 East 39th Street
New York, NY 10016

Printed in the United States of America

PROLOGUE - Part I: UFOs

Vicinity Newport News, Virginia
July 14, 1952
8100 feet

The night was sharply clear in all directions. First Officer William Nash and Second Officer Bill Fortenberry were piloting the Pan American DC-4 over Chesapeake Bay en route from New York to Miami. Visibility seemed unlimited. The only clouds were thin cirrus, three-tenths, at 20,000 feet, but they were practically invisible to the pilots. In the early evening darkness the two men could see the distant lights of Norfolk, luminescent with electric pulsings, flickering like candles. A little farther west, the lights of Newport news glimmered with a galaxy of colors. At 9:13, as Nash was pointing out various landmarks to Fortenberry through the V-shaped front windshield, a brilliance appeared ahead, low and to their right.

"What the hell is that?" remarked Fortenberry. Both pilots had seen the light together, at practically the same instant. And in another instant the men perceived that it consisted of six red objects streaking toward them at tremendous speed. The intense brilliance of the objects startled them. They radiated a red-orange glow with amber tinges and the glow had *depth*, like hot coals, and a brightness twenty times that of the city lights of Norfolk, over which the formation quickly passed. Each of the unknown craft had circular shapes with well-defined edges, not phosphorescent or nebulous, and the red-orange color was uniformly illuminating their upper surfaces. They held an in-line formation as they flew, with the lead object low, almost on the ground, it seemed, and the other objects in a stepped-up echelon.

Nash got up from the left seat and followed the objects with his eyes as he made his way toward the windshields on the right. Halfway to the big Pan Am plane, across the blackened waters of

Chesapeake Bay, the front disc abruptly slowed. The next two discs overshot the lead craft, sliding back and forth over each other as though the lead object had slowed too suddenly. *Loused up the formation*, thought Fortenberry. By the time Nash reached the right main windshield, the high-speed formation had almost reached them, a mile below the DC-4. The objects each looked big as the wingspan of a DC-3. *They're going to pass under us*, he thought.

Suddenly their glow diminished and the six coin-shaped objects flipped up on edge like a dazzling row of checkers. With that, they instantaneously reversed course, sliding past one another until they flattened out in formation and streaked through the sky in almost the opposite direction to their initial approach. Immediately, two new objects shot into the pilots' view from beneath the airliner's right wing, both bigger and brighter— perhaps higher than the others. The new pair of objects dived at the rear of the original six on an intercept heading.

The front six blinked out completely and a scant second later the other two blinked out. Then, all eight in line, they lit up and reappeared, heading west at high speed. Still low, they streaked across the western edge of Newport News and then the formation angled upward sharply in a breathtaking change of direction. As they climbed, they flew with odd, jumpy movements, bobbing up and down in the chainlike formation, slanted upward in a line 45 degrees from straight-up. At some extreme altitude the lights from the objects blinked out—not all at once, but separately, in a random, irregular order.

The pilots both finished their observations of the unknown craft twelve seconds after it had all begun, looking through the right side window into the ebony sky. They had open-mouthed, serious expressions on their faces by now. Nash returned to the left seat and they looked out the windscreens all around them to see if there was anything else out there, but there were no more unknowns. They both knew the fiery objects had been moving in excess of 10,000 miles per hour. And thus it dawned on them that they had witnessed some advanced aircraft, controlled by an alien intelligence they could only wonder about. A leading scientist of his day said later that the pilots had seen reflections—maybe a stewardess taking long, nervous drags from a cigarette seen in the darkened windshield, maybe searchlights reflecting off hoary layers of mist. Actually, a specter was haunting the earth—the specter of UFOs.

Prologue - Part II:
The Overshadowing

San Francisco, California
Summer, 1967

The crowd covered the sidewalks and shuffled along with slow, undeliberate movement. There was a lot of noise in the crowd and the streams of cars made noise in the streets that ran along the intersection of Haight and Ashbury, and beyond that, there was the murmuring noise of the city.

"This country doesn't need weapons," the dirty looking boy was telling the radio news reporter. Above them, the sun shone through the light-gray sky like a giant frosted light bulb veiled by overhanging mist. Behind them on the corner was the Unique Men's Shop with SALE signs plastered in the glass windows. "We just use 'em to stomp some poor peasants in Vietnam. We should get the hell outta there—leave those people alone so they can kinda be free to determine their own damn destiny—you see what I'm layin' on you?" The young man who spoke had stringy blond hair flowing out of his head like a fountain of fireworks at a professional show on the Fourth of July. He wore a purple-and-red-striped shirt and colored lines across his cheeks like Indian war paint. "You dig it, lady?" he added authoritatively.

Another unkempt looking older man interrupted by putting his V-shaped fingers in the woman reporter's face and yelling, "Ban the bomb!" His other arm was extended over and around the neck of a cold-eyed girl in her late teens with buck teeth, a huge, watermelon-sized-belly and mouse-colored, shaggy, long hair.

"We'll have to let the listeners decide," the reporter said into the microphone on top of what the last man had yelled. "Don't forget the Vietnam call-in poll that starts at nine tonight. This is Cynthia Quanta, live, reporting from Haight-Asbury. Back to the station." The thin-lipped newswoman thanked the first boy for the interview and handed her microphone to a man beside her. They got back in the white-paneled truck and drove away from the curb.

The van took them back to the small AM radio station and Cynthia finished up there, then waited until it was eight o'clock and her shift was over. She went to the "body exchanges" in the financial district of downtown and drank cocktails and ate large butterfly shrimp off the dark trays that the waitress brought around. She didn't meet anyone new there and so at twenty till twelve she left and took the Golden Gate Bridge to Sausalito. She drove past the lonely, closed shops for a while then drove out toward the Muir Woods, the pleasant sound of the Mustang GT exhausts stroking the air. Fifteen minutes out of town, she caught the time on the rally-pack clock and veered sharply onto a narrow road so she could turn around. It was just when she slipped the gear shift into reverse that the engine quit running. She tried to restart and pumped the gas until the cranking of the 289 High Output engine slowed to a grunting and a heavy petroleum smell flooded the air around her. Then, even the grunt wouldn't come.

There were lights on a hillside that lay in front of her in the darkness, so she got out and left the car gleaming faintly in the starlight. After moving on foot 50 or 60 yards toward the lights she paused and looked up to find the North Star. When she had found it and confirmed the direction of the distant lights as northeast she continued on. The woman could hear the drone of crickets and a few night birds call from around her. But after a few minutes it grew silent in all directions and she became aware of an odd, sharp odor. And it seemed like it was warmer then it had been before, though hardly noticeable, like walking by the brick building next to the station on a summer evening after the sun had set. She paid no attention to these sensations but, since it didn't look like five minutes of walking had put her much closer to the hilly lights, she checked the sky again to make sure she was still heading in the right direction. But the stars were gone and the night seemed to instantly heat up to where it was hard to breathe.

The sky was black as coal above her—and then she saw why. The stars were being blotted out by a round dark shape about three car lengths up. She had the feeling of being watched and it paralyzed her for a minute, it was so overpowering. She managed to step back a few paces until she caught sight of the edge of the object silhouetted against the sky. The air was cooler, less oppressive when she did that, and it helped her concentrate more clearly on what she was seeing.

She could see an edge on the object and, right above that there seemed to be tubular, protruding constructions that faintly reflected the starlight. A fury came up inside her. No sooner did she get this feeling than she noticed shadows move high along the curved side of the object. Above her, where she saw the shadows move, she heard a weird crackling noise and then a high-pitched whine. She froze where she stood as she watched a small ball of orange fire come out of the side of the UFO and begin to drift toward her. As it floated down it expanded into a cloud of orange mist. The woman let out a little shrill cry like a wounded bird as she crossed her arms over her face. When the mist enveloped her she lost consciousness and slumped to the ground.

1

A Desert Mystery Begins
May 3, 1998
East of Needles, California

It was just at the hour that separates one day from another, when the stars silently blaze. There was a glow up ahead of Jack O'Fallon. An oddly bright, red island of light in the sky had just popped onto the edge of his perceptions, like a concentration of fireflies glimpsed down a country roadway on a midsummer evening. As he steered the four-month-old black Cadillac through the desert night, a desolate part of east California flattened out on both sides of the road like the landscape from some eerie, alien planet. Around him the terrain was dark—scantily clad in a veil of starlight. *What the hell is that*? he thought to himself, eyeing the weird glow and tightening his grip around the pleasantly abrasive, black plastic steering wheel. The man had been mesmerized by the long, narrow highway rolling montonously under his automobile a moment ago, but in a scant millisecond that spell had been broken. In fact, because of the things that were about to come upon him, O'Fallon would never be hypnotized by a hurtling, darkened road again.

The stimulus that had halted the fixation of his eyes upon white lines darting endlessly along the continuous asphalt flow, was the most remarkable luminescence he had ever seen in the night sky. It was so different it could have never been mistaken for anything normal. It had appeared above the distant horizon slightly to his left, seeming merely to rise up from where the rounded surface of the earth slips from the curiosity of human sight. At that distance it was difficult for the man to make out a shape behind the light, even with his eyes squinted. But it resembled a grandoise flying amoeba as much as anything. There were curious, changing patterns inside its nebulous, ghostily perimeter. *Glowing red protoplasm* came to his mind as he watched the orb of glowing jelly move from his left toward the road. As it did that, it grew larger, eating up more of the blackness beyond the beams from the car's triangular headlights, out in the distance where the road seemed to drop off the edge of the earth.

O'Fallon's sweaty pants squeaked across the leather seat as he got the hunch out of his back and laid a finger on one of the power seat-control buttons, bringing the seat-back toward the vertical with a motorized whir, gathering his alertness from where it had been in the outback of his mind. The speed control on the supercharged Cadillac two-seater kept the car cruising at a steady 65 as the man rode toward the glow, increasingly fascinated.

How absurdly ironic it would be if it turned out this was a UFO, he thought. Surely they would have briefed him in Washington if the military had secret devices it was testing in public airspace over California; he had served on the Senate Armed Services Committee for years. He certainly didn't want any controversy over military escapades in his home state when he geared up to win the Democratic nomination for the top spot on the ticket, two years down the road.

As the car closed on the unknown light, O'Fallon gradually discerned an oval shape behind the glow. A craft of some kind seemed to be drifting his way, 20 or 30 miles ahead, stalking the air above the road. Looming larger, it looked like a football-shaped machine descending toward him, amid a glowing red haze, through the pitch-black night. The hair at the base of his neck tingled, then a chill ran down his spine, making it feel like an electrified wire. The UFO came on, and O'Fallon's mouth gaped open slowly, stiffly, almost as if it were being pried open by the sight of the unearthly aeroform's approach. He craned forward to get a better look.

Instantly the atmosphere in the car turned warm and thin; he had trouble breathing. His lungs felt like lead balloons. He gulped some air, then swallowed hard, spreading a bitter copper taste over the slick curves inside his mouth. Fear squeezed at him like invisible blackness clutching at his consciousness. He squinted as a flash of pain like hot acid poured on an open wound came from his belt-hugging gut where a doctor at Walter Reed had found an ulcer last year.

Thoughts assaulted the main isle of his brain and circled like dust devils twisting above a heated plain. The main one landed ke a bomb: *Why in the hell aren't there any other cars on this highway?* He verted his eyes and peeked in the rear-view mirror, but it was all lackness in back of the sloping line of the trunk lid beyond where he taillights spewed red onto the roadway. Then the other *whys* lammed into his thought stream as if to clamor that they had een held back long enough: *Why* the hell had he sent his wife on head; *why* had he decided to take a week and drive across from Vashington, alone; *why* hadn't he flown as he always did. Of ourse it had seemed a good idea at the time—to take his time, ee the out-of-the-way places, maybe for the last time for a long me. If he made it to the Presidency, he might go two terms. But ow the thought kept coming back at him as he turned this all over his mind and looked at it: *Why the hell am I here in the middle of this arren stretch of desert, alone . . . without an escort!*

O'Fallon was not one of those men who pause much and so he eached between the expensive seats, flipped open a padded over, and uncradled a thin, red phone. He wrapped his meaty ght hand around it, poked a single number on the lighted eyboard, then slid the earpiece to his ear. The phone let out a nelody of beeps as the 8666 microprocessor dialed his San Diego home. A burst of deafening static hit him in the ear. He erked the phone away, using the distance to attenuate the bsurdly loud noise that hissed at him like an electrical storm on M radio. He poked another of the dial's buttons and listened to he beeps as the phone rang his Washington office. He held the arpiece at a more respectful distance this time as the beeps topped and the static came on: more amplified seashell hissing. Hello, this is Senator O'Fallon." He tried a loud, public-speaking oice on the plastic-phone holes. Nothing came back but jagged udio haze. "What the hell can cut off satellite phones?" he mut- ered to himself, recradled the phone, and stared with wonder at he alien object as it swung down over the highway and came irectly at him. The tachometer lights went to zero and he knew he engine had died.

He pumped then at the brakes; nothing happened—no esponse! He braced himself against the steering wheel and ammed down on the brake pedal as hard as he could, over and ver, but the Cadillac kept moving at the same absurd speed. *Now e damn brakes are screwed up,* he thought, *or maybe it's the cruise-control.* Ie wanted this to be a dream and he wanted to wake up now in he bedroom of his San Diego home, climb out of bed, and get a glass of water. But he was in this hunk of metal headed toward some flashing, flying thing and he was more awake than he had ever been in his life.

To add to his immediate distress, the Cadillac's dashboard lights flickered off and on and then blinked out. The headlights faded next, and the light that had come out of them failed. Jack O'Fallon rammed the HEAD LAMP switch back and forth like a crazy man for a couple of frantic seconds, but the power was gone from the car and he knew it had been sucked away by that glowing spectacle in the sky. He knew it! And the road out in front of him was lighting up from the craft's blood-crimson light and the distant mountains were black forms with the red road winding into them like a fluorescent serpent.

Amid the dreadful silence in the car, the man became aware of a new sound—a swishing, liquid noise, pulsating like a mechanical wristwatch filled with water. He knew it had to be the artificial valve in his heart, pounding with hideous loudness in the absurd silence, like a Rolex failing the 50-fathom leak test. In rhythm with the swishings, he could feel his heart beat against his ribs like an enormous parasite. *How could it be*? he asked himself, knowing the Cadillac's engine was silent; and yet he was being tugged toward the UFO as it dived toward the Cadillac, displaying an oddly synchronized, every changing luminosity as it descended. By now O'Fallon could make out a thin, metallic ring around the UFO's perimeter, and on the edge of this rim, varied colored lights scintillated off and on—purples, neon blue-green, electric yellow, the strangest orange he had ever seen. On the underside of the craft, a blue-white beam of light flicked on like lightning striking the ground and stayed on, bright as a welder's torch. The beam swung until it pointed at the Cadillac, and light flowed into the car like sunbeams into a silver cloud.

As the size of the craft dawned on him, O'Fallon's mouth froze like a knothole in petrified wood, open in a silent gasp as he squinted against the brightness. He wanted a weapon at this instant—badly. He wanted to get hold of the director of Air Force Intelligence and the other generals who had given a classified briefing two months ago on the non-existence of UFOs.

Now the object was close, looming in front of the speeding Cadillac, big as a $700,000 two-story house. Gracefully, descended the last few hundred yards to eye level, switched on the blinding beam of light, and hovered over the road under which the senator would pass. O'Fallon jammed his foot frantically against the brake pedal once more—no effect. He tried to turn the steering wheel against the unseen force—nothing. The unidentified craft was almost on top of him now and the inside of the car was bathed in a reddish-orange light that gave him pinpricks at the back of his eyes.

The instant before O'Fallon would have passed under the huge, glowing machine, the Cadillac swerved right and headed down the shoulder of the highway, then shuddered to a halt. His body jerked forward sharply, digging the shoulder harness into his chest. He unlatched the restraint, rubbing his chest unconsciously while he fixed his gaze on the spears of UFO-light radiating toward him in a cone of dazzling bombardment.

On the other side of the windshield, the strange machine was rocking in the air like a rowboat on choppy water, as if it were unstable being this close to the earth. The thought came back at him again: *These damn things aren't supposed to exist.* As that absurdly immaterial thought died, the light radiating from the skin of the craft abruptly dimmed and he could discern faintly illuminated square panels above the central rim; the source of the remaining glow seemed to be a fluorescent gas that issued from small pipes along the rim. The center of the machine was rotating lazily and the whole thing reminded him a little of a giant's gyroscopic top, spinning on its axis in the middle of the air, throwing off luminous gases like pinwheel streamers as it turned. Like magnetic smoke, the gas drifted toward the shining Cadillac.

Without warning, the rim stopped turning and then the desert silence was broken by a grinding, whining sound—the kind big electrical machinery makes. It reminded O'Fallon of the whirring his old Buick Centurion had made in the seventies when he used to put the white canvas convertible top up and down. Then a square of dusty yellow light appeared on the left side of the craft, as if a door had opened. The whirring sound faded and shadows began flickering within the yellow light that showed through the opening. A sharp metallic taste permeated O'Fallon's mouth as he continued to gaze in awe at the floating machine.

Then he saw it: a dwarfish, alien creature appeared in the square of light. The thing was dressed in dark clothing and it reflected the yellow glow as if the clothing were made of black, mirrored metal.

"What's that?" asked O'Fallon aloud.

The creature dived out of the craft's opening and slowly floated through the glowing smoke toward the car. Then another of the creatures appeared in the opening; and then it dived out. And then another. As O'Fallon watched the grotesque beings come down at him, some previously unknown connection between his heart and throat tightened and ached. As ghostly apparitions descended through the glowing mist, he thought crazily of slow-motion movies depicting sky-divers who seem to float slowly down through invisible air. He looked around about him now and realized that the green mist had clotted around the outside of the Cadillac. And, all the while, the alien forms like miniature cadavers, approached. *Fog came in on cat feet in a Sandburg poem*, the curiously inappropriate thought flashed through his mind. *Now it was coming in on UFO feet—alien being feet.*

"What's that?" he muttered again in a quivering, anxious voice; a thin veil seemed to hang before his mental vision; his thinking seemed to slow. Ponderously, he tried to speed up his thinking, but there were more of these shiny obsidian creatures floating down through the strange mist and then they were at the car, grabbing at its doors. He punched the power-lock button like a man possessed. *Where in the hell are the cops when you need them* raced through his mind. He turned to check the lock on the other side of the car. The door was already opening and fog was seeping in, reaching out at him like tentacles from a ghostly octopus.

"Oh no!" he said in a high-pitched voice. He could feel his heart pounding, fast and strange like some piece of alien machinery gone berserk. The beating was fierce and it almost seemed he could hear the ebb and flow of his blood through the hidden valves and corridors in his heart as he saw the first of the creatures appear around the edge of the door. The misty smoke was in the car now and O'Fallon could see the nearest of the creatures looking at him through the thin, moving vapor. The only sign of life on its face was contained in its monstrous eyes, fixed on him, dully glistening in the light from the hovering craft, and O'Fallon could see the eyes stretch grotesquely around the sides of its head. As the creature leaned in the doorway, the man glimpsed insignia on its shoulders and wide straps slanting down but the smoke was dense and he couldn't make the insignia out.

He picked a glass soft-drink bottle up off the seat and raised it in self-defense. O'Fallon's mouth froze like an enlarged Cheerio and fear etched its furrows across his dry, lined face. His eyes, with an expression in them like that of a startled bird, seemed to bulge out to meet the menace that was now upon him. The senator spotted a rod the size of a fountain pen in a second creature's hand and then a pencil-lead-thin beam of violet light flashed through the front seat mist and struck O'Fallon in the head. He felt an electric jolt that seemed to vibrate his skull for an instant, heard a murmuring buzz, then blackness expanded against the light and he lost consciousness.

The next thing O'Fallon knew he was lying on a cold, hard slab in a round, lighted room. A great wave of heat passed over his face. He rotated his eyes in their sockets and saw the creatures nearby, then tried to raise himself up from the slab, but his body felt weak and numb. He couldn't even raise his head. As he tried to gather his thoughts, words came into his mind: "Are you a resident of this sector?"

"No," he managed to answer. The word had come out slowly and had sounded slurred. He exhaled a long, deep breath.

"You have slept a short time," he heard them say in his mind. I *sure as hell want to sleep now*, his own thought answered.

"Where do you think you are?" This question popped open in his brain like fireworks exploding and it hurt, sharp as a knife point, at the base of the skull.

"I have to . . ." he said weakly and then grunted as he lifted up on one wobbly elbow. His body felt sluggish and unresponsive, as if he were lying in a vat of molasses. He wheeled his head slowly leftward until his gaze met their ghastly faces, staring down at him.

"Sonavabitch," he mumbled under his breath as horror took over his mind: *Those eyes! Those horrible staring eyes, dark and liquid and big like a cow's eyes.*

The creatures had pear-shaped, grayish craniums with mouths and noses that were merely slits in their hairless, burlaplike skin. O'Fallon felt like he had been drugged, but he still wanted to jump out of his skin. His body felt like a useless instrument now. There were four of *them* and he wanted to get away from them—leave his body and flee. There was something dreadful and utterly sinister about these alien beings with their bulging, wraparound eyes and their domed, rigid heads.

Here is what O'Fallon thought next: *This is not like being in a movie theater when a monster from outer space is up on the silver screen and I'm in my seat eating popcorn. These damn things are here, staring at me with those cow eyes.* And while he thought that, he could see the creatures' eyes shift in the bright, white light as they approached.

O'Fallon glanced around desperately like a cornered animal. Everything in the room was one piece without seams—the walls, the consoles, the instruments he saw on a table next to him. Everything blended dully into everything else in the white light that came from the curved walls of the room, which glowed like electric mother-of-pearl. There was a sterile-looking white surface higher than the slab, close on his right, supported by one central leg; he could see where the pillar joined the bottom of the table—there were no screws, bolts, or seams. The leg simply seemed to grow out of the table like a natural appendage.

The creatures on his left edged closer, soundlessly, like dreams. "You can't get away with this—stay away from me!" screamed O'Fallon. One of the creatures had a small black box that flashed with varicolored pinpoints of light. As the alien operated a lever on the box, yellow mist wafted from the ceiling like smoke, curling in heavy wisps, and when O'Fallon inhaled its sour, pungent odor it made his head feel lighter than air and he blacked out again. The creatures gathered in a semi-circle around the upper part of the man's unconscious body. They operated on the man with peculiar-looking, transparent instruments that they retrieved from the work surfaces close to the slab, and the creature with the black box passed it slowly over the man's cranium, seemingly intent on the changing colors and patterns of flashes the box made as it moved.

One of the creatures carefully retrieved a tool that resembled a long, crystalline knitting needle and attached a tiny device the size of an early June pea to its tip. The new end of the tool resembled a miniature sputnik—gray and round with spiked, right-angled antennae protruding at regular intervals.

Meanwhile, a second creature had inserted a transparent tube up one of O'Fallon's nostrils, and a colorless liquid moved through the tube. Another of the creatures skillfully attached a cylinder to the human's cranium above the left frontal lobe. The cylinder flashed with bright prismatic lights. Overall, the team of creatures seemed to perform the complex procedure with great speed and expertise, like a well-practiced human surgical team that had done the same operation hundreds of times before. Then the creature holding the newly tipped rod inserted it up O'Fallon's free nostril, parallel to the tube of liquid, and the length of the needle would have put the tip well into the man's brain.

The creature depressed a small protrusion at the base of the tool and the crystal needle glowed momentarily with an intense blue light that gave the alien's hand a stark appearance, illuminating the long, clawlike fingers and shiny skin, giving it an uncanny resemblance to a fake plastic monster hand one might find at the last of the west-coast novelty stores. After another moment the needle dimmed and the creature slowly withdrew it from the man's nostril. The tiny device that had been on the tip of the instrument had vanished.

Above the table on the right side of the slab there were viewing screens that had complex symbols changing and flickering with different colors, and when O'Fallon woke up he noticed them for the first time. With his fear apparently gone, he became intrigued by the flashing symbols and the patterns of changing lights. He could feel a sharply throbbing pain in his head, but a numbness that permeated his mind and body made the pain seem small and faraway. With some effort, he propped himself up on one elbow and pointed toward the viewing screens. It almost looked as if he were trying to touch the screens with a weak, grasping reach.

"What do these symbols mean?" He asked the creature nearest him. His lips felt dry as dead leaves.

The creature O'Fallon had fixed his gaze on, whom he *knew* somehow to be the leader, came a step closer, then communicated the response silently to his mind: "If you could understand these symbols, you could rule the galaxy."

"Where do you come from?" asked O'Fallon, cool as an iced cucumber.

"A realm within a distant galaxy that we will not presently reveal. You will be given that revelation when we deem it appropriate. We will illuminate all the unclarities soon."

"Why do you visit us?" he asked, and then moved his lips over one another to moisten them. He felt tremendous thirst, not only in his mouth but down in the tunnel of his throat, which felt like it was sticking together.

"We travel here to protect your race from atomic destruction. We are creatures of compassion. You have evolved from the seas. Now you must evolve toward the stars. We are the overlords—the watchers." The creature's strange, dark eyes glittered in the harsh light. Its face was rough and rigid, like a mask. O'Fallon would never forget those deep-set, hypnotic eyes—it was torturous to look at them. The fact that he was conversing calmly with this alien life form made him feel like he was insane. He knew how insanity must feel now.

The leader began again, talking into the man's mind: "Our hour grows near once more. We will make ourselves known as we have in the most ancient of days. You will be a part of it. Most humans are foolish and have not the vision to be a part of our contact. You will help take the message to the masses of earth creatures. Before long, your planet's creatures will be praising the reality of our presence. Your earth will soon be projected into a higher vibrational plane.

"Our race has conditioned your world from time immemorial. Across two generations we have enabled the reality of visitors from other worlds to be absorbed into the consciousness of your kind on the earth. We continue even now for the good of all humanity. At the necessary time we will provide salvation to men and women of the earth so that they may survive to enter the new age where archaic and useless relics of man's self-destructive past will be discarded and, by creative thinking, man will learn to unbind himself from the limitations of conventional thought forms and the myths peculiar to your planet. It will be a new dawning."

O'Fallon understood what the creature told him perfectly: each word had lived in his mind its brief moment, then had seemed to sink into a deeper level. But this whole nightmare was still giving him plenty of pain. He felt a sickness in his stomach nag at him, he had charley horses in both sides of his butt. He felt dry as a bone inside and yet he was forcing vomit back. "What are you going to do with me?" he asked finally.

"Your memory of this will be erased until the moment of revelation." The words came powerfully into his head from the slit-mouthed leader. "We are gathering. Not three of your earth years will pass away before you will see us returning. Then we will do what we must do. We will communicate the essentials to you when they are needed. The initiates must be prepared to aid us in our plan. The higher vibrations will cause some of the earthlings to dematerialize off the face of the planet. These will be the less advanced forms, the dogmatists and the false prophets. The increasing densities of the solar spots and magnetic storms on your system's star will cause madness in other humans—your weaker ones. That has already progressed to preliminary stages."

There was a long moment of silence as the creature paused and then it picked up the black box from the work surface beside the man. In the next moment the leader's eyes riveted themselves onto O'Fallon's eyes with a strange intensity. There was no feeling or emotion in the alien eyes that told him this, but rather they seemed to grow larger and steadied themselves from the constant shifting.

"I say to you that we have chosen you out of many candidates. Be prepared. For at the appointed hour, if you are truly loyal, you will be given great power and dominion. For even you will aid the ushering in of the new age."

The yellow gas jetted out of the ceiling once more as the creature continued his mental communion, and as the alien leaned toward him, O'Fallon could see the red velvetlike insignia on the shoulder of the creature's uniform. It looked like a black winged dragon inside a white ring with dots like stars below that—*perhaps some giant ship journeying through a peculiar, elliptical galactic system,* he reasoned. As O'Fallon heard the last of the alien's thought-words move through his mind, he felt weak and dizzy and, when the last of the message faintly registered, he blacked out again.

The sun was still low in the sky when O'Fallon awoke, lying on his back beside the highway. He saw the shiny, metallic disk recede into the depths of the sky straight above him, and a red landing light blinking for an instant as if it were an airplane. He felt the spiny desert vegetation against his bare back. Moving his right arm slightly, he located a clump of clothing beside him which he knew must be his shirts. All the hair on his chest had been removed and, in the middle, a blood-stained red triangle was etched in his skin, its sides lying just inside the nipples.

In the gray early morning light, as the sun warmed his chilled body ever so slightly, the bizarre pattern on his chest resembled a work of modern surrealistic art. In fact, the entire body, with its almost white face, purpled eyesockets, reedlike lips, wounded chest, and slumped ragdollsque posture looked easily like something one might find on display in any large municipal art museum of note at the turn of the twentieth century.

The man got to his feet, glanced at the dark, dusty car on the shoulder in front of him and began to put on his shirt. He knew he had to get started, make up the time, think up an explanation for the strange wound, and reach San Diego by evening.

2

Edwards

Nestled in the difficult world of rugged high desert, amid the sparsely scattered creosote bush and mesquite, with distant blue-gray mountains that touch the sky, Edwards Air Force Base resides as an outpost of military technology. Sixty-odd miles from Los Angeles, this oasis for flying machines and pilots, larger than the distant metropolis itself, nevertheless had flourished in these lonely, open spaces, a bone-dry corner of the Mojave Desert where skies had shunned the clouds across the years.

The main concrete runway 4-22 is three miles long and extends onto the hard-packed grit of an ancient, immense lake bed, its waters long since scorched away. Runway 17-35 on Rogers Dry Lake gives the test pilots another seven and a half miles to land or lift off. Beyond that, if the sky would loose an air vehicle from its tenuous grasp, pilots could set down on another forty-three square miles of Rogers Lake.

Edwards had been the cradle of the nation's aerospace industry since the closing days of World War II and by the 1990s the massive Soviet espionage network and threats of terrorist sabotage had caused many areas on the base to be restricted—off-limits to those without proper clearance and a need-to-know. There were steel fences and military guards around the forbidden territory—protecting secrets. And, in rooms that seem small by desert standards, flights of the latest Air Force aircraft are electronically monitored by every sophisticated means known to man.

In Telemetry Room 655 the overhead speaker grille suddenly blared out a radio message, the words linked together so tightly it made them hard to understand. "Delta Red Niner to Edwards—ETA one minute—on final to leg zero-one, Alpha Corridor. All systems go. Climbing to fifty thousand—over."

"Roger, Delta Red Niner," a no-nonsense voice answered over the droning whine the blower motors made as they sent cooling air up through the racks of electronic equipment. The room was bristling with last-minute activity, its people scattered among the radar screens, which glowed with ghostly circles of blue and green and computerized data screens flashing with illuminated text and symbols.

Some distance from the base, in a California sky where Golden eagles once commanded the machine-less heavens, the streamlined jet sliced through the early morning air like a winged dagger, glistening white in the sunlight as its fuselage rotated slightly at the top of a climb. The main wings on the craft had an odd forward slant and in front of those, below the cockpit's bubble, another set of stubby wings caught the sun's gleam like knife edges. Colonel Jon Murphy was controlling the F-170, seated alertly inside the faintly roaring cockpit, almost 10 miles up in a clear May sky. His big hands rode with easy confidence on the black, cobra-headed control stick as the plane leveled off, the explosive sound of its passage left far behind in the stratosphere, where it funneled out and carried down in booming avalanches onto the brush-speckled desert below. The aviator examined the sky with casually alert eyes, their outer edges radiant with deep-furrowed crows feet; between them, a broad, pinkish nose ran down into the hard blackness of the oxygen mask, the mask covering the lower part of his face like a strange crustacean shell. As he examined the panorama around him, he could see the sky was cloudless and bright to the edge of the earth.

The airborne computer had just given Murphy a GO on the built-in test of all F-170 subsystems, and the confidence he had gotten from that crouched in his mind lingeringly as he angled his head sideways and glanced at the montonous expanse of desert far below. It seemed to shimmer in the sunlight as if millions of miniature gem stones covered the ground with a luxurious dusting. For a moment the pilot's eyes glazed over with a faraway look as he thought about the girl he had met the night before last. She had gone to bed with him, made him feel like a man in his twenties.

The thought of his wife back in Dayton flickered sullenly in Murphy's mind for an instant, but there was this 24-year-old, raven-haired, round-faced girl whom he was damned fond of now and so, to get rid of that thought, he pulled up the girl's image and looked at it with his mind. Like a strobe light freezing a moving thing, he saw different poses, the way Judy had looked one moment, then another strobe and another remembered slice of Judy; a coy look here, a flash of her body there. Perfectly still frames played the theater in his mind, but they didn't satisfy and so they made him want to be with her. He knew it wouldn't be long until he saw her and touched her; that's what fifty years on earth did to you, he thought; you learned how to muddle through, plot and scheme if you had to, then wait if you must.

After the flight there would be the debriefing at the base. Then he would head to his sparsely furnished quarters, take a quick nap, call the wife, and find out what the oldest kid wanted for graduation. After the shave and shower he'd pick up the girl fast as his little Corvette would carry him. They'd eat at the Desert Tee-Pee—a decent place, as he remembered—then he'd take her where they could dance slow and close, the old-fashioned way. *She had flashed a big smile after he had told her about a place where they could still dance that way.* After the dancing they would go to her apartment and listen to slow, sensual music while they made love. He could almost feel the touch of her soft, physical hands . . .

"Edwards to Firefly—what's your status?" The radio interrupted the train of his thoughts.

"Roger Edwards—Alpha is Go—markpoint in five seconds," he answered.

"Roger."

With practiced internal agility, he checked off a mental list of aircraft parameters that needed to be right before he thrust the slender jet plane past the next speed barrier. With those in mind, he riveted his attention to the array of instruments on the panel in front of him—checked the dials, the cathode-ray screens, and the rolling-tape displays for signs of trouble. Then, focusing his gaze on the Airspeed-MACH indicator, he eased the throttles forward. The jet gathered speed smoothly—*like silk on silk*, he thought pleasantly.

Suddenly, bright light flashed off the F-170's nose. With amazingly quick scans of his head the pilot searched until he found the source of the flash: an intense bead of light far to his left, slightly higher.

In the next split second, a strange craft splashed into view where he watched, as if the atmosphere were only a curtain and this strange phenomenon had punched through the hidden seam. Murphy's eyes took on a mesmerized glaze as he watched the unidentified machine streak toward his flight path at fantastic speed—much faster than any of the MIG-21s he had encountered as a 22-year-old over the North Vietnam of the seventies. The object had an oval shape and was moving in a smooth, arching path, and he could see it flash and scintillate blue-silver in the nine o'clock sunlight.

"Hey, Edwards—this is Firefly Red-Niner. What kind of traffic's out here in alpha corridor? I got a visual on a bogey at 9 o'clock crossing my track superfast," said Murphy into his mask microphone.

"Roger, Firefly," a voice answered, then hesitated. The voice was attached to an Air Force sergeant who was seated in front of the largest of the glass radar screens in the telemetry room. The screen was set at a steep angle in a gray metal cabinet and was as big around as an old-fashioned washtub—the kind they sell in antique shops in old, used-up farming towns. The display was crosshatched with a white-line matrix superimposed on a sea of green luminescence; across that background, yellow dots moved as an intense white thread of light circled the screen every 10 seconds. Projecting from the bottom of the screen, a smoked plexiglass control panel was sprinkled with embedded colored lights, black levers and coded push buttons, and it faintly reflected the image from the screen.

The sergeant was a big man, dressed in blue, with a lantern-shaped jaw, and the way his hair was cut made the top of his head resemble a triangular, horse-hair brush. "We're painting an unidentified target crossing in front of your track—nothing authorized in your sector, Colonel," said the sergeant. "You should be up there all by your lonesome. Do you copy, Firefly?"

"Roger, Edwards," the pilot radioed back. "What kind of velocity do you register on that bogey?"

Another military man in the blue-gray telemetry room punched at a set of buttons on the keyboard in front of a smaller radar screen. Amber numbers flashed on a window to the right of the radar's blue circle, and the airman read them out: "That's two-point-nine kilo, Colonel; it's makin' tracks. It's not painting a transponder. We confirm negative on traffic in alpha corridor."

"Roger. Well, there sure as hell is *something* up here with me. And, far as I can tell, it's damn near big as a naval cruiser!"

The sergeant sat motionless in front of the largest display, his eyes narrowed at what he was seeing. "It should cross your track . . ." the sergeant began.

"It's coming across *now* from eleven o'clock," radioed Murphy from the F-170.

"It's slowing," said the brown-haired sergeant abruptly. And then: "The fastest deceleration I ever saw, wow-wee!" A warbling excitement had entered his voice.

"That's affirmative," echoed the 50-year-old test pilot coolly. The strange machine had stopped suddenly in midair and was hovering to the right of the F-170—close enough so he could get a better look at it. The UFO glittered with dazzling silver reflections as it rotated, wobbling slightly while it hung like a beacon in the sky. To Murphy, the shape looked like an ellipsoid, a shape he remembered from a high-school textbook; it looked bigger than the biggest plane he had ever seen.

Glancing down at the F-170's radar screen, he saw a green dot registered just where it should have been. *Damn if it ain't solid*, the pilot thought, his left forefinger riding a push button for an instant to engage the Identification Friend-Or-Foe electronics.

The horse-haired sergeant came back on the air: "Edwards to Firefly Red Niner—what kinda visual you got on that target, Colonel?"

"Let me tell ya—it's not one of ours," said the pilot. "Negative on IFF."

"We copy IFF response, Firefly. This confirms our data," a balding captain on another console cut in. Besides him a woman with stringy black hair sat, elbows extended on a table as she monitored strip chart recorders that printed out telemetry from the test flight with pens thin as insect legs.

The pilot checked the symbols on the Heads-Up Display, which was set atop the instrument panel like a giant hooded lens facing the sky in front of the aircraft's nose. Overlaid onto the sky, Murphy could see the multitude of colored symbols that repeated, in cryptic form, data from the flight instruments, inertial navigation system, central computer, and weapons control system. He flipped on the target designator control, bracketed the radar image of the unknown craft, and pressed down for a radar lock on. Just as the jeweled green lock-on light illuminated and the red target designator box appeared on the head-up display, the UFO began to pick up speed. *It knows it's being tracked*, thought Murphy.

All the while, electronic symbology flashed and changed on the thick glass HUD:

TIP PROFILE 48%
D 11.8 KM
CLOSG - 38.6 DEG

"I make the raw target at twelve kilometers and starting to move," radioed the pilot.

"Roger, Firefly. That's what we're painting. You got a good look-see yet, Colonel?" The sergeant smiled a little uncertainly, the way people do when they're speaking to someone they can't see. The pilot pushed a button on the TISEO control panel. A magnified image of the unknown craft sprang up in front of him on the thick HUD glass.

"The thing's definitely a craft of some kind. I've got it punched up on the electro-optics. It's smooth and metallic, seamless—no insignia . . . no markings at all. It's a flattened sphere with a metallic ring around its equator—very definite double-convex outline. I think I can make out a rotation . . . that's affirmative on the rim rotating about a vertical axis. Negative on a vapor trail—I can't see one, anyway. It's at my two o'clock position now, heading away from me." There was a short pause. "Wait a minute! There's something really weird here. Something's jamming my electronics," said the colonel in a surprised voice that trailed off and garbled the words that came out of the big speaker box on the telemetry room wall.

"Say again, Firefly," radioed the sergeant.

"Ah, I'm picking up EMI from somewhere. I've lost some electronic systems. The object is accelerating. I'm going to abort the mission and get closer . . . What the hell, over."

"Colonel, I don't think . . . we don't have authorization for a mission abort," squawked the telemetry captain into his microphone. He nodded and waved a flat hand at an airman standing nearby, who immediately uncradled a telephone.

Colonel Murphy banked to the right and let the air combat machine slip through the air until he was pointed toward the fleeing unknown craft. The UFO instantly changed its course, moving away from the F-170's turn. Murphy realized whoever or whatever controlled the UFO knew precisely where the F-170 was *and* what he was up to, and that thought made his heart pound at the wall of his chest.

"Firefly Red Niner, that's a negative on mission abort," said the young captain in the telemetry room. "General Nobis is on his way over here. Maintain flight profile. Do you copy, Colonel?"

"Hell, I hear you. Sorry I can't wait for the red tape. I got to get after it. This damn thing could be on the moon by the time the general gets there," said the pilot. He switched off the incoming radio.

"Edwards to Firefly. The brass drew and quartered the last pilot who changed the flight profile, Colonel," the captain said into the microphone. "Do you copy?"

The speaker on the wall hissed like the inside of an electronic seashell.

"Edwards to Firefly Red Niner, do you read me?" Only the hiss came back.

Colonel Murphy clicked the throttles all the way forward and the triple-tailed F-170 jolted in response, the Pratt & Whitney J-960s gushing flames, roaring at the air like synchronized volcanos, the engine tubes lighting with purple-red fire like the inside of a steel blast furnace, and he could feel the engines kick him in the butt as the plane lurched from the most powerful jet-thrust in the free world. He shifted the control stick to one side ever so slightly and edged the nose of the aircraft toward the diving silver craft; the UFO was heading for the desert floor.

Colonel Murphy peered for an instant at the multicolored symbols on the heads-up display glass and then glanced a little further down, spreading his attention across the myriad of symbols that flashed on the various cathode ray tubes in front of him. As he rechecked the HUD, he saw the UFO's rate-of-closure numbers change from negative to positive. A glance out the canopy confirmed the UFO was changing from a pea-sized dot back to the discernable silver craft, growing in size—coming straight at him. He switched his radio back on.

"Firefly to Edwards—the bogey just turned back on itself—it's on an intercept to my position!"

"Roger, Firefly. It just did a one-eight-zero turn on our scopes," radioed the sergeant.

"Roger," replied Murphy. The silvery craft grew larger by the second as the colonel pitched the plane back up. He could see the UFO respond, maintaining its intercept course as it streaked toward the F-170. *It's going to hit me*! his mind screamed at him.

"I'm breaking left," he hollered into the helmet microphone, whipping the control stick toward the inside of his thigh. The F-170 seemed to shudder for a split second, banked violently, then flashed down and to the left. Murphy swiveled his head opposite the banking dive and saw the unknown machine flash by a few hundred feet above him. It was the biggest thing he had ever seen in the sky, and as it went by the most incredible thing he had ever witnessed occurred—or had it been only a trick of the mind confronted with an unknown danger?

As he blinked his lids hard against the eyes and replayed what he had seen, he was sure: When the object had been right on him, as it passed by, its shape had changed from that of a metallic aerial machine to something that looked for all the world like a pulsating, translucent jellyfish with tentacles rippling out the back of it, and with the sky faintly visible through its enormous, glistening body. And, as the strange craft had closed on his aircraft, he had glimpsed port holes below the central rim; but at the UFO's closest approach, the port holes seemingly transformed themselves into ugly, gelatinous eyes that peered out from some hideous denizen of the sky.

Murphy shook his head as if this strange remembrance were a steel ball in a pinball machine and he was trying to keep it alive for a few more chances at the high-scoring bumpers before it fell down a hole and was lost. He was dead sure he had seen the UFO change, but the whole thing lay outside everything he had ever imagined. And even though it had happened only a few seconds and a few thousand feet away, his belief in it was fading even now.

While he meditated on those thoughts, the G-forces from the turning F-170 plastered him against the seat, and that discomfort interrupted his thinking. Then, as if uncertain which way it would go, the aircraft shuddered and began to vibrate. Murphy adjusted his grip to hold the control stick steady against the buffeting and, as the plane rolled slightly, he caught a last glimpse of the UFO—an amorphous, gray dot streaking upward into the western sky.

The F-170 vibrated more fiercely the instant he tried to bring the nose up. *Something's gone haywire with the controls*; the unwanted thought stabbed at the marrow of his mind as the nose of the aircraft wavered up and down then side to side, oblivious to his commands. Suddenly the plane started to spin like a record on a turntable.

"Edwards to Firefly Red Niner," radioed the sergeant from the telemetry room. "We just showed a near miss on our scopes. Are you okay, Colonel? You must've got a hellava look."

"Roger, Edwards. This is Firefly. I got a problem up here. This bird's changing ends on me. We're into a hard spin and descending through thirty-six kilos. I'm going to try and bring her out. I've had some oscillation in the control system." The pilot's voice paused. Telemetry room eyes wandered from the ceiling speaker to other eyes, and then some stared down at the floor, some inward, until the voice came back on the air. "The main computer's not responding; the controls are out." Static came for a moment, then: "They might kick in further down."

Murphy jiggled the control stick to shake the spin, but the mindless plane kept turning as if its fuselage were trapped in an invisible aerial whirlpool that was dragging it down into the depths of the atmosphere. As quick and smart as he knew how, he flipped combinations of switches, glancing in short bursts at the spinning sky as the plane dropped.

"Edwards to Firefly," one of the engineers in the telemetry room broke in. "Try rebooting your central computer, then go to override."

"Roger," radioed the colonel. The colonel doggedly reset the computer with his right hand, all the while struggling to work the flight controls against the worsening spin with the other. The plane was gathering speed as it descended, whooshing through the air like a windmill, and he could feel the g-suit tighten against his legs as the pressure of the spin built up.

Murphy tried switching to a backup control system, then overriding the flight computers with the main computer, and when nothing changed the idea that this was a terminal spin began gnawing at him like a rat chewing on a wall. The flight controls left stiff and lifeless no matter what he tried, as if the aircraft were only an amusement park ride where the controls were fake, merely for children to work back and forth in a useless farce until the ride was over. The big metal bird was dropping fast. At 25,000 feet he knew it was time to get out.

"Edwards to Firefly—what's your status, Colonel?"

"Firefly to Edwards. I'm going down. My last radio fix was twenty miles north by northeast of sector twenty-three beacon. This is a Mayday."

"Damn!" said the sergeant, pounding his fist on the console. An airman at a communications console switched to the VHF emergency radio channels and began broadcasting: "Mayday—Mayday. We have a test aircraft, Firefly Red Niner, in trouble in alpha corridor fifty miles northeast of the northern perimeter. Zebra alpha and zebra bravo—this is a Mayday. This is not a drill. Let's get out there. We need equipment in a hurry!"

"I'm gettin' out," radioed Colonel Murphy. "See you on the ground." He disengaged his oxygen mask from the helmet and threw it down beside the seat. Above and behind his head were two thick cord loops, each striped like blue and white peppermint sticks, and he reached those and yanked on them, pulling them down and over his head as far as they would go. At that point in the ejection sequence the canopy was supposed to blow off, but it hadn't. The CANOPY UNLOCKED indicator on the WARNING/CAUTION panel stared back at him with disappointing non-illumination. This, then, was a test pilot's dilemma, he thought, this is what all that extra pay and extra status was for—to inevitably be in a damn-tight situation.

"Firefly to Edwards. Negative on canopy jettison. I pulled the face curtain to its stop, but the bubble's still on the bird—canopy unlock light is extinguished," he said. "Going to emergency override." The pilot found the yellow-and-black-striped, pyramidal PULL TO JETT handle and pulled it.

There was a pause. Back at the base, except for the equipment blowers, the telemetry room was silent until the horse-haired sergeant broke through it: "Roger, Colonel, we're with you. We got help coming your way. Get out of there, Colonel. Hang tough, buddy." Several people were standing around the sergeant, peering at the radar screen, watching the luminous yellow dot angle down past the graduated altitude marks. Their faces looked like those of wooden puppets with their mouths ajar before the puppet-show house curtain glides open.

"Firefly to Edwards." The strained pilot's voice broke the numbed deadness of the room once more. "Hell, it looks like this is it." Murphy paused a moment and the people in the telemetry room could hear his slashing breaths come quick against the invisible g-forces that they all knew were tearing at his body by now. "I'm going to punch out through the canopy. It's the only option. Negative on the canopy unlock light. If it's locked, I know it won't hurt for long . . . I'm preparing myself now."

"Oh God," said someone in the telemetry room.

Inside the F-170 aircraft, the pilot hunched over. The sky and edge of the desert showed through the canopy almost as a continuous, bluish-tan swirl around him as the plane whirled toward the ground. His face was distorted from the force of spinning, and little folds of skin stood out of his cheeks on each side of his mouth as he struggled against the pressure and slid the cam away from the seat emergency switch, then jammed it to the ARM position.

Colonel Murphy reached both hands down between his legs, jerked the D-ring and rocketed himself through the canopy. The pilot and the seat-coccoon tossed and rotated uncertainly in the violent blast of air for two-thirds of a second before the left tailfin separated his head from the rest of his body.

On the cathode-ray radar scopes in the telemetry room, the F-170's *blip* vanished, and the room came more alive. A couple of the equipment operators barked out stark, loud words into multitudes of perforations on red plastic telephones. "Oh God," cried one of the civilians. "God help him."

Ray Stone, lead engineer on Johnson Aircraft flight test operations, moved quickly to a phone, his cigar trailing smoke like a brown rocket. He was a short, pudgy man with a belt-testing belly, a square-jowled face, and slightly bulging eyes. On top he had a thick stock of graying black hair swirled to the right like Kansas wheat blown by a tornadic wind. It was only 8:57 A.M., but Stone's hair had already lost its part; he looked like he had put in a full day. He jabbed a button, and while he waited for the voice to come on the other end his eyes played over the front page of the May 12, 1998, edition of the *Los Angeles Times* beside the phone as if he were seeing it for the first time:

WEIRD WEATHER CONTINUES—STORM DUMPS 16 INCHES OF SNOW ON NORTHERN CALIFORNIA.

PROCESSING PLANT EMPLOYEE ADMITS POISONING MILK.

UFOS INVADE LOCAL SKIES—MAN CLAIMS FLASHING, FLYING OBJECT BLINDED HIM.

There was a burr edge to Stone's voice as he relayed the news: "A bird is down." His eyes squinted at the curses that came back.

3

The Tiger Team

On the second level of Johnson Aircraft's Test Operations Building at Edwards AFB, an office, huge as an airplane hanger, perched coolly in the hot morning sun. With its high ceiling and eye-stretching expanse, the office reminded Tom Kruger of the animal and crafts exhibition wing he first saw at the Georgia State Fair as a 12-year-old; instead of the sights of homemade quilts and oil paintings, pickles, jams, and pies, sewing and crafts, the vast area at the top of Buildings 67 was filled with engineers, technical specialists of various kinds, administrators, and too few secretaries, all sitting behind gray metal desks amid a constant din of conversations, computer printer clatter, and the shrill electronic buzzings of telephones pleading to be answered. Instead of the smell of prize hogs and cows, the sweat of the people in the room was neat and sanitary and disguised under the chemistry of 23 brands of deodorant.

This was the team that worked at bringing the Johnson prototype aircraft up to military expectations; they kept the bird flying. The contingent of engineers instrumented the planes, analyzed flight data, experimented, and made design changes, transforming advanced constructions of metal, epoxy, and plastic into the best aerial fighting machines that money could buy. The others made up schedules, added up the cost, processed the words and figures, drafted documents from which the planes were manufactured, expedited scarce parts—did what was essential so that planes could be built and delivered on time.

There was absolutely nothing colorful or unique in the entire barn of a room—merely a drab, cluttered dullness. Overfilled gray metal bookcases and file cabinets lined almost every inch of unwindowed wall. Where sections of walls were available, computer printouts and detailed drawings of mechanical parts and electrical circuits were hung with cellophane tape. Most of the faces at the desks and tables carried haggard, concerned expressions all the way across their brows, from temple to temple and into the eyes. Most of the mouths were drawn tight with serious expressions. The majority of the men wore white or blue shirts, some with collars frayed at the points, and polyester, dark-patterned ties four or five years too thin for the style in vogue at the turn of the twentieth-first century. Some of the women wore blouses with a little more color, but the women's short hair and lack of makeup made it difficult for Kruger to guess the gender of some of the people just looking at the faces.

Only a few of the hundred or so heads could be seen upright at any one time. Most of the faces were lowered toward one paper among the stacks littering the tops of desks and drafting tables. The draftsmen and design engineers seemed to be working unceasingly, huddled over rectangular wooden boards, drawing and redrawing symmetrical patterns and complex symbols, some onto large sheets of slick, vellumlike paper and some onto white drafting paper or blue-toned prints that smelled like strong ammonia. The drafting tables had fluorescent tubes of light housed in brown-enameled fixtures that overlooked the slanted boards from various distances.

There wasn't a green plant or a flower in the entire place except for several of the red flowers that bloom in parts of the desert in May that someone had gathered between the arches of a glass vase on a secretary's desk beside a computer's louvered cooling outlet. The flowers had been withered by the exhaust.

In the midst of the harassing noise of a nearby technical debate, with its multitude of voices bouncing off the hard angularities of the room, next to a windowed wall, Tom Kruger was just now lifting the pink cover sheet from a stack of papers that lay on the desk before him. Below the first page's blue sticker that reminded CONFIDENTIAL MATERIAL—HANDLE WITH CARE, he started reading the F-170 accident summary as the loud exchange in front of him waned. It was nearly lunchtime; he had missed breakfast and his mouth was dry and tasted flinty, like an Indian arrowhead. He had flown in on an early morning flight from Atlanta with three hours less sleep than he was used to, and had driven two hours from the City of Angels to the Lancaster Red Rooster Inn. After checking in there had only been time to freshen up and drive to the base.

As he scanned the first page, Ray Stone sat three desks up, a smoking cigar jammed into his mouth, waiting for Kruger to finish. Tom could smell the cigar smoke, and it struck him as a rotten, part-chemical smell that made him wonder how much Stone had paid for the cigar.

Tom Kruger's 26-year-old face had a handsomeness that had given his life more than its share of hostile men and friendly women. His cheekbones jutted out close below blue-green eyes and the skin on his face was tight and well tanned for the middle of May. The light brown skin contrasted against hair the color of a lion's body, weblike in its fineness from German extraction. His nose was well proportioned, slightly knobby at the bridge and, as he flipped the page over, his brows arched in response to the next thing he saw, and the redness of his eyes made them appear more blue than green. The man's lips parted a little as he paused, his eyes seemingly illuminated by an interest in something he had come to, then closed while he scanned on.

A small jet aircraft began taxiing on the runway outside the windows to his left, and he could hear the new sound that penetrated the window as a faint, high-pitched whine. There were two vertical creases that had formed in between his eyebrows in response to the noise, and they gave the illusion that his nose continued up into his forehead. He glanced out and observed the jet as it moved across the sun-drenched concrete then, shifting his glance upward, he squinted to cut the brightness of the blue-white sky and felt an ache at the back of his eyes. In his mind he related the pain to the half quart of Wild Turkey 101-proof bourbon he had consumed the night before.

He skimmed the six-page report quickly, knowing that all the key details would stay in his memory. In his freshman year at college he had first discovered a very useful talent; all he needed to do in order to memorize exact details was to open a door in his mind. And after he had practiced the door opening enough, he got to where he could control it, and anything he saw or heard would usually stay with him—in photographic detail if he happened to store it visually as he did now with the report. This talent had considerably eased the difficulty of obtaining a college degree and, later, it gave him a small reputation in his department at

Johnson Aircraft an engineer who had a genius for solving tough problems when actually he simply had a very good memory.

Just as Tom Kruger looked up to check if Stone was occupied, he saw Stone standing over him, looking down through an expanding cloud of grayish smoke. Beside Stone stood a young, beautiful woman.

"Tom, this is Melissa Delaney," said Stone, his cigar at his side now. "She'll be lending a hand, helping out with the computer programming on the flight data analysis and whatever the hell else we run into." As he finished Stone shifted most of his weight from one foot to the other, then poked his cigar into his mouth, clamping it between his teeth.

"Real good," said Tom Kruger, and he rose from the chair, extending his hand. Her dark eyes flickered almost with a look of surprise as they shook hands. Melissa Delaney was tall at five foot ten, with a modest, pretty build and wide, curving hips. Her hair was dark brown with a hint of auburn in it and she wore it neatly, in a style slightly longer than commonly popular in the late nineties. Her face had high rosy cheeks and small, finely shaped features. The most impressive thing about her, though, were her eyes—almond-shaped, chocolate-brown in color. There was something about them that seemed to draw your gaze into them. As fate would have it, Melissa Delaney had grown dramatically prettier the past few years and, at 23, most men who saw her considered her quite nice to look at.

She takes a lot of drabness out of the room, he thought, smiling. "Tom Kruger, here. Good to have you on board."

"Hi," she said in a husky-edged voice.

"You're not from Atlanta?" Tom asked her. A sonic boom suddenly jolted the building, thunderlike, and the windows rattled like stacked teacups in an earthquake; Tom and Melissa averted their gazes in comical synchronization, first to the row of windows beside them, then to each other. A faint chill flashed over Tom Kruger when her eyes locked onto his.

"I'm from the Huntington Beach office," Melissa finally said, a shyness flickering in her eyes.

"A native, huh," confirmed Tom. "Of California, I mean."

"Very perceptive," she said, then laughed, and the corners of her mouth turned down in a smirk. Her eyes locked onto his again, and he could see the way they smiled—and, even though the girl was attired in the most modern of clothes, the only outdated feature being the high cut of the black cotton dress she wore, she somehow reminded Tom Kruger of a heroine out of some romantic novel of the early nineteen hundreds—*The Beautiful and the Damned* was one that came to mind.

"Did you get through the report?" Stone asked Tom.

"Yeah—not much detail," replied Tom, giving Stone a blank look. It had seemed unnatural to pull his eyes away from Melissa, and he barely heard what Stone had asked him.

"I'll fill you in," said Stone, "whatever you need. They're wanting something concrete from us in seventy-two hours." Melissa looked slightly surprised.

"I've been through this routine before," Tom said to Melissa. "We're supposed to analyze all the surviving nuts and bolts—all the recovered avionics; tie in a time-sync with the flight recorder, then sort out all the crucial electronic paths, put the whole thing together, find the right answer, write it all up, and they give us a whole three days."

"They don't want to spoil us," said Stone. He let out a short, parrotlike burst of laughter that turned into wheezing and ended with a fit of coughing. "Clears out the pipes," he explained after a moment, red-faced from nearly choking. Melissa nodded slowly and smiled. Stone cleared his throat and went on. "Anyway, we'll get you whatever help you need, Tom. They tell me Melissa's a computer whiz-kid. We got a contract engineer coming in from Denver. We got top priority on the computer. This whole investigation's got tiger team authorization. The guys on mahogany row are behind us."

"By the way, Ray," said Tom, "what was the raw anomalous target the colonel was chasing?"

Stone glanced at Kruger's identification badge and then at Melissa's. "The pilot was chasing a UFO, and that little tidbit is classified Secret—so watch who you tell."

Tom Kruger's eyebrows became hyperbolas. "Well, even assuming the UFO didn't zap the colonel out of the sky, there's a lot more than seventy-two hours' worth of work here," said Tom, turning toward Melissa. "I hope you're as slick with a computer as he says you are."

"I play a mean round of 4D-Invaders," she replied. "They used to call me the Atari Kid in the old days."

"I played that fourth dimensional thing once at the Aerospace Lounge in LA," Stone remarked. "The computer beat the hell outta me."

"All a computer knows is ones and zeros, Ray, that's all you gotta remember," said Tom, smiling. Stone frowned, and brownish cigar spittle came sliding out of the right corner of his mouth, under one edge of his mustache, like vital fluids from a wounded caterpillar.

Melissa nodded politely, her pleasant eyes dancing a little. "You've got to watch those computers in bars. They're probably rigged—the odds are with the house," she said. "You know software—bad odds in, bad odds out."

Stone nodded his head. "You might be right. Those machines at the Aerospace could eat five-dollar bills like there's no tomorrow!" A wheezing laugh came out of him; he took a long pull from the cigar, then easing it from his mouth, tilted his head back and blew a stream of smoke up at the ceiling. "Well, why don't I take you down to the lab. We should be able to rustle up some desks."

Down a flight of stairs, at the end of a narrow hallway, Stone punched a keyboard and one-three-seven-nine let them into the laboratory past the door's red and white AUTHORIZED PERSONNEL ONLY sign, and Tom Kruger smelled the coffee right away. It made him want a donut, but he settled for the inky-black coffee, stray grounds and all—the last of a batch from a Mister Coffee atop a metal shelf against the blue concrete-block wall on the far side of the room.

The F-170's black boxes, which had survived the crash, were scattered around on top of wooden tables along one wall. Some were bent and mangled looking and had enamel-starved splotches where fire had licked at them. Tom already knew the type of data gathering that would be required. And then, too, all of the data would have to be transferred to their computer base, and the computer would process the critical flight information relevant to the last moments of the aircraft and its pilot's life—and, in time, he hoped an answer would emerge. After Stone left Tom and Melissa bought sandwiches and V-8 juices from a vending machine, bolted down lunch, and went to work.

Stone strolled back in the lab at three-thirty. He had puffy, dark purple arcs under his eyes and his hair was greasy and uncombed. His shirt collar was unbuttoned and the knot on his tie had slipped one and a half inches down his chest. "How's it going?" Stone asked Tom.

"Fair to middling," said Tom. "Some of these units are pretty torn up—I guess I've seen worse. A Stealth bomber came down like a lead balloon in Washington State last year—it took 'em a couple days to find it. We worked seventy-hour weeks on that one for a while—didn't get paid a cent for anything over forty."

"No overtime, huh," Stone said.

"Nope. After working about twenty days in a row we cut back to sixty-hour weeks for six months running—no OT. Our department head said the company didn't have any budget for crashes."

"Sounds familiar," Stone agreed. "I've pulled the same duty more times than I care to remember."

"Yeah, Ray, they sure didn't tell me about free overtime when I was in college working for the old engineering degree," complained Tom.

"Tell me about it," said Stone, chomping down on a cigar that had moved to the right corner of his mouth. "I've been at Johnson twenty-four big ones."

"At least you get five weeks' vacation a year, right?" said Tom. Stone took the cigar from his mouth and laughed, making his mustache stretch out and seem to gravitate toward his nose, and Tom noticed for the first time that Stone had no teeth—only pink gums that glistened with saliva in the laboratory's bright, shadowless light.

"We wouldn't have got that except the production people went on strike in ninety-two," Stone declared. "Engineers get some of what the union guys get." He winked, showing Tom a greasy-looking right eyelid.

"I knew there was a reason I went to college. I couldn't spell engineer a few years back, and now I *are* one," Tom joked.

"Hey, before I forget—we're getting some more talent in tomorrow, bright and early," said Stone. "A guy named Glidewell from Denver, by way of Vandenberg. We'll stick him on circuit analysis. I mean, they say this guy is the best in the west where electrons are concerned. We're supposed to get some extra computer people, too—they keep sayin' we're short of funds."

"Great," said Tom. "We need all the help we can get on this one."

"Hey, what are you doing after work?" Stone asked Tom. "I could give you a tour of a local watering hole or two."

"Sounds pretty tempting," said Tom, smiling faintly. "I imagine it gets awful thirsty in the desert at night." He put a crook in the left side of his smile.

"I should be able to swing a night out, away from the better half, if you're game," said Stone, scratching the backside of his pants with the cigarless hand.

"Count me in," said Tom.

"I got jus' the spot—a real oasis," said Stone. "Where you stayin'?"

"Then, I'll pick you up at nineteen hundred hours, okay?" said Stone, after Tom had told him, and went on, not waiting for a reply: "This'll give you a chance to unwind, you know, relax a little. Once you delve into those black boxes, you ain't gonna have a hellava lot of time."

"Sounds good, Ray." said Tom.

"See you then, okay?" said Stone, and he turned and headed for the door.

"Okay," Tom answered the retreating figure, which showed a penguinlike wobble as Stone raised a hand in a quick wave before he disappeared out the door, leaving clouds of smoke that hung sulphurous in the air for a moment after he had gone.

4

The Prospector

The Antelope Valley is a great saucer of land, elliptical in shape, bounded by the Santa Ynez Mountains on the west, the Tehachapi Mountains on the north, and the Sierra Madres to the south. The valley's eastern end extends to the edge of the great Mojave Desert. Further east, a little deeper in the earth, lays the parched, moonlike landscape of Death Valley.

The valley in which Lancaster had blossomed was named for the great herds of Antelope that once roamed its foothills, even before the Piute Indians came. Half the antelope herd was lost from 1882 to 1885, when unusually heavy snows drove the animals eastward to the railroad. The antelope would not cross the railroad tracks to get to their normal feeding grounds and 15,000 starved or were killed by predators and hunters. Long before 1988, the last of the antelopes had vanished from the valley.

The Antelope Valley Inn, like a thoroughly modernized descendant of earlier Western saloons, filled a comfortable niche between a doctor's office and a funeral parlor at the outskirts of Lancaster. The tavern was located inside a big flat-roofed, one-story building that was almost as sterile looking and featureless as it is possible to be—windowless and angular like vintage World War II German blockhouses, which scientists and engineers once used to hide from V-2 rocket launches. Nevertheless, one could guess it was a tavern by the sight of neon blue bubbles coming out of a red glowing bottle beside the blue AV INN on the big sign above the door. In contrast to the glowing display, the outside of the AV Inn was painted the color of ashes, and that effected a camouflage that had mingled the dimmer back edges of the building with the blue-black fall of night by the time Stone reached out and grabbed the heavy knob on the plain steel door.

As they cleared the doorway, Tom Kruger caught a whiff of the rotten grain smell of beer wafting out into the heated air. Once inside it was cooler the farther they went into the room and so the two men walked to the end of the bar and sat down on stools and planted their elbows on the varnished mahogany. It was crowded in the bar for a Tuesday night, and they could see blue smoke billowing up into the square ceiling lights.

The bartender, a big man with sunken, darkly circled eyes, came up, pointed a thick finger, and stretched his eyes wide: "What'll you have?" he asked. His voice made him sound Irish, but he looked German. The bartender's white shirt was opened two buttons down from the collar and bulged to its limits; a herringbone-patterned gold chain clung to his chest just below the neck, and it was so wide it looked like an artifact from an Egyptian tomb. His sleeves were rolled up high where they dug into his big arms.

"Coors Lite," said Ray Stone.

"Wild Turkey, one-hundred-one," said Tom.

"Any chaser?" asked the bartender.

"What?" asked Tom.

"Any mixer?" asked the bartender. His thick black hair looked like it had transparent Jell-o spread on it to make it lay down.

"No, on the rocks," said Tom. The bartender hustled away, and Tom glanced at the landmarks around the lounge. It looked to him like the kind of place where spiders probably hung in the corners of the room. The ceiling was made out of some type of black, sound-absorbent material, convoluted like the bottom of egg cartons. There were spotlighted photographs of military planes, rockets, and space capsules that hung in cheap frames on some of the walls. A white glowing glass panel sprinkled with black images of constellations and astrological symbols ran the length of the wall behind the bar. Their spot at the bar was just across from Libra.

"They're talking about cutting funds off for the F-170—you hear that?" asked Stone.

"You're kidding—what are they going to do for defense against the Russians?" questioned Tom.

"The senate armed services committee claims the plane's too complex, too expensive. You know, same old song and dance . . ." said Stone.

"Well, hell, if they want to save some money on defense, they just ought to order maybe a thousand Piper Cubs and stick machine guns on 'em," said Tom.

"Yeah." Stone eyed the prospect in his mind. "The pilots could carry grenades for ground attacks." He guffawed after he had said it. "They could toss 'em in through the bomber windshields as they come in over Los Angeles!"

Tom laughed and then continued in a loud voice, "Hell, they'd never even catch up with the Russians long enough to get a shot. They'd just be shooting at a whiz—just a whiz in the sky."

"Just a blue streak," said Stone. He pulled a cigar out of his shirt pocket, took a bite out of the end, and ran it through his lips to wet it.

"Just a red and silver streak," said Tom, and he laughed.

"Right," agreed Stone. "I forgot the communist motif—a hammer and sickle streak." Stone paused a moment while he lit the cigar, puffing furiously. "Well, anyway, it looks like they've got enough for the redesign. After that I don't know." He drew on the cigar, then jerked it from his mouth and coughed, and Tom could see his gums glistening and dancing in the sprinkle of light that came from behind the bar.

The bartender came back and stuck the drinks at them from the ends of his gigantic arms. They paid him and he went away and they sipped into the drinks.

"Man, that's good coffee," Stone joked, rubbing his thumb against the corner of his mouth, making the edge of his mustache frizz up, then squinting his eyes against the smoke from his cigar.

Tom smiled and said, "Nothing like good ol' Kentucky bourbon."

"I thought you were from Georgia?" said Stone.

"Yeah," said Tom. "I had a buddy at Georgia Tech used to always drink Wild Turkey. He even collected the special bottles. I kind of picked it up from him, I guess. He got a bleeding ulcer pretty bad when we were seniors—had to give up the booze and drop out of school." Tom paused a moment. "Where you from, Ray?" he asked.

"Hannibal, Missouri," replied Stone, pronouncing Hannibal as Hanibull. "Graduated from University of Missouri. Worked for McDonnell Aircraft when I first got out of school, then had to come out to California in seventy-four. There was a real shortage in engineering jobs. Lots of guys I knew never did get jobs—they had to get out of engineering altogether."

Tom nodded negatively. "Howdya like it out here?" he asked, chugging down the last of his drink.

Stone watched the younger man devour the drink before he spoke. "I like it in Lancaster; LA's too damned crowded. Say—you know—that hard stuff destroys brain cells."

"Yeah, but I figure they must grow back," said Tom.

"You sure 'bout that?"

"In college my drinking buddy and I calculated how many we had lost—brain cells, you know."

"You're puttin' me on."

"No—really. We found data on the average size of male Caucasian brains and the number of brain cells per cubic centimeter in a back issue of *Scientific American*, and then found a medical book with the figure for the number of cells each ounce of hundred-proof booze kills."

"What'd you find out?" asked Stone.

"Just using conservative estimates of the amount of alcohol we each drank from our freshman through our junior years, we calculated that we had destroyed our entire brains!" said Tom, breaking out in a laugh. Stone laughed, rocking back and forth on the stool, waving his cigar at a distance as if he were using it to help him maintain his balance on a wire.

"What got you into the aerospace game?" asked Stone.

"Guess I just didn't know any better," Tom began. "I always loved science ever since I started reading physics books when I was a kid. I used to stay up lots of nights and watch for meteors—I was nuts about science fiction movies from the fifties and sixties. They used to play 'em on our local TV station late on summer nights." Stone nodded knowingly. Tom continued: "My favorites were the ones where the scientific type is working in a lab or something and some really weird stuff starts happening out in the desert and he latches on to some equipment and takes the secretary and goes off to investigate the weird stuff and, of course, the secretary is real beautiful."

"Yeah," murmured Stone, nodding.

"And they run right into the space creatures, but the hero and heroine escape and they give mankind the clues they need to fight the invaders from space."

"Well, here we are in the desert," said Stone. "I haven't seen any space creatures yet—but, hell, the night is young." With that, he drained the last of the beer in the mug and signaled the bartender.

"How's the weather been out here, Ray? I hear it's usually pretty nice," Tom said.

"It snowed four or five days back—heavy," said Stone. "Some places got twenty, twenty-one inches—I mean, down at our elevation, not just in the mountains."

"You're kidding."

"No. It's like the weather's been getting weirder the last couple of years out here."

"We had some pretty strange weather back in Georgia last month—hotter'n hell," explained Tom. The bartender came back and gave them an expectant look. "Another round," Tom told him, raising two fingers in a vee and waving it between Stone and himself. The bartender took the empty glasses and wiped their section of bar dry before he hustled away, moving like an upright gorilla. "Hey, Ray—tell me—you were in the telemetry room when Colonel Murphy was on his last flight. What do you think he was chasing?"

Stone hesitated a little, then spoke in a hushed voice. "Just a UFO—hell, I don't know what it was. They picked whatever it was up on radar and all—you read the report; what do you think?"

"I don't think it was a sundog or a temperature inversion," said Tom, "but I tell you, Ray, I'd sure as hell like to find out what it was—I knew Colonel Murphy!"

Stone's mouth dropped open. "Is that right?" he said, surprised.

"Yeah," said Tom. "He used to come to all the crew-station meetings on the SFX project when I first started working at Johnson Aircraft."

"Is that right?"

"Yeah. And I'll tell you," said Tom, steadying his gaze, "he was the sharpest, most level-headed guy I ever saw sit down at a design review. He was one of the top Air Force experts on cockpit design in '94. And he could spot flaws that nobody else could even hint at." The bartender brought the drinks and after taking a long pull from his, Tom's eyes took on a dreamy, faraway look, as if he were on the edge of seeing something pop up from an alien landscape. "If Murphy said there was an unknown craft up there, I've sure as hell got to believe it wasn't anything secret outta the skunk works at Lockheed." Tom took another pull from the drink, exhaled the burn in his throat, and went on. "I'll tell you something else . . ."

"What's that?"

"If Murphy felt it was important enough to break off the mission and chase that thing, then whatever it was might be damned important to us all."

"Well, just assuming for a moment that people from outer space are flying around in these UFOs—how come they don't communicate?" Stone asked Tom.

"Maybe they look upon us like we're a bunch of amoebas or something—like we're primitive masses of protoplasm living together in groups, taking vacations at the same places, making war against other protoplasmic groups across the farthest reaches of this big hunk of rock we call home."

Stone nodded in agreement, his eyes staring at the thought "Maybe," he said. There were bottles lining the illuminated glass in back of where the bartenders made the drinks; most of the bottles were capped with spiggoted chrome tops, some of which glittered with little star points of light. Looking into that background, the two men used up their favorite stories about the aerospace business while they drank the drinks and watched the rest of the inn fill up with people—and the time passed that way until the best stories were gone.

The big hand on the Michelob beer clock was two orbits away from eleven o'clock when a white-haired old man climbed onto the last of the empty bar stools at Tom Kruger's left. The man was thin as six o'clock. He had a jovial face of a bronze tint, with skin furrowed by wrinkles the color of desert sand. A silver-white beard encircled his face like a garland and there were gossamer wisps of whiteness swirled across the top of his head. You could catch glimpses of the bronze skin under the hair on top as he ordered tequila, a salt shaker, and a lemon cut in half.

A little later, when Tom's conversation drifted to UFOs again the old man, who was working on his second tequila, joined the discussion. "They're landing out in the desert!" The old-timer's mouth broke into an odd smile, showing teeth that glinted in the light like rough-cut, opaque yellow gem stones.

"What's that?" asked Tom. He could see salt crystals at the corners of the man's thin-lipped mouth.

"Flying saucers," declared the old-timer, "landing—that's what I'm talkin' about!"

"You've seen one?" asked Stone, looking past Tom.

"I see 'em," said the old-timer casually. He sucked a lemon and sipped at the tequila.

"Where'd you see them?" asked Stone.

"Left three holes in the sand!" said the old-timer sharply. His voice sounded like that of a movie leprechaun.

"Holes?" repeated Tom as he looked into the old-timer's eyes incredulously.

"Yep—big ones." The old-timer's mouth crinkled up into a smile.

"I guess I don't quite follow you," said Tom.

The old-timer went through the last of the tequila in the glass. He sucked all the juice out of one of the lemon halves, and it looked dry and white on the inside after he had put it down on the bar. Stone brought out a new cigar and the old-timer caught the bartender's attention and ordered another drink.

"The holes where the three round things on the bottom of the saucers are," said the old-timer. "That's what they leave in the sand."

"I see," said Stone. His eyes widened as he nodded and puffed the fresh cigar to life.

"You ever see anything in the air?" questioned Tom.

"Yep," said the old-timer. "Out by my claim." He angled his head away from them to look at the bartender.

"Oh, I see—you're prospecting?" asked Tom.

"Yes sir, I'm a doin' it—out around Mojave, near the deep valley," said the old-timer.

"Which valley's that?" asked Tom.

"Why, Death Valley, naturally," said the old-timer.

"I didn't think there was much out there, 'cept Borax," commented Stone.

"There's gold, boys. Lost gold—stuff like that. I'm a lookin' for the yellow metal," crowed the old-timer.

"I thought the gold was all mined out," said Stone a little reluctantly.

"You don't have to find much at five thousand an ounce, boys," said the old-timer, and he laughed a short, high-pitched laugh that came from deep in his throat. Kruger and Stone nodded at the idea as the bartender came and went.

The old-timer's eyes took on a deep, liquid translucence as he recalled the night the flying saucer came near. Just as he started in, a small blond-haired man made his way over to the bar from a corner table and took the freshly vacated stool beside the old-timer. A long scar showed on the new man's forehead, just at the hairline, and he wore a checkered shirt and blue jeans; pointed-toed lizard skin boots dangled at the bottom of the jeans.

"My dog Pedro saw it too," said the old-timer. "He was real scared. He got to shivering, and that was funny 'cause it was a real hot night—the wind was a'comin' up from Mexico—a Santa Ana."

"Well, sirs, I can tell you I was nervous when that saucer floated in, all glowin' red, and it had these orange and blue rays of light flashin' out of it. The flashes hurt your eyes—made 'em sore as hell," said the old-timer. Beside him, the new man was listening, but pretending that he wasn't.

"Did you see any shape?" asked Tom. The old-timer grimaced and blinked, ignoring the question. There were several people at the bar listening to the story by now, and the bartender interrupted it by bringing fresh drinks. The old-timer sampled his tequila leisurely and the listeners seemed restless for the story to move ahead.

"Do you think there's any oil out there where you're at?" the new man in the lizard boots interrupted the old-timer. He took a quick drink from a whiskey sour and then smiled, showing small, sharp-looking teeth.

"There sure is a lot of hot air in here," said someone seated toward the middle of the bar, and a round of cackling laughter burst forth.

The old-timer looked over at the new man. "There jus' could be some of that black gold out there somewheres. But I can't say fer sure." The man nodded in reply, then watched as he took the last of the tequila from the glass, licked salt from his hand, sucked on one of the lemon-halves, then smacked his lips together. He put the lemon half with the other dry ones on the bar, then grinned, making the white whisker stubble stand out on his cheeks before continuing with the story: "Well, sirs, the saucer got up real close to where it jus' hung above the old Spencer mine shaft. It was shaped like a WW Two U-S-of-A Army helmet and it had those three round things on the bottom—they kinda looked like those metal balls that's inside toilet tanks, and they were rotatin' real slow and easy."

He turned his forefinger in a lazy loop to illustrate what he had just said. "I could hear it then—damn! It sorta sounded like a stirred-up hornet's nest—real unfriendly soundin'."

The blond man with the sharp teeth looked on and listened, his small rough face stiff and hard looking, like flesh-toned, vacuum-formed plastic.

"Any windows or port holes—anything like that?" Tom asked the old-timer.

"Nah! Nothin' like that. The thing was only around jus' a while. Then it took off—pronto tonto!" said the old-timer, gesturing his hand into an upward-turning arc.

"Where do you think they come from?" asked Stone. "Another planet?"

"Nah! People are bein' lead down the brimstone path," said the old-timer with a quiver of his eyelids. He looked like he knew something.

"How's that again?" asked Tom.

The old, white-haired man wheeled around on his stool, turning to face Tom, and pointed a finger straight down at the floor. "That's where they come from." He snorted.

"Under this beer joint?" said Tom.

"Way down," replied the old-timer, "that's all I know." He paused a moment. A couple of men swiveled on nearby stools, laughed, then went back to their loud conversations. Tom took another slug of bourbon. He could feel the warmth sliding down his throat.

"There's somethin' funny about the saucers—somethin' evil, somethin' dark—like they don't belong here." The old-timer gave his scalp a scratch, ruffling his hair, and it made the strands of white hair stand up and arch over like solar prominences eminating from his head. The old-timer's eyes seemed to be transfixed on something stretching out inside him for some distance, like a surveyor's eyes as he sights a distant property line through a telescopic transit—except he was looking back inside himself. He looked like he knew *something*.

Tom finally asked, "So you think they come from under the earth?"

"You got that right," replied the old-timer.

"Who do you think's flying 'em?" Stone asked the old-timer.

"People's goin' find that out when it's too late!" said the old-timer.

"You lost me on that one," said Tom.

"We are not contending against flesh and blood, but against principalities, against powers, against the rulers of this present worldly darkness, against the spiritual hosts of wickedness in the heavenlies," said the old-timer.

Kruger and Stone looked at the old-timer as if they were looking at him for the first time. "You sound pretty convinced," said Tom.

"It's in the Good Book—that makes it right fer as I can see," said the old-timer. "It all adds up—flying saucers is jus' the demons coming out in the last days of this old world."

The sharp-toothed man on the stool beside the old-timer dashed back the last of his drink, slid off the stool, and ambled away toward the door. He looked as if the whiskey sours he had been drinking had affected his personality.

"Maybe you're right, Old-Timer," Tom told the prospector. Stone nodded as if he agreed with some small part of the whole thing.

"Most people don' wanna think on it, but judgment's comin', sure as shoutin'!" said the old-timer.

"We've got a long day tomorrow," said Stone. "We probably ought to get cracking, whatdya think, Tom?"

"You boys work at the base?" asked the old-timer.

"Sure do," said Tom.

"Ah, I see them silver birds roar over my place sometimes," said the old-timer. "Keep 'em flyin'—red, white, and blue. We got a great country, that old U S of A. Don't want to let any fellers come in and grab it away from us."

"Hey, we're doin' our best," said Tom casually. Then, in a serious voice, "Say, if you ever get another rash of saucers out there, you know, for a couple days running or somethin', I'd really appreciate a call—I mean, I could give you my number at the base."

"Tom Kruger." The old-timer said the name out loud after Tom had handed over a scrawled piece of napkin. "You ain't by any stretch related to the Krugerrands of South Africa, are ye?"

"Nope, 'fraid not," answered Tom. "Only Krugerrand I ever saw was under glass at a coin dealer's. Wish I would've bought some 'bout eight or ten years back."

"I'll tell you what I'm fixin' to do here," offered the old-timer. "I'll draw you out a map showin' where my place's at. Then if you get an urge to drop on out some time, you're sure welcome. You strike me as pretty nice fellers." The old-timer took the pen Tom offered, grabbed a napkin from the bar, and scrawled quick, sharp lines on it until there were enough. He handed that and the pen back to Tom.

Stone and Kruger finished their drinks and slid off the bar stools. Stone moved his legs a moment to get the stiffness out and, after that, they left.

5

The Powers That Be

It took until 2 A.M. to make the old-timer come out of the inn. He was the last of the patrons, and the overhead parking lot lights had already been turned off for the night. The moon was nearly full, shining brightly up high like an electric white opal and the old man's hair and beard had the appearance of white phosphorescence as he poked along toward a far edge of the parking lot, just a white-whiskered form moving toward a dusty tan jeep. It was Wednesday morning and the life of the town had been suspended by human slumberings, and there were no car lights moving on the street that ran beside the tavern. There was an eerie quietness.

As the old-timer meandered toward his target, a black Lincoln automobile emerged from the rear lot, passing through the shadow of the building, then catching the strong silver moonlight with chrome-edged reflections as it rolled toward the slightly limping form. It was one of the big Lincolns from the seventies coming at him, and the muffled sound of the engine made the old-timer glance over, and then his body recoiled automatically, his mouth unhinged with surprise as the car lurched to a stop beside him. Suddenly a man with a wirey build stepped out of the car, grabbed the old-timer, and forced him inside with an ease normally associated with a well-conditioned and powerful athlete. The car door through which the abduction had come slammed quickly, and the car began to roll again.

"Hey, what is this?" shouted the old-timer. "What's goin' on?" Amid the silence, one of the men beside the prospector in the back seat brought out a small gray box, shaped like a pack of cigarettes and, when he pressed it into the old-timer's side it crackled like a powerful electric spark. The old-timer screamed in pain and lost consciousness as the driver of the car turned out of the parking lot, and the big car disappeared into the dimly lighted distance, the twin red taillights dwindling as the dark shape moved away from the city.

The Lincoln didn't slow until it reached a petroleum storage facility near the highway that ran between Edwards and Rosamond. The black car halted at a chain-link fence, then slid through a slowly opening gate back toward a corrugated metal building that loomed stark and white in the moonlight. A faint whine came out of the building, a door raised, and the driver eased the big automobile inside, parking on a section of floor marked off by blue runway lights. In a few seconds the Lincoln-laden section began lowering like a trap door, down past several levels of construction. The largest of the underground parking garages was on the lowest level, and when the elevator platform bottomed out the Lincoln rolled off, then traveled in a short semi-circle until it finally came to rest, neatly parking beside five other cars. Overhead, a square of peach-colored lights outlined the opening through which the car had descended.

Near the fifth car from the Lincoln there were several doors, each outlined by white fluorescent tubes, which seemed to give out a cold, bright light in the subterranean dimness. Three men in black suits got out of the Lincoln; they looked like the kind of men who wouldn't write on restroom walls. They stood very straight-legged and erect and resembled each other slightly, as if they were distant blood relatives. Their eyes carried a dry coolness and had elongated shapes, suggesting the men were oriental, although their complexions were pallid, nearly white. Two of the men had dark, black eyes; the third had odd, light hazel eyes, the colored part almost yellow in the dim light. Their faces had small features with abnormally wrinkled appearances, as if the skin were made out of wax that had cooled too quickly. With the wrinkled faces and necks, the ages of the men were hard to judge, but they gave the impression that they possessed an age much greater than they showed.

The tallest of the men pulled the old-timer from the car. The man with the light eyes took one arm, and the two of them dragged the old man toward one of the doors. There was a panel of switches beside the door and an illuminated legend composed of light-emitting diodes that read ARO INTERROGATION ROOM 52. The third man was first to reach the door, and he centered his left eye over an aperature that glowed with a steady light, six inches left of the door, halfway up the wall. A black-grilled speaker beeped several times; the door slid open sideways, emitting a vibrating, reedy hum that reverberated off the concrete walls around them.

Inside, around the rim of the room, there were eleven racks of electronic equipment, and on these monoliths, at intervals, patterns of numbers and snaky white and yellow curves formed moving displays on black screens. The men in black strapped the old-timer into a sparsely padded chair that had switches on the side with sufficient quantity and complexity to enable regulation of the dynamos at Boulder Dam.

"What the hell's goin' on here!" sputtered the old-timer as soon as the ebb and flow of consciousness returned. "Who in the sam-hill hell are you people—can't you say nothing!" The old man's face flushed red as he stared at the two men whom his sputtering was seemingly bringing his way again. The old-timer was still intoxicated from the tequila, and blood red lines were etched on his eyes like streets on a Rand-McNally map of LA, and they bulged a little as he writhed in the chair, flapping against the straps that held him in. Two men in black came up to him and stood for a moment, staring down wordlessly.

"Well, I guess you guys finally caught up with me," said the old-timer. "But I can't figure which ones you are—Weight Watchers or Alcoholics Anonymous? Then there's the FBI or Future Farmers of America—maybe the CIA or the Four-H Club, huh?" The old-timer cackled nervously, the laughter hollow and strange amid the mechanical whirrings, synthetic clatter, and electronic tones that filled the room.

The men seemed to glare for a moment at the old-timer with eyes lifeless, as if they had been drawn by a computer on a screen. The shortest of the men, the one with the almost yellow eyes, spoke first in a closely controlled voice: "We understand you've been spreading filthy rumors about so-called flying saucers."

"Maybe, maybe not. What's this all about anyway, governor?" asked the old-timer, hiccupping slightly at the last word.

The shortest of the men standing over him continued. "You'll have to reveal to us the details about these things you say you have seen—all of them. We prefer that you give us the full story of your own free will." The speaker paused, his face fierce in the artificial light, his slanted eyes narrowed into elliptical slits.

"What's my business is my business—it don't concern you,"

said the old-timer firmly. His mouth tightened; he looked surprised at what he had said.

"Let us simply say that your business is our business. In fact, it's not any business of yours at all. This UFO rumor is only our business. Ater you tell us the full story you can shut your fat, drunken mouth."

"What happens if I don't?" snarled the old-timer.

"You will receive an injection—a sample of a few of the pharmaceutical Frankensteins we carry on an in-stock basis," said a man in black nonchalantly.

"This is a free country, mister!" piped up the old-timer.

"That's a nice slogan," said a man in black with casual arrogance. His words had come out in a clipped fashion that made his speech sound mechanical and utterly ruthless. "Your name, please."

"Ben," came the reluctant reply.

"Last name!" said the interrogator, a mean impatience in his voice.

"Gibson!" shouted the old-timer.

"We will require confirmation of that name," said the interrogator, and he extended his hand expectantly toward the old-timer.

"Well, you'll jus' have to take my word fer it," snarled the old-timer. The interrogator reached one of the switches on the side of the chair and turned on a pair of high-intensity spotlights in the ceiling; the old-timer's leathery skin took on a gnarled appearance under the glare.

"ID!" shouted the interrogator. He lit a cigarette and let it dangle from his mouth while the smoke curled down out of the orange-lighted tip. "ID!" he said again with muffled hoarseness, the cigarette waving in his mouth. At that the old man reached his wallet and handed it over. The interrogator quickly glanced through it, then nodded to the man in black beside him, who walked away, took up a seat in front of one of the control terminals, and began typing information into a machine, the display in front of him responding with glowing words: NATIONAL SECURITY INFORMATION. UNAUTHORIZED DISCLOSURE SUBJECT TO CRIMINAL SANCTIONS. He paused a moment and then put more words up: PROJECT O—May98-606-155763/CC: NSA: SUBJECT: B. GIBSON/ ASO PROJECT/MOJAVE/EYES ONLY.

The interrogator's voice started again. "Now, tell us these flying saucer stories of yours—from the start to the finish."

"Tell me who you people are first and what all this stuff in here is for and why you have a right to do this to me," said the old-timer in a ragged voice.

"This is a national security affair," said the interrogator. "We are the people assigned to listen to all these weird flying saucer stories. It's all excrement as far as I'm concerned."

"Who are you—CIA?" questioned the old-timer.

"It doesn't matter to you," responded a man in black. "All you need to know is that we want the required information from you—and we have the means to get it." The chief interrogator's odd, red-rimmed eyes were dominant over the old-timer by now. "Now, you will tell us everything you claim you saw."

Multitudes of recording machines and the voice-stress analyzer were already running in smooth synchronization as the old-timer began to speak about the strange things he had seen, hesitating to the point of stuttering at first. The men in black were listening intently, eyes narrowed into thin ovals, pupils emotionless as marbles and, even under the harsh lights that beamed down with expensive regularity, each set of eyes seemed to possess a separate secret.

6

The Verdict Is In

Seated at the controls in front of the humming wind tunnel was a man in a checkered cowboy shirt who had thick, curly hair in which the white had almost, but not completely, triumphed over black. The man's face was thin and dry with unusually deep wrinkles etched across his brow like Frankenstein stitches. Inside the tunnel enclosure, through a dirty glass window, one could see a one-eighth-scale model of the F-170 fighter hanging at an odd angle, its nose pointed downward. The technician's murky blue eyes, magnified greatly by his silver-rimmed glasses, gazed in at the model as the powerful whine of the wind tunnel enveloped the room.

Beside the technician stood Leo Glidewell, peering through keen dark eyes with aloof interest into the hazy window. As he watched the miniature warplane begin to flutter, his mouth was curled in a slight smile and his lips were ajar, showing front teeth that were crooked and crossed like a rabbit's. His profile showed a long, slender nose that curved and extended over his mouth, beaklike, giving him a faint resemblance to a bird of prey. The front of his face was shaped like that of a narrow Valentine's Day Heart with a V-shaped, bony chin at the bottom and a pointed outgrowth of hair at the top that extended down his forehead a little, forming a widow's peak; combed back from that apex was a thinning stock of brown hair. His weakest feature was a receding chin that only served to make all his other features stronger by comparison. He was wearing a white cotton shirt and a tobacco-colored leather sports coat, and he had one hand pocketed in expensive slacks that hung creaseless above black, unpolished Weejun penny loafers with unfilled coin slots.

The wind tunnel technician worked a series of switches, his

glasses catching the light in the room like twin mirrors as he glanced at the controls, then back up to see the smokelike vapor begin to swirl over the fluttering airplane inside the tunnel.

Three and a half weeks after Glidewell had arrived from a lower-paying assignment, the two major causes of the F-170 crash had been isolated. Glidewell had located one crucial circuit within the aircraft's Roll/Yaw Computer that had failed, even though it had been designed to be failsafe.

"The catastrophic failure of one transistor produced a daisy chain of electronic events that caused the aircraft's flight control system to enter into irreversible oscillation," was the way Tom Kruger and Glidewell had summarized the first failure in the engineering report on the investigation. That particular mystery had been solved by analyzing thousands of possible circuit failures in the F-170 flight control system. Melissa Delaney's computer program together with 17 days spent by a team of specialists, round-the-clock on the computer, had given them the millions of calculations needed to find the electronic design flaw that correlated with the last fatal moments of the test plane's life.

Reconstruction of the F-170's final flight profile led the tiger team to the conclusion that Electronic Component AQ279 had burned out; it had died—subatomic electrons had ceased to flow through it. A gap, unbridgeable to electrons, had formed across a microscopic chunk of crystal and a three-hundred-million-dollar aircraft had crashed into the desert because of it.

Analysis of the surviving F-170 black boxes had revealed that the pilot had switched to the emergency backup control system, but he had waited too long. Using all the rules of reason and logic, an experienced test pilot should have switched to the backup sooner, but the pilot had been preoccupied with the pursuit of the UFO. The delay in pilot action had caused the second problem, which sealed the fate of the F-170. The aircraft had begun to oscillate irreversibly by the time he switched over and, because of a flaw in the F-170's aerodynamic design, the report read: "The vehicle became locked in a spin and none of the controls could have terminated the type of spin encountered."

This was all contained in the 42-page technical report the team had hand-carried to Johnson Aircraft's chief flight test manager. He would sign it and present it to the responsible Air Force officers; they would call a meeting and tell him to fix the problems. And so, a new series of wind tunnel tests were already beginning and, for the tiger team that had been gathered from all parts of the country, the days ahead promised to be less stressful. Only the key team members would remain at Edwards until the F-170 redesign was completed.

The tunnel's whine droned on for a moment before Tom Kruger walked up, clutching a half-eaten bag of peanuts and a white paper cup with cola in it. He finished the peanuts and the rest of the drink, watching the scene inside the wind tunnel as if it were a television show he had seen before.

"Going back to the office?" Glidewell asked Tom in a loud voice that overcame the sound of the wind tunnel. His accent was distinctively British.

"Yeah," said Tom. "How's everything look so far, Herb?" he asked the white-haired technician.

"I'm 'bout halfway through the series," yelled the technician. "I'll give you a buzz when we're done."

"Super! We'll see you later, Herb." The man with silver glasses nodded dryly and raised his hand in a silent wave. "We almost got it whipped, now," said Tom to Glidewell cheerfully as they walked away.

"Hell yeah," answered Glidewell. "It was trivial in the final analysis, wasn't it, old chap?" Glidewell was easily the taller of the two, but he took unusually short, measured strides for his height and, with his hawklike appearance and thin build, it made him look slightly awkward, like a huge bird who had trouble walking.

"Trivial for you job shoppers maybe," said Tom, and he laughed. He had used the slang industry name for short-term contract engineers, which Glidewell mildly disliked. "It's just another step down the glorious road to retirement for us regular guys."

"Close enough for government work, anyway," said Glidewell, then with suddenness, "Hey—you realize we're back on forty hour weeks, starting today?"

"Right!" said Tom, looking at his watch. "As a matter of fact, we get to go home at the regular time today. By the time we get to the office, we won't have to go into the office! We can cut through the building and just head out to the car."

"Jolly good idea," said Glidewell as they started up the metal stairs from the wind tunnel laboratory. They walked on out of the low-slung building, across a small parking lot, and into the Johnson test operations building, where they headed down the central hall;

halfway through, they passed an office that sported a well-dressed chubby man, feet up on the desk next to a fancy nameplate reading RONALD SWABODA—PROJECT COORDINATOR, who was reading the latest issue of *Scientific American* magazine.

"I say, old man, wonder what that chap does?" asked Glidewell after they had passed.

"I don't think anybody knows," said Tom. "He just seems to watch what other people are doing. He walks around with a clipboard sometimes. I heard he's even got a second desk in another building someplace."

A smile spread over Glidewell's lips. "Marvelous gimmick," he said, eyes flaring up with a cynical look. Then, after a second or two, "Ever notice how the damn bean-counters have taken over the engineering companies—RCA, Raytheon, GE, Johnson Aircraft."

"Well, I've only worked at Johnson, but I reckon they're probably takin' over the whole world," said Tom.

"I've seen it all over, old chap," Glidewell went on. "They have us engineering fellows busting our carcasses to get the plane or some other contraption out the door and there's a vast number of bean counters looking over our shoulders to make sure we don't go over our quota of file cabinets or number-two pencils or Pink Pearl erasers for the year."

"I don't make many mistakes; last time I used an eraser was a couple years back," said Tom dryly, and both men laughed.

Notices posted on the main hallway's bulletin board offered a good opportunity to pass the last few minutes of the shift, and so the two men stopped there to read. "Hey, look at this," said Tom as he examined one of the three-by-five-inch cards. "FOR SALE—STUFFED HEADS. Two large stuffed heads, must sell. Expertly mounted on walnut. Will separate! Mountain Lion and Grizzly Bear, both in perfect condition—$345.00 each. $550 for the pair. Must see to appreciate. RAY BENSON—Extension 75030."

A couple of snorts came out of Glidewell's nostrils. "Well, they *are* a good buy," he said.

Beside the first card, a pink sheet announced: ANTELOPE VALLEY UFO STUDY GROUP MEETING—LOWER LEVEL, LANCASTER PUBLIC LIBRARY, JUNE 12, 7:30 P.M. EVERYONE WELCOME! REFRESHMENTS PROVIDED.

"Hey, Leo," said Tom, jabbing at the notice, "why don't we head over to this thing? Maybe find out what's goin' on; maybe get a handle on what Colonel Murphy was chasing that day."

"I wouldn't mind delving into the matter. These UFOs are itching to be researched," said Glidewell. "Besides, the refreshments look intriguing, they may have UFO cookies or flying saucer punch."

"Okay, I'll even drive," offered Tom.

"Splendid," answered Glidewell as they started down the hall toward the double exit doors. Through the windows in the doors Tom could see a mammoth cloud floating in the sky. Glidewell pushed through the door first, and the men descended the worn and pitted steps, their shoes scraping across the concrete. A steady stream of wind blew at them as they headed for the cars, and there were cumulus clouds scudding through the sky and, in Tom's mind, the largest cloud changed to a fat-faced king with a curly white beard and a crown on his head; the king's cheeks looked like the sky. It amazed Tom when he came to himself and knew what he was doing. He hadn't seen a cloud that way for a very long time.

"Boy, this wind out here's somethin' else," said Tom. "You ever work at Edwards before, Leo?"

"Yes, in actual fact, I've served as an engineering rental unit out here on several occasions."

'No kidding."

"Right-o. Made a lot of bucks out here—like picking plums from a large, juicy orchard."

"Does the wind blow all the time like this?" asked Tom.

"Generally speaking, I would say it does, old chap. I mean, I've had gusts of wind blow fast-food hamburgers off the outdoor tables before I could consume them!"

"You're kidding me!"

"I wouldn't do that," said Glidewell. "Actually, I used logical deduction to solve the burger-wind dilemma."

"How's that?"

"Well, one day when the wind was quite beastly, I purchased two cheeseburgers and one without, went outside and plunked them down on one of the tables. Never lost a cheeseburger; the regular burger lifted off in less than a minute."

"That sounds real scientific," said Tom sarcastically, then he laughed, checking Glidewell's eyes to see if he was joking.

"It's the added weight, you see, cheeseburger versus regular burger," expounded Glidewell, "and a double burger is safe as hell. I would hazard to say one can turn one's back on a double burger in Lancaster, even in a blooming windstorm."

7

An Electronic Search

By seven thirty, there were nearly 200 people gathered in the meeting room of Lancaster's library and, like a hawk seeing prey from a great height, Glidewell spotted two of the last available gray folding chairs near the back of the room. They barely beat two teenage boys to the chairs and, after sitting down, Tom proceeded to thumb through a British UFO magazine he had purchased from an albino man who sold them from a table just inside the door. After lighting a pipe, Glidewell picked at a green sport shirt, which was still stuck to his skin in sweaty spots from the heat outside. As he rotated his wrist, Glidewell's gold and steel watch band caught the light and glittered and looked expensive.

"Polyester!" exclaimed Glidewell. Tom looked up from the magazine and nodded casually. "Inferior stuff! Synthetic abominations that pass for clothing these days," croaked Glidewell.

"I prefer the hundred-percent cotton stuff, myself," agreed Tom.

"Damned hard to find cotton anymore," said Glidewell.

After a few minutes a distinguished-looking man with graying hair at the temples walked up to a mud-colored podium and tested the microphone, which projected like a mast from the front edge. An electronic squeal issued out of black cloth-faced speaker cabinets, each stenciled with A-V and suspended atop chromium poles on either side of the podium; another man bent to adjust a pair of amplifiers that were stacked on a low table, just beside a ten-foot screen in the front of the room.

With the microphone adjusted the man called the meeting to order and there followed a flurry of people interweaving to find their seats. The man smiled sweetly as he waited for the shuffle to end.

"Welcome, both to our new guests and to our regular customers," said the man at the podium after the sounds of the commotion had faded. The overhead lights reflected off his eyeglasses as he surveyed the room a moment. "By way of introduction to you new folks, my name is Lester Madison. I'm the president of the Antelope Valley UFO Study Group. I'd like to invite the newcomers to formally join us if you find an interest in what we're trying to do here. Our dues are inexpensive, we have a lot of good clean fun, and we work in some time for UFO research as well." A flurry of laughter erupted from the crowd.

"Well, I imagine everyone's aware of the deluge of UFOs various people have been sighting in our local area the past few weeks. In point of fact there's a record number of reports coming in from around the United States and Canada. We're also receiving quite a few reports from Europe and the Middle East," said the president. He had thin lips and a sharp nose, which he touched with his forefinger from time to time, as if to scratch it.

"Hypothetically we must ask ourselves—what does this massive increase in sightings signify?" he said. "Maybe we'll get your ideas on that a little later."

"Our group has been literally deluged with hundreds of telephone calls from UFO percipients as a result of our media exposure on several LA radio and TV stations. Thanks go to Mary McNelly, our publicity director, for much effort to make the media aware of UFOs and the Antelope Valley Study Group. Stand up, Mary, will you?"

A small woman with curly golden hair raised up out of the crowd and lifted a hand. She smiled and sat back down, adjusting her thick-lensed eyeglasses, which had almost fallen off her head.

"So far we've been able to investigate a couple of excellent close encounters—some, I might add, involving entities observed outside a landed UFO." The man paused, fluttering his eyelids as if to organize some thoughts.

"And what we probably need to do is set up additional teams to investigate some of the better sightings people have already called in, and we still need to keep on the lookout for UFOs with our sky watches," continued the president. "If you wish to volunteer, please leave your name and telephone number with the group's secretary at the door before you head home tonight. Wave to 'em, Joe." A hulk of a man waved from the table beside the double doors.

The speaker straightened his tie and went on. "Uh, how many of you out there believe UFOs are vehicles flown by beings from a planetary civilization other than our own?"

Glidewell's hand joined most of the others that reached toward the ceiling to form a majority opinion.

"Well, for what looks like the majority of us, who believe that the UFOs are somebody else's spacecraft, I must say that the massive number of worldwide reports may signal a new phase in the activity of the UFOs—whatever they are planning. There seem to be a huge number of close encounter cases in this latest wave, especially in California.

"I just investigated one out by Palmdale yesterday. I was able to interview five of the six witnesses. The narratives they gave were consistent; the case has a high strangeness factor and involves three unusual humanoids they saw by the side of the road. I still have some work to do on this one, so it looks like I'll have to wait and give you all the details when the investigation's complete. Just out of curiosity, let me ask if anyone has any theory about the possible significance of the tremendous concentration of sightings in our local area."

A hand flapped up out of the middle of the front row: "It's possible that the UFO aliens may have a base around here," said the voice behind the hand. "There are reports that go way back that seem to show that UFOs prefer certain geographical locations. It seems like the southwestern U.S. has always been one of their favorite spots. Underground bases could certainly explain it."

"That's a definite possibility," agreed the president. "In fact, it might be productive to set up a project to search for signs of a secret base right around here; with the ton of reports there might be one right under our noses. Of course, it might take some fairly complex equipment." The president paused a moment and seemed to scan the back of the room where a man nodded and raised his hand. "Right now our trusty video expert is setting up a piece on the cattle mutilations. Please bear with us while we debug our new equipment; we're reading the instruction manual as we go along." He smiled at the laughter that broke out. "So, there will be a short recess while we get our act together."

Glidewell elbowed Tom, his voice hissing in a loud whisper. "We could use my van to pinpoint a hidden base—I've got most of what we need—the antenna arrays are already mounted. We'll probably need to borrow some specialized equipment—spectrum analyzers, things like that." Glidewell proceeded to draw his pipe out of his pants pocket and reached his tobacco.

"You really believe there's hidden bases?" asked Tom incredulously, "On earth?"

"It's a fair assumption," said Glidewell.

"You mean like a UFO Fort Apache, sitting out in the middle of nowhere?"

"Under the middle of nowhere," said Glidewell confidently as he rammed tobacco in the pipe. "There've been scores of UFOs reported coming out of the oceans, lakes, reservoirs, even rivers. They could have select bases under the land linked by tunnels to water. Three quarters of the earth's surface is underwater, and most of it's virtually unexplored. And we have no way of knowing what's happening to most of it at any given time." Glidewell paused to light the pipe. "A silent UFO with its lights off wouldn't be seen entering or exiting a secret base at night under cover of darkness. But, by jove, it might be detectable electronically."

Tom leaned forward a little, his eyes intent on the idea. "Sounds like you know some stuff about UFOs," said Tom.

"I've mounds of data and hundreds of books on these things, old boy," assured Glidewell. He drew on the pipe pleasantly a moment and whisps of bluish smoke rose in the air and gave it a sweet smell.

"Underground UFO bases still sound pretty incredible, Leo," said Tom.

"Let me give you the background on this particular deduction," said Glidewell. "I worked with an engineer in St. Louis at McDonnell Aircraft who was on a team that set up the first Air Defense Command satellite tracking system in Colorado. He swore that when they first set it up they tracked some kind of huge artificial satellites in four-hundred- to six-hundred-mile orbits. This was in the fifties, when nothing should have been up there, old chap. By the time we had something we could shoot up and check it out with, these things had bloody well disappeared."

"What the hell were they?" questioned Tom.

"Hold your horses," said Glidewell. "In that same time period there were zillions of UFOs being sighted all over the world. It was almost like they were making a reconnaissance of power plants, military installations, things like that. A few of the chaps this engineer worked with at NORAD thought the unknown satellites were mother ships for the smaller scout ships."

"You mean like aircraft carriers—except they were launching flying saucers."

"Exactly!" said Glidewell. "Interstellar class, something like that." He looked at his pipe and saw it had gone out. "And if they launched the smaller craft from orbit in the fifties, they still have to be launching them from someplace now. They probably can't use the moon; it's too distant for quick launch and recovery."

"So they moved their UFO carriers underground?" said Tom.

"It's possible, old chap," said Glidewell.

"Setting up a search effort might be worth a try," said Tom.

Glidewell scratched up and down one side of his nose. "The UFOs could be the biggest scientific game in town. If there are secret bases, whoever discovers one could solve the whole bloody mystery!" exclaimed Glidewell.

"Or get zapped by a ray gun from here to Timbuk-six," joked Tom. His eyes lit up and he smiled at the look that began to creep onto Glidewell's face.

"This whole UFO mystery is a window to scientific stardom," said Glidewell. "Hertz and Faraday played with electromagnetics before anybody else could see their true importance. Gallileo had the planets; Madam Curie had radioactivity."

"Dr. Jekyll had Mister Hyde," said Tom.

"And we've got the UFOs, old chap," said Glidewell. "This is where the new vein of scientific gold is. By jove, this thing is still wide open. Most of the technocrats in this generation are ignoring the data, scoffing at things they don't understand."

Tom nodded. "Probably don't have much to lose."

"Hell-yeah. Sure there's been private studies and spurts of government-sponsored appraisals in France, Russia, and America. But, hell, considering the bags of evidence, what's been done is just a drop in the bucket. Tom, I don't mind telling you, I've wanted to be famous ever since I was knee high to a grasshopper."

"Well, count me in. I'd still like to know what Murphy died tryin' to catch up with," said Tom.

The group's president walked back to the front of the room, leaned over the podium microphone, and announced: "Okay, I believe we're finally ready. If those of you who are standing would please take your seats, we'll roll the tape." Glidewell leaned down and tapped his pipe on his cupped hand, then disgorged the ashes onto the floor under his chair. He ran his finger around the inside of the pipe's bowl and put it away. The lights in the room were extinguished and the video projector cut a swatch of light across the darkened room. The image of a blood-drenched cow exploded silently against the screen, the sound of space-age music blaring out a split second later.

8

Death in the Night

A night bird shrieked out its lonely sound above the pleasant murmur the insects had put on for the evening. Hank Warwick, Jr., heard it while he sat on the front porch of the weathered farmhouse, gazing upward past the edge of the roof, letting the starlit night fill him so that he could feel small. In the blackness above him the stars were shining like stilled, luminescent insects.

It was a few seconds after the bird had called before Warwick saw the green-lighted craft glide down and land out beyond the alfalfa field to his left. It scared him, and he jumped up off the wooden chair slats and ran into the house, almost tearing the screen door off its hinges. He blurted out in a loud voice what he had seen, but there was no belief in there at first, no comfortable room for the story in the minds of his family. They didn't accept the boy's version of reality until later, when the creatures began approaching the house. In a few minutes members of the family began to hear scraping noises and sounds like animals would make walking on the roof. Then they saw one of the grotesque creatures drag its claw-encrusted hand across the window screen as it stood outside the window above the kitchen sink.

The father grabbed his rifle from the red oak rack and began shooting at the creatures that scurried and cavorted outside the house. The mother and two daughters began screaming when they caught sight of one of the creatures with its hideous eyes glowing red through the living room window; then the three women huddled together, sobbing in discomforting, rising and falling crescendos. The two sons grabbed shotguns and took up positions where they could get clear shots out the doors on opposite sides of the house. Hank Warwick, Jr., shot a barrelful of buckshot into one of the alien life forms, and the blast knocked the creature down, but then it flipped up again in instantaneous, dreamlike quickness, like the popping up of a toy jack-in-the-box, and then it fled behind the chickenhouse. The scene resembled that of a small engagement in the war with the Indians that once covered the land, except the creatures didn't shoot anything at the farmhouse and they didn't die when they were shot.

Under the starry night sky Hank Warwick, Jr., could see that the creatures wore shiny, tobacco-brown one-piece clothing that looked like the jumpsuits most of the upper classes in Europe wore at the parties the Warwicks were used to watching on television via satellite. The monsters' hairless, ugly heads protruded directly from their shoulders and their eyes wrapped around the sides of their heads. The central part of their eyes glared with arrogant, triumphant looks and seemed self-illuminated, except when they were caught in the floodlights that slanted out from the eaves of the farmhouse into the darkness.

The men of the house tried to fill the creatures with lead before the bizarre encounter was over. Most of the shots had missed, but each time it seemed one of the creatures took a hit, it would flip up like a gymnast and scurry off into the surrounding darkness. After two hours had gone by the creatures withdrew out of sight altogether and didn't approach the house after that. As Hank Warwick, Sr., looked out the front screen door, he saw a light rise up into the air slowly, and then it went from a big light to a little light and then shrank to no light.

The cattle out in the fields far from the farmhouse were silent. The moon had risen by now, a silvery sliver like the slanting smile of a big Cheshire cat up in the sky. A light bigger than the moon swung down from the western sky and approached the animals. The strange orb was pulsating between dim and bright and emitting red-orange beams and forming and reforming shapes in the air like a giant neon amoeba stimulated by powerful electric charges. The luminous spectacle set down suddenly on the darkened plain 50 yards from the nearest cow.

The animals watched the spectacle nervously while they pawled and scraped at the ground with their hooves. In the next instant unknown creatures began emerging from the glowing, ever changing blob of light. There were six in all, and they each had split hooves and dark, thick hair that covered their bodies. Their heads were hairy and hideous, and the eyes sparkled with a beastlike cunning as they approached the first of the animals.

Behind the creatures snakelike pointed tails twitched and slithered. A growling roar came out of the throats of the creatures as they closed on the nearest of the cows. The tremendous glow from the landed glob of light reflected off their dark heads and showed pairs of whitish horns bobbing and weaving through the night before the glow from the landed orb of light faded and only a dim, flickering luminescence remained, and then the dark, moving forms of the creatures blended in with the night.

The nearest cow stared at the approaching beings, bellowing in frantic tones as the first of the entities came on. The first animal's eyes were lame and stark as the first wound slashed across its body like a lightning bolt, ripping the flesh, and blood spurted out of the animal in a thick, pulsating stream. The cow gave out a final sound like a slaughterhouse death cry and went down on its front knees. One of the creatures bent over the animal and slashed a short deep wound into the cow's right side, using its long, pointed claw. The cow went down the rest of the way, then gasped at the air, and rolled over on its side. The strange being separated the wound with darting movements and placed its hairy face against the fountain of blood, beginning to drink in the liquid, an awful sucking sound issuing from the creature's mouth.

A second creature reached the dead animal, went to the rear of the cow, lifted the tail, and proceeded to remove the rectum by inserting a long, thick talon and working it until the rectum came free. Another of the creatures reached its thin arm up the hole the other had made and, after a frenzy of activity, pulled a hunk of flesh from the cow and began to devour it. Blood had plastered down the hair on its left arm and, as it ate the animal organ, it held the meat high between two hideously powerful-looking hands, one arm appearing only half the size of the other.

The other creatures attacked another of the cows and felled it where it had stood its ground, bawling, paralyzed with fear. They drank its blood after they had removed the ears and one of the eyes and the sexual organs with lunging slashes from their powerful, razor-sharp claws.

Hank Warwick and his two sons had left the house by then, searching for traces of the creatures they had shot at. As they neared the fenced pasture where the cows were kept, they noticed the dim luminescence of the landed light and heard strange, faint sounds in the darkness ahead of them. Hank Warwick, Jr., swung the heavy Ray-O-Vac lantern toward the spot where the sound came from until it caught one of the murderous creatures in its beam. Instantly the strange horned creature transformed its appearance into that of an extraterrestrial humanoid, clad in a coverall with boots on its feet, a belt around its waist, and with a bald, pear-shaped head sticking out of a hood at the top of his clothing. There was an instant when the Warwicks didn't know whether they were seeing the forms of alien animals or strange bipeds. But after the smallest part of a second the UFO creatures were perceived as two-legged beings with semi-human faces and bodies. Warwick swung the light to one side and caught the second creature in his beam, but all the demonic presences in the field had changed their appearance in that one instant of time, and so the thing that the light flashed across was a pear-headed humanoid just like the first creature they had seen. The farm people stood for an instant on the brink of the pasture, mesmerized as they watched the dreamlike scene filled with space creatures hurrying to their ship.

The father raised his rifle and tried to draw a bead on the closest of the humanoids as it glided with the others toward what had been a blob of light a moment ago. As the Warwicks perceived it now, the light had grown dramatically brighter, and it had developed structural details, looking now like a lighted 30-foot soup bowl resting upside down on the pasture in front of them. A ladder extended from the glowing machine, a hatch seemed to open, and as the first of the creatures scurried toward the opening, the father got off the first shot. He missed the creature and fired and missed again. By then the creatures had disappeared into the bottom of what looked like an advanced aerial machine, lighted by a dazzling illumination, and the three men ran toward the craft.

After 30 yards the men stopped to fire shots at the shrinking opening in the side of the craft, and they heard one of the rifle bullets zing off something that sounded like metal, and the big machine lifted off and flew straight up, out of sight in 826 milliseconds. After it had gone the men stared at the place in the sky where the machine had disappeared, and Hank Warwick, Jr., figured just as much as anyone could figure out anything that they had just happened onto creatures from another world in space and witnessed the departure of their spacecraft.

9

The Mystery Deepens

The telephone beeped for attention in the quiet room. Tom Kruger was in the middle of the most pleasant dream he had had in a long time. Melissa was with him in the dream, behind his eyelids. The two of them were sitting together on a hilly bank beside a silent stream, and he could see the stream flowing through the arch of a wide stone bridge that ran from one side of the stream to the other. The moment he opened his eyes, the place he had been was gone, and the sun was wafting a wide, fan-shaped ray of light through a slit in the beige curtains that hung at the motel room window. And so the first thing that registered when the stark light met his eyes was the sparkle of dust in the illuminated air above the bed. As he rolled to face the beeping, he could see a trapezoidal patch of light on the carpet beside him.

He stumbled sleepily out of bed and moved his bare feet through the sunlit patch of carpet until he was close enough to reach out and snare the strident-sounding mechanism from its cradle. Glidewell's voice was on the other end.

"Tom," said Glidewell excitedly, "get your clothes on—they're mutilating cattle out by Victorville! The UFO Study Group just rang me up."

"What the hell did they want?" responded Tom, his mouth distorting the words involuntarily.

"They wanted to know if we'd help set up a lookout for UFO activity. I volunteered us—I thought you'd probably be interested. The farmer with the mutilated cows caught some type of humanoids in the act. I'll be over to pick you up."

"Wait—hold it, Leo! I've got errands to do," said Tom. He scratched his chest through his pajama top.

"What bloody errands could keep you from pursuing the UFO

enigma?'' asked Glidewell.

"Well, I tell you, Leo—first I'm going to mutilate a bloody steak with my teeth at lunch. I've got a big urge for one. Then I've got to get some groceries and a haircut,'' said Tom.

"Why don't you get them all cut?'' joked Glidewell, and he screeched a laugh loud enough to distort the sound coming through the telephone.

"Very hilarious, Leo,'' remarked Tom. "Besides, I think I'm supposed to be taking out Melissa. I kind of said I'd take her to a movie tonight.''

"Ask her along,'' suggested Glidewell. "Hunting UFOs is a hellava lot more exciting than the movies they're putting out this decade!''

"Okay, I'll ask her, but I don't guarantee anything,'' said Tom.

"When do you expect your bloody errands to be completed?'' asked Glidewell.

"By four,'' answered Tom, a little annoyed at Glidewell's voice.

"I'll be by at five,'' offered Glidewell brightly. "We'll take the night shift at the mute site. Melissa's more than welcome. How does that sound?''

"Count me in,'' said Tom reluctantly. "I'll give Melissa a buzz and see what happens.''

"Good, good. Cheerio,'' said Glidewell before the connection clicked off. The silence sounded good to Tom; Glidewell's voice over the phone had been a little too raspy for pleasant early morning listening. Tom yawned as he tapped in Melissa's room number on the eggshell-thin plastic phone. The low-pitched ringing tone came and went three times before Melissa said hello from the other end of the line in a faint, husky voice that had all the indications of not being fully awake.

"How are you, sleeping beauty?'' he said cheerfully.

"I guess I overslept, huh?'' She sounded to Tom like a very young child would, wiping sleep from its eyes.

"No, of course not. In China it's only two in the morning.'' Melissa responded to what he had said with an uninhibited, sleepy laugh.

"That was a great dinner last night,'' said Melissa. "I really had a good time.''

Tom hesitated before he framed the words. "Well, I'm glad you liked it,'' he said. "That kind of brings up tonight. We kind of talked about going out tonight, right?''

"Yes," said Melissa, and she hesitated. "I seem to remember, yet I don't quite remember where we talked about going. I don't think my brain's working yet."

"Well," began Tom, "how about going with Leo and me on kind of a UFO hunt? We've got a hot lead."

"I thought we were going to a movie." said Melissa.

"Well, I thought—I mean, this is probably going to be a lot more exciting."

"Who's Leo bringing on this expedition?" asked Melissa.

"I don't think he's bringing anyone. Uhh—he's got to stay on his toes—you know—keep all the equipment going."

"I'm not real keen for UFOs tonight." said Melissa. "And I don't think I like the idea of double-dating with Leo and a bunch of equipment. Where is all this excitement taking place?"

"Some cows have been mutilated out by Victorville. It's about forty miles away—why don't you come?"

"No thanks," she said, and laughed. "Actually, Tom, I'm not too thrilled by the thought of watching cows cut up and dismembered in living color. Mostly, I like musicals like *Singing In The Rain* or *The Sound Of Music*."

"Well," he said, "if they cut up two cows simultaneously, at least the sound would be in stereo."

"How grotesque!" exclaimed Melissa. "Nope—I'll pass."

"Okay, I'll take you to a show. I'll call Leo and tell him to forget about me going."

"No," said Melissa. "We can see a show anytime—I'm serious. Go ahead and do what you have to, but I get a rain check on the show."

"You're not mad?" asked Tom.

"No," she answered. "I'll just curl up with a good book. But you definitely owe me. Just have a good time playing with the equipment, analyzing whichever cows you can rustle up that are still breathing. By jove, I've got it!"

"Well, don't give it to me!" he said. "We can hit the show tomorrow, okay?"

"I'll tell you what," she said. "How 'bout taking me to church tomorrow? It is Sunday tomorrow, isn't it?"

"Let's see," he said, hesitating. "Today's Saturday, and if you add one day—yep, I guess you're right."

"How 'bout it?"

"Ahh, I don't wantta ruin my reputation, you know," he answered.

" 'Fraid it might be real?" she said.

"Oh, I believe it's real."

"Well, don't we all want to kind of plan to go upward when we die? You know, I mean we don't want to go the other way, right?"

"I dunno—I might have to take out fire insurance before I croak." They were both silent a moment. "Well, what the . . ." he began again, expansively. "I mean, I guess I owe you one—sure. What time?"

"It starts at ten-twenty, so pick me up at least by nine forty-five."

"Gotcha."

"Don't forget—okay."

"Okay."

After they had said good-bye he cradled the receiver back on its hook and felt himself smiling.

After two fried seafood dinners at the Ranchhouse Restaurant, Glidewell and Kruger rode out Highway 14 south to Palmdale, then east on Highway 18 to Victorville. It was late afternoon and the sun was low in the sky, and a dust devil was whirling off in the distance, gliding toward them from the west.

"How far you think it is?" asked Tom.

"About thirty miles as the photon propagates," said Glidewell, and he smiled, showing his rabbit teeth.

Along the way there were low, thin wisps of clouds drifting overhead like small gossamer nebulas. As the van neared its destination the clouds in the sky thickened; the southern sky was bright and it made the occasional buildings off to the right appear dull and somber, except for some of the metal roofs, which sparkled as they passed.

They reached the Warwick farm a little after eight, and Glidewell took the first unpaved road that ran back toward the farmhouse, and 1000 feet down that road there was a tan Mercury automobile. The man inside the car had gray wavy hair combed back, straight black eyebrows, and penetrating blue eyes, and he was gazing out the car window at them as the van pulled alongside; Glidewell went past, angled in front of the Mercury, then stopped. As they got out of the van and strode toward the Mercury, the man opened his car door and got out, arching his back in a long stretching motion, then working his legs, bending one and then the other.

"Leo Glidewell and Tom Kruger here," Glidewell said to the man as he and Tom came out of the van and approached the Mercury.

"I'm Bill Scheider," said the man, offering to shake hands.

"Any activity?" asked Glidewell as he shook the man's hand.

"Nothing much," said Scheider, and then he shook with Tom Kruger. "I took about three rolls of film—mostly airplanes in the distance, I think."

"Lester sent us out to take the night shift," said Glidewell. Scheider nodded.

"How's the mutilation situation?" Tom asked the man.

"These people had a hellava time out here last night—first these creatures came up to their house—the men tried to shoot 'em but the suckers wouldn't go down for the ten-count," said Scheider. "He's had missing cows before, and one confirmed mutilation about six months back, but last night, after the UFOnauts left the house, they caught 'em mutilating their cows out in that alfalfa field." The man pointed to a distant field left of the farmhouse. "They got off a few rounds as the UFO was lifting off, heard a couple of shots ricochet off something metallic just before it accelerated out of sight."

"Is this guy gonna mind us parking out here?" asked Tom.

Scheider moved his upside-down forefinger to shake it briefly at the distant farmhouse and answered, "We interviewed them, got the report and all. Warwick said it was okay to park on the road here. I think he was glad somebody else would be watching in case something comes back for an encore. He just don't want people tramping all over his fields, you know. The local sheriff's been patrolling the area quite a bit."

"How'd the mutes look?" Glidewell asked Scheider.

"Dead as hell," the man said comically. "Most of the blood was drained from the bodies. The sex organs were removed from one of 'em, an eyeball and the two ears were gone, and two teats on the right side were cut out; the rectum and a couple of internal organs were missing from the other one."

"The blood was missing, huh?" asked Tom.

"Oh yeah," said Scheider casually. "The veterinarian found puncture wounds in the jugular vein of one of the cows."

"But not the other one," said Tom.

"No," answered Scheider. "The other one had a big gash in the side of him."

"How about the UFO—did they get a good look?" asked Glidewell.

"Oh yeah," said Scheider. "It was shaped like a domed craft of some sort; had a green glow and white lights around the rim. Lester was out here earlier—he got a sketch of it from the Warwick family. The episode last night was pretty scary evidently. They had UFO creatures climbin' on the house, comin' up to the windows . . ." Scheider stopped and shook his head from side to side. "It just don't make no sense."

Glidewell walked over to the van and took out the part of the *Los Angeles Times* he had saved from dinner. He brought it back over and offered it to Scheider. "I say," said Glidewell. "Our illustrious news media has solved Mr. Warwick's creature problem."

"I knew reporters had been out and interviewed the Warwicks," said Scheider. "I haven't seen the evening *Times*." Scheider held the paper up and found the headline, which read, CIRCUS MONKEYS ESCAPE AND CAUSE FARMER TO SEE SPACE CREATURES. Scheider shook his head in disbelief as he scanned the small article. The desert wind played with the edge of the paper, and it made the slightest of flapping sounds.

"What can you expect them to say?" said Scheider after he had finished and handed the paper back to Glidewell. "Monkeys attacked them, predators killed two of their cows, and they shot at the moon 'cause they thought it was a spaceship—musta not been their night."

"You can sure say that again," said Glidewell.

"Well, men," said Scheider. "After reading that story I think I'll be headin' home. My wife's got a roast in the oven and I'm lookin' forward to sinking my teeth into it." Scheider glanced at the dome in the top of Glidewell's van as he turned toward the Mercury. "Looks like you men are ready to get some data," he said as he walked away.

"Hell-yeah," said Glidewell toward the retreating figure. Scheider started up the old Mercury and pulled the gear selector lever down to REVERSE. "Good luck, men," said Scheider.

"Cheerio," shouted Glidewell. Tom waved as the Mercury backed down the small farm road, then reversed when it reached the highway and drove away. The sun was nearing the edge of the western sky and night would fall soon. That thought entered Tom's mind as he walked with Glidewell back to the van, and he wondered what book Melissa was reading.

"Let's get our logistical preparations underway," said Glidewell, back in the van. "I have a premonition we're going to get lucky tonight."

"I sure as hell would like to see something," said Tom with an acrid tone in his voice.

10

Pay Dirt

There was haze in the late afternoon air, and as the veiled red-orange sun made its way down the edge of the western sky, a few curious specators came and went, peering at the farmland where the latest published mutilations had occurred, lingering and pacing about with muted anticipation. They squinted at the distant farmhouse and gesticulated toward the fields with nodding heads and moving fingers. Some parked along the highway and others ventured down the dirt road where Glidewell's van rested. Glidewell and Tom Kruger brewed strong coffee on a small Coleman stove in the back of the van and shared it with some of the curious who came up to chat. Glidewell had several coffee mugs—white, decorated with the words SOLDIER OF FORTUNE in black above a picture of two crossed survival knives—and the people used those in turn to drink the coffee. A man and his wife from the UFO Study Group came by the van just as the sun's light was putting Dreamcicle-orange bands at the edge of the western sky, and Glidewell gave them a brief proud tour of his storehouse of equipment and made cascades of waveforms appear on some of the cross-hatched screens.

Soon the horizon flared with a red-ocher light as the edge of the sun slipped below the mountains, and the alfalfa swayed in the last copper rays of sunlight, caressed by a twilight wind. The daylight was beginning to grow fainter by degrees, and as the evening darkened the casually curious got in their cars and threaded their way back down the small road, the gravel making sounds like corn popping in a pot.

"Do you always carry this much stuff with you on the road?" Tom asked Glidewell as they watched night fall.

"Hell-yeah! One can never be too prepared. Too easy to

happen onto something important at any time—tornadic activity, extraterrestrial spacecraft, uncataloged creatures. This is an amazingly unpredictable cosmos we occupy, old chap. Really."

"Amazingly," said Tom.

"You can sure say that again," said Glidewell comically, and he forced a momentary grin that showed his slanted teeth. He reached into a canvas sack that was lying in the open console between the seats and took out a Meerschaum pipe shaped like a bearded man. Tom watched as the other man dipped the pipe into the sweet-smelling tobacco.

"What kind of tobacco?" asked Tom.

"Oh, it's just a mixture I have sent over from London."

"You're from London, aren't you?" asked Tom.

"No. Missoula, Montana, actually," replied Glidewell.

"Really," said Tom, giving a half laugh. "I never would've guessed that."

"Oh?" said Glidewell as he tamped the tobacco in the bowl of the pipe. He slid the tip of the pipe in his mouth and his cheeks went in and out like bellows as he held a lighter above the bowl. A pleasant vanilla aroma filled the air. "My parents are Ukranian," he finally said.

"Where'd you get the British accent?" asked Tom. He could feel the sweet tobacco smell inside his nostrils, warm and musty.

"I presume I acquired it from watching old British flicks—mostly old Sherlock Holmes movies with Basil Rathbone. I watched 'em hundreds of times—British stories are so extra-ordinary—vastly superior to American ones."

"Yeah. I remember ole Basil Rat-bone," said Tom. "I almost feel like Dr. Watson out here on a mutilation stakeout."

"You can sure say that again," said Glidewell, then he smiled, showing his rabbit teeth. Then: "Let's have at it, old chap!" They got out of the van then, and Tom threw his head back to check the sky. It looked to him like dark gray velvet sprinkled with tiny precious gems sparkling from some hidden light. He looked for movement. *Nothing but stars,* he reflected after a moment, and he found the five stars of Cassiopeia. It gave him a pleasant feeling, like seeing an old and wise friend. He thought of the times he had pointed out the five stars to girls he had known in the night. He remembered in detail their different perfumes, the different ways their eyes had looked in the starlight, the curves of their young faces. He looked inside his mind and saw those girls talking again and watched some of their smiles across the years.

All of that was still clear in his mind, and he wished for the smallest of moments that the last girl he had dated in Georgia were here, but now there was Melissa and the other girl was back in Georgia along with a house he had grown up in and his parents and the hills behind their house and all the rest he had left to come out here. But he hadn't really left the girl—he had broken up with her the week before he left, and he realized he missed her a little because his home seemed far away now. She had been a virgin when he had met her last summer. He had used all the right words at the right times and had seduced her with gentleness in the heat of August. But after a time she had been like the others—he had seen the flaws and grown tired of her, and so he broke it off, wanting someone else, never having met the one he knew he would stay with. Now, as the present seeped back in, the only thing that resembled any of the things he had left in Georgia were the stars in the sky, and it made him sad.

"Ripping good time if we spot something, old boy," said Glidewell as he climbed in the back of the van and turned on a power supply.

Ripping good time, Tom thought.

It was a little past eleven when they spotted a brilliant light flying at them from the south. "What the hell is that?" questioned Tom, pointing at the UFO.

"Well it isn't Air Force One, old chap." commented Glidewell.

"Look at the way it moves!" said Tom.

"Tallyho," said Glidewell. "Like a bat from the pit of Hades."

The light flew toward them like a lighted bat. It darted and accelerated, then slowed and hovered, then came on again. Glidewell pushed the flap of his ear forward the way people do sometimes when they try to detect a distant sound.

The two men watched in silence as the strange glowing object made a curved descent down from a high altitude—lower and lower until it leveled out, slicing through the air 1000 feet or so above the state road. Suddenly the thing stopped dead in its tracks.

"Leo," said Tom, "is that thing registering on the scopes?"

Glidewell spun around, took several long strides back to the van, then hopped up through the open doorway. Tom watched him a moment, then refastened his eyes on the UFO, moving sideways toward the van. "This is definitely the real McCoy," Tom said to Glidewell.

"Either that or those damn circus monkeys have escaped again and commandeered a UFO," responded Glidewell, tinkering with the maze of switches and knobs.

The UFO was less than a city block away from them now and there was a faint hum Tom suddenly noticed coming from the craft—a sound like bees swarming. The unknown craft had slowed, and it was floating like a ghost above the highway, enlarging. A very ghostlike way to fly, thought Tom, and fear danced at the edge of his mind.

"How's it goin' in there, Leo?" shouted Tom after the generator kicked in.

Glidewell was adjusting sliding control bars beneath a display screen like a country musician moving a bar across a steel guitar. He hollered out the door, "You're not going to believe this!" Tom strode toward the wide van opening and peeked in at the screen.

"I'd say that's a weird wave form," said Tom.

"You'd have a high probability of being wrong," said Glidewell, and he chuckled like a mad scientist in a horror movie.

"How's that?" questioned Tom.

Glidewell sputtered excitedly, dark eyes darting toward Tom Kruger, then back to the screen. "It's almost identical to a military electronics countermeasures pattern I've worked with before! Almost identical to the latest and greatest top-secret Air Force radar jamming capabilities."

"That's no Air Force bird out there, Leo," said Tom. "Check it out."

Glidewell bent down and peered out the windows on the other side of the van. "It's closer—looks like it's gonna land on top of us!" Glidewell snared a camera from an overhead shelf and tossed it out to Tom. "Well, whatever that thing is," said Glidewell, "I don't understand how it can radiate US-AF jamming. Shoot some pictures—I've got to get the video tape rolling."

Tom snapped off 16 shots before he knew it, the camera's power-winder alternately freeing and clicking the shutter. He took the last of the roll just when the craft's brilliant light dimmed, and he could see an oval shape appear; and on top of the thing a hump bulged out, like there was a canopy. The craft glowed faintly, blood red in color, while a central rim emitted an unearthly greenish luminescence.

"The ECM pattern just vanished," shouted Glidewell. "It's still putting out something centered on five-point-five gigahertz."

"Get it on the strip chart," hollered Tom, "and take another peek out the window."

"*Hell*-yeah," shouted Glidewell as he glanced out at the strange machine.

Suddenly a silvery square appeared on the bottom of the UFO and a beam of silver-white light blinked on and flashed down from the sky. It put a dazzling patch of light on the ribbon of asphalt, and Tom could see atmospheric haze and sparkling dust floating in the beam. The UFO continued drifting toward them, the square of light illuminating the road as if there were alien eyes peering at the lighted ground, perhaps searching for something. The search beam was strange as lights go—it didn't fan out—it was like an incredibly sharp-edged laser beam, and it was a square of light.

Tom felt somehow vulnerable out in the open with a creeping alien machine four football fields away now. Fear played with the edge of his mind again and he tried to push it out. *So this was one of those UFOs—one of those things people were seeing all over the world. Strange blobs of light in the sky . . . that some people reported and were laughed at because of it*, he thought. This thing in the air had to be made out of metal—he could tell by the way the light reflected off the rounded surface. And that meant it was a craft, his engineer's mind told him, maybe hundreds of years ahead of anything we have—maybe thousands.

The craft's vertical light beam shut off the next instant, and he saw for the first time that the equatorial ring was rotating slowly; it seemed to him the rotation was stabilizing the craft, like a giant gyroscope. It was funny, he thought, this thing looked exactly like it was supposed to—it looked like an advanced interplanetary vehicle should look. It was so simple in his mind that he wondered why there had been controversy and disbelief all these years as he noticed the huge craft rocking a little in the air as if the stabilization systems were correcting a momentary error.

Slowly he sensed a thought chasing after him; then, like a warm, sweet-smelling wind, it tugged at his senses and swept over him. The thought had come out of something that most people would have remembered only faintly, but he remembered the 10-year-old details now as though they were still right before him. He had been in the fanciest rare bookstore in Atlanta when he was 16, and he had seen a book in the science-fiction section with the title *To Mars via the Moon*, and it was a first American edition of a book published in Philadelphia in 1911. The owner of the store had priced the book at $500, which was $475 out of his reach at the time. But he recalled the book had a drawing of an imaginary Martian spaceship stamped on its spine in gold, and the same drawing on a slick illustration in the front of the book, and that other-worldly craft in the book had looked almost exactly like what he was seeing now a few hundred yards away from him. He wondered suddenly how that could be.

This thing had to be real, he thought, and anyone who saw it would know it was real and, yet there was something wrong just at the edge of his mind—something elusive. Something about this bizarre display went beyond what he could see. It was exceedingly curious how the object looked like a bookmaker's fantasy, conjured up by some human mind before there were supposed to be such things as UFOs. He strained in his mind a moment to track down exactly what it was that he was so close to discovering, but the glimmer of that *something* escaped as a vacuum vanishes when one opens certain jars of food.

Tom glanced back at Glidewell and watched him work the video camera. After he had run off a few feet of tape Glidewell locked the camera in place on its bracket, left it running, and walked back over to the illuminated screens in the center of the van. The high-frequency receiver showed a wave form that looked like a giant oceanic tidal wave, which slowly moved above the flickering waves and ripples of an electronic sea.

"Hey, Tom, take a gander at this," said Glidewell as he motioned Tom to come inside the van. Tom walked over and then up into the cramped, noisy interior.

"Whatdya got?" asked Tom.

"Check out this pattern," said Glidewell, pointing to the glowing yellow wave form that was spread out on the square blue screen. "I've got the loop antenna lined up dead center on that thing out there. Looks like a six-point-five center frequency, right?"

"Right," agreed Tom. "Hey—look at that pattern!" Spiked luminescent patterns had begun racing across the screen.

"It's totally different from before," said Glidewell cryptically. "It resembles panoramic radio frequency jamming except it's weirder—more advanced."

"Maybe it's some sort of communication," said Tom, his

words trailing off as the screen they were watching burst into an intense yellow glow from edge to edge. The two men stared for a moment in disbelief.

"What the hell?" said Tom.

"Advanced ECM," said Glidewell.

"Very!" Tom nodded and glanced at a row of gauges to his right. "Just got a glitch on the gaussmeter."

"I say," exclaimed Glidewell. "This thing knows its electronics."

"There's no aircraft in the world that can put out that kind of a magnetic field," said Tom.

"How much?" asked Glidewell.

"One-point-eight gauss."

Glidewell whistled at that. "About a billion times more than any earth-made flying machine, old boy."

"And the field's collapsing and reforming about one and a half times a second," Tom added.

He stepped down out of the van. The UFO was farther away now—powerful looking; and a kaleidoscope of colors were shooting out of it as it drifted away, following the highway. With great suddenness, the UFO shifted direction and began moving directly toward them again.

Inside the van, Glidewell changed positions and rotated the gray telescope around the upper dome's perimeter until he cross-haired the UFO and then began to click off exposures with the Nikon attached to the rear of the scope. The UFO approached, and the laserlike beam of silver light shot out of the bottom, shifting across the ground once more, and Tom saw the brilliant square of light coming right at him. He knew it would be on them in a matter of seconds.

All of a sudden he heard a new sound to his right and, as he turned to look for the source, he caught sight of a formation of aerial machines approaching from the direction of the Warwick farm. He swiveled on his heels and saw bright flashes of light were popping on and off along the bottom of the UFO—silvery orange, then red, roman candle green, violet-red like claret wine, and white like a welder's torch. As the laserlike beam of light from the underside of the UFO blinked out, Tom sighed, relieved that it had come no closer. Glidewell jumped out of the van and loped over to where Tom was standing.

"What the hell's going on?" questioned Glidewell as he turned toward the popping sound the four approaching objects were bringing toward them. "What the hell are those things?"

"I don't know," answered Tom, "but they sure as hell are something! And I don't think the UFO likes whatever they are." When they turned to check the UFO again the ring between the hemispheres on the craft was already a blur, and they had to shield their eyes against the new level of light that lit the terrain around them. Suddenly the UFO shot straight up into the velvet black sky as fast as a glimpse of a lightning bug's glimmer on a midsummer night—and it was gone.

They spun back around and faced the four machines that were swooping in from the other direction, and the pulsating noises the machines brought were familiar to them, but it was still hard to make out what was coming at them in the darkness. Scant seconds later the speeding machines skimmed over the Warwick farmhouse and flashed over the heads of the men with a great rush of wind and a deafening noise that rocked the air. Tom arched his head and watched the four black helicopters flash over, gaining altitude, homing in on the track of the vanished UFO.

"What in the hell were they?" asked Glidewell. "Helicopters?"

"You ever see helicopters that fast, with no external lights, no markings?" questioned Tom. "Hell, I doubt if those guys were more than a thousand feet in the air." Glidewell just shook his head.

They crawled back into the rear of the van. Glidewell ejected the video tape from the camera and transferred it to a player while Tom turned off the strip-chart recorder, examined the markings, cut off the portion that showed UFO signals, then rolled it up into a tube.

After that Glidewell played the video tape that showed the UFO on the ten-inch monitor in back of the van. "The fates have smiled upon us," crowed Glidewell as the last of the UFO video ended.

"We sure as hell saw *something*," said Tom. "Big as life."

"I doubt if a better tape's ever been made," said Glidewell proudly. "I'll have to copyright it. And then we'll present it at the next study group meeting."

"It'll probably blow the lid right off the room the way those people go for UFOs," said Tom wryly.

"Hell-yeah," said Glidewell, arching his eyebrows up and down a few times, and then his lips stretched in a dry, contented smile.

11

The Secret Game

Ron Swaboda drove in through the pseudo-petroleum company's automatic gate, which he had opened by flipping a miniature toggle switch on a radar transmitter he carried inside a brass pseudo-cigar case. He eased the sleek gray Mustang around the side of the building, past two trucks that had STUTZ ICE CREAM painted on the side panels and, beneath that, a portrait of white ducks swimming on slices of blue water. Swaboda operated another toggle switch on his transmitter and drove through the broad entranceway after the corregated metal door had lifted.

After parking the car neatly in a row with eight others on the lower level of the subterranean building he ducked his head a little to clear the edge of the gull-wing door and proceeded over to the solitary door that broke the montonous expanse of wall to his right. Tubes of fluorescent light gave his dark hair a greasy brown cast as he put his left eye up to a red-lighted aperture and paused nervously until the door swished aside, after which he walked briskly into the dusty white light that poured from the opening, his dark eyes darting quickly side to side as he cleared the doorway as if he didn't trust what he would find inside.

He headed straight down the center of a slightly curving hall and into a large conference room at the end, where he found eight people seated around the black-and-chrome rectangle of a table. Swaboda took a chair next to a man with a rust-colored crew-cut. A man who looked like he had swallowed a 20-pound turkey, its form lodged in his stomach beneath a shiny white shirt, swung the door closed, sealing the aperatureless room.

At the end of the table opposite the door, a very well-groomed man cleared his throat in a refined, intellectual way. His face was the only one in the room that showed no speckling of black stubble beneath the huge, bright lighting panel that overlooked the entire expanse of tabletop.

The clean-shaven man in a black, narrow-lapeled suit, who sat with an evacuated throat at the head of the table seemed about to speak as the new man sat down, but he made a great deal out of hesitating. Then he spoke in a sharp east-coast accent: "Baker, what's the situation in Victorville—all aspects."

The man with the fox-red flat-top responded: "We've covered it pretty well. Used our people in the media. What the public knows is zip."

"What'd it look like out there?" the leader asked. Confidence seemed to ooze out of him a full octave above that of the other men at the table.

"Well, it's probable they've experienced a combination of activity," said the fox-haired man. His eyes were small with black pupils, and they enlarged and shrank when he put emphasis on different words. "Type-Two humanoids put on a display at their farmhouse, then classic Type-Fives terminated two of their livestock about forty minutes later."

"Any residual traces?" asked the short man. His eyes seemed to carry a weary anticipation in them.

"We were fortunate here. We got a head start from our monitor on the sheriff's line. Our operative reached the site first. The scene had two-point-five-centimeter circular marks leading from a set of three depressions, typically made by NP vehicle landing gear—same MO as the activity that the project's monitoring in the midwest at the present time. The traces were taken care of."

"Any anticipated problems with the mute percipients?"

"There's a lot of awareness among the locals," replied the red-haired man with a look in his eyes just like that of a fox after he's raided a chicken yard. "A local farmer's association just posted a twenty-five-thousand-dollar reward for capture of the perpetrators or proof of the mutilators' identity."

"Pretty lousy reward," answered the questioner. "Well, keep on it." He nodded pleasantly and smiled, then shifted his attention to a man who sat on the opposite side of the table from the fox-haired man. "What's happening on the coast, Sedgwick?"

After taking a long drag from his cigarette and ejecting the smoke in an uneven, rapid breath a bald man responded in a precise, effeminate voice, "Two F-18s from Miramar were lost on a

Project-O intercept. The UFO was tracked at variable speeds—zero to twenty-two-thousand miles an hour. Both aircraft went down within a few seconds of each other—no final pilot transmissions."

"Any ideas?"

"Well," said Sedgwick. "Our sources out there placed together the ground control intercept tapes with several other factors and they evolved a fairly unconventional theory." Sedgwick hesitated a moment, stamping the cigarette butt with a yellowed tripod of fingers into a gray glass ashtray.

"Well," urged the older man. "Let's have it."

"Their contention is that the UFOs were possibly using the F-18s as drones for target practice," said Sedgwick. He puffed once at the cigarette. His eyebrows were a color that blended in with his skin; other than that, his face and head were so hairless and pale in hue that it made him look like a person who has been taking near fatal radiation treatments.

"Drones?" said the man at the head of the table in a loud skeptical voice.

"That's their theory, anyway," continued Sedgwick. "The entire encounter, as they reconstructed it, approximated a successful military exercise where pilots use live ammunition in simulated air-to-air intercepts on dummy aircraft. This is the summary of events and constructive speculation that the IR put into the comments section—the UFOs appeared to be simulating an actual air-to-air intercept with the F-18s before the lights went out."

"What's the purpose behind that?" said the leader.

"Their report doesn't speculate to that depth," said Sedgwick. He took a long, thoughtful drag on the white, smoking Salem.

"Well," said the questioner, "we sure as hell can't relay something that controversial to Washington. How'd you handle the media?"

"They've been notified that the Air Force had a runaway missile from Vandenberg—the missile's self-destruct mechanism failed and two on-station F-18s were ordered to shoot it down using a top-secret weapon. We told them the 18s were lost due to mechanical problems associated with the launch of the unspecified weapons."

"How about the runaway missile tiedown?"

"We listed the missile as impacting the ocean five-hundred

miles from the Hawaiian Islands.''

"Did they buy it?''

"Most likely,'' said Sedgwick. "When we listed the intercept weapon as top secret, the major TV and print media rolled over—a little reluctantly, perhaps. We're debriefing the personnel involved—no problems thus far.''

The leader of the meeting straightened his black-spotted burgundy tie for a second and slid it further down into the buttoned V of his black suit coat. He nodded slowly and then, wheeling his head to the right, he probed Ron Swaboda's eyes a second or two. "What's the status at Edwards?'' he asked.

"Essentially nothing of an updated nature to report,'' said Swaboda smoothly. "The management of all relevant information regarding the F-170 crash is on target. All crucial elements are classified top secret—that ought to hold it in. No present danger of public disclosure that a UFO was involved.''

The older man in black looked at Swaboda a moment, as if he were examining the pores in his face, and then spoke in a careful, unemotional voice. "I think it's becoming intuitively obvious that the UFOs are escalating their various activities. It is becoming increasingly more difficult to handle public relations. A major threat revolves around the growing number of close encounters. There is a certain vulnerability in this situation that I want you all to be aware of. I think the entire western operation needs to work more diligently in response to the challenge.'' He stopped a moment and forced a smile. "Agreed?'' said the leader in a vigorous tone. At that, the rest of the men in the room nodded their heads.

"To cover our regional hind ends,'' he went on, "I want each of you to build a report about escalations of the UFOs in your respective areas—it shouldn't be much of a hill. I'll collect them one week from today. Then I'll gin up an estimate of the situation out here and we'll get that to HQ.''

There was a pause, as if the group was waiting unsurely for the leader in black to speak again. A glance around the room would have shown frozen expressions on the faces, eyes shining dully in the overhead light, as some of the men took long drinks from white polystyrene cups of coffee. The leader snared a long pencil-thin cigar from his shirt pocket and put a flame to it with a slim gold lighter. He took a long drag, then released a slow, dramatic puff before he spoke again. "Now,'' he said abruptly, "for your benefit, the new man seated to my left is Frank Sloan from head-quarters. He's going to give us some help out here, and he's been brought in as second in command, Project-O, western region. His code name is Regis Littleton.''

Sloan nodded and smiled cordially at the other men who sat at the table. His small, closely spaced eyes maintained a guarded, unfriendly look as he scanned the faces around the table. ''It's nice to be aboard,'' was all he said.

The older leader continued, holding his cigar gracefully elevated at the end of the arm that rested upright on the table. ''Now. For Mr. Sloan's benefit, I should explain some of what is occurring immediately around us as I speak.'' He drew a puff from the cigar, exhaled, and looked at Sloan as he continued. ''We currently possess a new UFO candidate to throw out to the media when the opportunity presents itself. The subject is a derelict we recruited from the slums of LA a week ago. As we all know, there are officially no slums or derelicts in the Lancaster-Palmdale area.'' Knowing chuckles followed this from around the table.

''Of course,'' the leader in black continued, ''right at this moment, our man of the hour believes he's undergoing examination aboard an extraterrestrial spacecraft and when we're finished he will spout this story out for the remainder of his mortal days to anyone who cares to listen. And, as we all know, Mr. Sloan—a little disinformation goes a long way.'' The man's lips curled up and showed a crooked half smile.

''Quite true,'' agreed Sloan. ''It sounds like an interesting distillation process you have incorporated into the petroleum facility here.''

The leader rose from his chair at the head of the table and announced: ''Well, without further ado, let us go take a peek at the process.''

The men in the room followed him out, through the curving hallway, down an intersecting hall and then through a double door labeled SIMULATION—CEIV. The group of men gathered at a 20-foot-long rectangle of glass, standing tightly against each other. Through the gray glass they could see a lean, unshaven man seated on a padded chair. The man's wrinkled face was staring blankly ahead at a screen while a younger, perfectly bald man talked to him slowly and carefully. The older man wore a hospital gown and there were shiny, round patches on his flesh, devoid of hair, where electrodes had been implanted into his head, neck, and wrists.

"Cut in the mic," the leader said to Swaboda. Swaboda reached the wall at the right of the glass and pressed a black push button, which allowed sound from the room beyond the glass to come out of a metal grill at the left corner of the room where two walls angled into the ceiling.

"The leader has big, red eyes and a bald head with veins sticking out of the forehead. You look for his mouth when the words come, but you see only a slit—a fold of flesh where a mouth should be," the young man was saying to the derelict. The bald youth who coached him was wearing a one-piece tobacco-colored coverall. "The creature has a hairless face and ears shaped like pointed ice-cream cones." The shaved and groomed derelict was staring out into the space over the instructor's shoulder and his eyes showed a man with an intense, obsessive day dream.

"A good-looking charm-school student," said Swaboda to Sedgwick casually.

"Tailor-made to be our next space cadet," replied Sedgwick in a low voice that broke into a chuckle at the end. They both chuckled softly as they stared through the glass.

"They're taking you through outer space," continued the instructor. "Through blackness and stars until you reach their planet." The instructor operated a switch on the arm of the chair he sat in and a lighted moving picture appeared on a huge curved screen that encompassed the entire wall in front of them. On the screen an alien creature was operating an array of controls on a panel. "The creature is controlling the flying saucer, navigating through the solar system," said the instructor. "You're approaching Saturn at this exact moment." In a moment the images on the screen changed to an aerial view of a green planet's surface, and the man stared as if hypnotized.

"What if someone rehypnotizes him and he remembers the screen or the instructor?" Sloan asked his boss.

"We use a particularly effective combination of drugs and electric shocks to preclude that particular scenario from ever occurring," answered the leader. Sloan's thin lips curled in a smile.

"Now, Elwood, you will remember at this exact moment that you asked the spaceman for some proof of your voyage to Saturn—is that right?" asked the instructor.

"Yes," said the derelict weakly. His thin hair looped and

swirled around the two electrodes on his skull like electrically charged spiderwebs.

"And they give you some plum jelly from Saturn and some of their Saturnian cornbread—each slab is shaped exactly like a cone and they bake them in cone-shaped pans." The bald instructor handed the derelict some pieces of corn bread and a glass jar filled with a bluish-purple substance and sealed with a brassy top. "You keep these, Elwood—these are yours now. The creatures from Saturn gave them to you as evidence of your trip to Saturn."

"Yes, this is my evidence," agreed the derelict in a monotone.

"Now we are going into a deeper sleep, Elwood—*deeper* and *deeper* and *deeper*. In this deeper sleep you will forget about me and this room—you will remember the pictures on the screen because they are real and you will remember the creatures and the spaceship that landed and how they picked you up."

"Yes," said the derelict.

"There is a block in your mind that no one can go past," said the instructor solemnly. "If anyone tries to see me or this room, your body will cease to breathe. You will die! No one will be able to see me or this room. You can only remember the moving pictures and you can only tell anyone what you know about the space creatures and their planet. From this moment in time there is a block where you will not remember this room or me or anything except what you have been told to remember—no matter how deep you sleep in the future. You see only the inside of the spaceship and the creatures that operate it now. They are bringing you back to the earth, landing in the desert and letting you out. You float down on a blue beam of light that comes out of the bottom of their spaceship at two in the morning."

The instructor tilted his head from side to side as he examined the eyes of the derelict from various angles. The convolutions and bony depressions on the instructor's head shone like random geological formations on a slick, flesh-colored moon. One of the group of men at the glass viewing window yawned and then another man caught it and yawned sleepily, making a sighing sound at the end. The leader in black leaned over toward the intercom switch and cut off the sound. "Well, there you have the essence of the process," he said to Sloan.

A man wearing a white laboratory coat entered the room beyond the glass now and, after the bald-headed instructor rose, sat in the vacated chair. The new man worked a hypodermic needle until fluid squirted out, and then the two men slid the derelict around on his seat, pulled down the elastic waist of his pants, and the man in the white coat implanted the needle into the base of the derelict's spine. With that accomplished, the code-named men who had been watching through the glass window filed out of the room, resembling a group of bored gentlemen of leisure after seeing a mildly interesting Broadway show.

12

Angels of Light

After the church service Tom and Melissa went to the fanciest Sunday buffet they could find in a desert town. It was half past noon by the time the waitress sauntered up and from lack of breakfast they were both ready to get their money's worth. The waitress took their order and they waited until she took two steps away from the table before jumping up and heading toward the long counters laden with food warming in copper, steel, and glass receptacles. There wasn't any line and they shoveled spoonfuls of the waiting food onto too small dinner plates and carried them back. As they settled behind the plates heaped with food, Tom pointed to his and said, "Looks like one of the great pyramids, huh?" They both laughed deep laughs and then the eating began. Outside the window beside their table the wind was whipping through the dry leaves on the trees that were growing along the sides of the road. "That sermon brought the UFO to mind," said Tom after downing two eggs and part of a pancake.

"What you and Leo saw?"

"Yep."

"The angel of light part?" guessed Melissa.

"Yep—at least that could be part of the answer. There was something else really odd—I can't quite place my finger . . ."

"I think of UFOs as omens, I guess," said Melissa. She drank some of the orange juice the waitress had left on the table and gave him a curious look.

"Omens?" questioned Tom.

"Omens of the last days before the Second Coming," said Melissa. "The Bible says that there will be signs in the heavens right before the Lord's return—did you ever read *The Late Great Planet Earth* or *Rapture* by Lindsey?"

"I read part of the *Late Great Planet* one a long time back—I guess I really couldn't get into the writing style," said Tom, and he cut off part of an egg Benedict and devoured it.

"I really believe we're in the last generation," she said, her eyes mellow. "The prophesies are being fulfilled left and right, all over the world."

"Man, this egg is good!" he said.

"Oh, is Benedict back in the kitchen?" joked Melissa.

Tom gave her a questioning look with one eye squinted. "What are some of the prophesies?" he asked.

"In the last days, people will run to and fro and knowledge will abound. Then there's the one where Israel would be conquered and the Jewish people scattered to all nations and persecuted. The conquering part was fulfilled in AD 60 or something like that. Jesus predicted the Jews would reestablish the state of Israel and that would start the countdown to the end of the age—I think that was in 48 when Israel became a state."

"Yeah—I think that was after World War II."

"The Lord said Jerusalem would be conquered and trodden down by the Gentiles until the days of the Gentiles were over—Israel took back Jerusalem in 1967—another prophesy fulfilled, big as life."

"What's supposed to happen next?" asked Tom. He was busy eating the crispy part off his fourth strip of bacon.

"After seven years of world tribulation, the anti-Christ bites the dust at the battle of Armageddon and Jesus will rule on the earth for a thousand years—the millennium, you know."

The waitress walked up, checking on what they needed. She had closely cropped bleached-blonde hair and a fat round face that elongated periodically as she chewed the gum she had in her mouth. "Do you all have grits?" Tom asked the waitress.

"Sure do," said the waitress.

"Lay an order on me if it's part of the buffet," said Tom.

"Sure-nuff, hon," said the waitress, and she sauntered away, her stretched uniform making a swishing sound as she walked.

"What are grits?" asked Melissa as soon as the waitress was out of range.

"You're kidding. I thought everybody . . ." His voice trailed off and turned into a boyish grin. "You don't know?"

"Nope," she said sheepishly. Her face changed color a little and gave her rouge some help. "I've led a sheltered life."

"It's a southern dish—I'm surprised they even have it here."

"What are they made out of?" she asked.

"Kangaroo claws." Tom's lips pressed together in a subdued smile as he nodded his head in mock seriousness. "From southern Australia, I believe."

"You wouldn't kid me now, would you?" she said, and then laughed.

"Everybody knows 'roos are from down under," he responded. He carefully spread grape jelly on his buttered wholewheat toast. Melissa bit into a crescent-shaped slice of melon. Tom bit a large piece out of the toast, chewed it, and swallowed. He followed that with a swig of coffee, and then spoke on top of the swallow: "Where are you from again?"

"Santa Barbara."

"Must be a nice town."

"It really is—I really like it there," she said softly. "Not much computer work, though."

"The better the spot, the thinner the jobs," observed Tom.

"I really like your accent," said Melissa, and she smiled. Her cheeks were set high on her face and they had the loveliest curve to them when she smiled, he thought. The fact that she was lovely to look at flashed through him as he took another bite of toast. The jelly on the toast tasted like the grapes had started to ferment a little. He checked the list of preservatives on the ruptured container. "I bet where you live in Georgia is nice," she said.

"I miss it," he said. "My parents have about two hundred acres north of a little town called Duluth. When I'm back there, I live with 'em—commute into the Johnson office every day. Traffic's gettin' kind of dense, is the only thing I could kick about—the place is boomin'. But the farm's still nice—we got peach trees and we grow a lot of vegetables and stuff." He paused a moment to fork some potatoes into his mouth, and then went on. "That's enough about me—how 'bout you?"

"Well, let's see," started Melissa, feeling her way through the words, "I'm twenty-three years old. My father owned a book shop in Santa Barbara; he went away when I was twelve—ran off with another bookdealer. The book shop wasn't doing very well, and he took the few rare books with him when he left. He died in San Francisco a year and a half ago."

"I'm sorry."

Melissa cast her eyes at the near part of the table, then back at

Tom. "My mom was very religious—she took me to the local pentecostal church at least once a week after the separation, sometimes twice. We ran the bookstore to make ends meet. I graduated from Santa Barbara college in 1996, but the most important thing that ever happened to me was when I found out what Jesus really died for, and that set me free."

"You look like you would've been a pretty good kid. I mean you weren't a dope addict or anything were you?" said Tom.

"I was a sinner like everybody—the Lord gave me joy I never knew—he saved me from judgment and whatever might come after that," she answered matter-of-factly.

"You mean like Hades or something," he prodded.

"I believe there is a real Hell—someplace where there's an unquenchable fire."

"I guess it's hard for my engineer's mind to get that abstract—I mean, the Bible was written way back, there's been a lot of human translators—there's probably a lot of symbolism, you know." Tom realized when he looked back on the words that he had spoken to her the way he used to talk to his younger cousin who lived in the hills 80 miles north of his parents' farm.

The waitress brought the order of grits and refilled their coffee cups with steaming coffee from a glass carafe. "How's everything?" she asked.

"Just great," answered Melissa, smiling. After the waitress walked away Melissa leaned over and peeked into the bowl of buttered grits and spoke in a low voice. "So that's what kangaroo claws look like." Tom chuckled as he dug into them with his spoon.

"Want some?" he asked.

"No thanks," said Melissa, and she took a bite from a fried potato and chewed it slowly while she watched Tom attack the grits. "What were you saying about Hades?"

"Engineers aren't used to working with intangibles—I guess I'm trained to be skeptical," he replied.

"It's really the same as engineers taking physical laws into account when they design an airplane. I mean, I think there are spiritual laws just as real as the law of gravity."

They were both silent for a minute, then Melissa took the lead again: "I've got a favorite story about these other laws, if you'd like to hear."

"Sure, fire away," said Tom, spooning grits into his mouth.

"Well, I was born at a very young age," said Melissa. Tom slowed his chewing and put on a helplessly trapped look. She gave him a tight smile and then went on, suddenly serious. "And, well, I kinda had a deformed left leg—it was just about an inch shorter than my right one." Tom stopped chewing completely at that and tilted his head like a dog hearing a high-pitched whistle. What he was hearing surprised him more than anything he could remember.

"It was really strange," she continued. "My left foot was twisted inward. It was awful—besides uneven legs, I had a real bad case of pigeon-toe in one foot. In the sixth grade I started to do little things to cover up the one shorter leg and all—I walked a certain way that covered it some, I wore special shoes. I was pretty good at it, so most people didn't know about my leg. But when I made Jesus the captain of my life, things changed—a faith came in. I became a new creature—I really did. When you ask Jesus into your life he *really* comes in." Melissa's eyes took on a misty look.

"It took a year or so of reading the Bible every day, and I built up my faith that the Lord could heal me—that he wanted to. I learned a lot about prayer with little things at first. But I had to build up my faith for my leg, 'cause I needed a miracle, and we're taught all of our lives not to believe in something like that." She hesitated enough to get some more coffee in her.

"One of the things that stood out as I read about the life of Jesus over and over—Jesus healed every person who ever came to him to be healed—those who had faith and quite a few that didn't. The Bible has a lot of promises, and healing's just one of 'em—it was like a spiritual law that God wants us healed and perfect, you know. But it doesn't work unless we have faith." Melissa paused and took another sip of coffee.

"In the summer of my fifteenth year I went to an old-fashioned tent revival—I knew in my heart something would happen if I went."

"You mean you had precognition or somethin'?"

"No, it was more like a power had taken hold of me, deep down inside—it was kind of like I could feel the Lord telling me—go to that meeting. Anyway, in the middle of the healing service, the preacher called me forward—he told me my exact condition. I sat on an old wooden chair up front and they propped my legs up on the seat of another chair. The preacher laid his hands on my ankles and prayed for my miracle in the name of Jesus. I felt something come over me like an electric current, and Tom, it was really *something*—I watched my left leg untwist and grow one-inch onto itself. It only took a couple of seconds."

Tom's head remained completely motionless as he took in the testimony with blinking eyes that held a gaze not unlike that of the most modern of astronomers hearing an astronaut say the moon was square.

"What did it feel like?" he asked.

"I don't remember feeling the leg move or anything—I trembled and I just felt this warm feeling run through me, powerful, like electricity. And I knew then, beyond a shadow of a doubt, that Jesus was the one who did it. It didn't matter what the world thought that night—he did it anyway."

"That's the first time I've ever heard anything like that first hand and all—I mean, it's really great," said Tom. "I never would have thought you ever had one leg shorter or something like that."

Melissa picked up a piece of melon and took a nibble out of it while she glanced out the window. Tom shot her an inquisitive look. Her skin was smooth and she had a few faint freckles over the bridge of her nose, and her mouth was full and well-shaped. Her eyes were the color of dark chocolate in the light and had a beautiful shape to them. He realized that he had never before seen any eyes shaped exactly like hers. It seemed like he had never seen eyes that had the look of hers, something almost haunting, down inside them, and the thought struck him that it was exceedingly pleasant to see something that pretty nibble at a melon across the table.

She looked directly into his eyes then. "You can't beat Cranshaws," she said with a piece of it still in her mouth.

"You know, you've really got pretty eyes," he told her, and it surprised him a little that he had said it. He picked the last strip of bacon off his plate and smothered it with his mouth.

"Thanks," said Melissa, and she smiled shyly. The light from the window was reflecting in her eyes, and he could see the movement of the blowing trees in them faintly.

He nodded at her. "Just thought I'd tell you," he said.

"Yours aren't bad either," she said gaily. Tom laughed. She retrieved another piece of Cranshaw off her plate and nibbled at the end of it. "I'm probably supposed to use my utensils more," she said. "I hope you don't think I'm uncouth."

Tom grabbed the last arc-shaped slice of melon off her plate. "We could practice up—utilizing, you know—some night maybe," he offered, realizing he hadn't made sense. Before she tasted the Cranshaw he followed up with: "Maybe get together and go out to dinner again."

"And we could go on complimenting each other," said Melissa, laughing.

"And maybe I could tell you about your ears," Tom joked, trying to keep the Cranshaw juice from running out of his mouth.

The slightest of smiles came onto her face, and her mouth looked amazingly like that of a young child's. "What's wrong with my ears?"

"I'll tell you later," he said, "when we go out to dinner, if you'd like to."

"Okay," she agreed. "Only if it's a place where they set the table with at least two forks—I can use the practice."

The trees outside the window swayed, and more of the white cauliflower-bud clouds drifted past, and they ate until they couldn't eat anymore. They finished up by drinking more coffee and watching the birds play in the trees outside the window.

13

The Starlight Room

"Leather seats and everything," said Tom Kruger as he drove Melissa's aging yellow Oldsmobile down the main boulevard of town. He had just spent a week working on the night shift at the base and he was brown from days spent in the high desert sun. His full-cut hair gave him a leonine look. Melissa was beside him wearing a high-cut cotton dress the color of a lilac flower.

"You noticed," answered Melissa. "I really think leather's kind of neat—especially brown leather. I guess I'm partial to stuff that's natural."

"The seats are still in great condition," observed Tom, feeling the texture of the patch of seat beside his right thigh. "What year car is this, anyway?"

"Nineteen eighty-three—one of the last of the big ones."

"Really fun to drive," he said.

"Yeah," she said slowly. "I put special stuff on the seats all the time—about every two months, whether they need it or not."

"Whatda you use?"

"Neat's Foot Oil and lanolin," she answered, gazing at him from the unaccustomed right-hand side of the Oldsmobile. "You have double rows of eyelashes—did you know?"

"No kiddin'?"

"No kiddin'," she said. "By the way, you didn't tell me where we're going now that I think about it."

"You'll probably want to get your two cents in—your two-cents' worth," said Tom, correcting himself.

"Yeah," she answered slowly, caressing the word. She stared at him with dark, smiling eyes.

"Well, here, now, there, then," he said in quick succession, "what're your feelings concerning destination? I mean, what preferences would you entertain at this point?"

"*Well*," she said, "I usually eat two or three times a day whether I need to or not."

"Food! That's an idea! I take it you haven't eaten," said Tom humorously, a brisk southern accent coloring the words.

"I thought you'd like the idea," she joked. "First, since you told me not to eat anything before you picked me up, and then there's the way you cleaned 'em out at Sunday brunch." Her cheeks rounded out in pretty curves and a broad smile came out.

"Very funny," he countered, stopping the car at a traffic signal that showed a hooded red eye.

"What kind of cologne do you have on?" asked Melissa.

"Canoe," answered Tom. "I guess I've been wearing it ever since I was just a young whippersnapper." The traffic light swung a little in the afternoon breeze and when the green light flashed on he eased the car away from the intersection.

"It's nice," she said. "I've smelled some pretty awful cologne in my days. I'd swear some guys wear liquid fire and brimstone."

"Frijoles or flapjacks?" Tom shot the question out casually as the big Olds 88 rode with quiet smoothness down the street.

"Oh, do I get to pick the spot?" asked Melissa happily. Her eyes darted over at him.

"Sure," confirmed Tom.

"There's a nice Mexican spot in Santa Barbara," she said.

"Really," he said, his voice carefree. "Sounds enticing for a weekend jaunt, but—I tell you—it's past my dinner time. I gotta eat somethin'—put your thinkin' cap on—we're running out of town." He stopped the car at another red-eyed traffic light at the edge of town. On both sides of the road there were new shopping centers going up, the thin-timbered shells of the buildings in various stages of construction.

"Well then," she said, "I've just got to tell you. I have this tremendous urge for German food."

"Do they cook that stuff in California?"

"Of course!" said Melissa.

Tom glanced over at her, laughing, and then accelerated after the light had changed. "Let's see," he thought aloud, "there's somebody around here that whips up a mean wiener schnitzel—if I can just think of who. *Vos es los*? Who is it?"

"You sound like a bilingual owl!" she jested.

"My feet don't fit no limb," said Tom. "Turn right here," he said to himself, pointing with one hand and turning the steering wheel with the other. He stepped down on the gas pedal and accelerated quickly—the restaurant lay five blocks away.

At the restaurant, in the low light, Melissa's eyes surprised Tom—like he had known her all of his life. He had seen galaxies in the night sky and comets and nebula for the first time through a $12,000 16-inch Newtonian telescope, but he knew all those sights had been quite ordinary, now, compared to examining her eyes, a tabletop away over the top of the cardboard menu.

They ate the sauerbraten and wiener schnitzel with German red sauce. There were fresh green beans and potatoes cooked into brown-crusted, flat cakes. And after they had finished that there was coffee and almond-strawberry cheesecake.

"Do you ever watch the stars?" she asked wistfully, tilting her head to one side.

"I used to have a real good telescope a few years back," recalled Tom, "There are really some amazing things up there—nebula—galaxies—clusters of bluish-white stars. Stars are gregarious, you know—they like each other. They like to hang around each other, I mean."

"Really," she said. "I guess I've never heard that before."

"That's the first thing that really struck me when I got my telescope—how a lot of stars hang around together in pairs. I even saw Halley's comet back in '86. I really used to get into the sky—I watched it all hours of the night."

"The heavens declare the glory of God," she offered.

"I never heard it put that way. . . ." he said, sipping into an after-dinner Galliano. The yellow liquor seemed to glow like liquid gold in the light from the floating candle that sat between the transparent, pyramidal salt and pepper shakers.

"It's from the Bible," she said. "I forget exactly where."

The piano chords of the *Moonlight Sonata* were playing out of the Klipsch speaker cubes that hung from the ceiling at the end of thin black rods. It was turning into the rare kind of evening where everything around Tom seemed to blend into everything else. Things inside him seemed to match things outside him. Thoughts that went through his mind seemed to find their way into the things he could see and hear around him. It had happened two or three times before in his life, but this time it all seemed more pronounced than it had ever been.

When they came out of the restaurant into the twilight

beginnings of night, the air was fresh and blowing, intoxicating to breathe, and Melissa's dress billowed in a spurt of wind and Tom Kruger's navy sport coat flapped open like a sail. Inside, a white lining showed shiny as silk.

They strolled to the car, which waited under an aluminum pole that flickered on top with a peach-colored light just as he unlocked the door. Tom drove them out to a lounge that he knew of while the disc jockey on the car radio played songs from another decade—the best of the old songs. A black Porsche whisked past them and accelerated off into the distance out in front of them, the sleek, beetlelike rear end turning into red dots and dashes in only a moment. "Must be goin' at least a hundred," he said.

"Some people are nutty as fruit cakes," said Melissa. She squinted her eyes and leaned her head forward to watch the shrinking taillights.

It was a Monday night, and so the crowd in the High Desert Inn's Starlight Room was sparse. Tom found them a good table, tucked in the corner away from the bandstand. In the center of the room there was a big circular bar and, above that, a cove in the ceiling that resembled a violet-blue twilight sky embedded with blue and white stars that shone with flickering electrified light. Centered in the cove was a brass-rimmed four-foot opening, like a port hole, with black night showing through it, and there were deep blue floodlights around the port hole that were shining onto the starry, indigo-painted sky. The walls of the room were painted a royal blue and there was a raised circular platform at the far end of the room where the musical instruments stood illuminated by bluish stagelights.

Tom ordered bourbon and sweet soda and a tomato juice for Melissa and when the band began to play they got up and went over to the parquet wooden floor. Tom put his cheek against hers, looking past her at the dark-skinned man who was nodding his head as he punched piano keys. Melissa's perfume had a clean, citrus smell to it, and her cheek was soft, and the dress she was wearing felt like silk where his hand pressed against her back; he could feel the vertical curves in her back through the dress.

"I've really never gone dancing that much," said Melissa in the middle of the third dance. "I mean, I'm probably not a very good follower."

"You're doing great," he said. "You're not looking at your feet or anything." He pulled his face back to look at her. Her eyes had a look of concentration as she worked her feet, but she moved well with the music, and he had somehow known that she would.

"How tall are you?" she asked.

"Four foot eleven." He lied by 15 inches.

"You seem taller." Her eyes smiled and the corners of her mouth turned up in a little smile, and two small dimples formed above each corner.

For a moment his thoughts took over, and his mind went back to nights he had spent watching the evening sky on his father's farm the twelfth summer after his birth. He felt again the cool earth as he rested his spine against one of the farm's old pine trees, gazing at the myriad lights rotating above him while the foliage swayed and rustled in the night. He remembered feeling a part of it all on some of those nights—and some presence greater than himself would come in and, with that, he would feel this wisp of peace inside him, at the core of him. Then, at those times, he had sensed there had to be a designer of these things—some power who had fashioned the infinite beauty of the night—a master architect for galaxies and snowflakes, someone who had brought the sky into existence.

On some of those same nights, he had ached with the feeling that there would be a girl he would meet someday, and she would be unlike any other girl in the universe. He didn't know then if she was on earth or whether she was on a planet out there among the distant stars, but, like an invisible spore that had come out of the starry blackness, a thought had taken root inside him on one of those nights—a faint thought that grew more pleasant across a boyhood of silent watching in the night, until he believed that he would find this right girl someday and finding her would somehow be automatic. Although he didn't know when, except he knew he would know when she came. And he came to believe that when they met they would spend part of a life together, and somehow they might be able to do something important that would mean something to the stars and to the soft presence he had felt within on those nights.

Melissa's words interrupted his thoughts—they seemed to come out slowly and move past him as if they were riding on a breeze that softly blew chimes made from onyx and silver slivers: "You really dance well."

"Well, thanks," he replied. "Fun, ain't it?" He broke out in a belly laugh, pulled away, and saw the way her eyes reflected the overhead lights as she threw her head back, laughing with him. Her eyes looked very pretty.

After that they danced while they looked at each other without saying anything for a moment. It seemed to him that he wasn't just seeing her brown velvet eyes now, but they were inside him somehow, penetrating to the depths. They were into some deep part of him—those eyes that looked a darker shade at this moment than he had ever seen them look. There was a lot in those eyes, and they had little creases underneath them and seemed to speak of things he had always wanted to hear. He drew her back toward him and put his cheek against hers and they danced closer than before.

He knew now that Melissa was the girl he wanted to marry. Something in his mind told him, very logically, that he barely knew her. But a deeper whisper flashed through him then: *Ask her to marry you.* And a confidence shot through him like like an electric chill full of charged particles, and he felt if he asked her, she would say yes. Without a doubt he knew that the girl he had always wanted to be with was dancing inside his arms and the strange yearnings that had come to him long ago on those warm starry nights were closer to fulfillment than they had been before. A relaxed stillness came to him when he realized all this—a certain quietness that seemed to make the song in the room stretch out time itself.

Those thoughts flowed wistfully through his mind like a song once remembered, like a quiet stream of water in an uncharted land, and it struck him as exceedingly strange to be thinking these things. He felt as if a hidden part of him that had been there in a 12-year-old on his father's farm was here now, bringing these thoughts, and would always be.

When the set ended Tom and Melissa sat back down at the corner table and drank the drinks and talked, the light reflecting from their eyes. A stalk of celery jutted up from the cloudy red juice in Melissa's glass, and there was a slice of lemon straddling the rim of the glass, and she chomped on the celery in between her words until it was gone. Tom ate the fruit from the lemon slice, and it was still on his breath when he kissed her good night outside her room at the Red Rooster Inn.

"It's pretty early," said Tom, and he kissed her again.

"It's late," she whispered back. She looked up into his eyes with a blinking, sleepy gaze.

"I haven't seen your place yet," he said. "I wonder if it's like mine."

"They're probably pretty much the same," she said in a slightly shaking voice and laughed, and her eyes danced. They looked golden brown in the harsh light.

"I'm beginning to think that you're not going to invite me in."

"Remember work," she said brightly. "We've got to get a good night's sleep so we can give old Johnson our best tomorrow. And we'll get to see each other and everything."

"But there'll be all those other people there," he said, and he kissed her again, tenderly holding her face. She parted from the kiss after a long time. Her eyes had a soft look.

"I definitely think we'll see each other tomorrow," she said.

Tom pleaded his case. "What about tonight? The night is still young."

Melissa stuck the key she had been holding into the door and turned the lock. She kissed him quickly, swung the door open, and backed into the open doorway. "The night is old—I remember it from way back when the sun went down," she said quickly. "And if there's anybody I'd invite in, it would be you. But I'd better not."

"Why?"

"I'll tell you later," she said softly as she went in. "Maybe. 'Night."

"It sure is," he said to the closing door.

14

The Presentation

"Whatdya think they'll say when they see these babies?" croaked Glidewell as he held up a glossy photograph he had retrieved from a thick folder and gave it an admiring look.

"We're liable to turn into instant UFO gurus," said Tom Kruger, and he yawned as he shifted gears on the Chevrolet that the Johnson Aircraft travel department had allocated to him. It was small and cheaply made, and the engine ran so poorly, he was glad he didn't own it. He glanced to his left and saw a dust devil begin to whirl in the distance. The funnel glided lazily toward them for a few seconds and then vanished. "They'll go ape over the video tape," continued Tom. "Hell, Leo, we could prove the UFO case in a court of law with the stuff we've got!"

Glidewell put the photograph back in the folder on his lap and gazed out the windshield a moment as the automobile turned from motel row onto the first cross street they came to. "Damn straight, old chap—the UFOs have opened a door and all we have to do is walk through and see what's-up-doc on the other side."

"You know, Leo, have you ever wondered . . . I mean, there's been a few scientists try to figure this UFO thing out and nobody's come up with much about where they're from—how they fly. Hell, we're just electronic types—our big expertise is supposed to be in squirrel-cage motors, microchips, diodes—stuff like that."

"Science!" said Glidewell, his tongue powdered with sarcasm. "A bunch of blody egoistic eggheads long on tenure and short on insight. It's all a big joke." His eyes enlarged at the thought. "I've read their officious journals wherein they analyze trivialities while completely ignoring momentous data which every day stares them in the face. I've heard their bombastic ridicule of promising data and new theories of the universe. They alter data to fit their pet theories—make it up as they go along—it's in the record. A bloody lot of conmen—that's what most of them are, old chap—conmen." Glidewell brought out his yellowed Meerschaum pipe from the right-hand pocket of a blue cotton sport coat, packed tobacco into the bowl, and lit it.

"Tom, we live in a very materialistic society," continued Glidewell after a time. "I'm afraid what the world calls scientists today are people looking for more status, better automobiles and houses, more security—maybe even a more sexy wife, eh?"

Tom Kruger glanced out the window at the pale houses with rock-covered roofs along the side of the road. The rocks were crystalline and they sparkled like jewels in the late afternoon light. The sun was low on the horizon and red from haze in the air, and it made the westward windows on the houses blaze like squared-off sheets of fire—like gateways to hidden infernos.

Glidewell puffed at the pipe and the smoke drifted into the path of the car's air-conditioning ducts and gave the air inside the car a honeyed smell. Glidewell continued. "It never ceases to amaze how the pious kingdom of science weaves an elaborate theory out of the most minute, inconsequential garbage while ignoring UFO data that pours in on mankind like a deluge! Their sense of inquiry must be dead as doorstops."

"Hell, most people just believe what they see on TV, Leo," said Tom, squinting his eyes against the big red sun that stared at them through the windshield.

"Hell-yeah—somebody's got to get to the bottom of the mystery—give the public the truth—might as well be us," said Glidewell, puffing pleasantly on the pipe as thoughts seemed to course through his mind.

At the meeting Glidewell projected images of the UFO they had seen onto the big screen while the crowd sat and watched like a multicelled living thing hushed by what it saw. He had edited the still 35-millimeter UFO photographs onto the video tape and showed those first, commenting on the sequence of shots Tom had taken, as the whir of the equipment became audible between his words and the white ceiling-mounted projector showed red, green, and blue circles of light.

The next part of the tape showed the UFO in motion, and there were surprised murmurs from the crowd as it watched the huge lighted craft grow in size, all the while darting and dipping toward the earth. "The craft maneuvered in a series of right-angle turns as it approached our location," Glidewell told the crowd. "The equipment I utilized to obtain this video is the best currently available. The camera mounting device I used is extremely stable under a variety of operating conditions and so the wobble that the UFO exhibits periodically is not due to any sort of equipment malfunction or camera vibration but is a real attribute of the UFO as we observed it."

Next Glidewell changed the speed of the tape and showed the UFO's approach in slow motion. Some of the people in the room leaned forward a little in the darkness, squinting their eyes as they stared at the pictures on the screen. The man directly in front of Tom had a small head with closely shaved silver-gray hair and darkly tanned skin that reminded him of a coconut. He glanced at the faces of two more old men and a woman with dyed black hair next to the coconut-headed man and their eyes seemed fascinated at the sight of the glowing UFO.

"We also managed to obtain some amazing data of an electronic nature during the UFO encounter," said Glidewell. "Our analysis of that data is currently in progress and I would rather not present the raw data until completing the analyses.

"In the future, if we are fortunate enough to encounter another UFO-type craft, we will be prepared to use a pulsed laser beam device that I have mated with appropriate audio circuits. Since the main visual attribute of UFOs are changing light patterns, as you can readily observe on this slowed-down version of the video tape, we feel communication might be feasible utilizing coherent light beams. It's certainly conceivable that complex coded light waves could be the key to establishing communications with them. At least, that's one of our current operating hypotheses."

When the room lights blinked on at the end of Glidewell's presentation a fat man sauntered up to Tom, smiled and addressed him unexpectedly. "You don't need all that sophisticated gear to contact the intelligences who operate the UFOs."

"Is that right?" responded Tom, his eyes peering at the fat man quizzically.

"That is indeed correct," said the fat man, who had a thin black mustache, black slicked-down hair, and thick lips pursed in a faintly expectant smile. "Allow me to introduce myself." The man reached out a meaty arm and offered to shake Tom's hand, exhaling heavily with a slight wheeze. "Al Vilchek."

"Tom Kruger," said Tom, shaking the weighty hand. "Nice to meet you."

"My pleasure," said Vilchek.

Gildewell strolled up with a cola someone had bought him and gave Tom an exaggerated grin as if he wanted to air out his upper teeth. In the well-lighted room, his two middle teeth showed yellow and thick where they crossed on top of each other.

"This is Leo Glidewell," Tom said to the fat man.

"Al Vilchek," said the fat man. Glidewell nodded, and they shook hands. "Interesting presentation and the video quality was quite excellent," commented Vilchek. He had a deep, hoarse voice, and that gave an impression it was difficult for him to enunciate the words.

"Thank you," said Glidewell.

"I was just telling your colleague that you really don't need lasers and electronic gadgets to contact the intelligence behind the UFOs," said Vilchek matter-of-factly.

"I am curious as to why you would say that, my good man."

"Do you like good chile con carne?" Vilchek asked them.

"Absolutely," said Glidewell, his eyebrows lowering and taking on a sinuous curve.

"One of my top-ten dishes of all time," said Tom, nodding a couple of times, throwing Glidewell a puzzled look.

"My private plane's about ten minutes from here," said Vilchek. "It just so happens there's a session relating to UFOs planned for this Saturday at a place out in the desert. Usually, for lunch, they prepare the most magnificent chili in the western states, and I'm counting Texas."

"What kind of session?" Tom asked Vilchek.

"Why, a flying saucer communication session, of course. And you don't need to bring all those gadgets," said Vilchek. He smiled at them broadly, his cheeks swelling like tumorous growths seen by time-lapse photography, and the fat around his eyes crinkled into folds. "You certainly are welcome to join me if you so desire. I'll be lifting off from the local airstrip at eight A.M. Saturday."

"Where's this place at, again?" questioned Glidewell.

"We simply call it Desert Rock," answered Vilchek. "It's about an hour's flying time."

"Can we bring a colleague along?" asked Tom.

"Yes. Four is not too many for my little flying machine," said Vilchek.

Kruger and Glidewell glanced at each other a second or two. "We'll be there," said Glidewell in a chipper voice.

"Superb," said Vilchek, and his smile puffed his tumorlike cheeks out again.

15

A Desert Place

It was the seventh day of the week, just past ten in the morning, and the gray dawn had come a while before. The canopy of sky above the airstrip was covered with murky gray cumulus clouds, which made the desert look dismal and monotonous, and the mid-morning air still had a dampness Tom Kruger could feel on his skin as he boarded Vilchek's Cessna with the others. A few minutes later the plane droned up through the clouds and the morning brightened as they flew toward the sun and then, as they lifted, the clouds became jumbled gray-white masses below them.

Vilchek flew the plane casually, like a farmer driving a Ford outside a rural town on a lazy summer afternoon. He was wearing an expensive-looking, cream-colored linen suit, a white silk shirt, and a red ascot was loosely clustered around his broad neck. From his jaw to the ascot there were dark blue veins that stood out like embedded plastic tubes.

"I somehow assume that you all are employed at the base," commented Vilchek. He adjusted his sunglasses to get a better fit over the crooked bridge of his nose.

"You could say that," responded Glidewell from the seat beside Vilchek in the small, bright cabin. "We're all migrant workers in the aerospace plum orchard."

Tom chuckled, and Melissa followed his with her own high-pitched laugh from the two seats in back. "My hyenalike short-haired colleague back there and myself are engineering types," said Glidewell. "Melissa is more a computer guru—a jolly good one, I might add."

Vilchek smiled and, with the slightest of glances back at Kruger, addressed Gildewell. "People with the knowledge of electronics that you displayed at the meeting don't usually bag

114

groceries at the food mart." Vilchek laughed with a little wheeze, and his belly shook.

"Yep, electrons are our game," observed Tom. "You'd be surprised where those little ras-cules can show up."

"And where might that be?" asked Vilchek.

"Everywhere!" said Tom, laughing. The steady drone of the engine gave him a good feeling, and when he looked over at Melissa she gave him a half smile, half smirk that made her mouth seem very small and made deep ridges form above it like rivers that ran down to her lips.

"Very nice aircraft," remarked Melissa from the left rear seat. She fingered for a moment a turquoise and silver necklace she was wearing, and the loose-fitting knit top she wore matched the color of the stones in the necklace.

"Thank you," answered Vilchek. "I usually trade for a new one every year. It eases my fears to fly a plane with low mileage."

"May I ask what profession you're in?" she said.

"Certainly, my dear," answered Vilchek, craning his neck toward Melissa. "I own a small print shop in Lancaster. I'm involved in book publishing and, for that matter, quality printing of every conceivable type—pardon the pun." Vilchek hesitated a second. "When I was just starting out I published a flying saucer magazine up in the great Northwest in the sixties. Had a couple thousand subscribers at the peak in 1968. I gave up after a few years."

"How come you quit?" asked Tom.

"I'm afraid I wasn't making any money," answered Vilchek. "The journal, humble as it was, required an extraordinary amount of time. I was young and naive. We didn't know very much back then."

"The printing business must be getting along fairly well these days," commented Glidewell in a slow, deliberate voice, arching his brows, tilting his head birdlike to look at Vilchek.

The fat man laughed and launched into an explanation. "I speculate in the precious metals market from time to time, concentrating mostly on gold. I like the look of the damn stuff. Besides, buying and selling very expensive commodities is where the money is, Mr. Glidewell—if one does it wisely and the right hunches manage to outnumber the wrong. And that's where I obtain the means to pursue my lifelong passion of quality typography. My small shop is merely a labor of love where I publish limited editions of little-known literary gems. Most of the book printing today is unadulterated garbage—cheap bindings, inadequate type. Even money and postage stamps are cheaply printed today. If any of you ever need any quality printing, come over to the shop. I'll show you some samples.'' He hesitated to take a deep breath, and then: "Sorry about that sales pitch—sometimes I can't help myself.''

Tom looked through the window, down at the patches of clouds below them. They looked like mountains made of gray-white wool. The sun was higher now, and Tom could see the dark shadow of the Cessna moving along the tumbled cloud tops. The moving shadow was surrounded by a perfect ring of rainbow colors, and the airplane's image frolicked over the uneven clouds, enlarging in the hollows, diminishing on the nearer prominences and, with it, the colored ring enlarged and diminished.

"How much farther, Al?" queried Glidewell.

"We've got an ETA of eleven fifteen," said Vilchek cheerily. "Just in time for lunch.''

"I'm famished," said Melissa.

"You'll like the chili," Vilchek told her. "But the main attraction at Desert Rock, of course, is the pursuit of knowledge. It has only a word-of-mouth notoriety. You see, people have gathered there for more than a decade to contact our brothers and sisters from outer space.''

"Brothers and sisters?" parroted Glidewell.

"You see, our galactic neighbors are quite intimately involved in the UFO appearance you seek to study, Mr. Glidewell," explained Vilchek. "Advanced civilizations in this galaxy formed an alliance that has been responsible for monitoring our earthly activities for many years. They've helped man on earth in the past and they've waited for the day when we would be ready to join them as the rulers and keepers of the galaxy.'' Vilchek gave Glidewell a penetrating look, then, looking back into the bright sun, he said, "I think that may be rather soon now.''

Tom's eyes narrowed and he gave Melissa a long look. She met his gaze with quizzical eyes and pulled the right corner of her mouth to one side a little in a frown. If Tom would have had to guess her thoughts, he would have guessed she was thinking: *How did I let you get me into this mess?*

Vilchek's bulging eyes showed a lot of white as they peered around at Glidewell slightly before his head followed. "There are more than eighty different civilizations coming to earth at the present time," said Vilchek, appearing to gauge the effect on Glidewell.

Glidewell looked down at the instrument panel for an instant, then, whipping his head back up, he looked at Vilchek and spoke abruptly. "I say, how did you happen upon this knowledge?"

"The leaders of this galaxy communicate with initiates and disciples around the world, directly. Of course, these galactic contacts are part of a larger intergalactic federation."

"Amazing," said Glidewell simply. "And how do these entities go about this communication?"

"They use human vocal cords," replied Vilchek.

"Like mediums?" questioned Melissa. She squinted her right eye as if it had hurt to ask the question.

The fat man eagerly responded. "It's actually very simple. The space brothers have a method whereby they open up something similar to what we know as a telepathic channel in a suitable earthling just as one would tune an electromagnetic or radio receiver to the proper frequency in order to receive the transmitted signal."

"This all sounds mad," observed Glidewell.

"It may sound incredible at first, but I assure you it is absolutely real, gentlemen and Miss Delaney," said Vilchek confidently. "That is why I'm bringing people of your caliber out here, incidently—so that you may experience it first hand and believe. Oh, we have doctors and lawyers and architects and such in our group, but the world today respects the scientists and the engineers who have revolutionized our way of life. And the world must come to the truth about what UFOs really are; they must be prepared for what is to come shortly and, who knows, you may just want to aid the cause. Now I'm afraid I've probably said too much for you to digest in one sitting. Would anyone care for a brandy?" Vilchek hunched over to the right, strained against his stomach to reach under the instrument panel, and popped back up with a pint of liquor.

The three passengers passed on the brandy. Then Glidewell spoke. "These communications—how do you know they're not from the subconscious of the person involved?"

"Excellent question," said Vilchek. He paused while he placed the brandy bottle between his legs, unscrewed the cap, and then carefully poured some into a white ceramic cup he had set on the

center console. "You must realize that the entities behind the
flying saucer phenomena have proven they are who they say they
are."

"How?" questioned Tom.

"They make prognostications," said Velchek. He recapped the
bottle, then swirled the cup of liquor, sniffed at the brandy, and
drank it down in one pull.

"And so these predictions come true?" asked Melissa.

"Why yes. Of course," answered Vilchek.

It was just before eleven thirty when they landed. The Desert
Rock Airport had hundreds of light aircraft parked along one side
of the flat, sandy air strip. Sagebrush encrusted hills ran along the
other side of the dusty air strip, and at the end of the runway they
could see boulders sticking out from the base of a short, squat hill
like ladyfingers from a generous pudding. The largest of the
boulders resembled the front half of a gray-black whale angling up
from the desert depths. After Vilchek had taxied and parked the
Cessna and paid a man who came to meet them, they made their
way toward the rocks, past parked campers and RVs, where most
of the people appeared to be in various stages of lunch, some
outside sitting on webbed lawn chairs under light-colored
umbrellas, others inside their luxury vehicles hiding from the high
wind that was whipping up and sweeping across the desert as
across a sea. They could see it stiffen a blue flag that rippled in the
air beside the giant slanted boulder. The flag was decorated with a
white, lens-shaped space craft resting on a white meadow, and a
mass of humanity were shown standing around the craft with
upraised arms.

When they reached the base of the mountain there was a
weathered wooden building adjacent to the giant rock, and next to
that was a speaker's platform and a long rectangular food-serving
area covered with white canvas. The canvas was flapping in the
wind like a sail. Above it all, the oblong giant rock stretched high
as a four-story building and dwarfed everything around it. Vilchek
led them to a line in the big tent where they bought bowls of chili
and lemonade and tea, and then sat down at a picnic table to eat.

"Great chili," said Tom, spooning the third spoonful out of the
bowl, his napkins lifting off the table, then flying through the tent
with a gust of air.

Vilchek's face beamed. "The secret ingredient is Swiss bittersweet chocolate."

"It *is* good," agreed Melissa, passing Tom a napkin, which he tucked inside his belt.

"Absolutely smashing," Glidewell added his verdict.

"I'm glad you folks like it," said Vilchek, getting up from the bench, holding an empty bowl. "I think I'll sample some more."

After they had finished eating, Vilchek led them in through the side door of the sun-bleached building beside the giant rock. They went through a corridor, down a curved flight of stairs, and Vilchek stopped beside a wide, open doorway. He extended his hand politely, gesturing them through the door. "Please enter," urged Vilchek. "I should think we are just in time. This chamber, lady and gentlemen, is the inner sanctum." They all hesitated an awkward moment at the doorway, and Vilchek finally laughed his raspy, wheezing laugh. "Go on in, they won't bite!"

Tom Kruger went through first.

"I've brought some guests, Norman," announced Vilchek, waving a meaty hand at the man who stood behind the podium. The man returned the wave with a spindly arm and smiled, his teeth flashing brilliant white within his bronzed and wrinkled face, his light gray hair forming half a globular cluster over the top of his head. On first seeing the new man's face, Tom was reminded of the way Harpo Marx looked in classic Marx Brothers' comedies.

"Grab a group of chairs for your friends, Al," said the Harpolike man, gesturing with his long, bony arms toward an empty patch of used school desks. "We're ready to begin the session." His deep voice echoed surprisingly loudly off the walls of the room.

As they went for the seats the coolness in the room reminded Tom of his grandfather's cellar in the house outside Atlanta. After they had taken their seats Tom nudged Glidewell and Melissa, who sat on either side of him, and then spoke in a loud whisper: "I sure hope this is worth it. At the UFO meetings in the library at least we can go upstairs and charge out books and read magazines if it's dull. It looks like we're stuck if this turns out to be a loser."

Melissa covered her mouth and laughed. Glidewell whispered back in a perfect British accent, "It's highly probable that this will be the least dull meeting we've been to all year, old chap."

Melissa nodded and then smiled, and Tom watched the freckles ride up on her nose. She looked around the room, fingering her necklace again as if to confirm it was still there, the silver shining dully in the dim light. She shielded her mouth with her other hand and directed her words at Tom in a low voice. "This is absolutely the weirdest place I have ever been and these people are the weirdest people I've ever seen in my entire life."

"You're just easy to please," whispered Tom.

16

The Space Brothers

"Fellow seekers, I believe we're ready to begin," said the man with the Harpo Marx hair. The buzz of conversation hovered in the cavernous room for a moment, then drifted away. "Now," the speaker continued, "we shall begin the meditation. And to our new guests we say welcome and please join us in silent meditation—eyes closed—with an attitude of reverence. Try to clear your mind of all thoughts. When the channel is opened questions may be addressed to our heavenly brothers. Let us now prepare. And now—we begin."

The room became very quiet then, and people closed their eyes and sat utterly still like slumbering house-of-wax figures. The room became like a rock-enclosed lagoon of expectant faces—very quiet—as the people sat motionlessness at the hard wooden desks. Tom closed his eyes and began to feel the silence, hard like the concrete around him. The room seemed to grow colder and damper with his eyes squeezed shut, and his body shuddered involuntarily with a chill for a second or two.

A few minutes passed before a stout woman dressed in shining black clothing began to speak aloud in a slightly mechanical voice. When the silence was broken it took on an air of importance, like a lone seagull's shout in first or last light. Tom eased his eyelids up, turned toward the solitary voice, and saw other people opening their eyes and eagerly looking at the woman who had broken the silence. He saw that the voice belonged to a gray-haired, middle-aged woman whose facial skin was slack and loose and whose eyelids were pressed so hard against her eyes, it made them look like oversized grapes covered with a thin layer of flesh.

Words were issuing from her mouth very precisely and in an

eerie voice, harsh and deep in tone. The voice made Tom think whatever controlled it was arrogant and aloof. "I am known as Tantaur of the sixth realm," said the voice. "I open this channel in the name of the elder brothers of light. Look to nature for signs of the new age that, even now, comes to your planet, which we know as Terra."

Like a bird that has spotted its prey from a great altitude, Glidewell focused a hawkish gaze at the woman who was speaking. His lips mumbled almost silently, "What-the-hell," as the voice started up again.

"Your planet now enters new realms of higher vibrations. Every phase of your culture on Earth will eventually be benfited—politics, economics, medical sciences, religion. Earthlings are involved with the death forces of atomic weapons. Human civilization is misguided by forces of fanaticism; even now we prepare to come. We are your ancestors and overseers from space who come as brothers to save you from your self-destruction.

"This should fill your essence with satisfaction, those who shall be called the disciples of light. Know the nearness of our coming. We have tarried in the heavens, but even now we prepare to descend to earth with great light and love. Prophesy this, you who walk in the light—for the hour of our coming approaches. For the elect's sake the days of this closing age will be shortened. This is why we communicate with you bearers of the light on the surface of earth by transference of thought—so that there will be workers when we come. Many of your faulty concepts must be cleansed. Then you shall become vessels of truth."

There was a pause in the communications and the woman who had been speaking sat motionless with eyes staring straight ahead, strangely intense and liquid, as if she could see beyond the walls of the room. Then the voice started up again, speaking a little slower now. "This entity awaits your questions."

"Why are your craft specifically appearing now in greater numbers worldwide, and especially here in California?" asked a bone-thin handsome woman with red-rouged cheeks, who sat against a wall in the rear of the room.

"We are presently monitoring virtual earthquake zones and other unbalanced conditions," answered the alien voice.

"Let me ask if there is any danger of further serious earthquakes in the near term for the western coast of the United

States?'' asked the Marx Brother-lookalike from his spot at the podium.

"Yes," answered the alien voice. The word had come out abruptly and the voice had clipped off the end of it.

"Are you still with us?" inquired the frizzy-haired leader.

"Yes," the voice came back uncertainly, as if it had been a great distance away. "There will be passive disruptions in your planet's crust. Space civilizations are studying the Earth in great depth during this chaotic period."

"What steps do you recommend that we take in the coming days?" asked the leader with perfect enunciation.

"Warn others. We are not yet authorized by the council on high to intervene in the situation. We of the intergalactic council offer our Earth brethren eternal gifts of exceeding value. You and all of mankind have only a brief time to accept the saving light. In the coming days there will be great destruction."

A glass-mantled candle was sitting on a small empty table adjacent to the dark wall in front of Tom, and he could see the reflection of the flame and the darkened wall as it flickered and swayed in response to some circulation of air. He stared for a moment at the reflection as he listened to the alien voice echo faintly off the walls of the cold, dim room. He seemed to consciously form the mental question, *Can this be real*? His mind came back at him with, *Probably more real than the six o'clock news*.

"Our joint mission is one of assistance," the strange voice continued, the woman mouthing the words like a remote controlled mannequin. Her eyes seemed to refocus a short distance out into the room. "As we have told you, the Earth is one of our experimental colonies. The creation of life on your Earth was in the hands of the Masters of the intergalactic council. Your more enlightened writers have tried to hint at this. We are the forerunners of the return of the Elder Brother. We increase our missions in your realm to present truth and foreknowledge."

A man in the back of the room shouted, "What is truth?"

"It involves light and love," said the alien voice.

"Who are you?" asked Glidewell suddenly.

"We are the Elders of light."

Tom shaded his mouth with the back of his right hand and whispered into Melissa's ear, "Is that anything like the Sons of the Pioneers?" he joked.

"Who?" she whispered back, her lips curling up in a curious

smile, her eyes playful and sparkling.

"On second thought," he whispered, nodding slowly, "I guess they were before your time." A woman who was seated on the other side of Melissa looked across at Tom and gave him a sour frown.

All the while the alien voice droned on. "We have come in past ages to survey and guide humans. But in this generation brothers from different worlds live among you without recognition. We are planetary governors. The new age approaches, and with its nearness your vibrational levels must be raised. Then you will be suitable to work with elders of light and love. In that day we shall speak to you face to face, and you shall know the truth, and the truth shall make you like God—of course, that's only a word to you."

"I'll be damned," said Glidewell under his breath. He glanced over at Melissa and Tom only to find them looking back at him.

"No spacecraft or projection from another level or world outside our intergalactic council is permitted atmospheric entrance. An unauthorized ship entered the earth's atmosphere, and was destroyed above your Siberian region in your year 1908. We are the guardians."

"What is your appearance?" a heavily wrinkled man croaked from the first row in the front of the chamber.

"My form is similar to your own," answered the alien. "We utilize our bodies as vehicles and we have evolved the type of vehicles we use to contain our intelligence and past life information. We keep the same vehicle for hundreds of thousands of your years before we replace them. There is no sickness, little aging of appearance, only mechanical wear."

"Tell us more about the dangers of atomic devices," said the man at podium. He seemed to fill in with questions whenever a hesitation came over the room.

"Your atomic power plants and experiments continue to endanger your race. Your epidemic of cancer is one result. This condition will continue to worsen. Your people in close proximity to nuclear facilities are exposed and vulnerable. It happens slowly over many of your years, even across generations. The very soils and rocks of your planet have become infected. It is a slow and deadly process."

"How can we reverse the process?" the leader followed up. "Or can we?"

"It is too late for you without our help. But that will soon come."

Tom stifled a yawn. It seemed like he had heard a lot of this somewhere before. A *monotonous extraterrestrial voice speaking bombastically*, he thought.

"How should we prepare for the new age and the return of the elders of light?" asked the man at the podium. Tom sensed an unseen harmony of some kind between the man with the Hollywood hair and the being whose captivating, parasitic voice enthralled the audience in the room.

"You must live without darkness in your life and control yourselves, always lifting your brother, to reach perfection. You must desire the light."

"What would you have us do?" asked the leader.

"Your society must unite as one," replied the alien voice. "The people of Earth are entering a higher plane of existence. Perceive all of nature for great cataclysms that will exhibit themselves soon. Tornadic activity, cyclones, earthquakes, and tidal action will intensify as your planet's timepiece ticks on and the chosen hour nears. Your weather will modify. Great signs will be seen in outer space. Few humans on Earth are prepared. I say to you, raise your vibrational levels. The remnant will be limited."

"Where does your communication originate?" asked Vilchek. "You are a new voice. You have not transmitted to our group before."

"I represent elements of the same alliance that has communicated with you on past occasions. My most recent incarnation occurred on a planetary system in the depths of what you term Orion—one of the six-hundred sixty-five planets from the seven local galaxies that belong to the intergalactic council. Jesus was one of our group, as we have said. He came down to act as a teacher although he never took on a fleshly body as some dogmatically believe. We possess bodies of light that can appear real in your terms. We can pass through your walls with our light bodies, or walk on your water, or rise in your air. Our brother Jesus came to earth and left in his light body. He did not actually die in your terms." Melissa's face seemed to flush a little at that. Her eyes squinted as she stared at the passionless face of the woman through whom the voice had come.

"Why do you need craft if you have these light bodies that can travel through the cosmos?" asked Tom. He leaned forward in his chair, as if to try to concentrate on the response when it came. When the voice from beyond hesitated his body angled forward a little more until it stopped at the second bowl of chili that had bloated his stomach.

"I must leave this realm for now in your terms . . . This communication terminates." The alien voice was different now, more mechanical, wavering like an offspeed tape recording.

"Can you not stay with us longer?" asked the leader, who rested his bony elbow on the top of the podium.

The alien voice dwindled as it answered. "I bid you ever shining light and love." Then the voice shut off, like a switch had been pushed.

"For some reason the entity had to go, I suspect," observed Vilchek apologetically as they filed out of the room. "Usually the message is more extensive; this one confirmed a lot of things we already knew. At least you were able to hear one of the space brothers first hand. Any striking opinions?"

"Well," said Melissa, "even assuming what we saw was real, I have only one observation."

"And what is that, my dear girl?" responded Vilchek, hesitating halfway between the chamber door and the rise of steps.

"What if they're lying?"

The fat man's face hardened into a pained expression for a split-second and, at the same time, the tightness seemed to vacate his mouth, allowing folds of flesh to hang down below his chin as the crowd filed past him.

"I don't think the elders of light are lying," said Vilchek with a little laugh. "But if they are—then, my child, we are all in a lot of trouble."

"How's that?" questioned Tom, seriously.

"It's very simple," said the fat man. "The people from outer space who control the UFOs can only be bad, good, or indifferent —right?"

"Right," agreed Glidewell.

"If they are inherently good, as they claim, they would most likely be incapable of lying, and it would also be unlikely that they would seek to harm us," said Vilchek.

"Okay," Melissa agreed halfheartedly.

"If they were indifferent, it would not be likely that they would bother to lie," continued Vilchek. "That means if they are lying, as you have suggested, they are probably bad—and, at the same time, they are most likely thousands of years advanced technologically and therefore extremely powerful in relationship with our puny race! I don't particularly relish entertaining that combination of possibilities."

"Defense against something like that might present a hellava problem," said Glidewell.

Vilchek nodded affirmatively before going on. "Nevertheless, I hope you will tell some of your aerospace colleagues what you have observed here. Of course, I would test them individually before you reveal the nature of these communications. If they are in the least bit skeptical about UFOs or the possibility of life on other planets, do not reveal the things you have witnessed today. The message would fall dead on the ears of an unbeliever. I must tell you that we've been in contact with many different beings. A creature with a high ranking by the name of Ashtar comes through on many occasions. He confirms that there are a vast number of extragalactic civilizations that will make themselves known at the proper moment. As incredible as it may sound, the various extraterrestrial life forms who have entered our atmosphere may well number in the millions."

"Fascinating," murmured Glidewell as they started up the stairwell.

"But what if these aliens are trying to deceive us?" asked Tom at the top of the stairs. "What if they are, in fact, hostile?"

A smile slowly curled onto Vilchek's fat, purplish lips until his upper teeth showed like an ivory rim. He was puffing from having gone up the stairs too quickly, and after a deep inhalation, an awkward swallow, and a wheezing exhalation of breath, he answered, "I'm afraid, given their obvious ability to manipulate matter and energy at will—why, if they were hostile, Mr. Kruger, they could have conquered us on any Sunday afternoon, a very long time ago."

17

Messengers of Deception?

"Judging by the shape the world's in, mankind could probably use some high-powered help," Tom said to Melissa. "These UFO creatures might just be the ticket. Whatdya think?" He forked the first bite of salmon off the octagonal dinner plate and into his mouth, the plate was made of a new plastic, just on the market, and it looked and felt expensive, as if it were carved out of marble.

"I can't believe you said that!" said Melissa, searching his face for some sign of hidden humor. Tom put his fork down, elbowed the tabletop, and stuck both hands up in mock surrender.

"Whoever or whatever was speaking through that woman was phony as a three-dollar bill," continued Melissa. She leaned closer to him, across the table. "The voice in that cavern claimed Jesus Christ was one of them, a space creature, no less. It was beating around the bush, saying Jesus wasn't flesh and blood . . . that he didn't die . . . it was definitely a spirit of anti-Christ!"

"Hold on, we know Christ had a lot of power. He could . . . I mean, it's possible he was sent by the intergalactic civilizations and maybe half flesh and blood and half advanced spirit vehicle, you know," said Tom in a mild voice.

"Tom!" said Melissa. "There's a spiritual battle going on—Christ is on one side and you-know-who is on the other. . . . And you-know-who wants to claim the territory Jesus already won."

Tom shot her a quizzical look. "You mean the Devil or something?"

"Sure—the Devil's real. Jesus talked to him in living color two-thousand years ago in Israel."

Tom made his eyes shrink and gave her a skeptical look. He spoke carefully, as if picking his way through a mine field of words.

"In the space creature game, maybe you oughtta kind of take off your Christian hat a little and put on your computer expert hat, you know."

"Well, all I know is that I was blind before I met the Lord and now I see," she said calmly. "I know a lot of people think the Bible's an obsolete document, but the deeper I get into it the more I see—a kind of careful internal agreement beyond the talents of the greatest authors, men who never met, who didn't even all speak the same languages . . . fishermen and the uneducated . . ."

"Hey, I'm sorry, I didn't mean to . . . cut down the Bible," said Tom.

"No, I didn't mean you—" Melissa tilted her head, making one eye larger, biting her lip as if to hold back a smile. "It's just . . . since I've known the Lord, I was given a steady urge to read the Bible, and I don't even automatically believe a minister or one of those men on television who preach the Gospel. But I always check it in the Bible first, and I sure don't believe some disembodied voice that spouted some obvious lies."

Tom squinted at her again, lodged his right thumb nail between a gap in his lower teeth, and nodded as if he were humoring a small, precocious child. He really believed what she was saying was oversimplified, too much of a legend to believe it all, but she was damned beautiful saying it. "Well, I think the Bible's great," he told her.

"Good," she said, smiling slyly. "The Lord shows all of us things individually. I mean, it's a personal thing." Melissa reached into her purse and brought out a thick, blue-covered paperback. On the front it read *The Book*. She handed it across the table and held it out above the salt and pepper shakers. "Have you seen this version?"

It's the Bible in disguise, he thought immediately. "No, I don't think I . . ."

"You can have it then, I've got extras. It's really a neat translation—modern English and all." Tom nodded, smiling close-mouthed as he took it from her, feeling the warm softness on the underside of her wrist, and he delayed pulling his hand back for a second.

He lingered over the softness in her eyes, then gave the slightly worn book a glance as he flipped through a few pages. "You don't waste any time," he said, and then laid the book down beside him on the seat.

"To me the Bible's like a teaching machine," she said, stabbing at the pile of French fries on her plate, then dabbing the one she had speared into a pool of catsup. She nibbled off the red end, dabbed the last half, then finished it off. Tom had dug into his cheese-covered cauliflower by then. "You know, it's like there's more than words in the Book," she went on. "It's like the Lord shows me things in there when it's time for me to see them—no matter which hat I've got on."

Tom fingered a string of cheese from the corner of his mouth. "Hey, I didn't mean . . ."

"I know," she said, flashing a smile. Then, after another couple of French fries, "I still think we're in the last days," said Melissa. "The signs are all around us."

"I knew they'd find a way to cheat me out of my social security," said Tom. Melissa gave him a smirk, and he held his hands up in surrender.

It was cool in the restaurant. Electronic Spanish guitar music was playing in the background. The booth they were sitting in was large, and they sat on aquamarine-colored padded squares of vinyl. The blue seats dully reflected the late afternoon light that came in through the stretch of wide windows on their left. Multi-colored prints of sailboats scattered on deep-blue lakes, and fishermen in boats on rippled blue-green water, with sea gulls hanging above them, sprinkled the wall on their right, as if they represented apologies for the dry desert heat outside the building. A short wall jutted out behind Tom and on that, a very large brownish-green turtle shell was mounted a few inches above his head.

The shell was patterned with etched squares that curved out at him, and when he turned in his seat and saw it, *matter tells space how to curve* popped in his mind from a physics class, as if the turtle shell were a small space-time continuum affected by a local gravity field. Tom turned back around and glanced toward the front of the restaurant, where the band of windows to his left met rough, weathered cedar in the corner of the room. He could see the big plate-glass front window with its three-foot black letters, backwards on the glass, announcing THE FISH PALACE.

He dug into the brown rice and followed that with another chunk of the grayish-pink salmon flesh. Melissa dipped a large friend shrimp into white-speckled red sauce and bit into it thoughtfully.

"How's the shrimp?" he asked her.

"Pretty swell," she answered. "How's the fish?"

"Just medium swell," he answered. Then, provokingly: "So what do you think about the UFO message—overall, I mean?"

There was a pause. Melissa looked at him seriously and began in a slow, slightly strained voice, "Tom—they flat lied about historical records. Jesus of Nazareth *was* flesh and blood. The Romans beat him within an inch of his life with a cat-o-nine-tails and ripped his back open and bits of his flesh flew out into the air. They spiked him up on a cross, pierced his side with a spear—blood and water spurted out. A body made out of light, or however that UFO voice put it, wouldn't have flesh and blood in it."

"Maybe," said Tom. "But, you know, I still think the intergalactic voice could've been sayin' the same thing that's in the Bible—maybe their terminology's just a hair different. I mean, Christ was advanced, right? He could have been one of the top guys in the universe like one of the time lords on *Doctor Who*, you know."

"There are many false prophets gone out into the world," said Melissa. "I believe Jesus suffered so people's souls would not have to be destroyed when the world is judged—that supposedly advanced space turkey gave itself away as far as I'm concerned. It had the gall to claim that humans had to earn their salvation themselves, which directly contradicts Jesus. He said He was the way, the truth, the the life, and that the way to God is through Him—not through some space creatures."

Tom laughed. "You're really somethin' else when you get started—you know that?" The things she had been saying almost irritated him, but not quite. Something inside him rebelled against what she was telling him, but not all the way. He knew there had to be advanced extraterrestrials out there in the sea of stars that filled the sky, and the UFOs had to be advanced spacecraft—he and Glidewell had seen one for themselves in all its dazzling glory a few hundred feet away. And to his mind, the intelligences behind the UFOs could damn well communicate any way they wanted, and telepathy at a distance even seemed the logical choice for ETs to use—no transistors to wear out, no big electric bills. So what she was saying seemed old-fashioned, but she was still beautiful sitting there, enthused, across the table from him. And he would have listened to anything she wanted to say.

"I didn't mean to sound preachy," she said in a silky voice. She elbowed the tabletop and held her thin, tan arms up in mock surrender this time.

"No, I'm just not quite on the same wave length, you know."

"You're not on Vilchek's wave length, I hope—I mean, you question that mumbo-jumbo we heard down there, don't you?"

"Sure," he answered while Melissa stabbed at another fried potato. "But just let me throw one more thing out here, okay?"

"Okay." She bit into the fry and seemed to relish the taste.

"These creatures who control the UFOs could be thousands of years ahead of us, right?" he reasoned. "And in the old days if men met up with them, they probably would have thought that these creatures were gods."

Melissa's eyebrows bent downward—she squinted a little and seemed to examine his eyes—then moved her head side to side slowly, and her voice came out filled with steam. "The record still shows that Jesus was born in Bethlehem, he was flesh and blood, he died and rose from the dead—why would an ET lie about it?"

"Well, I still say if they're advanced, they could have used artificial insemination—anything's possible."

A pained look flashed onto Melissa's face. "So what you're saying is because these space creatures are advanced, that's a guarantee they're telling the truth. They could say that UFOs brought the Satute of Liberty to New York City, and we should believe them!"

"Well, you got me on that one," he answered with a big grin. "I think the French gave us the Statue of Liberty—maybe the ETs put 'em up to it, though," he mused. Melissa gave him a full smirk this time, and little arcs formed at the corners of her mouth.

"I kept looking at the people around that room while that entity was speaking," said Melissa. "They all looked transfixed, like they were under a spell or hypnotized or something! I think those people at Desert Rock are shaking hands with the Devil and they don't even know it."

"I'm beginning to think you don't like the good old space creatures," said Tom, still chewing. He swallowed and stretched his lips in a big crooked smile. "You think they're all monsters, I bet."

Melissa laughed at the way he had said what he said. "You remember when you took me to church?" she asked. He nodded back at her. "Reverend McDougall talked about the Devil posing as an angel of light. Satan's not a dummy—he's not going to leap out at people with horns and a pointed tail!"

"So he's like an angel or something," said Tom. His eyebrows arched up; his left eye widened and fixed its gaze on her.

"Right, he can change his appearance—on the outside," she said. "And he's got a bunch of demons under his command." The tempo of the music that came from the speakers in the ceiling changed abruptly and the music became fast, with wailing electric guitars, a heavy, thumping beat, and words that seemed to be screamed instead of sung. Melissa stabbed at the red sauce with another of the curled pink shrimp, nibbled at it, stabbed and nibbled again until she discarded the pointed tail on the plate beside the others. Three lines broke out on her forehead, her eyes suddenly brightened.

"Tom," she said, "lemme ask you this—would you want to die trusting in some group of space creatures to save you instead of trusting in an inheritance Christ offered us all?"

Tom looked at her a meditative moment. "Well, I guess I'm kind of an agnostic right now," he said. "I believe in a prime mover or a life force in the cosmos—I don't personally think we know much about him and all—but I'm really grateful to whoever or whatever he is for giving me life. And I just try to live the best I can—and I hope when I die this power in the universe will accept my life. I guess that's how I think about death and all." He turned the upper part of his body toward the wall in back of him and rapped his knuckles on the turtle shell that hung on the wall. "Knock on turtle shell."

Melissa glanced around the room quickly. "Tom," she said and grimaced. "They're going to throw us out."

"And good riddance, too," joked Tom loudly. His eyes had an inward look when he turned back around from the turtle shell. He grinned at Melissa and she caught his smile. He waited a moment for her to counter what he had said, but she just nibbled on a few fries and then pulled at her ice water, the ice clinking against the side of the glass as she drained the last of it. Her face was perfectly serene as she lowered the glass and looked out the window. He glanced past her and could see the big crystal chandelier in the middle of the room. The light played through the cut glass and made prismatic flashes that radiated through the room and put colored bits of light on the walls.

"In the spirit of UFO research—I mean, to really check out the evil spirit possibility—why don't we chat with Reverend McDougall about our Desert Rock encounter," suggested Melissa. "He's been a missionary all over the world. He's seen a lot of demonic activity—stuff like that."

"I guess it's worth a try," Tom agreed reluctantly. "If you set it up, being the true scientist that I am, I'll go."

After they had finished with dinner and the waitress had cleared the table they got up and headed for the cashier. Melissa tugged on Tom's shirt sleeve as they passed a television set that was turned on at the near end of the horseshoe bar. On the luminous screen there was an image of a man who had just mentioned unidentified flying objects. Melissa and Tom veered from their course and edged up to the black vinyl bartop where they stopped, staring up at the screen. The washed-out picture showed a reporter interviewing an older grubby-looking man. *Probably needs a new picture tube*, thought Tom automatically.

"So then the UFO touched down?" prodded the long-haired reporter, stretching the microphone toward the old man's mouth.

"Uh huh," said the old man. "It whizzed past me goin' 'bout a couple or five thousand miles an hour and crash landed, you might say. It kinda hit a glancin' blow, ya know. It slid along the ground until it hit this pile of boulders and these two little silvery dwarfs jumped out and jus' took off after me. My jackass was bellowing like I never heard before."

"Were you frightened, Mr. Bagley?"

"Call me Elwood, son. Yeah, I was downright scared, 'specially after they caught up with me!"

"And that's when these beings took you inside their ship?"

"Yep. These things grabbed me and drug me off! Flew me to Saturn. Took about forty minutes—the better part of an hour."

The announcer's eyes were squinted slightly in a serious look, his thin-lipped, straight mouth curved up at the corners as he spoke. "And what did Saturn look like?"

"Oh, there's lots of Evergreens and Mimosa trees and other plants that look like what we got here on Earth. They had lots of kangaroos and opossums—the 'roos were chasin' the 'possums. Kangaroos are different on Saturn—faster and more ferocious." The old man smiled crookedly and showed spaces where teeth were missing.

"I see, Mr. Bagley—I mean to say Elwood. Did these extra-terrestrials give you anything in the way of evidence?"

"Well," continued Elwood, "I asked 'em for some proof that I had been on their ship and all, and he gave me some Saturnian cornbread and a jar of jelly—I thought that was right nice."

"What flavor jelly?" asked the reporter.

"Plum—it's green, kinda light colored. They got green plums on Saturn."

"I see."

"Yeah, ever' plum jelly I ever seen was kinda purplish red, here on Earth, ya know."

The reporter withdrew the microphone from the older man and turned to face the screen. "Well, there we have it. Finally we are face to face with a UFO report containing real evidence we can sink our teeth into. But don't look for green plums in your neighborhood stores just yet, folks. Not until we establish trade with the planet Saturn. This is Nelson Bryers, reporting from the high desert somewhere east of Los Angeles."

The national anchorman flashed onto the screen and said with a smile, "CBS *Evening News* will continue in a moment." The screen faded to black and then to a four-inch-high can of deodorant.

"I don't understand why the networks do stories like that, and it's damn lucky if the good reports make the local papers," said Tom as they walked away. "These nuts always pop up out of nowhere and give the whole thing a bad name."

"Old Elwood probably wants to write a book and make some money," said Melissa.

"He looked like he needed some money," was all that Tom said in reply.

18

The Preacher's House

It was a beautiful evening at the end of July. The top of the sun had just slipped below the horizon and above the distant mountains there were clouds textured like the fleece of lambs, glowing with a rosy-pink color, floating in a golden stretch of sky. It was half past eight when Tom Kruger and Melissa Delaney arrived at the small beige house that sat behind the local Church of the Nazarene.

"Hi," said Reverend McDougall at the door, with a slight wave of his right hand.

"Hi," said Melissa and Tom.

"Come right in. Oh, it's a glorious sky," said McDougall, looking past them as he held the screen door half open. "Red sky at night, sailor's delight," he said, letting the door close behind them.

"Hello." Mrs. McDougall came up and spoke to them before they had taken the second step past the screen door. "Hi, Mrs. McDougall," replied Melissa. Tom stayed behind Melissa, nodding shyly and smiling as the preacher's wife motioned for them to sit down. It was a small kitchen, decorated mostly in white and beige with Armstrong tile on the floor, and a white table with chrome legs the diameter of a half dollar sat in the center of the room.

Melissa and Tom sat down on red vinyl seats at the table and Mrs. McDougall brought a pitcher of lemonade out of the small GE refrigerator and set it on the white tabletop. She brought four expensive glasses over and set them in front of each of the people at the table. She poured the lemonade into the glasses, the ice cubes ringing against the sides of the glasses as they rushed in. "I just really think everything tastes better in real lead crystal," said Mrs. McDougall. "We got these when Jim was a missionary in Germany—must've been about fifteen years ago."

"They're beautiful," said Melissa, smiling.

"Thank you," said Mrs. McDougall.

"What's all this about UFOs?" Reverend McDougall asked Tom.

"Wait," said Mrs. McDougall, sitting down. She raised her glass in a toast. "Let us toast the end of a beautiful day." Everyone linked their glasses together above the center of the table and then took long pulls from the crystal glasses.

"Now," said Reverend McDougall, "we were just about to get to these UFOs."

"Well," began Tom, "it seems like we encountered some strange happenings at a place called Desert Rock. There's a group there who receive telepathic messages from what appear to be highly advanced, extraterrestrial beings."

"I see," said Reverend McDougall, nodding thoughtfully.

"One of these beings spoke through a lady who was in kind of trance," added Melissa. "And this entity or spirit claimed they were part of an intergalactic council and this council was monitoring earth—preparing to make some kind of contact. I personally felt the woman was under control of a spirit, and we just kind of wanted to get your opinion."

Reverend McDougall's blue eyes seemed to glitter from inside his rough, craggy face as he looked at Melissa and then at Tom longer. "Let me ask you," said Reverend McDougall, "did this voice prophesy and reveal some unusual new gems of knowledge about the history of man on earth and perhaps the relationship between humans and the universe around us?"

"As a matter of fact, it did," said Tom, a little surprised. He lifted the glass of lemonade and took a short pull. Mrs. McDougall sipped some of her lemonade, and smacked her lips a little as if she were carefully testing the taste.

"Do you think it has enough sugar, Melissa?" asked Mrs. McDougall.

"It's really good, Mrs. McDougall," Melissa answered.

"Tom," said Reverend McDougall, "did the entity say that the end of the age was near? And—this is important—did it claim that humans must overcome their evil natures by doing good works—something along those lines."

"Yes," answered Tom, glancing over at Melissa, who was taking a swig from her lemonade, trying to hide an ever expanding smile. "I believe it *did* said something about humans needing to

raise their vibrational levels. These intergalactic types were gonna
help in some way."

"Tom," said Reverend McDougall, "Melissa's told me what
kind of work you both do at the base."

"She has?"

"Oh yes," said Reverend McDougall. "And so I'll try to put
things in scientific terms as best I can." The preacher was seated
opposite a window that looked out at the western sky, and he
paused for a moment, seeming to examine the contours of a
golden haze that clung to the distant mountains before he went
on. "Superior extraterrestrial beings in this universe have
communicated a great deal of material to mankind concerning the
true nature of cosmic reality and concerning laws of both the
universe we perceive with our senses and another universe that is
outside the spectrum of what our physical senses can detect. That
second universe is normally invisible to us and to every instrument
devised by man. These verified extraterrestrial communications
are contained in the book known as the Bible."

Tom nodded at the idea. "I guess I never thought of it like
that."

"It's true," said Reverend McDougall, his eyes illuminated by
an impassioned brightness, "but lad, I must tell ya, the Bible's not
communications from just *any* extraterrestrials. Not on yer life. I'm
fully persuaded it was written under direct control of the Holy
Spirit, and so, you see, it contains God's message to us about
everything we see and plenty more we don't see—He's the one
who made it all."

"It's the message from the top," chimed in Mrs. McDougall.

"So," continued Reverend McDougall, "I think any
dissertations that come from UFO beings, or the announced spirits
of dead people, or from the vocal cords of an entranced human,
to put it in scientific terms must be tested, just as you test a piece o
equipment to see if it's safe to rely on it once it's up in an
airplane."

"What kind of test could you run?" questioned Tom,
interested in the notion.

"Ah," said Reverend McDougall, lifting his eyebrows, "you
see, this entity who spoke to you sounds similar to ones I've
encountered in various locations around the world, and I've found
them in every case to be part of an organized group of spiritual
terrorists who are under the control of the Prince of Darkness—the

Bible calls them spiritual forces of evil in the heavenly realms. The Bible says we must test each spirit—whether they be of Christ.''

"This spirit claimed that Jesus was a member of some intergalactic council and they sent him to earth to teach light and love,'' said Melissa, ''and the thing claimed Jesus didn't have a real flesh body when he was on earth, and he didn't really die.''

"Well, now,'' said Reverend McDougall. ''That's a dead giveaway. The spirit that communicated with you failed the test, don'tya see. By denying that Jesus of Nazareth lived in the flesh and died on the cross, the spirit speaking through the medium showed he was on the devil's side—the enemy of Christ and all He stands for—and thereby we know this entity is bent on the absolute destruction of humans, not on saving them!''

"It sounds like you've researched this pretty well,'' said Tom.

"It's a familiar pattern throughout the world,'' offered Reverend McDougall. ''And Satan and his gang of demons are very real, I can assure you—unlike what the modern world believes—and that bunch is quite deceptive, never tires, and they're organized. They don't have nine-to-five jobs. And they're not playin' poker and shootin' craps all the time. They got plenty of time to think up schemes to fool people. Our Lord had a long encounter with the Devil in the wilderness of ancient Israel.''

"And you've run into similar communications before?'' Tom asked Reverend McDougall.

"What you two encountered was the 'high-technology' state-of-the-art version,'' replied the preacher. ''But we've seen evil spirits coming through people in some pretty backward places, and these spirits are known to adapt their 'act' to the surroundings. I've sat out in jungles around the evening fires, and the people I was sitting with didn't have any pot on the fire for the evening meal and I can remember one occasion when they handed me a piece of meat from the pot and it still had the feathers on it,'' said Reverend McDougall, chuckling pleasantly. ''And then I can remember this other time when a tribesman passed me a pot with the evening's dinner in it—you were supposed to reach in and help yourself—well, I dipped my hand in there, pulled a piece of meat out, and when I looked at it it was lookin' back at me.'' Mrs. McDougall groaned after he had said it, but her husband kept on. ''You see, they liked to cook the head with the eyes still in it, and gettin' that particular piece was the luck of the draw for me!''

"How grotesque!" said Melissa.

"You think it's bad sittin' here, I had to eat the darn thing!" concluded Reverend McDougall.

The minister's wife nodded and smiled at Melissa. "Awful, isn't it?" she said calmly. "I'm glad I didn't go with him on that assignment."

The golden light slanted in through the western window and beads of water had formed on the lemonade pitcher, which glistened faintly in the light as Reverend McDougall took another sip of his lemonade and then continued, some of the lemonade still in the process of being swallowed. "Some of those dinners made me miss Ann's cooking somethin' fierce. Well, anyhow, a person can run into some pretty nasty demons possessing some of the natives in some of the tucked-away corners of the world. These people are so primitive, you can usually look at their faces and see when there's demon possession. Some fairly powerful spiritual entities come out through witch doctors, and all the ones I ever ran into were anti-Christ in nature. But these spirits can come out anyplace and pose as anything." The preacher paused a moment to take in a swallow of the juice.

"I pastured a little church in Los Angeles several years back," continued Reverend McDougall. "And I was called in to witness a seance some pretty fancy people were conducting in a big house in Beverly Hills. They proceeded to contact a spirit through a little old gray-haired woman who acted as the medium, you see; and this particular spirit was all sweetness and light. It spoke about the need for everyone at the table to help the starving millions of people that the worldwide famine had produced. It talked about giving money to help stop the new diseases that were popping up, left and right. It even talked about the need for people to have some type of religion—gave dietary suggestions that would supposedly help a human live longer—things like that. People at the table looked like they had a real sense of joy just hearing all this. Like everybody, these rich people were looking for simple answers to their problems." The preacher pulled down what seemed to be the rest of his lemonade and sat the ice cubes back down.

"Who needs more lemonade?" Mrs. McDougall interrupted her husband. Everyone nodded, and so she rose and refilled the glasses.

Reverend McDougall took the top third from his glass before

ontinuing. "I had been brought in by a number of relatives who
uspected the spiritual motives of whatever was coming through
his medium—they wanted me to test this thing from a Christian
rospective. So when the spirit finished its spiel and finally opened
he floor to questions, I popped up and asked it whether Jesus
lied on the cross. It said to me, 'My son have you not heard me, I
m for all religions.' So then I said to it, 'Then you agree that Jesus
lied on the cross for human sin.' Well, a few seconds later the
nedium's chair started shaking so hard it dumped her on the floor.
he seance was over for tht bunch, and I don't mind telling you
aere were some movie stars that walked out scratching their
eads that day. They couldn't quite understand what had
appened, but they smelled a rat. And I doubt if they ever went to
seance again. The spirit had shown its true nature."

"But this entity at Desert Rock—I think it called itself
antaur—it said some things that go along with things I've read in
ne Bible," said Tom.

"Ah, but you see, lad, the Devil and his demons are a subtle
unch. The Devil quoted Biblical scriptures to Jesus in the
ilderness, but he took the quotes out of context," answered
everend McDougall, his words lilting against each other.

Sipping quickly at his drink, the preacher went on, "Most
eople, when they contact something from the supernatural—why
ney're so awed at first they usually assume what they're
ommuning with is all sweetness and light. But the Bible plainly
ates there are two forces in the supernatural world. The apostle
aul said even if an angel from heaven appears and gives a
fferent message than what's already in the Bible—let him be
irsed! Pretty strong, pretty strong."

"I guess we still get back to the key then. How can one be sure
e intelligence behind the UFOs is evil?" asked Tom.

"It's the message, you see, lad!" said Reverend McDougall.
t's always in the message. You'll always see this, whether they
ose as angels of light or departed souls, Satan's gang always
storts the good news of the scriptures. It's the one message the
evil doesn't want the world to know: That Jesus shed his blood to
ve us from our sins and a human being only has to accept our
ord's sacrifice to escape the Devil's clutches. I personally believe
e visions and apparitions at Garabandal and those at Fatima,
ortugal, were extremely subtle deceptions of the Devil. The
ntities in those encounters threw in a little prophecy, a little truth,

and a big lie about humans earning their own salvation at the same time."

"Why does all this UFO and space creature stuff seem to be increasing all of a sudden?" Melissa asked the preacher.

"I believe this old world is headed for the sunrise," said Reverend McDougall, and he smiled, showing dull white teeth. "And this is the generation when the Lord Jesus will come like a thief in the night to take the believers away. And you know astronaut Ed White, when he orbited the earth in the old days, saw four great ridges on the surface of the earth, and these are the four corners where the Bible prophesied the angels would stand and gather the believers in the last days." The expression on Tom's face stagnated with surprise for the slightest of moments when he heard that. The preacher took up his glass and drained the rest of the lemonade, the ice cubes clinking softly when he set the glass back down.

"Let me pour you all some more," offered Mrs. McDougall. "I'll just have to throw it out if we don't use it up." She got up again, lifted the pitcher, and topped off the glasses around the table. The ice cubes were smaller now, and they floated up toward the top of the crystal glasses. "How 'bout some more ice?" she inquired. The others stood with what they had, and so Mrs. McDougall took the pitcher over to the old white GE, lifted some cubes out of a plastic bowl in the freezer section, and stuck some in her glass and in the pitcher.

Reverend McDougall took a sip of his drink, then continued afresh after his wife had come back to the table. "Anyway, the Devil and his evil ones know the time is short. The Bible told us they would. So they are fighting for the minds and souls of all the people they can use their deceptions on. And we live in the space age, so they are going to use space-age delusions and lies to try to deceive the modern man."

"The Devil is the expert at deception," said Mrs. McDougall. "He'd probably be called a senior deception specialist at a big corporation."

"And I personally think these UFOs are only illusions appearing real," said Reverend McDougall. "Fearful signs in the heavens prophesied to occur in the last generation before the Lord's return. Now, without the armor of God, they might be dangerous—I'm not saying they're not evil in their intent."

"I've seen one myself," said Tom. "It sure as heck looked

solid, and we got photographs and all kinds of electrical emission data. Besides, UFOs have been known to leave marks on the ground."

"A master of deception such as the Devil would make it indistinguishable from reality," said Reverend McDougall. "He's like a magician. I don't know how he does the trick, but he is capable of altering the physical world as we know it. A good example would be poltergeist activity. When I was twenty-nine years old I fasted for forty days—I only drank fruit juice. I've never been the same since that."

"That's why he drinks lemonade like it's goin' out of style," interjected Mrs. McDougall. The others at the table roared at what she had said, the preacher winked at his wife, red-cheeked from his laughing.

"Besides a love of fruit juice," he began again, "after the fast, God gave me a gift that lets me see the world more as it really is sometimes. I have, on occasion, seen all manner of spirit beings. I've even seen some of the evil, pot-bellied runts that infest the world around us. During these times when I've been allowed to see through that dark glass between the two worlds, I see the unseen world everywhere, hiding among the flesh-and-blood part. So I have been blessed and allowed to see for myself the reality that the Bible describes is absolutely true—that those who believe in Christ don't battle against flesh and blood—we battle against powers and principalities of the invisible universe. Never forget these demons and other fallen beings are organized for one purpose—to keep people from the truth so that they'll end up forever in a burning lake of fire. The head of this disinformation campaign to influence the eternal destiny of human souls is anti-Christ—the Devil himself."

"John gets pretty gabby when you get on demons," explained Mrs. McDougall politely. "He's not usually this long-winded, 'cept on Sundays in the pulpit."

"That's good. We needed some answers," said Melissa. In the sky outside the window two white birds arched upward suddenly, and Tom could see the quick-moving shadows follow faintly on the dusk-darkened ground as they passed over.

Reverend McDougall went on. "You see, most people in the world don't realize what the most important thing in the world is—or something inside them doesn't want them to realize. Here in America, they think it's fame or fortune. I've sat across the table from a lot of unhappy millionaires in Beverly Hills. And every one of them, if they had any age on them, knew something was missing. I've ministered to actors and actresses in Hollywood who had bodies and faces most of the rest of us would like to trade with, but their smiles were just pretend. I told all of them that ever came to my office at that little church that their souls were the most precious things in all the Earth. It didn't matter what was on the outside. And the only answer to set their souls and spirits right was Jesus.

"I remember one very famous actor who possessed great wealth, and you could tell he had lost his zest for life. All the actor went out of his eyes after I told him that Jesus was the answer, and he said 'But nothing can be that simple.' I told him it was. He said he'd go home and do some deep thinking. Later I saw him—he had accepted Christ and he was a different person—he had this contentment."

"Let me just ask you this," said Tom.

"Sure."

"Well, you likened the Bible to a set of extraterrestrial communications given to earthlings by the power in the universe—a power some men call God."

"One and the same," said Reverend McDougall. He winked at Tom and Melissa, and his eyes sparkled in the artificial light.

"Well," continued Tom, "do you believe in physical life on other planets beside our Earth?"

"Sure, Tom—Jesus said that he had sheep that were not of this fold and we would be together in heaven. But I don't think we will encounter them until then. All the science fiction ever written about travel between the stars and alien life forms who visit the Earth is just fiction as far as I can tell. I've never considered it worth reading. But, you know, somebody, someday, could write a piece of science fiction worth reading." The preacher nodded like he knew something and, looking straight at Tom, he winked again.

Mrs. McDougall brought a fresh peach pie to the table after that, sliced it, and they ate the thick, triangular pieces off transparent plates with silver forks. It was dark outside by the time they finished second helpings, and Mrs. McDougall poured everyone coffee, and they talked while they drank it. Then Tom and Melissa got up to leave.

"In your investigations of extraterrestrial communications, never forget," Reverend McDougall summed up, looking at Tom, ''the price for a human's sin doesn't have to be paid twice. Any intelligence that would ignore the mission of our Lord and tell humans they need to look for another savior tells a lie. And the Bible points to the Devil as the father of lies. Satan tries to disguise the truth about human souls; he wants to hide the fact that punishment is reserved for unsaved sinners, that we must believe in Christ to be saved—and that's the most important thing we'll ever do in this one life we have to live.''

''Well,'' said Tom, edging toward the door, ''we sure thank you for your help. It sounds like the UFO phenomena is up to no good. If that's the case, somebody needs to warn people.''

''Yes,'' agreed Reverend McDougall.

19

The Theft

Tom Kruger had just stepped into the narrow kitchenette of his motel room when the telephone beeped at him. It made a sound like an intermittent, electronically simulated rattlesnake—coiled, rattling. A phone ringing that way after a full day always irritated him. He flipped on the square of overhead light in the entryway, made his way slowly across the room, and turned on the lamp beside the bed, taking his time as he went, hoping the phone would give up. It didn't. He hesitated another moment and reluctantly plucked the receiver from its cradle. "Hello," he answered.

"Tom," said Glidewell's Basil Rathbone voice. "Get over here straightaway!"

"Over where?" asked Tom, eyeing the bed wistfully.

"To my room," said Glidewell, a sober urgency in his voice.

"What's wrong? What happened?"

"I can't divulge anything over the wire. Get down to my room as soon as possible," pleaded Glidewell.

"Okay," agreed Tom. "I'll be right there." He recradled the receiver, wheeled, and stepped around the bedroom wall to the kitchenette, where he filled a glass with water and chugged it down. Then he went out the door, scurried down the short hall to the stairs, went down them two at a time, and 71 seconds later he was at Glidewell's door, knocking.

Glidewell had a sour expression on his face as he ushered Tom Kruger into his room. When Tom stepped further in he immediately saw the disarray that had caused Glidewell's dismay on the telephone. The layout of Glidewell's two rooms was a mirror image of his own, and the big closet he was used to seeing on the left was on the right side here. But the closet's louvered oak doors were spread wide, and clothes were strewn on the floor in rumpled piles. Further in, he could see dresser drawers lying on the floor with their former contents littering the floor.

"Is your housekeeper doped up or somethin'?" quipped Tom.

"This isn't humorous, Tom," said Glidewell.

"What the heck happened?"

"They got the UFO photos and the video—that's what happened," said Glidewell. "And I'll be damned if I can find anything else they took."

"*That's* weird," said Tom. "You still have a duplicate set stashed away, right?"

"Hell-yeah, in the van," said Glidewell, his eyes searching inwardly for a thought. "Oh no! They couldn't—I've got the alarm on. I don't think . . ." Glidewell wheeled around and headed for the door all in one sweeping motion. As he turned in the motel hallway, he broke into a trot. All Tom could do was try to catch up.

Glidewell rushed through the beige metal EXIT door and ran to where the van was parked. The side door of the van was closed, but as he pressed the handle to check the lock the door slid open. By the time Tom trotted up, stopping himself with one hand against the van, Glidewell was already cursing, peering in at the van's contents, his face sullen in the peach-colored light that came from egg-shaped globes atop aluminum poles.

"Son of a bitch!" hissed Glidewell. "How could they bypass a thousand-dollar alarm?" He stepped up into the shadowed interior as Tom looked on, dumbfounded. Glidewell hurriedly examined equipment, stumbling over objects on the floor, cursing as he went. "Sabotage," cried Glidewell, "pure and simple."

"Who the hell did it?" asked Tom.

"I don't know," said Glidewell, his voice faint with resignation. "But they've destroyed some damn expensive equipment—my gaussmeter and the CRO are total losses. This is utter madness. I cannot believe someone would do this!"

"What about the extra set of photos?" questioned Tom.

Glidewell eyed up the small black file cabinet built in under a Formica slab on the far side of the van's interior. Glidewell opened the file drawer and then cursed some more. "Gone," said Glidewell, shrugging his shoulders. "They took them all! Every shred of UFO data—gone. Those lousy sonsabitches!"

"Who, Leo? Who?"

"Hell, it took something damn sophisticated to get around the alarm. It's some kind of fox-clever bastard," shouted Glidewell. He dropped down from the van and slammed the sliding door behind him. "Let's get back to the room. This damn thing makes me sick."

"Let's think this thing out," offered Tom as they walked back into Glidewell's motel kitchen.

"What's to think out, old chap?" said Glidewell in a high-pitched voice while he retrieved two tall glasses from the kitchen cabinet. "Somebody wanted those UFO photos in the worst way and they sure as hell knew how to get them. I think we're playing with the big boys now. Maybe those half-witted UFO skeptics and explain-them-away scientists are smarter than I give them credit for. Maybe they know what's good for them. Want a drink?"

"Sure," said Tom. He pulled a chair, translucent plastic with black seat panels, out from under the small kitchen table. Tom sat on it slowly, carefully testing his 188 pounds.

"What flavor?" asked Glidewell.

"Bourbon and sweet soda."

Glidewell made the drinks and sat down opposite Tom. The two men were speechless for a moment, taking long draws from their glasses, eyes focused on their separate thoughts.

Tom broke the silent mood first. "The way I figure it, somebody in the local UFO study group has got some peculiar friends."

"I'd sure like to find out who the hell it is," said Glidewell. "You don't think it's Vilchek, do you?"

"Could be anybody," said Tom, wolfing down the rest of his drink.

As if he didn't want to be outdone, Glidewell tossed the last of his drink down. "Damn—I'd find it an ecstatic pleasure to get hold of whoever's behind this."

"You might be better off not getting hold of 'em," remarked Tom. "It looks to me like whoever did it was damned professional about the whole thing. I mean—I think these guys know some things."

"You can sure say that again! Somebody should have heard the alarm—hell, I would have heard it! I was in the restaurant eating my curds and whey right after I pulled in," said Glidewell. He stared out into the white entryway for a moment, then got up and brought the glasses back to the kitchen counter. The beep of the telephone interrupted his drink making a few seconds after he had started. Glidewell moved with haste into the bedroom and snared the receiver from the end table's cradle. "Hello," he said to the mouthpiece.

"Don't concern yourself with the misplaced pictures you faked. I would forget them," said the voice on the other end.

"Who the hell is this?" shouted Glidewell. The way Glidewell he said it surprised Tom, and he stirred in his chair, staring at Glidewell through the square opening in the wall that separated the kitchenette and bedroom. Glidewell's body appeared to stiffen while he listened.

"This is a warning against you and your accomplice," the voice on the telephone said. "Stop spreading that pack of lies about flying saucers before some unfortunate accident befalls the two of you!"

"What business is it of yours, jackass lips?" shouted Glidewell, spewing spittle into the mouthpiece perforations. Tom got up from the table and ambled into the bedroom.

"As you recently surmised in your conversation, if we can get around your overly complex alarm, we are able to perform other more serious indignities—eh?" The voice on the phone seemed almost to hiss like a cobra. It had a peculiar electronic quality, as if it was being filtered by a voice-altering device. "And I wouldn't worry about Vilchek—he's not one of ours," continued the telephonic voice, and then it broke into laughter, oddly rhythmic in a metered cadence that gave the laugh an air of unreality.

"Buzz off, bastard!" shouted Glidewell as he slammed the receiver down against its mating base.

"Who in the hell was that, Leo?" asked Tom. "Your face is red as a tomato."

Glidewell's head seemed to quiver at the edge of perceptibility as he squared off to face Tom. "Somebody's got this room bugged! They've heard everything we said in here!"

"You sure?"

"You should've heard the bastard—he laid a death threat on us—told us to quit talking about the UFOs. He told me not to worry—Vilchek's not one of them. I tell you, they've got this room bugged, man!"

"Don't panic," urged Tom.

"Right," said Glidewell in a sarcastic tone. "Next time the phone rings, *you* get it!"

"Who the hell's behind all this stuff?"

"I haven't the foggiest," said Glidewell, heading in a straight line for another drink. His hawklike eyes stared at the moving liquor as he filled his glass with Chivas Regal scotch.

"How about yours?" he asked tom, nodding toward the empty glass.

"Gimme·the same quantity, only bourbon," said Tom.

"You got it." Glidewell filled the glasses seven fingers high. He brought it with his over to the table where they stood and touched the glasses together for a couple of seconds in an unspoken toast. Tom wondered if someone was listening at that very moment. I *don't like people eavesdropping while I drink*, he thought.

20

The House Near Santa Barbara

The next morning at seven after seven, Tom Kruger telephoned Melissa. "Hi," he began in an uncertain voice. "I'm surprised you're awake and everything."

"I am now," answered Melissa with soft words that slurred together. "The big question is—what are you doing up at this hour on a Sunday?"

"I'm just a morning person," he joked. A husky laugh followed out of the earpiece. "I guess we kind of have a tentative date tonight," added Tom.

"Yes, those words came from your lips, I seem to remember. You'll have to excuse my brain; it's just starting to warm up."

"Can you give me a rain check?" asked Tom. "I think I'm just gonna go out and get bombed."

"On Sunday?"

"Sure," he answered. "Long as the bars stay open—it ain't Election Day, is it?"

"What's the matter?" asked Melissa.

"Somebody's broke into Leo's motel room last night. They sabotaged his van and stole the UFO photos and video tape," answered Tom.

"That's why you're going to get drunk?"

"I guess so."

"Why don't we drive down to Santa Barbara instead?" suggested Melissa.

"Maybe some other time."

"It would really be nice," said Melissa. "I'd like you to meet my uncle—he's my buddy."

"How about next weekend?"

"I just talked to him last night. He invited us up today. Honest.

151

I've told him all about you," she said.

"I'd like to," said Tom. "But this UFO business is buggin' me right now, and I'd just like to forget everything for a day or two—maybe three or four."

"I really think you'll be interested in what my uncle could tell you," she said mysteriously. "He's a retired Air Force colonel."

"Tell me about what?" questioned Tom.

"Trust me," she said. "I'll tell you later."

"You wouldn't lead me astray, would you," he said, and laughed.

"Sure," said Melissa. "He's not really my uncle. He's a creature from outer space in disguise. He and I are in it together. I'm a creaturess from space. We're going to trap you, suck your brains out of your head, and spread them on cornbread from the Milky Way."

"You won't get much," said Tom. He thought over what she had said for a moment. There was something she wasn't telling him, and it intrigued him as he rubbed his hand across the morning stubble on the right side of his face. "Okay," he said finally. "Since you put it like that."

Santa Barbara lay lovely and serene in the late morning sun. The day was already warm, and there were fluffy cumulus clouds that seemed to hug the mountains that overlooked the town. On their left as they drove, Tom and Melissa could see the dark blue of the Pacific Ocean, glittering and sparkling with the movement of wind and waves. Tom rolled down the car window and glanced left, catching sight of the gulls wheeling and soaring in the breeze that wafted across the ocean. The sea breeze felt cool as it came in through the window, and the bird calls pierced the fresh moving air like shouts. He could smell the salt of the ocean in the air.

As Tom drove past the string of motels and restaurants there were people strolling under the palm trees that lined the beach. Once they were past the boat harbor, he wheeled the Chevrolet right, onto a road that led up toward the mauve and tan amphitheater of mountains. There were patchy shadows on the mountains where snow white clouds blocked out the sunshine, and they watched the shadows move across the land as they angled up the slope from the ocean. After snaking around a mile or two of road Melissa spoke up. "Okay, now, slow down, Tom. The driveway's just past this next curve. It's kind of hidden by bushes and stuff."

"Okay, kid." Tom turned in, centering the cheap hood ornament on a brick driveway that curved like an S up toward a rustic, tan stucco house. The car bucked and rolled over the rough undulating road. The house protruded between two close stands of trees that overshadowed its red-tiled roof, and Tom stopped the car in front of the beige adobe of a walled-in porch that ran the width of the house, interrupted only by three open archways.

Up on the porch a man was reclining in the webbing of a ten-foot rope hammock that hung amid white wicker chairs, stereo components, a pair of aged Schwinn bicycles, and large gray concrete columns from which hi-fi music blared.

The man began the process of getting himself out of the depths of the hammock as Melissa and Tom got out of the car and crossed the patch of red bricks between the car and the porch. He swung one side of the hammock low, placed one foot on the floor, then hopped upright, like a bunny sprung from a trap, then stumbled and almost fell as he tried to get his balance.

Melissa led the way up the stone steps that led to the porch. The older man smiled and whisked his hand across his hair to pull it back from his eyes. He was a husky, barrel-chested man with a strong frame and big brown arms. He wore a thick gray beard, and the coarse black hair on his head had swirling patches that matched the color of his beard.

"Hi, Uncle Jim," said Melissa.

"Hi, Lissa," said the colonel. He bent down, Melissa kissed him on the cheek he turned toward her, right above the edge of his beard.

"Uncle Jim, I'd like you to meet Tom Kruger," said Melissa.

"Hi, Tom," said the colonel, shaking the other man's hand, "Jim Delaney." The colonel had the kind of eyes that crinkled up when he met people, independent of what his mouth was doing, and there were lines that formed to the sides and below his eyes like those variegations on the skin of a musk melon.

"Pleasure to meet you," said Tom.

The colonel shot a look at his stainless-steel watch. "Did you eat lunch?"

"No, Uncle Jim—all the good spots looked pretty crowded so we just came on up."

"Well, you guys must be starved," declared the colonel. "Come on inside—how 'bout that music, Tom?" Nat King Cole warbled out of the speaker boxes, and the violins contrasted starkly against the singer's smooth, husky voice.

"Not bad," said Tom.

Melissa turned to Tom and took hold of his hand. "Uncle Jim likes all the music they produced before civilization kind of disintegrated. Nat King Cole's one of his favorites."

"Nat's okay. At least he had a voice," commented the colonel as he led the way into the house. "Most of what I like, though, is classical—written before the twentieth century, of course. The music all went downhill after 1860, I'm sorry to say." Tom nodded at what the colonel had said, and smiled. The song played out, with unusual realism from the concrete-anchored speakers as the three of them walked past the softly closing screen door and into the house.

"This is a great-looking ranch," Tom said to the colonel a few minutes later out in the kitchen. The colonel had pulled a plump cooked chicken out of the refrigerator and dangled it by its legs before Melissa grabbed it. She was busy now, making sandwiches out of slices she had taken from it.

"I like being up high like this," said the colonel. "It's kind of pretty even in the winter, when the storms roll in."

"I bet," said Tom, looking out the back window at a treeless expanse.

"I just lease the place, though. The rent's a little steep, but what the heck, I liked the area so I took it. Most of the stuff in here isn't mine—just the matresses and a few odds and ends."

"Really," said Tom, surprised.

"Time to eat," said Melissa's moving voice behind Tom as she carried plates over to the table in the adjoining room. She set the sandwiches on the dining-room table and they sat down and started on those, and had iced tea to drink.

"Melissa tells me you're looking into UFOs," the colonel said to Tom.

"Yes, sir—been doin' a little research," Tom replied vaguely.

"This chicken is delicious," said Melissa.

"It's all organic," said the colonel, laying his sandwich back on the plate in front of him. "No chemicals in the feed," he said, holding his hands with the fingers curved like chicken feet. "And the farmer I get 'em from actually lets 'em walk around on the ground." He moved his fingers comically, back and forth across the table. "They're happy chickens—that's why they taste better.

The farmer even puts roosters in the chicken yard." The colonel's blue-gray eyes smiled, and the skin around them formed deep grooves.

"Oh, really, Uncle Jim," said Melissa, trying not to laugh.

"It does taste pretty good," said Tom, a little chicken still in his mouth.

"Lissa tells me you had a close encounter," said the colonel.

"One of my colleagues at Edwards has a modified van crammed with electronics," said Tom. "We got lucky first time out—spotted a UFO—got some closeup photos and a video."

"How close?" questioned the colonel.

"Maybe three hundred yards at the closest approach," said Tom. "Something had mutilated some cows the night before—could've been connected with what we saw."

"I see," said the colonel, nodding, rubbing his whiskers a little. "Melissa mentioned that you had some sort of problem holding on to the pictures."

"Yeah! Somebody stole 'em," said Tom.

"How many people knew you had them?" asked the colonel.

Tom eyed the colonel suspiciously. "Well, we showed the photos and the video at a meeting of the local UFO group in Lancaster. I think there was a reporter from an LA radio station there—I'm not sure. Somebody broke into my colleague's van, and they ransacked his motel room. They knew right where to go to get the photos. They stole all the video and some strip-chart recordings we had made of the UFO's electromagnetic emissions."

"Pretty professional jobs—the break-ins?" questioned the colonel casually.

"Well, yes," said Tom. "But they didn't stop at that. We're getting crazy calls. It's like somebody's monitoring us with eavesdropping devices, tapping our phone lines and stuff, but we couldn't find any bugs—we swept both our rooms after somebody phoned my colleague's room and played back what we had been saying to each other in private."

The colonel stroked his beard a few times thoughtfully, then left his forefinger lying on his mustache.

"Tell the rest," Melissa urged Tom.

"Well," began Tom slowly, "whoever's calling us made some threats—warned us to cool it as far as UFOs are concerned. The phone woke me at three A.M. this morning—some turkey told me to stay out of lonely places and forget I ever saw a UFO."

The colonel finished off the last of his sandwich and washed it down with the tea. "I'm afraid you may have encountered a certain government agency and they don't particularly care for what's under the little rock you've turned over."

"CIA?" questioned Tom. The colonel sat motionless for a moment, looking carefully into the other man's eyes.

"Can he be trusted?" the colonel finally asked Melissa, then winked his right eye.

"Almost like family, Uncle Jim," replied Melissa, grinning mysteriously again.

"I certainly hope we can trust him more than some members of our family," said the colonel. "Some of the shadier elements of our illustrious family are only a small step removed from the horse-thief stage, I'm afraid."

"I'm cleared for top secret with the DOD," offered Tom, confused.

"I'm afraid that what our government knows about UFOs goes quite a bit beyond top secret," said the colonel. "And for that reason what I'm about to say here must not be repeated to anyone, including your colleague." The colonel clasped his hands and planted his elbows firmly on the tabletop. "You see, Tom, the Central Intelligence Agency can be compared to the outer layer of an onion. Other networks and secret agencies exist, hidden from view behind the CIA. The CIA takes all the heat while more secretive agencies carry out their missions with little public knowledge that they even exist. In this country there is an extremely large, totally clandestine effort devoted to the so-called UFO situation, and the project's at the core of the onion where no one can get at it."

"You were in intelligence?" Tom asked the colonel incredulously.

"Yes," said the colonel. "I spent my last eight years in the Air Force working mostly on what's known as Project O. It's the biggest secret project since they developed the atomic bomb as the Manhattan Project. I was assigned as liaison to the National Security Agency—that's the second layer of the onion."

Tom's eyes enlarged, and a glaze seemed to cover them for a moment. "Project O," he repeated.

The colonel continued. "Project O is the real UFO project—the one most people don't know exists. The O stands for OINTS."

Tom looked at the colonel with quizzical eyes.

"OINTS is short for 'other intelligences,'" offered Melissa. Tom looked over at her, startled at what she had said.

"You're in on the secret stuff?" Tom blurted out, tossing a questioning look at Melissa.

"I've let Lissa in on bits and pieces of this thing," said the colonel. "But she was a good trooper and kept it quiet—she couldn't even tell you. I signed several documents pledging secrecy before I left the service—they can get pretty nasty if they find anyone leaking information that hints at the core of the UFO onion. It's the part of the onion they want to keep hidden. They'll do almost anything to keep it quiet. So, leaking a tidbit related to Project O is a good way to get a free ticket to electric shock and drug therapy at a federal installation up in Alaska."

"What's at the core of the UFO onion?" asked Tom suddenly.

The colonel smiled at the directness of the question. "Hostility and malevolence." He paused and looked at Tom for a moment without saying anything. "Tom, it appears as if you've managed to land smack dab in the middle of this UFO thing, and for your sake and Lissa's sake, I'm going to reveal some things now that only several hundred people in the free world know. You see, what the governments of the free world know about UFOs is the best-kept secret on God's green Earth."

"You mean Uncle Sam's got hard evidence? A crashed spacecraft, something like that?" said Tom.

"No, Tom," said the colonel. "Quite the contrary. The powers that be want the masses to think UFOs come from outer space—they operate a fairly complex rumor mill about captured space ships and alien beings."

"Huh," said Melissa.

"I don't . . ." began Tom, and the sentence died.

"UFOs don't emanate from outside our atmosphere!" said the colonel. "They've been with us many thousands of years."

"Well, somebody's sure been leading us down the primrose path, then," said Tom, his southern accent showing. "That's hard to believe!"

"I sometimes wish it weren't true," said the colonel, getting up from the table. He walked over to a black slate wet bar that resided in a recessed alcove adjacent to a large picture window. The window faced north, and through it the mountains above the ranch could be seen, hazy and serene. The colonel opened the right-hand door of the cabinet underneath the bar, stooped down, and brought out a crystal brandy decanter and a glass. "Tom, care for some brandy?" asked the colonel.

"No—no thanks," said Tom.

"You don't happen by any strange coincidence to have any of that strawberry leaf tea you used to have?" asked Melissa.

"Sure, hon—just got a fresh shipment in."

"I'll take some, Uncle Jim," said Melissa. The colonel filled a Corning Glass pot with water, sat it on a grate, then rotated a knob until a flame popped out, flickering like living blue tongues under the blackened grate.

"Fine old German lead crystal from the late eighteen hundreds," said the colonel, turning toward Melissa and Tom, raising the decanter high, admiringly, as the brandy rocked and flashed. He poured some out into a large wide glass and then swirled the liquor around, rotating the brandy snifter in slow, circular movements until he sniffed at the brandy and took a drink.

He seemed to linger on the taste of the brandy as he continued. "The ultrasecret project has accumulated a great deal of evidence of UFO-related hostility in its thirty-odd years of existence—some of it much worse than cattle mutilations, most of it never reaching the public domain in recognizable form. There were human abductions, disappearances, and mutilations, as well as low-level interference with military operations, disruptions of top-secret nuclear weapon manufacturing and storage—pretty serious stuff!"

"And they don't come from space?" said Tom.

"No," said the colonel. "I don't think so. We've got highly sophisticated detection equipment now—in the early days of UFOs we didn't. But now we can identify anything entering the atmosphere from space. Once you look at all the data on that the idea that UFOs come from outer space seems absurd. There's more evidence that they come from beneath the sea."

"Under the sea?" said Tom.

"I guess I've never ruled that possibility out—at least for some UFOs," said the colonel. "There's a lot of things that point to a near earth source—there's a lot that points to hostile intent. The kicker is that Project O was always ready to pay a high price to suppress any evidence of UFO hostility that could enter public awareness. They even financed and infiltrated some Hollywood projects to condition the public through films and TV shows to accept the existence of UFOs as space ships carrying advanced beings who were portrayed as godlike friends from other galaxies."

"Well, hell—that's probably why somebody came after the photos," remarked Tom. "They proved at least the UFO was at the site of cattle mutilations. Chopping up some farmer's cow isn't exactly what I would call a neighborly gesture."

"Precisely," said the colonel.

"The part about the godlike UFO beings is similar to some of the things we heard at Desert Rock," said Melissa.

"It's a message these creatures have been communicating to various groups for at least forty years. At NSA we had huge files detailing messages groups allegedly received from space creatures on a worldwide basis." The colonel swirled the brandy again, savored the smell for a moment, then took a long pull. "Some of the top Hollywood screenwriters and producers were associated with a couple of groups who claimed on-going communications with advanced space creatures. Between these UFO creatures contacting the cream of Hollywood at UFO rap sessions and the covert movie producers in the upper echelons of the government, they've stuck their message in big-time science fiction for the past thirty years!"

"The Hollywood types believed the communications?" asked Tom.

"Yes. They must have bought most of it—we saw correlations that proved certain screenplays were based upon what the space creatures told California-based UFO communication groups even when we didn't finance the movie. As someone said a long time ago, the media is the message."

"Selling the UFO pilots as good guys," said Tom. He tilted his head, and a smirk took over his lips.

"That's where a big internal struggle of Project O comes in," continued the colonel. "One group believed the public would panic if they found out the UFOs are hostile. I was in the minority that believed the public has a right to know the truth."

"It's amazing they could keep evidence of hostility quiet this long," said Tom.

The colonel swirled the brandy in his glass and sniffed it for a moment. His eyes closed and then opened slowly as he drank what remained in the glass. "That's precisely why you must be careful in your UFO activities from here on out," the colonel told

Tom. "The agency in control of Project O will do anything to keep the lid on any evidence of hostility."

"Anything?" questioned Melissa.

"Some private UFO investigators have died under mysterious circumstances," said the colonel. "I don't want to scare you, but I'm not going to put a pretty face on something that's ugly," said the colonel. "I'm just trying to warn you that you're dealing with the biggest thing that any government's ever had to keep quiet. Watch your step. And, if it gets too hot, or if you sense further danger—at the first sign of any trouble—call me. Anytime of the day or night."

"Gottcha," said Tom. He squinted his eyes and went on. "If these things are hostile, and if they're not from outer space, where are they from?"

The colonel took a few steps up to the big window on the far side of the room and gazed out at the sunlit scene for a moment. Clouds were still drifting close to the tops of the mountains. "There are other worlds besides the physical. Scripture tells us there are both physical and spiritual levels of existence—the seen and the unseen worlds." The pot on the gas burner was boiling away by now, making a low, gurgling sound. The colonel turned and walked over to the wet bar, got a tea bag and cup from a wooden shelf, and poured the boiling water into the cup over the bag. He dipped the bag a couple of times, removed it, and brought the cup to Melissa.

"Thanks, Uncle Jim," she said, sniffing the vapor that rose from the cup.

The colonel sat back down at the table. "Let me put it this way," he continued, looking at Melissa. "A true UFO is much like the chameleon lizard I gave Lissy when she was in junior high school—remember?"

A slow smile crept to Melissa's lips. "Sure," she said. "Old Carl the Chameleon—he was a real cutie!" Melissa glanced at Tom, extended her left arm, and let her fingers walk up his arm. "He used to crawl up my arm real gently," she continued. "And then he'd change colors to try and match whatever I was wearing. I really got attached to that little guy."

"Whatever happened to him, hon?" asked the colonel.

"We lost him in the backyard," she answered. "He crawled under the fence, I think." Melissa raised the cup to her lips and sipped the tea.

"Besides missing the point on some other things, I guess I'm missing the connection here," confessed Tom. He squinted at the colonel. "You've saying that the UFOs are like Carl the Chameleon?"

The colonel laughed at his own analogy. "Let me explain. Back in the late eighteen hundreds, people across America reported unidentified air ships that navigated the skies and sometimes even landed within view of witnesses. Goggled, helmeted aviators would get out of the ships and converse with the locals. One witness reported that an air ship even captured a cow. People who had not yet read Jules Verne science fiction had described ships similar to those he had written about in books an ocean away. UFOs are great mimics."

"The Old Testament recorded sightings of fiery chariots in the sky," offered Melissa.

"Right you are, Lissa," said the colonel. "In the modern era of UFOs, Americans have seen beings step out of advanced-looking space craft and gather soil, plants, and rocks."

"Like our early astronauts on the moon," said Tom.

"Exactly," said the colonel. "South Americans observed hairy dwarves stepping out of UFOs in the sixties, seventies, and eighties. Rural people in France saw similar creatures come out of landed UFOs in the fifties. People in rural Spain saw creatures step out of more primitive UFOs, wearing suits like underwater divers wear. The UFO and its occupants can take many forms—all of them modeled somehow on the thoughts of human beings."

"Any idea of the purpose behind the whole thing?" asked Tom.

"Unfortunately, the eyes-only files at NSA contain a massive number of reports where UFOs appear to be taking steps that an advanced military force would take if it were planning an invasion."

"So the recent increase in sightings might mean they're ready to make a move," said Tom.

"I'm not sure," answered the colonel. "Their presence en masse certainly indicates that the human race isn't alone on this planet—I don't think we've ever been alone—they won't let us alone, I'm afraid." The colonel gazed down at his glass a moment. His eyes had a strange, faraway look as he raised the glass to his lips and drank the last of the liquor.

"What were some of the hostility cases you ran across, Uncle

Jim?'' asked Melissa.

The faraway look oozed from the colonel's eyes as he answered, ''I can remember a UFO incident I personally investigated in September of '90. A woman was driving down a deserted highway in Kentucky at three in the morning. Suddenly her vehicle was struck from the rear by something that caused a severe impact. She thought in her mind that she had been struck by a tractor-trailer truck and, for a split-second, she thought she had been killed, the impact had been so great. She turned completely around in her seat in time to see a huge aerial object, bright as a welding torch, lift up above the rear window. The back end of the car was up in the air by then and the front end was tilted forward, so when she turned back around she was looking down at the road. She tried the steering wheel and the gas pedal, but the car was out of her control. The UFO was controlling the car—half-way up in the air.''

The colonel paused a reflective moment and drank the last of the brandy. ''The woman told me that there were some kind of vibrations flowing through the car—like an electric current. And it made the car shake fiercely. There was a small river ahead of her, and she could see the superstructure of the bridge coming up. She knew then that the UFO would have to either get her all the way up in the air, hit the bridge, or drop her. At the last moment it let loose of the car and she saw a round, lighted object fly up and out in front of her. The car swerved so badly that she barely regained control and got the car back on the road before she went across the bridge.

''She reported the incident to the local sheriff's office—that's how we learned about it. I interviewed her within forty-eight hours, posed as a newspaper reporter. The car was interesting in a way. The only damage consisted of two small indentations on the edge of the trunk. They were lined up on the center line of the car within a quarter of an inch and they were quite unusual. The mysterious thing about these two concave impressions was that they looked as if two three-inch-diameter hard rubber balls had hit the trunk with about twenty thousand pounds of force. But no paint was damaged—not even a scratch. I looked underneath the car at the frame and the bumper, but they hadn't been touched. I can attest to the fact that the trunk of an '87 Mercury Cougar has an adequate latch—the marks showed that the back end of the car had been held up in the air totally by the trunk lid itself.''

"I always did like Mercurys," said Tom.

The colonel smiled. "The witness ended up with internal injuries and profuse issues of blood from quite a few exits. We maintained a file on her. Her condition degenerated steadily after the UFO incident. She finally developed open sores on her body and then died a few years later, still in her early forties. There have been scores of encounters where people have been wounded and even killed by UFOs. After I'd investigated a couple of cases like that one—saw what the phenomenon does to people physically and mentally—I knew that UFOs were evil."

"Was that thing trying to carry her off, Uncle Jim?" asked Melissa.

"That's a very real possibility," said the colonel. "There are thousands of missing people listed in police archives who may have been abducted by UFOs and never returned. Some of their automobiles were listed as stolen and never found. We correlated quite a few of these."

"Now I don't understand how that could be kept secret—thousands of American citizens taken away, car and all," said Tom.

"We've got a pretty leak-proof society, Tom," said the colonel. "Most people purchase the brand of soda crackers they see advertised on television, and they believe and repeat the news stories and philosophies they've been programmed to believe. The media is rather easy to manipulate no matter what they tell you. The intelligence community doesn't have a monopoly on it. By utilizing the tried and true bribes and favors, the entertainment industry does it all the time. But if you ask people, they won't admit they're being programmed like a computer every day. It's extremely hard to see through one's own programming; it's a flaw in the human brain—I believe Freud first discovered it."

"So there are a lot of parrots around these days," said Tom.

"Excellent analogy," said the colonel. "It's the problem of outwardly directed men in an electronic global village," he added.

"Polly want a Ritz cracker," croaked Melissa. The two men gave her a strained look.

"Well, I must say it seems like I've been giving a seminar here," said the colonel, his eyes twinkling a little. "Why don't you two join me downtown for an early dinner. I know of some excellent eating establishments around here, and it's my treat."

"Great. I could talk about UFOs all night," said Tom.

"I'm afraid I won't be able to discuss the subject in a public place. Just one of the precautions I've followed for years."

"I understand," said Tom.

"I've got to freshen up," said Melissa.

"Okay, hon, you know where everything's at," the colonel said. He rose from the table and put his hand on Tom's left shoulder. "While Lissa's doing that, why don't I give you a little tour, Tom."

"Great! I need to stretch my legs anyway," said Tom.

The colonel and Tom went out through the screen door, down the porch steps, and circled around the left side of the house. On the backside the colonel pointed toward the distant town below them. "Great view," he said.

"Boy, it sure is," said Tom.

The house was set slightly on the down side of the crest of the hill and, as they strolled along the slant, Tom could see a three-story structure attached to the rear of the far end of the dwelling. The single door in the structure looked as big as some of the hangar doors at Edwards.

"That's the biggest garage I ever saw!" said Tom, pointing to it.

"Oh that," the colonel said nonchalantly. "I collect pieces of war surplus aircraft. I'm trying to restore two of the old birds. They're in pretty bad shape at present, but I'll give you a peek next time you come out, hopefully. Still have a lot of work to do before I piece it all together."

"Well, if you ever need some help, give me a buzz," Tom offered politely. "What type of aircraft are they?"

"Oh, an old Army attack helicopter and a P-51 Mustang from World War II. I hope I've got all the pieces—parts are pretty hard to find, especially for the Mustang." The colonel put his hand on Tom's right shoulder for a moment and gave him a brisk pat.

"That's what, a triple-decker garage?" asked Tom.

"It's more like a small aircraft hangar, but it has an upper level where I store all the spare parts I come across from time to time. They don't manufacture the parts I need."

"I guess you must've flown in the Air Force," said Tom.

"Yeah, I was a fighter jockey—flew F-4Es in Vietnam and F-15s for a while. Then a slot came open in intelligence and they stuck me in it."

"Ever run into any UFOs up there?"

"Nope, but I knew plenty of pilots that did."

21

The Prospector's Cabin

The motel swimming pool was unoccupied, and the wind stirred little ripples in one continuous pattern across the face of the water. On the mint green concrete that surrounded the pool, bodies tanned in the August sun. The motel was an L-shaped building, flanking the pool on two sides with a few thin palms showing their green clusters above the roof. Tom Kruger emerged from the leg of the L, a white-brick expanse on the north side of the pool, through a glass door that flashed behind him. He weaved his way toward the least crowded corner of the poolside by the spa and exercise rooms. When he reached the farthest of the empty chaise longues, he took off his tennis shoes and socks and plopped them down with a brown bottle and towel under the chair. He stretched out on the chair and lowered his sunglasses into the shadow of the chaise longue until they rested on his left-foot tennis shoe. The sun was two thirds of the way toward the top of the sky, so he adjusted the back of the longue chair to get the best angle, then let his body sink onto the rough, warm plastic.

There were little holes in the chaise-lounge's plastic, and he could feel wind coming from the south cool his back, so he reasoned the day would be another hot one. While he dwelt upon how the water would feel once his body heated up, voices caught his attention the way many normally overlooked pieces of life capture the curiosity of someone who lies awake with his eyes closed. So Tom concentrated on the chattering while he let the warmth of the sun soak into his skin.

"This sun is fantastic, isn't it?" exclaimed the younger of the women.

"Yes. It is very therapeutic," said an agreeable older woman's voice. "Instead of a couch and psychoanalyst and all that—this is my therapy. When I'm well tanned I simply feel so positive, you know."

"Yes. It is positive," said the younger woman. "We try to go to Palm Springs at least once a month—though it wrinkles me so!"

"Oh yes—if you stay out in it too long," said the older of the women matter-of-factly. "With all the weird weather this country's having, we're fortunate we have the sun to lay in. I mean, with the rash of ice storms in the north and the floods in Arizona, and terrible tornados on the east coast. And we have the sun."

"Some of our friends just got back from the south of France," commented the younger woman. "They had an awful time. They said the weather was just hideous—it shattered all the gloominess records. Strangest weather France has ever had."

"From what I've read, the weather's been terrible all over the world," offered the older woman.

"It would be dreadful to be on vacation without sunshine," said the younger woman. "I'm a sun sign—that's probably why I want to stay out in it and roast all the time. I'm a Leo."

"On really." The older woman pretended surprise. "Yes, that is a sun sign. Did you know there's a new book out on sunbathing techniques—it's reached the *New York Times* bestseller list! Written by that girl on *All My Children*, you know the blonde that had the two abortions."

"I'll have to pick it up," said the younger woman. "It makes me sick about my skin though. I'm wrinkling up. I've tried everything from the department stores—no one seems to have a good program though."

Tom shifted on the lounge chair, quietly, trying not to miss any of the exchange. He was curious about where the womens' words would lead them, and his skin felt warm from the sun already so he began putting on suntan lotion.

As he smeared the milk white creme, the older woman continued, "My dermatologist, who happens to live two houses down our street, has loaded me up with samples of this marvelous conditioner. It comes in a yellow tube—manufactured by Jon Palvee of Beverly Hills. It conditions as well as filters out all the ultraviolet rays when you wear it in the sun—prevents the actual damage to the skin."

"What do they call it?" asked the younger woman. "I don't think I've used that."

"It's called Infinity Three," said the older woman. "I'll let you try some. It is really marvelous—protects the skin from burning. Of course, your tan is held to the absolute minimum."

Tom heard one of the women light a cigarette with a sharp solid click from an expensive piezoelectric lighter. He heard her draw the smoke into her lungs and, by the rough, turbulent sound of the lungs exhaling, he guessed it was the older woman. The smell of smoke drifted by his head and made his right nostril begin to itch. He wiggled his nose against the itch, and after a moment he heard the sound of bare feet slapping the concrete, coming toward him.

"Yes, I certainly need to try something new," lamented the younger woman. "I'm allergic to so many things. I've had to throw tons of the stuff out, you know."

"I *know*. That's so frustrating," said the older woman, then she changed her tone to a more formal one and said, "Have you met my husband, Bill?" The sound of the slapping feet stopped abruptly. "Bill, this is Myrna."

"No, I haven't," the younger woman said politely. "Glad to meet you, Bill."

"My pleasure," said the man.

"The sun is nice, isn't it?" the younger woman said to the man.

"Very nice," agreed the man in a strained, uneven voice as his body landed heavily in a lounge chair. The chair's legs scraped the concrete with a grating sound as he maneuvered it. "I'll lose two pounds an hour out here."

"Oh really! By sweating?" asked the younger woman.

"No—by dehydration," answered the man.

"Yes, it is very hot," said the older woman.

"What's your opinion of all these UFOs they've been sighting out here, Myrna?" asked the man.

"I don't really believe in them," she replied.

"Me either, Myrna," the older woman chimed in. "I don't know why Bill constantly has to chatter about something so silly. It's probably because he has a brain the size of a pea."

"Females don't appreciate interplanetary life," said the man in a whimsical voice.

"Balderdash," his wife said. "Some people can't recognize a sea gull at twenty paces!"

"I'll probably lose about a pound in the sauna," said the man, ignoring what his wife had said. "It looks like a three-pound afternoon."

"Did you know there's something wrong with the Jaccuzi?" the younger woman informed the man.

"No. I haven't been in yet," he answered.

"It's turning people green—their fingernails, their swim trunks, even their hair! I think it's the chlorine or something."

"Has the management been informed?" asked the older woman.

"Yes," said the other woman. "They're calling in a sanitary engineer, I believe."

"I don't think I'll go in till it's fixed," said the man. "I don't look good in green."

The sound of metal sliding on concrete interrupted the conversation suddenly. Tom's eyes slid open. As he looked toward the new sound, he saw Leo Glidewell coming toward him, dragging a lounge chair behind.

"Cheerio," said Glidewell after he had scooted the lounge chair parallel to the one Tom was in with a final high-pitched etching of the concrete.

"I just had a whole bowl of those with a banana and milk," replied Tom.

Glidewell put on his exaggerated smile, which made his upper lip curl inward. "You can *sure* say *that* again," said Glidewell in a sing-song voice. Glidewell sat down in the chair. "How's the sun?"

"Gettin' hot," said Tom, squinting his eyes against the sunlight.

"Let me borrow your suntan lotion," said Glidewell. Tom handed it across to Glidewell. The other man squeezed the creme onto his legs right below a khaki-colored pair of swim trunks that looked like they were ten years old, then began stroking it into his pores.

"Save me some, will ya," joked Tom.

There was a pause while Glidewell worked on his legs, then he moved the squeezing and stroking up to his chest area. "Say, Tom, you mind if I ask you something?" asked Glidewell in a low voice, barely loud enough to be heard.

"Sure, fire away," answered Tom, puzzled at Glidewell's tone.

"Has anything terribly weird been happening to you lately?"

"Like in the past twenty years, or since we started getting our stuff ransacked and phone calls at all hours of the night, or when?" said Tom.

"Besides all that rot," said Glidewell mysteriously.

Tom reached under his chaise longue and retrieved the sunglasses from the tennis shoe. He slid them on, raised up a little off the back of his chair, and peered at Glidewell, the pool winking with a flash of light through the sunglasses. "No, the weird phone calls are all I'm getting," said Tom finally.

"Well, I dare say there are some strange psychic manifestations bouncing around in my arena," declared Glidewell.

"What type of manifestations?"

"The particular nature of what I'm experiencing I would say is a little hard to describe," said Glidewell. "Perhaps the way to say it simply is that I know more about some things than I did before all this UFO business happened."

"You lost me, Leo," said Tom. "What things?"

"Some pretty esoteric things about the true nature of the universe—comprehensive things from the macro to the micro," said Glidewell confidently. Tom nodded, then Glidewell recapped the lotion bottle and handed it back. Then he continued, more slowly, more carefully. "This may sound incredible at first, but I've had a revelation that there are two more as yet undiscovered planets in this solar system—I think they'll be discovered in the next five years."

"Anything's possible," said Tom, his eyes widening under the sunglasses.

"I also somehow know that Einstein was incorrect in certain areas of his field theories and, just this morning, the correction to these theories came to me out of the blue!" said Glidewell. "At least part of it. I know the rest will come—this phenomena to be automatic, like a universal computer data base or something."

"Whoa—wait a minute!" said Tom. "How is this stuff coming to you—are you picking it out of the air or what?"

"It's like this stuff just started seeping into my mind since we saw the UFO, slowly at first, but now it's speeding up," replied Glidewell in a puzzled voice that Tom had never noticed before. "It's as if some psychic mechanism has bloomed inside me, and it's connected to a source of all the knowledge in the universe!"

"Well, Leo, you sure got a hellava lot more out of that UFO sighting than I did!" exclaimed Tom in a low voice.

"I knew it would sound quite bizarre, but I had to tell somebody," explained Glidewell. Then, after an awkward silence,

"I can assure you, Tom—it *is* happening. And it *is* real."

"Well, keep me posted then," said Tom. "And let me just throw somethin' else out."

"What's that?"

"How about another UFO safari?" said Tom.

"I'm game," countered Glidewell without hesitation. "When?"

"How 'bout tonight?" said Tom. "We'll give whoever's keeping tabs on us another thrill. We'll give 'em some action."

"I would've thought you'd have a date with Melissa tonight," observed Glidewell.

"She's staying overnight in LA with a girlfriend, so as far as I'm concerned the night is ripe for UFO action," said Tom. "You got anything goin'?"

"Hell no, let's do it!" said Glidewell. "What madness do you have in mind?"

"Well, there's this prospector I ran into at the AV Inn when I first got into town," explained Tom. "He claimed there was a lot of UFO activity out by his place—landings, stuff like that."

"Where at?"

"In the Mojave, pretty far out—I figure there could be a base or something out there," said Tom in a low voice. "We could scan the area—try to pick up somethin'—maybe talk to the old-timer."

"You know how to get there?"

"Yeah, he gave me a map."

Seven hours later they drove past the edge of Lancaster, and headed for the heart of the Mojave. The night had inked the sky with bluish-black by the time they found the final turnoff to the prospector's cabin. Tom had matched up the landmarks on the napkin map he had memorized with the landmarks along the road as they went. They didn't stop until they found the cabin, several hundred yards off the road, nestled against a rise of mountains.

Tom and Glidewell got out and stretched their legs, then hiked toward the desolate cabin with its two rectangular eyes of milky white light that stood out against the dark mountains. Overhead, Vega twinkled with an intense blue-white pinpoint of light near the zenith of the sky as they approached the small cabin. Tom could make out the sinuous rills and ridges that ran along the mountains that loomed over them, silhouetted faintly by the starlight. In the distance a coyote gave its eerie howl. They mounted steps that led to a rickety porch, and Glidewell rapped on the rough, weathered door—silence came back in response. They tried the doorknob, and the door rolled open and the two men walked inside the cabin. "Leo, there's somethin' fishy here," Tom said warily.

"When's the last time you saw this chap?" asked Glidewell.

"June—no, May," replied Tom.

"He may have expired by now, out here in this God-forsaken place," said Glidewell.

The main room inside the cabin was sparsely furnished. A solitary, unfrosted 75 watt bulb hung from the ceiling, giving the room a harsh glare. The largest things Tom could see in the room included a rollaway bed, an oak table and three chairs, a Sony ten-inch battery-powered television set, and a tan wicker couch with two matching chairs. At the windows, white garbage bags hung in neat overlapping strips.

Tom penned a note, using paper from a small notebook he carried in his breast pocket. The note asked the prospector to telephone the base whenever he could, since there was no phone they could see in the room. They left the note lying on the kitchen table and walked back outside, closing the cabin door behind them. The two men walked around to the back of the cabin, halting at the sight of a cubical hunk of yellow light radiating from the base of the mountain. "What the hell is that?" said Tom, taking a few more paces toward it.

Fifty yards away they saw the light was coming from a rectangular, timber-lined opening in the side of the mountain, and the glow spewed out fan shaped, spreading along the ground a few yards into the darkness. "Probably a mine shaft," said Glidewell.

"How come it's all lit up?" asked Tom.

"Maybe he's on night shift this week," said Glidewell.

As they walked into the light of shaft they glimpsed rough-hewn steps leading down into the rocky glow that made them halt at the edge of the opening and peer down into the dimly lighted interior. In the hollow of the opening, a cylindrical lantern hung from a rusted chain, swaying gently from the wind that came into the chamber. The light glowed from step to step, fainter and fainter as the steps angled downward into the earth, leaving at the bottom the vagueness and mystery of a hole of shadows.

"I want to see what's down there," said Tom, slowly beginning a descent of the first steps. "I've never seen a real gold mine."

"Somehow I don't imagine he's left any of the stuff lying

about," answered Glidewell, a bold edge to his voice, as if he wanted to frighten whatever might be lurking down below them.

"You never know—we might spot a couple of nuggets," said Tom as he edged down the steps.

"I really would hope that no one blasts us for trespassing," said Glidewell, carefully picking his way down the steps a short distance behind Tom. At the end of the steeply angled stairway the shaft leveled out. Tom could hear the wind whispering tremulously at the entrance of the shaft as they made their way a few yards into the dimness lurking beyond the bottom of the steps, their heads constantly turning as they looked around them. After stalking past the third frame of timber braces, Tom spied an overhead door with a thick rope dangling from it. His crunching footfalls stopped, then Glidewell's.

"Wonder what's up there?"

"Pull it" urged Glidewell.

Tom hesitated a moment and then yanked the rope with a hard pull, and the trap door swung open. A body fell out of it, straight past Tom's nose, and plopped on the dirt floor in front of his feet with a lifeless thud. "Ahhhhhh," yelled Tom.

"By jove!" exclaimed Glidewell from behind him.

In the dim light that shifted with the swinging lantern above them, the thing on the ground resembled the body of a large snub-nosed dog; it was stiff like it was dead but, oh!—Tom thought he saw it move and then he knew it was moving! And he sensed at that instant some odd peculiarity about the way it moved. Tom could smell the rot and decay of a dead body, but still, the corpse was moving.

"What the . . ." said Tom. He squinted his eyes against the dim light and, holding his breath, bent over and edged his head nearer the body. Then he saw why it was moving. Hideous crawling forms were spewing out of the dead body. Giant white maggots issued from its rotting mouth like living vomit, and there were more of them slithering out of a wound in the neck and from an opening in the belly. One of the dog's eyes was missing and a stream of the many legged insects poured from the empty socket. As the two men watched in disgust, another group of maggots erupted from a hole where the left ear had been. For whatever reason, the dog's stomach was almost entirely gone.

Tom ran up the steps with Glidewell close behind him. They exited the mine shaft and headed quickly toward where the van was parked. Tom shot a glance at the sky as they sprinted toward the road, and he could see Mars, orange and brilliant halfway up the black bowl of night.

"Mars must be fairly close," he shouted to Glidewell.

"Hell-yeah." Glidewell barked out his reply. At that precise instant a dark figure jumped out at them from behind a jagged, immense boulder—ahead and to their left. The running men stopped in their tracks and froze at the sight. Tom stared at the top of the figure to see if he could make out who or what it was that blocked their retreat.

"Gotcha this time." A voice spoke out of the darkness as it moved toward them. In the starlight Tom made out a human figure at the other end of the voice, and the human had a long gun pointed directly at him.

"Man or beast?" said Glidewell uncertainly.

"I know who and what I am," said the approaching figure. "Just who mighten you be?"

"We're engineers from Edwards Air Force Base," offered Tom. "Tom Kruger here."

"Kruger? Without the Rand—yeah I seem to . . ." said the unknown voice. "What are ya doin' out here? This here's private property!"

Tom recognized the prospector's voice. "You invited me out, remember? At the AV Inn you told me about the flying saucers landing out here—remember?"

"I remember," said the voice. "You ain't got nothing to do with that bunch of guys driving the black limousine around, has ya?"

"What guys?" answered Tom. "I don't think so."

The old-timer came within a few yards of the two frozen figures and stopped, steadying the gun onto Tom's chest. "Now, turn around and head for the cabin so I can get your face in the light." As they neared the white light that came from the cabin's windows, the old-timer saw Tom's face and slowly lowered the weapon. "Go on in the cabin," said the old-timer.

"Recognize me?" asked Tom.

"Yeah I reckon so," said the old-timer. "Can't be none too careful. There's people and forces out to do me harm. I saw you come out of the shaft."

"That we did, old boy," said Glidewell. "We stumbled into it quite by accident."

"We found a dead dog in there," said Tom. Glidewell gave Tom a hard, surprised look.

"The devil killed my pup," said the old-timer. "I put him up in storage to keep the predators off." His eyes were red rimmed and watery in the stark light. He walked over and leaned his shotgun in a corner. "You boys just come out to see some saucers—is that the story?"

"That's about the size of it," said Tom.

"You want some coffee?" asked the prospector politely.

"Sure," said Tom.

"Make it a pair," said Glidewell.

The old-timer took a chipped, white porcelainized pot and filled it from a spigot that protruded from the bottom of a blue plastic tank on the counter top beside the stove. "Well, I tell you, chief—a lot's happened since I seen you last. I can't piece all of it out, but I guess it ain't goin' to hurt to let you in on the whole thing." The old-timer lit a flame on the stove and put the pot on to boil. He paced back over to face Tom. "I got no reason to suspect you of nothing," he said to Tom. "You seem pretty square. Why don't we all grab a seat instead of standing here like mules."

They sat down on the wicker couch, and the old-timer sat facing them in one of the wicker chairs. "After one of the big quakes last year I was out looking for fresh cracks in the mountains round here. Sometimes a big quake'll do that, and there's just liable to be a mother lode sticking out someplace—ya never know."

The old-timer scratched his tanned head through white wisps of hair and then continued. "I found something strange out there. Somethin' that's probably pretty danged important. Something that most all people in the world would never believe."

"What the hell was it?" Glidewell asked impatiently.

"I'll tell ya what I found out by that there mountain," the old-timer pointed in the direction of the door of the cabin. "It was a tunnel made by somebody and it was leading down into the ground like a snake hole, and the earthquake had tore the covering off and there it was—big as life! There that sucker was—a big black tunnel built right into the side of the mountain. Like a bunch of educated giant moles had been diggin' there, makin' a nest."

"I'll be damned," said Glidewell.

"What happened?" queried Tom.

•

"Well, no sooner than I started toward the hole, I felt something hit me like a jolt of electricity and I must've blacked out." said the old-timer. "That was all there was to it." Tom nodded slowly at what the old-timer had said. Glidewell had an odd smile on his face as he listened.

The old-timer got up from the chair and poured three cups of water out and spooned instant coffee into the cups. He brought the coffee over to Glidewell and Tom Kruger, then brought his own. He sat down, slurped at the coffee, and continued. "Naturally, when I woke up the tunnel was gone."

"Did you remember—I mean could you find the spot where it had been?" asked Glidewell.

"No," explained the old-timer. "I went up the side of the mountain a little and tried to find where the hole was, but it all looked like solid rock. It was like it had never been there. But it was there all right. I saw it!"

Glidewell twisted his body and snatched his wallet from his left rear pants pocket. He opened the wallet and slid something out from a hidden fold. "Here's my mobile number—call me if you ever discover another tunnel," said Glidewell to the old-timer. He gave the old-timer a business card with his van's permanent phone number emblazoned in red.

"But my God, don't tell nobody else about all this. Don't tell nobody or we're all in trouble," urged the old-timer as the two visitors nodded. Then they finished the coffee and made ready to leave.

Glidewell drove the van fast for a long while after they had left the cabin. "What the hell's happening out there, Tom?" Glidewell finally broke the silence.

"I guess I don't know," responded Tom. "But I can tell you, I think the old-timer is crazy as a loon. His brains have been out in the lucky old sun too long."

"He seems pretty coherent to me," countered Glidewell.

"I'm not so sure."

"A couple of hundred years ago nobody believed stones or chunks of metal fell from the sky," said Glidewell. "And it was all very logical to the scientists of that day. Since there were no stones in the skies then certainly no stones could fall from the skies. Today we're up to our butts in meteorites."

"I still say the old-timer's story bordered on fantasy," said Tom.

"What would cause him to see that tunnel after all the years of looking at those mountains?" asked Glidewell.

"All the years of looking at those mountains," replied Tom. "I don't think his elevator goes all the way to the top anymore."

"Hallucinations didn't mutilate that dog," reminded Glidewell.

"Well, you got me on that one," said Tom.

"You can sure say that again," said Glidewell. Tom shook his head and gave Glidewell a look that one gives when a bad joke has been told for the fiftieth time. As they drove back to Lancaster, the van's headlights pierced the night like a jack o' lantern's triangle eyes.

22

Their Human Prey

The desert was quiet and cool. Beside land where Indians once roamed the gray car rushed along the desolate road straight as an arrow. The man behind the wheel had just cranked the left-hand window open an inch to bring coolness into the car. His dark eyes looked like those of a man hypnotized by a swinging pendant in the movies as he drove through the flat desert night. There was a small muffled roar of air that came rushing through the window now, so the man lifted his right hand off the wheel, snaked it over and onto the radio volume control knob, and increased the sound level a few decibels. A radio announcer was chattering well-enunciated words like a well-trained, human magpie on a five-minute news broadcast: "The woman's body was found yesterday in San Francisco Bay. Police said she was clothed only in a T-shirt that read SMOKE ACULPULCO GOLD. Meanwhile, in other news around the world, a series of killer earthquakes ravaged parts of China and the Soviet Union this morning at eight-thirteen Eastern Standard Time. The death toll is still being revised upward and currently stands at two-hundred thirty thousand Chinese and ninety-eight thousand Russians. It appears to be a catastrophe of major proportions."

"That means it was *big*," said the driver to his wife, who sat pensively in the right-hand seat.

"Radio Moscow was off the air for six hours, but has now resumed limited operation," said the voice on the radio. Just at that same moment an orange globe of light appeared in the distance, behind the car, and began to follow from a mile or so back. The light from the aerial object was soft and dim and it flew unnoticed for a moment behind the speeding auto, then brightened an octave before the wife noticed it.

"Harry! Look in your mirror," said the woman. She was looking in the mirror to her right; it was convex, inset in an oval cove, mounted on a metal stalk outside the window. The man glanced into the rectangular rear-view mirror at the top of the windshield. Through that, the automatic dimming material in the glass made the light appear darker than what the woman was seeing.

"What the hell is that?" asked his wife.

"Probably a Russian spy satellite," answered the man, glancing between the road and the mirror a couple of times before he spoke.

"Well, it's orbiting right above the highway then," said the woman in a bitter voice.

"Probably an airplane," the man suggested.

"I never saw a plane like that before," she said as the lighted object visibly gained on them.

To better observe the spectacle, the woman angled her thin legs onto the car seat and twisted herself toward her husband. As she rotated in the seat, her left knee nudged the stack of books that lay between them. The top book in the stack moved as her thigh came into it and the title on the cover, *Secret Lore of Alchemy*, rotated with the book until it was diagonal to the rest of the stack. Once she had turned to look out the rear windshield, she gazed at the unidentified aerial object in total fascination for a while. The man flipped off the radio and listened out the window, but the light was silent as a flying tomb.

"You know, Harry, whatever it is—it's quite beautiful," the woman said after a long pause. Her eyes were wide and round as she gazed out the rear window at the strangeness of the glow. "It looks just like a Japanese lantern. You ought to take a good look."

"Unfortunately, somebody's got to drive this heap of metal," answered the man sharply.

"Well, stop the car then," she said.

He looked over at her warily. "I don't think so."

"Well, you just should see it," said the woman.

"I *can* see it—in the mirror," said the man while he reached the radio volume knob and turned it back on. The news was over and jazz music was being broadcast, but the signal seemed weak and it started to fade. Then a hissing, popping sound came out of the speakers. "Get something on that thing, will you?" the man asked, pointing at the green-lit digital display.

"All right," she said reluctantly. The woman wheeled back

around in the seat and depressed a triangular button at the right side of the lighted display, released it, and the display began to flash with ever changing digits. The static hissed intermittently from the speakers as faint, short-lived snatches of broadcasts broke onto the speakers and were removed while a microprocessor in the radio searched for a strong signal along the frequency spectrum.

"You know, one year of a car radio's life is about equal to twelve years of human life," said the man. "When they're six years old we ought to throw them away and get a new one."

"You're not going to throw me away, are you, Harry?" asked the woman.

"Nah, turkey knees—you still got some zip," answered the man. Just then, as he checked the rear-view mirror again, he could see the glass in it darkening automatically as he watched, and his eyes widened in surprise as he saw the light double in size in a fraction of a second. Then it doubled again. The car drifted to the edge of the road as he riveted his eyes on the light in the mirror and the vehicle shuddered as it lurched and jostled onto the shoulder; he twisted the wheel to the left and brought the car back on the road. By that time the unknown flying object had increased to a dazzling brightness and accelerated toward the car and, in a few seconds, it was trailing them a few hundred feet behind the trunk.

"Turn that damn radio off!" hollered the man. He saw the dashboard illuminate in front of him and, in the mirror, he saw the object swoop down toward the car. The UFO rammed the car like a giant sledgehammer, causing the heads of the man and woman to jerk back into the headrests like the heads on lifeless dummies.

When the man recovered from the impact he grabbed at the steering wheel and tried to get the car under control. The woman turned backward in the seat again and caught sight of the UFO, big as a house, rising up above the car roof. Intense orange lights were flashing off and on around the central rim of the strange object, and they reflected off the craft's metallic structure the way powerful searchlights would floodlight a steel water tower at night.

The man and woman could feel the rear end of the automobile lift off the road. The blue glowing digits on the speedometer flashed up to 99 and stayed there. The car began to shake in waves of vibration that buffeted their bodies. The hood of the car pointed down, at an angle, toward the road, which ripped by the headlights faster and faster.

Blood was trickling out of the man's ears by now and his face was white as a sheet, shocked, very old looking. Suddenly the man's head heaved forward and he regurgitated a stream of vomit straight that splattered the windshield and dash and steering wheel with its thick, sticky mass. Orange and red pieces of his supper clung to the T-shaped control pod that nestled inside the steering wheel, and the half-digested slimy morsels shook and moved with the car as it vibrated fiercely.

Then the big UFO lifted the front end of the car upward into the air with two protruding appendages that reflected the light from the rim. The man's wife let out a scream then and the gurgling, piercing sound went out into the desert silence around them and died quickly in the open land like a coyote's howl or a night bird's shriek or any other strange sound the desert hears from time to time. The woman shook her head violently from side to side and grabbed at her long hair, pulling out massive clumps of it as she continued to scream and move her head like a helpless animal, beset by a pack of wolves. As she ripped the patches of hair out of her head, her eyes had an icy faraway look, and saliva dribbled out of the corners of her mouth.

The gigantic aerial craft held the same speed while the four gray appendages, like robotic arms, drew the automobile through an opening that appeared in the bottom of the craft. When the last of the car had disappeared inside the UFO the opening instantly closed and, after a few seconds, the light on the craft grew dim and ghostly again and the big object accelerated straight up into the night, receding in a moment from full size to an orange speck, almost invisible among the stars. The sounds of crickets crept back as if brought by the night wind that blew gently where the car and the unknown object had been moving a moment before. The moon came out from behind angry-looking clouds and, with its thousands of shadows, it shone across the land.

At the same hour the television in Tom Kruger's motel room at the Red Rooster Inn was lighting up one corner of the darkness as he lay relaxing on the queen-sized bed with stacks of library books strewn on the right side of the bed and a tall glass of Galliano on the nightstand to his left. *Flying Saucers from Outer Space* and *Passport to Magonia* were right beside him. He reached left and brought the glass off the nightstand, raised it to his lips, and drank two slow swallows of the sweet, yellow liquor; he liked the taste—like licorice with the alcohol in the background. He replaced the half-empty glass and his eyes seemed to come alive as the commercials ended and the dark-skinned newswoman who anchored the network overnight news came back on, saying, "The United States Air Force released a statement yesterday concerning the rash of recent unidentified flying object sightings being reported around the country and particularly in the western states." The woman's voice was very sophisticated, older than her years.

"The Air Force says the UFO sightings are being caused by misperceptions of known objects under unusual sighting conditions. The unprecedented amounts of haze in the air from worldwide volcanic eruptions have created atmospheric conditions that are ideal for illusionary effects, according to the Air Force spokesperson. This new layer of material in the atmosphere is causing people to misidentify common objects such as weather balloons, high-flying gulls, satellites and other space debris, reflections of ice crystals in the upper air; and, of course, people are being fooled by astronomical objects at night—bright stars, Mars and Venus, and meteors. For more on this, let's go now to Michael Morgan in New York."

Tom frowned, reached for the Galliano, brought it to chest level, and swirled it around in the glass. As the scene at a plush hotel banquet room popped onto the screen, he tipped the glass up, tasting the heavy liquor, then letting it slide down his throat. The television screen changed again and illuminated two fresh faces. One of the men wore a lilac-colored shirt and black necktie, and he was holding a pencil-thin microphone close to the other man's mouth. The other man had moderately long black hair, a large crooked nose, and slick confident eyes. He was casually attired in a sage-colored turtleneck shirt, and as the announcer started to speak, the professor had an eager look of anticipation.

"Yes, Melody—I have here with me Dr. Eric Clayton, best-selling author and professor of astronomy at Princeton University," began the announcer crisply. "Doctor, tell us—do you accept the Air Force's findings regarding the recent UFO sightings?"

"Yes, very definitely," answered the professor with an air of secret knowledge only billions of study hours could have given. "I've looked over the recent Air Force analysis of the major sightings. My considered opinion is that the study was carefully done, and I concur with their findings." The professor had a thin neck and his Adam's apple had a way of jiggling at the top of the turtleneck as he spoke.

"Do you consider it a possibility at all that we may be experiencing visits by intelligent beings from other planets?" the reporter asked.

"I consider the possibility that extraterrestrials might visit Earth very remote indeed," said the middle-aged professor. "And, frankly, I have yet to see any meaningful UFO reports from credible observers."

"And why is it unlikely that so-called ETs would visit the Earth?" asked the reporter.

"Well, you have to remember that interstellar space is very large, and it would take an awfully long time to travel from the nearest galaxy or even from the nearest star capable of supporting life to the Earth. Einstein's discoveries put an upper limit on how fast a ship can travel in the universe as we know it. And that limit is one hundred eighty-six thousand miles a second—which, I'm afraid, is much too slow to make interstellar travel feasible," concluded the professor.

"So, in other words the idea of UFOs may appeal to our sense of mystery, but, in the real world, it's just not very likely," the announcer summed up.

"Exactly," said the professor, chuckling a little, his face shiny under the television lights. "I'm fond of reading some of the science fiction of today as much as anyone. And that's what UFOs are, I'm afraid."

"The Air Force has mentioned special conditions that may be contributing to the sighting of UFOs," said the reporter. "Since you are an expert in astrophysics, Doctor, I wonder if you could comment on that."

"Certainly," replied the professor. "Ah—the recent increase in volcanic activity has produced a fine layer of dust and debris in the air. When people observe a known object in the sky under unusual lighting conditions and with the layer of dust adding to the distortions, peoples' minds tend to play tricks on them and they sometimes think they are observing lighted spaceships. It's as simple as that." The professor paused in a reflective manner, almost dramatically, as if he were in a movie. "I was once misled briefly myself by the planet Saturn, low on the horizon. It took me awhile to identify it and thus change it from a UFO to an IFO."

"IFO stands for identified flying object, is that correct?" confirmed the announcer.

"Indeed," replied the professor.

"Have you found any other causes for the recent outbreak of sightings?" asked the reporter.

"Well, yes," said the professor. "It so happens that we have also been experiencing unprecedented levels of sun spots and solar flare activity. And this has been interacting with the earth and producing intermittent displays of aurora borealis across the United States."

"Now, doesn't this appear as a red glow, Doctor?"

"Yes, and with the clearer skies in the western states, the phenomena is visible more of the time."

"And you say it's intermittent?"

"Yes, this phenomenon is rare at these latitudes so consequently the displays are localized and only persist for, oh, half a minute at most—and with the human brain and its imaginative faculties, this combination can produce some real way-out UFO reports." The professor flashed a smile. "You've had some of the resulting reports on your network—you know, huge glowing space craft that hover, then disappear in a few seconds, apparently flying off in the distance or, as some people imagine, out into space, back to all the comforts of their home planet." The professor chuckled understandingly; the announcer caught it, and both their heads shook as they laughed a few seconds.

"Well, we certainly appreciate your being here with us live this morning, Dr. Clayton," said the reporter.

"Thank you, Michael," said the professor. "Always a pleasure."

"Now back to you, Melody."

Tom raised the glass of liquor to his mouth, angled his head against the back of his neck, and tipped the glass enough to get the last of the Galliano out. "And so it goes," he mumbled to himself. "Now that's one of the great scientific explanations of all time." He touched the lowest button on the remote control unit and the television picture flashed white, then extinguished. He shifted his position on the bed, turning toward the books, propped himself up on his right elbow, and opened the one entitled *Missing*

Time. A small black spider ran out of the spine of the book and disappeared down the side of the bed. On the insect's back Tom had clearly seen a marking like a red hour-glass; inside the wedge-shaped bottom of the hourglass there had been more red than in the upper wedge.

23

The Book Fair

It was recent custom in Lancaster to erect a tent of circuslike proportions in the parking lot of the largest shopping center the third week in August. Inside the tent they crammed donated books and held a sale, using the proceeds to help a local home for abused children. Most people didn't read nearly as much as they once did so old and new books came in truckloads from donors as far away as San Diego. On the first night of the sale Tom Kruger and Melissa Delaney drove leisurely to the shopping center and bought first-night admission tickets for thirty dollars. They stood waiting, touching and talking, laughing and gay, in a short line of people until the low sun made the clouds flame with orange and red. At seven thirty the official volunteers snatched a rope away from the tent's entrance and the line of people rushed into the tent and separated into its individual people, who ran toward the various tables. People began snatching at the choicest items among the rows of books that were arranged spine-up on the tables. With quick movements their hands slid books out of the rows and eased them into tan cardboard boxes, varicolored canvas bags, and even metal grocery carts.

Tom had brought an olive-colored army-surplus duffel bag and Melissa had brought a smaller canvas shopping bag, white with a gold-and-black bee decoration on it, and, before a half hour had passed, each of them had the bags half filled with carefully selected quarry. Tom had found four books on UFOs, a paperback copy of *Invasion of the Body Snatchers* by Jack Finney, and several lesser works of science and literature. The Finney paperback was in good shape for its 1978 publication date, and there were people on the cover running from powerful golden light rays and, above that, the original price of $1.95 was printed.

By eight o'clock the tent was crowded with people and the sides of the tent flapped and quivered in the wind. There were light bulbs strung at intervals on the ridge pole of the tent, and it was very bright and hot inside. Tom's pink sport shirt was saturated with sweat in spots and that made it darker under the arms; perspiration was rolling off his face in great liquid beads by now. As he slid the hairy side of his left arm across his face, wiping the sweat, he looked down and suddenly spotted an old astronomy book on the science table; he speared it, turned it, and examined the dark blue cover, which announced in gold leaf: *Astronomy with an Opera-Glass*. There was an illustration of a pair of binoculars stamped in gold on the front cover, and the title page showed a 1910 date on it. He smiled and dropped it gingerly into the bag that waited beside him on the floor.

Without warning, a loud voice suddenly spoke out, above the buzz of the crowd. Tom turned away from the table of books and looked in the direction the voice was coming from. He caught sight of a young wiry man walking very slowly away from him, beside a table of books, with slightly startled people around him. The man had on a white short-sleeved shirt and green corduroy pants, and he carried several books under his right arm. He was moving in a straight path 20 feet distant from Tom, almost as if he were inspecting a crop row in a farmer's field. His voice was so loud, some of the crowd stopped to listen, while others ignored it and continued to rummage through the books on the tables.

The man's voice seemed to cut through the hot air like a knife. "These are the last days prophesied in the Bible. Man must accept Christ," he said in a very powerful voice. "God is giving you a chance right now! Jesus Christ was tortured and died for you. You must accept his sacrifice and turn from your sins to be saved."

The man in the green corduroys reached the end of the aisle, turned around very slowly, and began retracing his steps. As he came toward Tom he could see the man's serene sky-blue eyes peer through the crowd, and a gust of air wafted through his coarse, sandy hair. As he approached his loud, clear voice seemed to hang in the air inside the tent like a living presence: "If you do not accept God's sacrifice and God's son Jesus, you are condemned to burn in the eternal lake of fire. The lake of fire is real. There is no other way to escape.

"Satan wants to deceive you. He doesn't want you to know what God has told me to tell you. Satan does not want you to believe there is a hell. His demons are out in the world, trying to deceive mankind at this very moment. Satan is the master of deception and deceit. He will be sending a strong delusion onto the Earth, but Jesus rose from the dead and his Spirit is here right now. Turn away from your sins. Ask Jesus into your life and you will be saved. Now is the hour of salvation. If you will live in Christ and his word abide in you, then you will know the truth and the truth will make you free."

The wind outside the tent came up and the light bulbs at the top of the tent danced and the shadows on the ground shifted. The man speaking in the loud voice grew closer to Tom as he paced of the row and, for an instant, it seemed he looked directly at Tom—straight into his eyes. The lean man's eyes sparkled and burned with more intensity than Tom had ever seen before.

Tom suddenly felt a twinge of guilt inside him. A sick feeling flared up in his mind, the same feeling that had haunted him when he had lied and cheated and stolen and seduced God-fearing girls in Georgia—the same feeling that sometimes shadowed him like a faraway presence. Why did I do those crummy things? his mind cried silently. Tom stood transfixed as the stranger neared him and passed by, heading for the rear of the tent. Perspiration rolled down Tom's face—beads of sweat streamed over the thick curves of his lips, and he could taste the wet salt. Tom Kruger felt the dark shudder of fear move through him now—he didn't want to burn in a lake of fire. But was this strange message really as true as it sounded?

The stranger with the booming voice turned around again, altered his path, and began walking through a row between the tables that held the five- and ten-dollar novels. He started speaking again in his careful, clarion voice, full of authority. "This is the good news that God wants you to know as the end of the age comes near. God wants to save you from the Devil's trap!"

The walking speaker stopped and stood perfectly still, looking at Tom again. It made a faint chill come up Tom's back and into his neck, and the hairs on his scalp tingled. After what seemed like a long time the stranger began walking again, speaking as he turned his head from side to side to look at the people in the crowd. "To be saved you must be willing to let Christ change your life. You must turn away from the sin in your life and be willing to change. And you must accept God's son, Jesus Christ!" The words had come out of the man slowly like the pouring of thick molasses and they filled every corner of Tom's mind and seemed to reverberate inside his head. The words had seemed more real than anything in the tent when he heard them. And he didn't understand why.

"Whosoever shall call upon the name of the Lord will be saved. Jesus came not to condemn the world, but that the world might be saved through Him," the stranger said. "Jesus aid unless you eat my flesh and drink my blood you have no life in you. He said you cannot inherit the Kingdom of God unless you are born again." His face appeared very peaceful and confident as he strode away, silent now. His eyes were bright with a thick layer of moisture that reflected the electric light inside the tent. To Tom, the man appeared more real than the other people in the tent—an oasis of gracefulness amid the hub-bub of the now murmuring crowd. The stranger was silent as he continued walking toward the front of the tent until he disappeared amid the crowd at the check-out lines.

The murmuring buzz in the tent picked up again, and Tom could see the sides of the tent move with the wind. He could feel a stream of air cool his wet face as it came in under the tent and blew against him. And while he felt the rush of air he prayed a silent, small prayer in his mind that if God and Jesus were really there and could hear him, that they would show him the way. Then Melissa came up to him, reached out, and held his hand.

"That guy was somethin' else," Tom told her.

"Really," she answered, smiling faintly.

"Whatdya think of the whole thing?" Tom asked her.

"I thought he did a real good job," she answered simply. After that they checked out at one of the cashier's tables.

"Do you have anything goin' Friday night?" Tom asked Melissa over a pot of Hawaiian Kona coffee at a motel coffee shop down the street from the book fair. The walls around them were painted orange and creamy white, and the color scheme reminded him of his favorite boyhood stick ice cream—Dreamsicle.

"Not a one," answered Melissa as she poured coffee into his empty cup. Tom sampled the hot drink while she poured hers. The coffee had a nutlike undertaste, and it was strong and good.

"Would you care to go to dinner in LA?" he asked her. "We can get an early start, leave work about two, hit a good restaurant, and then maybe ride around the city."

"Sounds super!" said Melissa. "Gee, do you think we'll have to work Saturday?"

"I don't know, but whatever they say about Saturday, turn 'em down. We'll really make a night of it. The heck with gettin' up early to go to the sweatshop. I figure if we can't get the job done in forty hours we're overpaid. Besides, they don't pay time and a half for Saturdays."

"I'm torn," said Melissa. "Why is it that we don't get overtime, again?"

"Boy, I tell you, I learned a lot from Glidewell about that particular subject," answered Tom. "He says it's a federal law that workers on a government contract get paid time and a half for any hours over forty in a week or over eight in a day. But the way the big aerospace companies like Johnson get around it is by calling you and me 'salaried' rather than 'hourly.' It's all in what they put down on the employment papers."

"Pretty clever," said Melissa.

"That way they can work the two of us sixty hours a week each instead of working three people forty hours a week," said Tom. "By having one less person on the payroll they save facility costs, corporate social security payments, company benefits, and a bunch of other stuff. And multiply that by the thousands of salaried employees they don't have to employ 'cause we work overtime at our regular hourly rate even though we don't *have* an official hourly rate."

"Because if we had an officially hourly rate, they'd have to pay us one and a half times our hourly rate for working overtime on a government project," reasoned Melissa.

"You got the picture, kid," said Tom. "Did you ever hear the anti-defense people in the media mention this little cost-saving fiasco—this little violation of the intent of a federal law? The media's always harping on the downtrodden steel workers and auto workers and clothing workers. These people all get time and a half for overtime; some of them get almost their full salary while they're laid off. If the TV networks wanted a real story, they could report about us not getting overtime pay and then, when Congress cancels the contract, how we get to scurry around for a few months to try and find a job in some other city. Meanwhile, the steel workers sit around in their hometown, let Uncle Sam pay their house payments, the auto workers are down in Florida relaxing for a month or two in their RVs. And who does the media constantly hammer away at for waste—the aerospace companies!"

"Well, maybe the good ol' Johnson family and the board

of directors who own the lion's share of the company are pocketing the money they save on us," said Melissa.

Tom wagged his finger at her. "You've got a real good point there," he said. She grabbed the finger that was pointed at her and pretended she were going to break it off.

"It's not polite to point, you know," she said, letting go of his finger. Melissa chuckled, and her eyes seemed to light up with a tired, happy look. Tom laughed with her then, and the laugh kept going like it wouldn't stop. He didn't even know why he was laughing except he felt good being with her.

She seemed to gaze deep into his eyes without saying anything for a moment. "You know, you don't even have a trace of crow's feet around your eyes," she said.

"That's not surprising," he replied. "I generally keep the birds off my face—I don't like the way their claws feel."

"Very funny," she said, her face looking fresh and sweet, like a little girl's.

"Anyway, put your eating shoes on for Friday night. I'm goin' take you someplace nice," Tom reminded her.

"Marvy," she replied.

24

The Proposal

The place in Beverly Hills where they went for dinner on Friday night had Rolls-Royces and Mercedes-Benzs lined up like airport taxicabs in front of the entrance, which stared through stained glass at the street under the lid of a purple-and-white-striped canopy that ran out to the curb. Melissa was dressed in a fuchsia-colored linen suit with a fancy white silk-and-lace blouse. The suit was the color of Santa Rosa plums, and under the crystal chandeliers in the restaurant it looked to Tom Kruger more purple than red. There was a white linen tablecloth on the table that draped halfway down toward a slickly glazed red-tiled floor; the walls were covered with an incredible silver-and-blue wallpaper patterned like modern art.

After a few minutes Tom and Melissa ordered from the leather-colored menus, and the dark-featured waiter straightened his tuxedo, then jotted the order on a small pad he cradled stiffly in his left hand.

"What would you care to drink with your meal?" asked the waiter.

"How 'bout Perrier?" Tom asked Melissa.

" 'Fraid I don't know the chap," she countered.

"You know, the H-2-0 from France that bubbles up from the bowels of the earth," he enlightened her.

"I'm not sure I want to drink stuff from the bowels of the earth," she said, her eyes laughing at Tom.

"We'll pass on the barbecued water," Tom told the waiter. "I'll take a little Wild Turkey 101 and sweet soda when you get a chance."

"Yes sir," said the waiter. "Thank you, sir."

"This is quite a place, Tommy," said Melissa.

"I'm glad you like it, kid," said Tom.

"You made a haul at the book fair, huh?" she said.

"Not bad," he said. "My ultimate find was the copy of *Invasion of the Body Snatchers*—I've been lookin' for that one for a while—out of print, you know."

"There were two movies based on it—one made in '56 and the other one in the seventies," he said. "I liked the first one better."

"Me too," she said.

Tom showed surprise. "I wouldn't take you for a science fiction fan," said Tom.

"Ever since I was a baby. I cut my teeth on the good stuff," said Melissa. "My dad used to sell a lot of science fiction in his store. I think *Invasion of the Body Snatchers* is my absolute favorite of all time, though."

"Yeah, it's one of my favorites too."

The waiter glided up with the whiskey and set it in front of Tom. "Thanks," said Tom.

"Yes, sir," the waiter said as he hurried away.

Tom sampled the top part of the drink and found it pleasantly strong. Melissa glanced around the dimly lighted room slowly, watching the people.

"Did you ever notice that people have different looks in their eyes these days?" said Melissa after the waiter had brought a cold bowl of shrimp.

"How do you mean?" said Tom, unbuttoning the front of his tan, black pin-striped suit.

"Well," said Melissa, looking around the room quickly. "I think they're here!"

"Who?" asked Tom.

Melissa leaned toward him and her eyes widened. "The snatchers," she replied in a low, secretive voice.

He leaned toward her across the table. "At the next table, perhaps," he whispered.

Melissa put her index finger up to her lips. "Shhhhh." She took another drink of water from the tall, thin glass, then, lowering it, she held the glass with her left hand and wiped at the beads of sweat that had formed near the rim with her right forefinger. Then she looked up from the glass and gave Tom a fond look. "You can tell if they're body snatchers by the eyes. Remember the scene in the older movie where the hero and Dana Wynter are trying to escape, and he tells her not to show any emotion, but she sees a

dog just about get run over by a bus or something and so she lets
out a little cry? And then the body snatchers know they're not
really body snatchers.''

Tom took a fork with miniature tines off the table, speared one
of the shrimp in the bowl, and sampled the pink flesh. "Boy, old
Dana Wynter was really good in that one,'' he said, blinking his
eyes at the memory. "I really went for her. I mean, she was one of
my all-time favorites.'' He took the rest of the shrimp off the fork,
ate that, and followed it with a long pull from the whiskey and
soda. Melissa lifted a shrimp out of the bowl and paused to eat it.

''Well,'' said Melissa. ''Promise you won't laugh at me if I tell
you something?''

''What is it?''

''The shrimp are really good.''

''That's it?'' questioned Tom. ''That's what I'm not going to
laugh at?''

''No, not really,'' said Melissa. ''You have to promise not to
laugh and then maybe I'll tell you.''

Tom speared another shrimp. ''Okay—I promise.''

They both were silent while they ate the shrimp and then
Melissa began again in a very serious voice. ''Well, I think more
and more people are like the body snatchers today. I mean, they
act like they have no emotions—but mainly their eyes are cold.
They say the words like they care about things, but they don't really mean what they say. Don't you know what I'm talking about?''

He had rushed a couple more shrimp in his mouth while she
had told him, and he spoke with some remaining to be swallowed.
''You've guessed the truth, I think. I am actually a vampire, myself.
I didn't want to tell you, but that's why my eyes have lacked that
certain intensity lately,'' joked Tom, curling his hand into a clawlike
shape. He took a swipe at her with the claw across the table.

''Not your eyes, looney-bird,'' she said, and laughed and
counter-swiped at Tom's clawlike hand with her own clawlike
hand. ''I'm serious, Tommy. I've even seen the difference in the
eyes by looking at old photos, movies, even video tapes of old TV
shows. People's eyes used to be warmer—they were usually
smiling eyes or sad eyes, but at least you could tell. There was
more feeling of some kind in them.'' Melissa bit into her lower lip.
''Look at any of the old movies like It Happened One Night, National
Velvet, A Summer Place, The Homecoming—you'll see what I mean.''

Tom ate more of the shrimp and finished his drink. The waiter brought the salads up to the table then, and Tom and Melissa started in on them after he had gone. "Come to think of it, you're probably right," said Tom. "I remember some of the old movies with Jimmy Stewart, like the one they show at Christmas about the angel who gets his wings. Those *were* different. I think the name of that one is *Mister Belvedere Rings the Bell*."

"*It's a Wonderful Life*," said Melissa.

"I guess that's true," said Tom, a little confused.

"That's the name of the Jimmy Stewart movie with the angel," explained Melissa. "*It's a Wonderful Life*."

"Oh, okay, I guess that's right," said Tom, digging a fork into the salad. Melissa started on the salad, and the waiter took the bowl of shrimp away.

"He took our shrimp," complained Tom after the waiter had gone.

"There was probably ten pounds in that bowl," she said.

"I was goin' to have 'em put it in a doggie bag," said Tom. Melissa laughed, and her shoulders shook.

"Just take out some old photographs sometime," said Melissa. "And take out some recent ones of people and just compare them—compare the eyes. The older they are, the better."

Tom grinned. "Well, you know Eastman Kodak has made miraculous progress in film and development techniques—it makes the eyes come out more solid looking, less nebulous, less hazy, less soft looking."

Melissa tilted her head to one side, squinted one eye, and looked at Tom sideways. Her eyes looked very soft and beautiful. "You're something else," was all she said. An instrumental song from the eighties named "Memory" played softly in the background of the large room, and it sounded very pretty to Tom. Then the waiter brought a large oval tray and set it on a stand beside the table. He brought the octagonal crystalline plates off the tray and set one in front of Melissa, then Tom. And he set separate dishes with baked potatoes beside those and placed a black straw basket of rolls toward the center of the table. He refilled the water glasses and said, "Is there anything else you require?"

Tom looked up at the waiter's dark eyes. They seemed full of cold arrogance. "No thanks," answered Tom. And the waiter walked away.

Melissa looked down at the beef Wellington she had ordered, puckered her lips a little, and said, "Ouuuuuu, it looks good."

There was a fat sprig of parsley lying between the thick brown steak and a candied peach on Tom's transparent glass plate, and he could smell the faint green smell of the parsley as he lowered his fork and knife into the tender meat.

"This is absolutely delicious," said Melissa after sampling the pastry and meat combination.

They were silent for a moment while they savored the food. Then Tom said, "I hope you brought your money."

"Very funny," said Melissa. "How's your steak?"

"Just great," he said, smiling, flourishing his knife like a sword in the air for an instant before he made a display of cutting his steak as if it were tough as shoe leather. As he sliced off the left end of the meat his knife slipped and slid across the plate, knocking the pickled peach off. The peach skidded of the table and landed on the floor with a dull, wet, smacking sound. Unhurriedly, Tom bent down and reached the peach with his left hand. He brought the slimy piece of fruit back above the tabletop and nonchalantly put it back on his plate. Then he picked up the knife and fork and proceeded to slice a small piece of steak off and fork it into his mouth as if nothing out of the ordinary had happened.

Melissa's eyes danced while she watched him and the way he had done what he did. When he bit into the steak she burst out laughing so hard the people at the nearby tables looked over with icy stares. Tom laughed before he had completely finished the meat in his mouth and, after a while, tears came to their eyes.

They ate more of the food and after a short time the recorded background music faded out, the lights in the restaurant dimmed, and a woman wearing a red-sequined evening dress strolled out onto a small stage at the other end of the room. The woman began to play "La Vie en Rose" on an illuminated violin, slightly mechanically. The bow she used glowed with a bright blue light, and the giant sequins on her dress, like bunches of red grapes, shimmered and danced as the glowing bow moved. The color of the violin changed with the pitch of the music—red on the high end, violet at the lower frequencies—and the song seemed to grow warmer and less harsh the longer she played. "I love that song she's playing," said Melissa.

"I'd like to get close and examine her eyes," joked Tom as he looked toward the violinist. "She sure doesn't sound like a body snatcher."

"You're making fun of me now," said Melissa.

"No, seriously, you've converted me," said Tom. "I mean, I think you're right about the eyes and all. There's snatcherism all around us."

Melissa looked at him a moment without saying anything. "You know, I think the type of eyes were predicted in the scriptures," she said to him.

"Oh, no, not again," he said.

Melissa squinted her eyes as she remembered something she wanted to say. "The Lord said in Matthew twenty-four—another of the signs of the last generation is that iniquity will abound, the love of many shall wax cold."

"And knowledge shall increase and people will run to and fro," said Tom.

Melissa tilted her head, surprised for a second. "I didn't know you had . . ."

"I've read the Good Book the last couple of nights before I went to sleep," declared Tom. "I don't know, maybe the guy at the book fair got to me."

Melissa nodded. "If he was a guy," she said, and smiled mysteriously.

"Well, he wasn't a girl," offered Tom.

"Was he human though?" she suggested, and grinned at Tom.

The waiter brought the coffee after that and took away the dinner dishes, opaque now with leftover food. The two of them talked more and sipped the steaming coffee from time to time.

"You want to know something?" said Tom, halfway through his refilled cup.

"Yes," said Melissa.

"I don't know if I should tell you," said Tom. "You're liable to get a big head."

"Tell me."

"You remind me of Dana Wynter in the body snatcher movie," he said.

"Before or after she was a body snatcher?" asked Melissa, curling her lips up in the smallest of smiles, the skin above her mouth forming a few deep, short lines. Tom laughed. He was already fond of the way her skin rippled when she gave him her little half smile.

"Before," he offered.

"Well that's a relief," exclaimed Melissa. Her smile expanded.

and her eyes seemed to dance for a moment as she looked straight into Tom's face. The music from the glowing violin reflected off the walls in the room, and Tom watched the people at the tables around them for a long while, off and on. In the dim light most of the eyes seemed cold, like the eyes of some sort of intelligent fish; and the people seldom looked at the violinist or at people at the other tables, but something about the corners of their eyes made Tom think they wanted mostly to be looked at. The people around about them wore expensive clothes, and the women had on a lot of makeup, expensive charms and jewelry with large, varied gemstones prominent in the light. And the women had expensive-looking hairdos and the men had thick, well-groomed hairstyles. The few people Tom caught peering around the room gave the impression that they were checking up, curious as to whether other people were looking at them, and there was more fire and life in the diamonds on the women's necks than in their eyes while they checked.

Melissa sampled the second cup of coffee the waiter had brought and it was scaldingly hot. She put the cup down hard on the saucer, making a clinking sound, and she fanned her mouth with her left hand. "I burned my tongue," she said, sticking one of her fingers on the top of her tongue. "It's numb."

"Better numb than no tongue at all," said Tom.

The woman at the other end of the room stopped playing music after a few more minutes, and Tom paid the $436 check and left a $50 bill for the tip.

It was late by then, and they drove from the restaurant to the hills above Hollywood and stopped at a wide place beside the road. They slid out of the Chevrolet and stood together by the edge of the hill. Spread out below them, the lights of the city flickered like a field of fireflies. They kissed, and the breeze stirred and blew across their bodies, and they saw the moon rise above the horizon, huge and golden. The craters on the moon made it look a little like a man's face.

Then they got back in the car and drove out of Los Angeles toward the desert beside the invisible shadows the rising moon made on the electric-lighted land. The classical music they were listening to on the radio turned into jazz, and Tom clicked the radio off.

"Jazz sounds like music guys from other planets would make up," he said.

"I don't like it either," she said.

As they neared Palmdale the moon went behind a cloak of misty vapor and the gray-white sand along the road shone faintly in the light, with the shadowy sagebrush scattered in the distance as far as the eye could see. Between the islands of clouds that floated above the desert the stars were out, bright as diamonds.

Tom stopped the car at a small park the government had built at the edge of Palmdale, and they got out again and walked in the moonlight. A coyote, on nocturnal patrol in the distance, howled its lonely desert cry. "I wonder what the coyotes are doing out there tonight—if they're having a good time and all like we are," said Melissa after a kiss.

The park was deserted, and so Tom hollered toward the distant moon-lit mountains that surrounded them like an amphitheater. "How you doin' out there?"

While they waited for an answer they kissed again and, suddenly, the coyote howled loudly, as if it were finally responding to what Tom had yelled out. Melissa laughed in the middle of the kiss, and Tom ended up kissing her teeth on purpose when she stopped laughing and for several seconds he just kissed her smile. "I'm sorry I laughed, you know, while we were kissing—that coyote just tickled my funny bone," she explained finally.

"I don't mind kissing your smile," he said in the moonlight. The small young trees were swaying in the desert breeze, and when the mist moved away from the moon, the moonlight was bright on the terrain again and the stars seemed to grow dim. A night bird called out a sound up high in the air as it flew over them, and they could hear the beating of its wings, hard against the silent air.

"My smile kind of likes for you to kiss it," said Melissa softly. "I mean, it doesn't mind that much." Her mouth looked very young an shy as she looked up at the moon. "That moon is awfully bright tonight, Tommy," she said. "Don't you think?"

"I should've brought my sunglasses," said Tom.

"Next time, don't forget," she said, looking at him softly. Her voice had come out slowly, a little hoarse, the way people sound when they're sleepy, and the moonlight was on her face and she looked very beautiful to him. "I love the clouds on a night like this," said Melissa as she watched the white glowing clouds ride through the sky. "They just ride through the heavens free and easy, and you can watch them all the way to the edge of the sky—they're so bright.''

''It's almost better than the Goodyear blimp.''

There had been a thunderstorm in the desert that afternoon as they were leaving the base, and they had driven in it as they headed for Los Angeles. But now the clouds were moving away to the east and the air was washed clean, and the faint odor of sagebrush saturated the air. A plane appeared in the west and gradually flew toward them and, overhead, they saw it was a small two-engine plane with two white lights and one red one.

''I really like being here—with you—you know,'' Melissa told him as the drone of the airplane's propellers died in the distance.

''I'd like to be with you for a real long time, kid,'' he said, and sneezed.

''That would be nice,'' she said in a soft, slow voice.

Her lips curled up in a little smile, her teeth showing white as ivory, and her dark hair glistened in the August moonlight. He drew her close and kissed her. ''I love you,'' he whispered into her ear when the kiss was over.

''I love you, too, Tommy,'' she whispered back at him. He looked at her, and her eyes looked beautiful and sad. Little tears formed in the corners of her eyes and flowed down her cheeks, reflecting the moonlight like drops of silver that had been refined until they were perfectly pure. She put her head on his shoulder and cuddled in his arms and after that they went back to the car and Tom turned the radio on. There was music fading in and out on the San Francisco station that the radio was tuned to. The music, with its velvet melody, played very faintly while they kissed and caressed each other inside the car. It gave Tom a nebulous, faraway feeling, like the world was contained within the radio's sound, and those times when the signal faded it was like the world was drifting away from where he was.

The music seemed to echo faintly across his mind as he kissed Melissa's warm, full lips, and then he noticed static on the station—*probably some disturbance in the upper atmosphere,* he thought. They were breathing heavily with the kisses, and she broke away for a moment, and they looked out the windshield at the moon, higher in the sky, with small white wisps of clouds around it, illuminated by the silver-white light.

Then they kissed again for a long time, and he tried to touch her where she didn't want to be touched, and she pulled away and said, "I can't, Tommy." They stayed parked there, not saying anything for a while after that, listening to the faraway songs. The night was like a warm cave around them.

"I love you more than anything," he finally told her. "Maybe we could get married if you want to." A night bird flew by the open window and made a lonely cry.

"Yes," said Melissa, her eyes reflecting the moonlight. "I want to." She was silent a moment as she looked into his eyes and gently caressed his face beneath them. "I've never met anybody like you before, Tommy, and after I met you—you want to know something?" Tom nodded at her, silently. She hesitated a long while and then spoke very softly. "After you I never wanted to meet anybody else." When she said it little tears trickled out of the corners of her eyes again, and after that she hugged Tom tightly, crying, streams of tears flowing down her cheeks. He kissed her again and pressed his face against hers, feeling the moist, warm tears against his skin—kissing her over and over, tasting the tears on her cheeks.

They listened to the wind as it cleared away the last of the clouds, and after that they drove back to the motel at Lancaster, looking at each other and talking, happy with love and thoughts of future things, and the wind whispered a restless, warbling moan across the land.

25

The Earthquake

During the day the air had shimmered over the land like hot waves from a jet exhaust and had even bent the light like an infinity of lenses, creating false illusions appearing real on the land. The high desert had been baking in the eye of the sun during the day, and whenever that happened the hot air would rise quickly from the land and nature would force in air from the west to replace the rising air. The worst of the heat had died down by the time Tom Kruger came out of the motel side door for dinner. The wind outside was still whistling and whipping up, and a strong gust hit him and Melissa as they stepped onto the parking lot outside the door. The heat was like a bear's breath in your face. It was the last of August, and temperatures in Death Valley had been creeping over 140 degrees every day, and the temperature in Lancaster had climbed past 120 each of the last six days.

It was evening now and the last glimmer of light had just faded from the western sky and the soft early darkness lay around them. They walked past the decorative rocks and the spray of water from the irrigation pipes was just cutting off, leaving the island of plants glistening, when the earth began to roll gently under their feet. At the very start of it they kept walking toward his car without saying anything, but the ground continued to move in uncertain waves that took on an unexpected fury. To Tom it felt like he was standing on a huge rubber raft, starting to hit rough white rapids. He felt suddenly dizzy as his body staggered and canted at a slight angle that he hadn't ordered. He recalled feeling the same way 11 years ago, after he had made a down-field tackle on a sprinting, burly fullback in high school football. He had hit the 255-pound boy in a way that made his head woozy, and his young body had drifted unsurely for a moment after he had gotten up from the pile. The hit in the head had made the ground start to move. Now, walking in the middle of the parking lot, he wondered for the smallest of moments if the booze had finally reached into the crucial part of his brain.

"This definitely feels like an earthquake," said Melissa after several seconds. Before a relieved Tom could answer they heard an extremely low-pitched rumble, like the distant sound of the firing of heavy guns, and the earth started a violent shaking. They were both thrown to the ground by the rocking, heaving earth like rag dolls knocked from a pedestal at a state fair midway. When they tried to pick themselves up the undulating asphalt kept them from it like a magnet against metal. Once, after struggling halfway to his feet, Tom fell back down to the ground. He could feel himself breathing heavily, and there was a sickening nausea in the pit of his stomach.

The deep, agonizing rumble, which seemed to come up from the earth, now clattered and transformed into a loud continuous roar. Melissa reached over and gripped Tom's hand. They both lifted their heads off the asphalt in time to see the lights on the poles above the lot and all around them flicker and then extinguish. Tom raised himself on one arm and watched the street on their left slant toward them a little, then crack and open up, showing a sand-filled interior. The pavement closest to them slanted upward toward the crack. He could see debris from the Golden Hoof restaurant across the street fall from the top of the building and bounce several times in syncopation with the trembling ground; pieces began falling off the front of the building, and plate-glass windows shattered and flew out on the parking lot and into the street.

The tops of the small palm trees around the motel shook vigorously; the darkened light poles about them swayed to and fro like they were going to come down, and the cars in the parking lot shook like toys. They heard the motel creak and groan and the sound of shattering glass mingle with the earthquake's roar and the sounds of destruction on all sides. Because the roar of the earthquake was so loud and filtered all but the loudest of sounds, it seemed almost like watching a silent movie of the outskirts of destruction that was only occasionally punctuated by thuds and the slashing of glass from close portals. Just at that instant Tom did hear, above it all, the uncertain clanging of the bell of a nearby church.

He could feel the ground under him undulating like a living thing—vibrating like the skin stretched across a huge drum. But in less than two minutes it was over, and the deep subterranean rumble gradually faded. Tom and Melissa climbed to their feet and looked around them in the eerie darkness. Tom looked up at the few dull stars in the darkening heavens. The sky seemed to have dust in it, and he smelled a sulfurous odor.

Glidewell stumbled out of the motel's front door a minute later with a mournful look on his face, like a doctor off to deliver another baby at 2 A.M. on a stormy night. He came around the corner toward the parking lot and brightened when he saw Melissa and Tom slowly walking away. Glidewell hurried awkwardly toward them on a diagonal to the corner of the building, occasionally changing his gait to longer strides in order to clear the rubble. "I say—that was a real rocker!" said Glidewell cheerily when he caught up. "I couldn't hardly get out of the motel. The side doors were jammed—the front one didn't want to open. We had to put our shoulders into it."

"I wonder how bad the coast got hit," said Melissa.

"I dunno," said Glidewell. "The power's all out inside the motel—nasty situation." Glidewell glanced across the street at what had been the restaurant. "Did you two eat yet?" Glidewell asked.

"Not a bite," said Melissa. "We were just going out to dinner. The quake knocked us down."

"The power's out; looks like we're stuck," said Tom.

"Never fear—Glidewell's here!" crowed Glidewell. "I've got some emergency provisions in the van. Why don't you two join me for a good old-fashioned dinner by fluorescent tube? We can check out the quake reports on my portable Sony—it's got short wave as well as the conventional bands."

"Sounds good, Leo," said Tom. "We were just goin' to crank up the car radio ourselves." Glidewell took the lead and they followed him to the van, which was parked under a light pole at the end of the parking lot that faced the road. In the background they heard the first sirens of the evening.

Inside the van they ate dried apricots, beef jerky, and imported British hard crackers from a metal tin. They split a bottle of Arkansas spring water, drinking from white plastic cups that had DIXIE CUP embossed on the sides under the rolled rims. Glidewell turned on the portable radio, worked another switch to hook in the matched outside antenna, and the three of them sat there on the floor in the back of the van, listening to the emergency broadcasts the radio brought in from Los Angeles.

"Scientists at Cal Tech say the quake was centered twenty miles northwest of Los Angeles in the Pacific. The University of Arizona seismograph recorded the quake as an eight-point-one on the Richter Scale, while the University of Colorado reports an eight reading," the radio announcer said. "From all the information we are able to gather, this appears to be a devastating catastrophe. Highways are blocked by rock slides up and down the California coast and on up into Oregon. Numerous overpasses and buildings have collapsed in Los Angeles. Tens of thousands of people are thought to be dead. The streets in downtown Los Angeles are littered with broken glass and debris from buildings. Officials have issued an emergency travel advisory; all persons in the affected areas are instructed not to attempt to travel unless it is an absolute necessity. We will keep you informed as to when the travel advisory is lifted. The National Guard has been called out to guard business and private property. Fires are still burning as a result of ruptured natural gas piplines, and electrical power and water are unavailable in most areas in the city. Communication to many areas is cut off. The California state government is in emergency session. We are on the air using the emergency broadcast system, and we will stay on the air until this terrible crisis is over."

The three of them were silent as they sat around the radio, listening. Their eyes stared out blankly into the interior of the van. Tom focused his eyes for a moment on the portable fluorescent light that glowed amber-white in front of them. Images flashed in his mind of things a man was talking about hundreds of miles away. At first it was hard to believe that it was a real story he was listening to. The announcer was talking about people and things that no longer existed, and he listened, nibbling at the food slowly, staring into space.

"The casualties in Los Angeles alone are estimated to be in the hundreds of thousands," said the announcer on the radio. "A black cloud hangs over the city, apparently from the many fires that are still burning. Transportation and communications in and around the city have been disrupted, hampering fire fighting and rescue efforts. We have reports that parts of the coastline have been inundated by giant waves, causing loss of life and property in Malibu and various marinas along the coast. Ships and boats all along the coast have broken loose from their moorings and have been lost. Ladies and gentlemen, this is an incredibly devastating disaster! Reports just handed to me indicate that the railway along Highway One is twisted and buckled in numerous places. Highway One is closed and has dropped into the ocean at several locations. San Francisco has fires burning throughout the city and has sustained substantial damage. I repeat—San Francisco has also sustained substantial damage." The side door of the van was open, and the strange quiet outside was punctuated suddenly by a another siren rushing by on the street that ran beside the motel parking lot. They could hear the vehicle slow and crash past the severed part of the street with a tremendous noise as it went by.

"Looks like it's another big one a lot of people said was overdue," said Glidewell.

"It's hard to believe," said Tom. "It's like the whole coast is torn up."

"Those poor people," said Melissa sadly. And then, as an afterthought: "They haven't mentioned how bad Santa Barbara got it."

"They're bound to mention it before long," said Tom.

"A bulletin has just been handed to me," said the radio announcer. "We have been asked to announce that martial law has been imposed on the city of Los Angeles. Travel is restricted to designated emergency personnel and a curfew of nine P.M. will be in effect beginning tonight. Emergency shelters are being set up at various locations in the city. We will be giving you those locations in just a moment."

It was as if the earth had trembled in its slumber and part of the west coast of America was gone now. The sea had claimed the part of San Francisco closest to it and Los Angeles was a ravaged ruin. San Francisco had stood unscathed for almost a century, a beautiful city on its seven hills, looking over the Bay like the queen of the western United States. The earthquake had descended upon it like a demon, almost exactly at 9:30 in the evening, careening through its thronged streets, its corporate enclaves, and its abodes of good and evil. The main shock had rolled in like a strange, earthen tidal wave, from north to south across the city, leaving destruction in its wake like a powerful, invisible fiend from the earth's mysterious interior realms.

It was upon the artificial environments of man that the terror from the depths had spent its force. And it was inevitable that the quake of August 28 was the worst quake people living on the California coast had ever experienced. It was the last and worst thing tens of thousands of people experienced in this life before falling artifacts of civilization destroyed them. In the cities and towns along the coast from Mexico to the state of Oregon there were fires and smoke and debris everywhere. And soon there would be the putrefied smell of death in the air.

26

The Hound of Heaven

Twilight had fallen on Lancaster and the shadows crept, long-faced, into the streets as Melissa drove the big Oldsmobile onto the parking lot that faced the front side of a large monolithic building in the north end of the city. The church had a beige anodized metal exterior and a flat roof, and it looked like a huge Kleenex box set on asphalt like many of the buildings she and Tom were used to seeing at Edwards.

The revival service had started a short while earlier, and when Tom got out of the car he could hear the sound of a piano and a multitude of voices singing in slow harmony, coming out of the large double doorway: "Some glad morning, when this life is over, I'll fly away."

Melissa took his hand and led him like a reluctant bear across the parking lot, in through the doorway, and on into the main part of the church. While they made their way the voices sang on: "... to a home on God's celestial shore, I'll fly away. I'll fly away—oh glory—I'll fly away." They hesitated as they surveyed the room, standing just inside.

"When I die, hallelujah, by and by—I'll fly away," sang the chorus.

Melissa gave his hand a squeeze, and they started down the aisle toward the front. In the next instant Tom tugged gently on her hand to get her attention and, when she turned back, he brought his face close to hers. "Why don't we kinda sit around here. I'm farsighted," whispered Tom, pointing halfway between the back two rows.

"Sure," agreed Melissa, giving him a crooked grin. They sat down on the hard, wooden pew in the third row from the back of the spacious, austere church. Tom glanced around at the church's interior. Among the hundreds of singing people there were not many empty seats. And the hundreds of voices blended in with each other and echoed off the low, flat ceiling.

All the walls inside were the color of ripe yellow peach flesh and the ceiling was white, with modern, saucer-shaped lights hanging down at intervals from brass rods. A rough wooden cross stood high in the front of the chapel and, beside that, an illuminated white dove with wings unfurled adorned the wall. To the right of the transparent podium a middle-aged man in a white shirt and tie sat, adjusting controls and switches on a large electronic console. Out of the console a shiny black cable ran to a large spherical microphone that sat atop the podium. The microphone displayed a sign on it that read WJIL.

"What's the name of this church?" asked Tom.

"Church on the Rock," said Melissa in a low voice. "Really a super place." The crowd had started to sing another song in response to a word projected on the front wall, and Melissa began to sing with the other voices and, after a moment, Tom joined in, singing the one word over and over, slow and softly: "Hallelujah . . . Hallelujah . . . Hallelujah . . . Hallelujah."

The singing of the one word took on an elegant beauty in the crowded room, and they sang the same song for what seemed to him a short while, until a few more stragglers had come in and taken up seats, but it had actually been a long time.

The evangelist got up from his seat and began speaking after the singing had faded out and the people had taken their seats. The preacher was a black man, unusually thin, as if he had been raised on a planet that had very little gravity. He had a close-cropped, raven black beard, and his hair was gray-black, like used steel wool. It was hot inside the church, and there were large fans with ringed metal guards that were set up in the front of the room, humming steadily, blowing air over those who had gathered.

"Welcome to our service tonight at Church on the Rock. I feel the Lord's presence and so I say you'll be a different person when you leave here than when you came. We're not going to pass a collection plate or anything like that—God supplies all our needs and we praise Him for that." Some of the people applauded their agreement and across the gathering there were scattered pairs of hands that raised straight up toward the ceiling.

"If you have your Bible with you, turn with me if you would to Matthew twenty-four. Matthew twenty-four." Melissa leafed quickly through the pages of a brown leather Bible she had brought as Tom looked over her left shoulder.

"I wish we could've gotten Leo to come," said Melissa. She had on a high-necked, chalk-blue blouse with a latticelike design above her collar bones, and there was tan skin that showed through the tiny square holes in the design.

"I don't think he's too keen on this stuff," explained Tom. "I think he's kind of scared of revivals."

"He needed to come and hear the Word—faith casteth out fear," said Melissa. Tom nodded as he looked down at the opened Bible they shared between them.

The preacher hesitated a moment as he shuffled his notes, rattling the microphone on top of the podium until it spit a few electronically amplified thumpings out into the room. "Read with me, if you will, starting at verse number three, 'And as He sat upon the mount of Olives, the disciples came unto Him privately, saying, Tell us, when shall these things be? and what shall be the sign of thy coming, and of the end of the world?

" 'And Jesus answered and said unto them, "Take heed that no man deceive you. For many shall come in my name saying, I am Christ; and shall deceive many.

" ' "For nation shall rise against nation, and kingdom against kingdom: and there shall be famines, and pestilences, and *earthquakes*, in divers places. All these are the beginning of sorrows." ' " The preacher closed the book and set it back on the platform on top of the podium. He stepped out from behind the podium and began to pace back and forth before the crowd. While he paced off steps he was silent, and whenever he stopped pacing he spoke.

"Just as sure as you are sitting there the signs of the end times are here. We've just had another terrible earthquake in California. People's homes were destroyed and thousands lost their lives. It was a terrible thing. But Jesus said these things are just the beginning of sorrows. A storm of unbelievable proportions is beginning to sweep across this planet. We've had earthquakes before and tornados and famine and disease. But now, as prophesied in the Bible, *we are getting all of the signs at once. . . ."* The words trailed off abruptly and the evangelist paused, pacing. Tom could see flecks of white in his dark hair, radiant in the light.

"I'd like to share with you very quickly the experience I had about eighteen months ago," continued the evangelist. "Jesus appeared to me and told me there's not much time. He told me to go around and have meetings and to help with the harvest—like what we're doing tonight. Friends, brothers, and sisters—the time is at hand." The evangelist paced then, examining the faces before him. His eyes were keen and friendly and his lips had an expression as if he couldn't wait to say what he had to tell them. He shook his head negatively and continued talking in a tremulous voice that fluctuated like a reed in the chamber of a pipe organ. "We don't have long. I don't know the day or the hour. I can't say he's comin' on a Monday or Tuesday. But I know it's at hand." Tom glanced over at Melissa. Her clear, dark eyes were glistening; her lips stretched in a smile that seemed on the edge of curling into crying as she gazed at the evangelist. She turned and caught Tom's eyes, and he could see the tears rimming her eyes.

The evangelist had on a black suit and under that there was a white, Egyptian cotton shirt that shone like sunlit snow in the harsh artificial light as he faced the crowd directly.

"God always warns the people before destruction is coming," he went on in a shaken voice. He smiled, and his cheeks stood out like polished prunes. Tears were starting to bead their way out of his eyes. "Jesus will come brighter than the sun. The whole night will light up when Jesus comes to get those who believe. People on the ground will be running away, terror struck." The evangelist had emphasized the last word. "My job tonight is to tell you that whoever calls on the name of the Lord will be saved and whoever does not is damned. It's as simple as this—if you don't accept Jesus and you die . . . when you open your eyes, you will be in hell." The pacing stopped and he stared at them intently for a moment. Tears were flowing out of his eyes by now. "My friends, my dear friends—the world and the powers of darkness are trying to keep this from you," he said, trembling. "There are no exits in Hell! The Bible tells you that in the gospel of Saint Luke, Chapter Sixteen.

"I know that society today considers the word *sin* an archaic term—huh? Isn't that right?" He posed the question in a voice that came out high-pitched on the last word. He took a white handkerchief from his pocket, wiped the sweat and tears from his face and, as he stuffed the white cloth back into an inside pocket in his coat he started the pacing once more. "The world teaches a spiritual equivalent to Einstein's theory of relativity. They say morals are all relative, but they failed to tell you that the modern moral philosophy is itself a theory. And I'm here tonight to set the record straight. The theory the world has told you—the one that says there's no such thing as sin—is a lie." The preacher had reached the podium again in his pacing and, as he went by, he picked up the black Bible and held it up above his head. "The book I have here contains the truth, and it says that sin is real and men and women have a terrible destiny unless they accept Christ.

"So—I'm going to ask you right now—'Are you ready?'" The evangelist stood very still for a moment and scanned left and right before he continued pacing. It was very quiet in the church for a moment as the evangelist seemed to reconsider the audience. "There may never be another moment where you are as close to the Kingdom of God. A soul has a season. There's a time to plant and a time to harvest. Your heart may never be the same as it is tonight."

He laid the Bible back on the podium as he passed it on his way to the edge of the crowd. Then he stopped short of the front row and started talking again: "You know, it's kind of a strange world we live in. If someone came up with a potion he sold and you could take it and then live forever, and if the media puffed him a little, hey—I mean to tell you people would stand in line to buy it. Isn't that right—huh? But when I tell people that eternal life in God's Kingdom is a free gift if they accept Jesus, a lot of people say, 'No man—that's religion.' But it's not! Jesus Christ is not the founder of the Christian religion—He is the Son of God who came in the flesh. Accepting Jesus is not going to make you some kind of religious freak! It's going to give you everlasting life!

"Once you accept Christ you pass from death to life. God cannot stand to look on sin, and all of us have sinned. If we do not take on his righteousness, we will not get into heaven."

The evangelist paused for a moment and smiled to himself, reflectively. "You know, about the only television I watch in these evil and corrupt days are some of the reruns of a show from the eighties called *Highway to Heaven*. But I tell you tonight that the only highway to heaven is through Jesus Christ. He is the only door."

The black man spoke the next words softly, with great quietness between each word. The words seemed to seep through an unused doorway into Tom's mind, where they expanded into a very still and silent presence. "Jesus said, I am the way, the truth, and the life; No man comes to the Father except through me." Then he stretched his right arm out and pointed his index finger out. His mouth was open in a grimace and his cheeks stood out like polished prunes. "Listen! Jesus Christ went to hell so you wouldn't have to—even you!" Like a wind, a feeling swept over Tom: *This is real . . . This is something very ancient and simple and true.* Then, right after that, *Jesus forgave men even though they killed him—if he forgave that, he will forgive everything.*

"The apostle Paul said that in the last days perilous times will come," the minister continued. "And someday soon Christ will come like a thief in the night. Do you want to be ready? If you have any doubt where you would wake up if you died, if you want to be ready if Jesus comes before you die, we're gonna ask you to come forward as we sing the hymn. First, I want to say a few special words to those of you listening by radio tonight. You see, I believe there's two arguments the Devil tries with people. One is that they're so good, they don't need to be saved. On the other hand, he tells some of you you're so bad, you can't be saved. To that person who thinks he's good enough, the Bible says we're all sinners. Jesus Christ did not come into this world to make bad men good—he came to make dead men live.

"To that person that thinks he's gotten so far away from God there's no way back—don't believe it! There is no sin you have committed that can keep you from the love of God. Don't let that prevent you from getting the help you need. Jesus paid the price for every bad thing you've ever done—don't let Satan fool you. If you take this free gift from Jesus, you will be saved from eternal condemnation.

"Some of you that hear me now know that you've done wrong and just don't care. Let me tell you, you can drink and get high and curse God, but Satan still hates you—he'll torture you before he kills you. Right now Jesus told me to tell you he's searching for you, looking for you, telling you he loves you. He said the door to eternal life is open. He's giving you an invitation to come in.

"For all you folks listening to me over radio, you don't have to be here—you can accept Jesus anyplace, right where you are. Jesus will meet you wherever you are—in your kitchen, laying on your bed, in your car. Get it out of your mind if you think accepting Jesus won't work—all the devils in hell can't stop it from working. It's goin' to work. God has the power to end the enchantment Satan has against you, so pray this prayer we're about to pray with me, right where you're at."

The preacher again pointed an amazingly long, bent finger at the audience in the church and held it still as a rock. "On the other side, Satan's primary purpose is to get you to worship him! Some of you don't believe in Satan—that he has power over men. Well, I would ask you to look at the Communists. In the Soviet Union alone, more than seventy million people have been murdered. In China, more than sixty million. The Communists think of humans as animals. They are the most barbaric and powerful force to ever inhabit the earth—and the Communists are Satan incarnate.

"But I'm telling you tonight that Jesus is coming again—and those who are alive and who believe in him shall be changed in a moment of time. And we shall rise to meet him in the air. He's the same Jesus that walked upon the water and healed all the sick who came to him, and cast out demons, and rose from the grave.

"He's coming to get us first and take us back in glorified bodies for a little while. Then we'll come back with him to battle the anti-Christ at the final battle. The future doesn't belong to the Communists—it belongs to those who have accepted Jesus Christ.

"Here in the church or wherever you are, you might ask, will Jesus take me as I am? Folks, that's the only way he will take you. Tonight the door is open. Right now, as the choir sings, I want those of you whom God is speaking to to come on up. And I believe no matter where you are he's speaking to you now. Those of you in the church who are not sure where they stand with God, come on up while the choir sings."

There was a small choir in the front of the church, and they began to sing the melodious chords of a song Tom had heard before but couldn't remember where. ". . . I wandered away from God. Now I'm coming home, coming home, never more to roam. Open wide that unsaved life. Lord, I'm coming home."

While Tom listened to the words of the song he knew he wanted whatever it was that Melissa had inside—call it vibration or call it a presence, but it was peaceful and it seemed to flow out of the very air in the room now. He knew that the peace was what he had always wanted. He had tried different things to find it, but he never had. And on this hot night at the last of the eighth month, he was ready to try something that he didn't quite understand, but that wasn't what got him up to the altar in front.

For the first time in a long time in his mind's eye he saw some of the things he had done in his life without his usual coloring of rationalization. Unretouched feelings and pictures flowed through him. They weighed heavy on him; they battled against the peace he felt flowing through the room. The guilt of things past—seducing small-town and big-town Georgie girls, the thefts, the lies, the hurting of other people—were all eating at him now, rising up like a bitter hell inside, expanding within his realm of awareness, and he felt that he would explode if he didn't go up to the altar.

People began getting up out of seats all around the chapel and coming forward, up the three main aisles. Tom went forward and Melissa tagged along, holding on to his hand. After the choir finished the hymn, there were 136 people gathered in front of the three-foot-high altar railing. The preacher spoke in a quiet way to the people who stood before him. "I thank God for everyone that's here. Every time I stand before people on the edge of salvation, I tremble and pray that I say the right words. Let me tell you that Jesus loves you so much. Jesus is telling you to stretch forth your hand. He's telling you he will help you start a new life. He said he would go out looking for that one lost sheep out of His flock. He's out looking for you and he's found you!

"Two thousand years ago Jesus stood before Nicodemus, a ruler in ancient Israel, and said 'You must be born again.' I don't know a better way to put it. You're about to be reborn tonight into the Kingdom of God.

"For those of you here with me, and those listening by radio, wherever you are, I kind of know what you need to say. I'm going to pray, and I want you to repeat it and believe it with all your heart the best you can. He will want you to give up the bad things in your life and he will give you something else instead. It's worth a trillion times more! Jesus called it eternal life. Pray after me now. Don't be afraid. Just bow your heads and pray out loud right where you are."

The preacher bowed his head and squeezed his eyes shut so tightly you could see folds of skin protrude on his dark shiny eyelids. He spoke clear, simple words that seemed to etch the air with their presence. "Dear God in heaven. I'm a sinner. I cannot save myself. I'm sorry for my sins and I'm coming to you." Melissa and Tom and the other people who had gathered in front by the altar spoke the same words the evangelist had spoken, out loud, a half sentence at a time.

And all of them continued, "And, Jesus, I know that you died for my sins and I ask your forgiveness. I believe God raised You from the dead and You're alive right now. At this moment I turn away from evil and sin. Lord Jesus, come into my life. Live your life in me and save my soul. I will live my life for you from this moment forward. Cleanse me and make me a new creature. I believe right now that I am saved. Thank you, Jesus, that you've heard my prayer. Thank you that you've forgiven my sins. Thank you, Lord, that you've made me a child of the most high God. Amen."

After the prayer had ended and the people raised their heads the slightest of smiles crept on Melissa's lips and Tom could feel himself smiling back. He had meant the prayer when he prayed it—he had prayed it sincerely, like he would have if he were a young child again. He sensed this strange ancient peace come into him for a moment, somewhere beyond any place he had ever felt before. In this place within, a still, small voice whispered powerfully, "You won't ever drink alcohol again." And after the whispering had ended, which he had felt more than heard, Tom was fully persuaded that he would never touch booze again. The soundless, ancient voice had emanated from deep within and he knew the voice had been from God. And in that smallest of instants, when important things are perceived within a human, he knew where he would go if he died. It was a deep knowing in the heart of him—in his heart of hearts.

After that the people in the choir handed out small pamphlets to those who had prayed with the evangelist, and then, before they went back to their seats to sing more songs, the evangelist said, "The Bible says that if we confess with our mouths Jesus Christ and believe that God has raised him from the dead, we shall be saved. So, for those who prayed that prayer with me, I want you to tell people that Christ has come into your life, because he has. And no matter if you feel different or not, if you invited Jesus in, he is living inside you now. And, I want you to get a Bible and read it every day."

Melissa beamed at Tom and they hugged. "I've been praying for you," she finally told him, and the tears erupted from their eyes and shot down their faces. It was like he had passed into another world, across the subtlest of divides. Deep inside him now there was that unearthly peace, and he felt an inexplicable joy when he realized what he had just done.

When he got back to his room that night Tom undressed for bed and retrieved the Bible from the nightstand. When he had crawled under the covers he read across the black and red printing on the Bible page he had opened to and, for the first time in his life, he understood what the words really meant.

27

Appointment in the Desert

It was 7:40 P.M. by the time Leo Glidewell strolled into Vilchek's Printing Shop in the heart of Lancaster. The business was located in a long narrow wood frame building, and Glidewell had followed the numbers on the row of colorless, nondescript storefronts until he found Number 2466, almost at the end of the block. The service had been slow at the Old English Surf and Turf restaurant and so he arrived 20 minutes later than the time he had told Vilchek he would be there.

As Glidewell entered the neatly decorated store, a bell rang; a wheat-field-colored oak door at the rear of the store rolled open a moment later, and Vilchek's rotund form came sauntering out of the opening in the beige-colored wall.

"Ahh, Mr. Glidewell—how nice to see you," said Vilchek effusively.

"Sorry I'm a bit late," said Glidewell politely.

"You've had supper, I trust?" asked Vilchek.

"Yes, yes—the service was bloody awful. It took me forever to acquire some cooked lobster," lamented Glidewell.

"Where did you dine?"

"Oh, actually, it was that surf and turf place," said Glidewell sourly. A chemical smell seemed to permeate the office now, and Glidewell's hawk nose seemed to twitch ever so slightly.

"That's usually pretty good," commented Vilchek. "But the aftermath of the earthquake has everyone a little out of kilter. Well, shall we get started? Tonight may truly be a rare adventure—your telephone call was fortuitous in that regard."

"You believe the landing will definitely take place?" questioned Glidewell.

"Oh, most definitely," said Vilchek without hesitation. "There have been two of these predicted landings in my experience with the group at Desert Rock. I attended both of them and I must say it was well worth the effort." Vilchek smiled, keeping his mouth closed, and his huge cheeks rode up his face and popped out at Glidewell. "The rendezvous point is approximately an hour away. We better get started."

"I'll drive," volunteered Glidewell.

Vilchek accepted, flicked off a bank of light switches beside the front door, locked the door on the way out, and, halfway down the block they climbed into Glidewell's van, pulling away into the heavy traffic on the street. Glidewell drove east and then northeast toward the waning part of the day. As the van rolled along the lightly traveled highway, the white sun went down behind the jagged mountains, and the wispy high clouds took on a pink glow. And as they drove the light gradually seeped out of the landscape.

By the time the van made the turn off the main highway onto a narrow, well-worn asphalt road, the light in the sky had faded and the last of the pink fringes had melted into a cloud-covered, dusky grayness. After several miles of that, Vilchek pointed to a turnoff, and Glidewell whipped the van into a tight right turn that led down a driveway and past a comfortable-looking, two-story farmhouse. Beyond the farmhouse, at the end of the driveway, was an asphalt parking lot sitting in the dim light like a medium-sized black pond, and there were almost three dozen vehicles parked in rough rows. Glidewell pulled in between a white Ford Bronco and the edge of the asphalt; where he had parked the surface had cracked, and its edges were bent off into the desert.

They got out of the van, and Glidewell retrived what looked to be a brand-new electric lantern from behind the front seat, locked the van, and turned a key in the alarm lock on the left front fender.

Then the two men hiked out toward a distant spot in the desert, where a golden glow of small lights already flickered in the gathering blue-black darkness. A smattering of stars were out by now; the landscape was dimly lit all around, and the faintly illuminated hills in front of them seemed to project upward from a dark sea of sand.

When they reached the gathering of lanterns Vilchek was wheezing and breathing in long profuse spasms. It took a moment for the fat man to get his breathing under control and he waited until then to introduce Glidewell to several of the people that he knew. The gathering was clustered in small groups of two and three, and the people in each group were chatting excitedly among themselves. After introducing Glidewell to the first group of people they came to, Vilchek nodded at Glidewell and said, "He's sympathetic to our cause—possibly a new recruit." The fat man wrinkled up one side of his face when he said that, and his right eye squinted in half a wink at Glidewell from atop his cherubic, ballooning cheek.

There was a second group of people Vilchek led Glidewell toward which consisted of two men and three women. All of them wore dark windbreaker jackets, and the women in the group wore slacks. All the women had extremely short hair, and it was difficult to distinguish them from the men in the semi-darkness. Vilchek knew each of the people in the group, and in the low light from a Coleman lantern, Vilchek pointed to each of the people in turn. "Mr. Robandzo, Mr. Asnezy, Ms. Atkins, Ms. Harkness, Ms. Quanta, let me introduce Mr. Glidewell. He's an electronics engineer working out of Edwards air base."

The people in the group put on smiles, nodded, and said hello. The oldest of the women had hair that appeared silvery gray in the unsure light, and she spoke first. "I have a thermos of cold herb tea with me here. If you two get thirsty, just give me the high sign."

"Fine," said Vilchek. "That's fine." Vilchek and Glidewell turned and looked in the direction of the farmhouse and the closer parking lot with its collection of vehicles. Several parcels of land had dark vegetation that moved slightly in the wind that came off the desert. Vilchek began walking toward the distant range of mountains. When they were out of earshot he spoke to Glidewell in a low, deep voice. "The younger Quanta woman back there is a top network television newsperson—did you know?"

"No, afraid not," answered Glidewell. He unzipped the lower right-hand pocket in his safari jacket and, fumbling for a moment, retrieved his pipe and tobacco. After he brought out the golden-yellow Meerschaum he thrust the bowl into the tobacco pouch and tamped it down . . . a couple of times he pinched more tobacco from the pouch and tamped that until he was satisfied, checked the draw, then returned the pouch of tobacco to its pocket, and lit the pipe. "You've been fairly quiet about what's supposed to occur out here, Albert," said Glidewell after a few puffs on the pipe. "What are the space brothers going to do besides land?"

"During the last communication session at Desert Rock the

high command of the intergalactic federation set up this physical contact. This farm has been used previously for similar encounters. This is an event that most of mankind is unfortunately not ready to witness. The space brothers only desire the presence of earthlings with expanded consciousness and other special qualities," said Vilchek. "I invited you because I perceive that you have an advanced psychic awareness."

"Good show, old chap—but I'm not so sure about my mystical capabilities."

"I believe you have a very advanced aura, Mr. Glidewell."

"Is that right?" said Glidewell, then he took a long draw from the pipe.

"Yes—I have the sporadic ability to see auras around people," said Vilchek. "The patterns and colors vary according to a person's physical and psychic qualities. Your aura is very advanced psychically."

"I'll be damned," said Glidewell without much interest, puffing on the pipe, brightening the bowl's orange glow against the gathering darkness. "So, the craft that's supposed to set down out here tonight is from this intergalactic federation?"

"I believe that's a correct assumption," replied Vilchek as he peered down at the faintly luminous digits on his black plastic wristwatch. "And they should be making an entrance very soon now, I would imagine."

"You want to know something crazy?" lamented Glidewell suddenly. "I completely forgot to bring the video equipment out of the van. I best scurry back there and retrieve it!"

Vilchek shot his meaty arm out and placed it on Glidewell's left forearm. "No!" said Vilchek in a deep voice. "The sons of light wouldn't permit it at this time. They expressly forbid photography in a case such as this!"

"Surely you jest! What we're talking about here is damn important evidence. I'll just stand back here in the dark and shoot a few choice shots," said Glidewell. "Surely they wouldn't mind something at a distance."

"They know what's in your mind, Mr. Glidewell," said Vilchek. "If you had your equipment ready to take pictures they would not land, I'm afraid. It's happened before that way."

"You're serious?" questioned Glidewell. "They can read thoughts at a distance?"

"Absolutely," said Vilchek. "We have been told to have

patience in these things. You see, Mr. Glidewell, the end of the Age is very close. They have told us that the Earth will shift and the north and south poles will lie on the new equator, and the places that are tropical will become frozen. And the closer mankind approaches to the great catastrophes, the nearer the UFOs will come to the human race, for they are our only salvation. The major earthquake that just struck is only a small, bitter taste of things to come."

The wind picked up and blew steadily for a while across their faces, and there were fine particles of sand in the wind. They could feel the sand fly against their faces. "So, after they land, what'd you say was on the program again?" asked Glidewell.

"I'm convinced the space brothers will choose a willing member of this gathering and that person may be allowed to go inside the craft. They might well be taken for a ride," said Vilchek. "At least that's how I interpreted the last intergalactic council communique."

Glidewell gave Vilchek a skeptical look. "Well, that would certainly add a little savor to the evening for the lucky one," observed Glidewell. "Frankly, Al, I'll have to see it to believe it."

"You shouldn't have to wait too long," said Vilchek, pointing his thick tapered arm at the light that glided toward them quickly from the back side of the tallest of the distant mountains. The crowd of people stirred and began murmuring to one another. Glidewell watched the light carefully as it glided silently toward them. Suddenly the light began to describe a zigzag path through the blackened sky, and then it would stop dead and instantly start up. It was obvious that nothing man had ever manufactured could move through the sky like the unknown light was moving. And the people, seeing the light approach, looked up in awe at the wonder that they had been expecting.

28

Prince of the Power of the Air

As the UFO descended from the distant celestial darkness its erratic right-angled swervings and levitations and plummetings changed to that of a controlled, sloping flight path—as if it were an airliner on final approach to an airport runway, smoothly correcting its altitude and heading to adjust for wind drift and speed. And as it grew closer the brilliant, eye-piercing light faded, and a shadowy, elliptically shaped craft became visible behind the glow.

"Glory to the intergalactic brothers!" shouted one stocky, pleasant-faced woman. Her dark eyes were bulging out at the sight of the glowing craft, as if it were a magnet pulling them from their sockets. The light from the UFO reflected in her dancing eyes as the UFO floated down and hovered a few hundred yards away from the group of people, maintaining its height about 50 feet above the ground. The UFO wobbled erratically side to side in the air, and the rotating outer rim of the saucer was covered with flashing, multicolored lights that lit up the sky like an electric kaleidoscope. Its surface glowed with an eerie bluish-white light. Gradually the brilliance of the surface glow subsided and the inward-facing lights on the rotating rim projected rounded triangles of red, green, and blue up on the egg-shaped surface, and these moving ghostly forms swirled around the craft in precise, rapid arcs. The only sound that the UFO made consisted of strange, hollow clickings. It sounded almost like millions of cicadas and locusts were concentrated in one aerial spot, and the intensity of the noise rose and fell in a harsh, alien crescendo.

The gathering of people stood their ground like cosmic sight-seers, gazing at the UFO expectantly, waiting, it seemed, for the intelligence that controlled the aerial craft to carry out their appointed task. Several moments passed before the unknown craft began to descend the last several feet to the desert floor. As soon as it had landed, a man emerged from the crowd of onlookers and proceeded toward the UFO. The outer rim had ceased its rotation, and the man was halfway toward it, walking in mesmerized, stiff-necked fascination. Without warning, with silent suddenness, an orange ball of fire shot out of the dark shadows on the far side of the craft. The flaming ball whizzed by the approaching man's head and he turned on his heels and ran in blind panic, stumbling and falling several times before he reached the waiting crowd.

A small interval of hushed conversations ensued, and then Cynthia Quanta began to slowly separate from the crowd and make her way toward the blue-flashing UFO.

"She is the chosen one," Vilchek said in a low voice to Glidewell. "The TV newsperson. How astounding! They've chosen her."

"I'll be damned," said Glidewell slowly. "How does she know to walk out there like that?"

"The space brothers have advanced telepathic technology, I can assure you," said Vilchek. "Evidently, she's receiving some telepathic signal—they're tuned in to her brain waves, telling her to approach the ship."

"Amazing!" said Glidewell.

The thin-lipped, painted woman had reached the edge of the ship's hull by now, and she hesitated for a moment while she looked up at the massive structure that towered above her in the night. She took a few short steps and walked underneath the craft, which sat on a tripod of long, shiny legs. The bottom of the UFO was still several feet above her head, and when she reached the central point beneath it a sharp-edged greenish beam of light flashed out of the bottom. It was so bright there was dust kicked up by the landing people could see floating in it. The woman seemed to go limp as the beam bathed her in green light, and her body began to levitate off the ground.

As the astounded gathering looked on, the woman rose until she disappeared through an opening in the bottom of the strange machine. Several seconds later there was a high-pitched whine that began to screech at the night; the outer rim of the craft began to rotate again, lights began to flash, and the blue glow encircled the craft.

At that instant a woman in the crowd began to speak in a loud, mannish voice. Her words had sharp edges to them, and the way they flowed out of her frozen-looking face made them sound slightly like a mechanized chant. "Do not worry about your companion. The leader of the intergalactic high command in charge of this region of the galaxy is aboard the ship you see before you. He has chosen the woman so that he may fill her with power and great light. The advanced being of light who rides this silver ship would be called a great prince in your world's terms. All humankind will know about him soon for he will lead the rescue of humans out of chaos when the appointed hour has arrived."

The next sentence was the last controlled utterance from the woman, and the words were broken and faded as the communication ended. "The powerful being on board this ship is one whom the intergalactic council has chosen to save a remnant of the human race. And your civilization will say to him, 'He has come to deliver us.'"

Immediately after the strange voice ceased its surrogate speaking, the UFO gained altitude, the blue glow intensified, and then the strange phenomenon disappeared from sight in a 45-degree climb. It had been an incredibly fast departure for a machine that supposedly inhabited the same physical creation as man.

Inside the ship the woman lay limply on a gray circular platform. She was a thin, gaunt, athletic-looking woman, but she nevertheless had great difficulty getting to her feet. She felt cold and afraid—terribly afraid. When she had managed to stand three strange humanoids approached her from an entrance in a curved gray wall.

The beings were all about four feet tall with extremely long arms and strange bony faces. They had wraparound eyes, thin pointed noses—each wore a red slash where a mouth should be and, beneath that, an ugly cone-shaped chin. There were hoods that extended from the top of the one-piece black uniforms they wore, and the hoods covered the sides and top of their heads. Each of the creatures had insignias on the shoulders of the uniform that resembled starfish with disclike centers and long, curving arms; two had five arms, one had four, another had only three.

One of the beings placed his feeble-looking, long bony-fingered hand on the woman, and her body jerked involuntarily.

Inside her head she heard the creature say to her, "Hear the unspoken. We want only that you come with us." The woman tried to back away from them when they said that, but as the second of the unearthly creatures grabbed her, another being, wearing a six-armed starfish emblem, appeared from her extreme left, almost behind her. When this new creature came into her field of view, she instantly recognized it. She wanted to sleep and then felt as if she would faint, but instead she closed her eyes and her mind flashed back to a time, many years ago, when this hideous creature had been with her.

I can't see the stars—where are the stars! she thought, beginning to panic. *She stepped back and saw the edge of the strange craft and it was hovering silently right above her head and she wanted to reach up and smash it. But it's so huge and it's horrible, how it can be that big? What are those little pipes on the rim . . . There's hot gas coming out. What was that? Something moved up there. . . . Sonavabitch! The orange fireball popped out of the shadowy craft as if a flame-eater had belched. Oh-oh it's comin' right at me! No . . . no. It can't . . . be. She saw the mist float down at her like it was a dream. Why can't I move—get away? Why can't I? She covered her face and tried to move her head, but it wouldn't move. Then a black tunnel formed in her mind, darker than the summer night across the years, and the sides shrunk suddenly and all went black.*

When she woke up two hideous creatures were dragging her young frail body across a smooth floor (like warm ice, she remembered) to a part of the floor that had been marked off in a perfect circle. When the two had positioned themselves inside the circle with the woman's body lying askew beneath them, the piece of floor began lifting like the elevator on an aircraft carrier. She had tried to scream, but only a rush of heated air came out of her mouth.

On the next level of the craft the first thing that had met her eyes was a jet of yellow gas that hissed in murky layers out of the wall nearest her. The gas had an artificially sweet odor to it, but, underneath, there was a stronger odor, like the smell of ammonia. Her face drew away from the smell and contorted as if it sickened her. She swallowed hard the way some people do before they're about to regurgitate. The cabin around her was circular, with several cone-shaped seats and strangely shaped storage cabinets and tables. The ceiling had a slight concave dome to it, and all around the room the lighting had an even, pure white cast and no shadow could be seen. The woman had been lying on one of the tables, restrained by wide gray straps made out of a lightweight, metallic material.

Before much time had passed an extremely tall creature appeared from an open doorway to the woman's left. He wore the same seamless one-piece garment as the other creatures, except the color appeared dark brown, and as he walked up to the table on which she lay she could see that the material resembled some kind of plastic—smooth and without fibers. The eyes on the creature were gigantic, with small black pupils and large irises, which were transparent, with only a trace of orange in them. The being was close to nine feet tall with a large orange symbol on the front of his uniform. It looked like a shepherd's staff, with a crook at one end, and with a horizontal bar attached halfway down (like a backward small-letter f). There were several unknown symbols or letters of script beneath the main symbol and, as he bent to stare at her, she first saw the starfishlike symbols with six curved arms, one on each shoulder, like military epaulets. As the beast stood over her, glaring and leering at her, she had lost consciousness once more.

When the woman awoke again she was naked—the tall creature was lurking grim-faced beside the table she lay on, and it was completely nude! The being's eyes had a strange look in them, the pupils large and dark like a beast, shifting liquidly in the bright white light. The creature had broad shoulders, skinny arms, and an absurdly small, skinny chest. The skin on it's body was a bluish-white color with the texture of an artist's canvas.

The smaller creatures scurried out of the cabin then, making no sound whatsoever; and as she had laid uncomfortably on the flat, hard table, as the entity stood over her, looking askance at her, she remembered how the sickening presence of the creature's eyes had made her feel death was somehow near. Her own eyes began to feel stiff and hard, as if a shell was growing over them—glazed and cold, as if she had been drugged.

She gasped a little as the creature drew next to her and outstretched its hand, placing the tips of the left hand on her forehead. The creature reached beside the table and retrieved a transparent tube from an aperture in the wall. The bestial entity extended the tube, put it close to the woman, and a warm, heavy liquid came out, flowing onto her naked body. She had watched the creature's hands passively as he moved the tube backward and forward over the length of her body. The creature's hands were ugly, and looked almost like the plastic monster hands that were still sold in novelty stores. As the fluid from the tube covered her body, her breathing slowed and she felt paralyzed, unable to move. Her eyes stared fixedly at the creature as it returned the tube to the wall. Her body became numb then, and she had trouble feeling it. With great effort she had been able to move her eyes downward, and she saw her own nude body limp and unmoving like a drugged laboratory animal as the creature pushed a glass button on the wall and lowered the table.

Then the ugly, alien creature awkwardly climbed on top of her and began moving, doing something to the bottom part of her—she felt a dull sensation. Her eyes squinted to oval slits and she screamed a penetrating, hideous shrieking wail

*that turned into a crying catch in her breath as the creature began to rape her
with vicious movements that pounded on her body and hurt terribly deep even
through the numbness. The creature's red slit of a mouth curled a little in a
preposterous, hideous smile. Its eyes were like an animal's eyes. She screamed
again, but the creature ignored her, and there was no one else to hear. And like a
hideous nightmare she could feel her body rock and writhe from side to side from
the creature's hard, unhuman thrusts.*

*In a little while a trance had taken her over and she made no more sounds.
Her face became impassive and lifeless as she lay there, her body quivering
involuntarily, as the creature moved within her. With its throat the monster
made a hideous, hoarse roaring sound in rhythm with its thrusts, and as it
opened its mouth each time it drew near she could smell a sour manurelike smell
and feel its hot breath. When the creature was finished with her it climbed
quickly off the table and hurried down through an aperture in the floor of the
chamber. She tried to move again, but her body was lifeless and she couldn't feel
anything or move. . . .*

In the cabin with her now the same hideous creature stood
dressed in maroon one-piece clothing, and beside him was an
extremely tall human man who looked to be in his thirties—and
the woman came forward toward them, almost automatically it
seemed, and embraced the young man. It had been a year since
they had taken her son away, and she couldn't help being glad to
see him. As for the alien leader, she had absolutely no feeling
about him whatsoever—only a quivering remembrance. *We will be
landing in a short time,* the leader said to her mind. *Our son is ready for
the task he was predestined for. He will go with you when we land—you are to do
his bidding. The time is at hand. The world will soon see the power we have given
him.*

The young man smiled a little cynical smile. His face had an
odd, fierce look for his age, as if he were an old man whose life
had been bitter and hard. His eyes had a faraway look as he
looked at his mother, who backed away from him now in a slow
awkward way. She looked at him as if she were trying to make sure
it was her son. The ship they were in was descending already,
hundreds of miles distant from the spot where the woman had just
been—toward the exact spot outside Sausalito where she had
been overshadowed many years before.

29

The Conversation

t was the last day of the eighth month, and the hot desert night hovered outside the glass sliding door of Room 119. Tom Kruger had changed rooms to get away from the multitude of crashing and thumping noises that had become almost constant through the ceiling in Room 210. Now, in the pleasant quiet of the new room, he could feel the heat radiate off the glass as he read the blue, paperbound version of the Bible at the round table beside the sliding door. Above him there was a frosted globe of light hanging beneath a brown mushroom-shaped cover.

Living in a pair of motel rooms since May had begun to take its toll on him. But the cramped lifestyle that he had increasingly tired of would be over in less than a week. He had put money down on a two-year-old trailer that Melissa was putting her touches on at the edge of town. Among the planners, managers, officers, administrators, and other big-picture men at Johnson Aircraft, it seemed no one knew about how long he or Melissa were needed at Edwards—but the job at hand looked like it might need another 10 or 12 months.

Finalization of the F-170 redesign was still several months away, and then a revamped flight test program would commence. Assembly of the custom-made skeleton and sinew of two redesigned prototype aircraft had begun at the Johnson Aircraft Palmdale plant eight days before, and people there were working 24 hours a day to speed up completion of the twin test planes.

Tom knew the military wanted the aircraft in a hurry. After the Soviets had taken over Iran through a proxy Communist government the world was not as safe as it once had been. Some thought it only a matter of time before the Soviets launched a push toward

the African continent, through Israel. And with the cuts the
American defense budget had suffered the past decade, it wa
doubtful if anyone in the world could stop the Russians with
conventional forces once they started their next Middle East
armed expansion.

The United States Congress had vowed not to allow U.S
military forces to be sent to the Middle East unless the United
States were directly threatened. Otherwise approval of any direct
involvement would have to go through the various committees
And the public's sentiments would be gauged to assess the
stances needed to help reelection campaigns. But in the event
America ever faced the Soviet military machine a well-designed
F-170 might do some good.

Tom realized just then that he had been attempting to read the
same sentence on the black-letter-dotted page over and over
without the words registering on his mind. So he put a marker
between the pages, closed the book, got up, and walked over to
the small refrigerator in the kitchenette. Thoughts were still
coursing through his mind. The defense industry had been hurt by
too many years of low pay levels for aerospace engineers and
print and electronic media that somehow managed to say what the
Kremlin would have wanted them to. An influx of foreign
engineers of all nationalities had increased the supply of engineers
in the business and decreased the demand for engineers. Some
engineers, like Glidewell, followed the uncertain government
military contracts across the country as if they were migrant fruit
pickers following the ripening fruit of rich and large corporate
growers. But Congress seemed always in a mood to cut down the
trees.

Tom bent down as he slid the Health Valley Grape Juice bottle
across the wire rack and straightened as he lifted it past the
refrigerator door. He grabbed a tall glass from inside the kitchen
cabinet above him and filled it with slivers and small cubes of ice
from the freezer tray. Then he emptied the purple juice over the
slick, frosty cubes, recapped the restowed the bottle, and took
long pull of the sweet liquid.

A rapping sound on the door interrupted the flow of grape
juice over his tongue. He lowered the glass and hesitated. At the
motel it was the habit of well-dressed men to make their rounds at
regular intervals down the halls to knock on doors. Like Fuller
brush men a half century before the men carried big commercial

cases. Instead of an assortment of fine household brushes, inside were drugs that the men offered for sale to anyone who could pay U.S. cash. The national epidemic of drugs had overtaxed the government's power to stop them, and it was widely known that a call to the police to report drug selling was generally met with the same response as reporting a UFO landing in a parking lot. So Tom was in the habit of ignoring certain occasional knocks on the door since he first found out what a knock followed by a $2000 suit in the peephole meant.

But the present knocking quickly turned into a heavy, impatient pounding, and that made Tom set the glass down hard and hustle to the door. When he looked through the peek hole he saw a big nose with Glidewell's face behind it, so he unlatched and opened up. Glidewell seemed almost surprised the door had come open. He hesitated on the threshold, beyond the door jam, eyes wide and filled with a great quantity of reddened veins. And then he spoke. "I've made contact with them, Tom."

Glidewell looked disheveled and sweaty—his eyes looked grotesque in their redness. "Come on in, Leo," said Tom as he swung the door all the way open. "Rest your weary bones."

Glidewell stepped in quickly. "I tell you, Tom, I've made contact!" Glidewell told Tom again.

"With who, Leo?" asked Tom. Glidewell strode forward, his eyes inwardly fixed, seemingly unaware of anything in the room, his legs moving almost as if they were separate robotic limbs.

"With our brothers from space—the men of light." Glidewell ended up turning on his heels at the round table by the curtained window, and then stood facing Tom, who was in the kitchenette getting the grape juice back out of the refrigerator.

"Are you serious?" asked Tom incredulously. Almost unconsciously, he topped off his glass with grape juice.

"Certainly, old chap," said Glidewell. "I mean, hell-yeah. I applied the methodology they taught me at Desert Rock, and it just happened. They contacted me and there was a series of precursors that happened to me and a certain chain of events occurred as they always do when the intergalactic brothers condition a channel. That exact sequence proved to me the reality of the whole thing. Tom, the most important thing in history is really happening. They are here!" The skin on Glidewell's face was drawn and white, as if his skull rested only slightly below the surface and his bloodshot eyes protruded like exotic red-veined fruit as he talked.

"What are you saying, Leo?" asked Tom.

"I'm saying I'm in touch with the superior minds in this entire galaxy," said Glidewell soberly. His voice had a higher pitch than Tom had remembered. "It's indeed feasible to communicate directly with the intelligence behind the UFOs and the value of the hidden knowledge they hold exceeds all bounds of comprehension."

"And this all came through telepathy?" queried Tom.

"Hell-yeah," said Glidewell. "Similar to the methodology used by the people at Desert Rock, but it's an internal technique. It's best to go about it the first time in a comfortable chair—you must keep the spine vertical," said Glidewell.

"Why don't you pull up a *chair*," suggested Tom. "We can both give our spines some verticality. Would you like anything to drink?"

"How about some scotch?" asked Glidewell.

"Sorry, I'm fresh out," said Tom.

"How about some bourbon then?" asked Glidewell. "Some of that high-class juice you drink."

"Fresh out," said Tom. "How 'bout some grape juice on the rocks?"

"Hell-yeah," said Glidewell.

Glidewell sat on the brown cushion of the white-plastic contoured chair. Tom dropped some cubes in another glass and poured until the purple reached the top. Then he brought the two glasses over to the table, setting them down while Glidewell continued. "Actually, the process involves clearing the mind of all extraneous detail. The way I implemented it was to visualize a night sky with my eyes closed, of course. Then I concentrated on one of the stars and then I wiped out that last star mentally—I just let it fade away. It's kind of hard to explain."

"And then these space people talked to you?" questioned Tom.

Glidewell's eyes seemed to enlarge at the thought of what Tom had said. "Yes," he said. "Then, certain things happened and then they talked to me."

"What were the certain things that happened?" said Tom.

"I can't tell you," said Glidewell. "Because what I say could influence you if you attempt the communication. If they channel through you, the same sequence of events will happen, and you

have no way of knowing what these signs are supposed to be. So
when you ask another channel, he will tell you the certain
sequence. And, if the sequences are the same, you'll know that
this thing is real like I do!"

"And so you found out the sequence after it happened to
you?"

"I called Vilchek tonight after the brothers came through—and
the same sequence happened to me as to all the others," said
Glidewell. "This thing is real!"

"Leo, I know you think you know who you're communicating
with," said Tom. "But if you could get the idea of spaceships out
of your head for a . . ."

"What are they then?" interrupted Glidewell as if he knew
what Tom was going to say.

"The evidence points at a fourth dimensional source—a place
where races of spiritual beings live—some angels of the Lord and
some angels of the Devil—and they have access to our physical
dimension."

"Oh, come on!" said Glidewell. "Next thing you'll be saying
the end of the world's coming."

"The end of this Age," said Tom.

"Look, Tom," said Glidewell. "These beings are thousands of
years ahead of us! Their entire philosophy is one of light, life, and
love. That's what makes them tick. I could almost feel their over-
whelming compassion, but it's a totally advanced, rational
compassion."

Tom took a sip of grape juice and tightened his lips, holding
the swallow a moment in his mouth before he let it go. "That
woman at Desert Rock," he began. "These beings spoke, using
her vocal chords. Is that the way it was with you, Leo?"

"No, definitely not," replied Glidewell. "They spoke inside my
mind, clear as a bell, more pronounced than my own internal
dialogue—superfast, more material than I could comprehend all at
once." Beads of sweat were making their way down Glidewell's
face, and he wiped at them and paused to take a drink of juice.
"Tom, I wish you could see what I'm saying. This is the most
important thing that's ever happened to mankind."

"Jesus Christ dying on a cross for the sins of the world and
rising from the grave are light-years ahead of anything that's been
on the program so far," said Tom. "At least until the day of his
return."

Glidewell smiled a small, enigmatic smile and seemed to look right past Tom as he continued. "They've given me power, Tom. Incredible power. I've got to make you see how limited your programming is."

"What are you telling me, Leo?" asked Tom. "You're talking in circles."

Glidewell took another drink of juice and smiled with a peculiar look in his bleary eyes. "I have powers," he explained. "After they made contact I went over to the bowling alley to imbibe a little scotch. Bill Drexel and a bunch of guys from work were out on a couple of alleys, bowling."

"Yeah?"

"And I sat behind Drexel at one of the tables."

"Yeah?"

Tears began to form and well up in Glidewell's reddened eyes and started coming out the corners. He uttered the next words slowly and carefully, "I could control the bowling ball with my mind."

"Huh?" said Tom. "Run that by me once more."

Glidewell bent his head down and dabbed at where the tears were about to come out of his eyes with his thumb and index finger. He made a snorting sound with his nose and said, "It was simple. Hell-yeah. When I wanted Drexel to get a strike it was a strike, every time. When I didn't, he would miss the strike. Then I got to where I knew which pins would be left standing after every throw."

"Just your mind playing tricks, Leo—you know, inverting events like when we dream, we dream backwards," offered Tom.

"It wasn't!" shouted Glidewell, and his voice echoed unpleasantly in the small room. "I did it every time, Tom. It wasn't event inversion at all."

"Come on, Leo," said Tom incredulously. "You're trying to tell me that space creatures are going around using their vast power to control bowling balls."

"This was only a test—preparing me for the real work ahead," said Glidewell. "It's so simple, but evidently you can't see or you won't see. They're here to help us. And we sure as hell could bloody well use it."

"They're going to help raise all our bowling scores or what?" quipped Tom. His voice had a hard, sarcastic edge.

"Don't give me a hard time," said Glidewell.

"All I've got to go on is what you're telling me, Leo," said Tom. "And what you're tellin' me just doesn't make sense!" A siren shrieked outside the window, moving by with a high-pitched warble that lowered an octave or two as it passed.

"There's infinite power for other things," said Glidewell solemnly. "The UFOs and the space brothers are coming to Earth in order to usher in the New Age."

"Listen, Leo—whoever or whatever is behind the UFOs is not extraterrestrial—they don't act like extraterrestrials!"

Glidewell laughed convulsively at that, his face reddening like someone with severe high blood pressure. "How the hell do you know how ETs act?"

"Leo, I thought you were the one who said we needed to always adhere to the scientific method," reasoned Tom.

"Hell-yeah."

"You're ignoring data just like the guys you used to make fun of—you're saying worlds outside our ballpark don't exist," said Tom.

"What am I ignoring?" asked Glidewell.

"All the cases where UFOs and their pilots abducted and abused humans and animals—and then there's the mutilations," said Tom, then paused, examining Glidewell's eyes to gauge the response. They still had the same wild look they had when he entered the room. "We both know what's responsible."

"Everything I've seen has been circumstantial evidence only," said Glidewell. "Even out at Victorville, we only have the farmer's biased report that UFO beings were responsible."

"Leo, we photographed a UFO out there—why was it there?"

"Blasted if I care!" said Glidewell. "You see, being present at the scene of a crime one day later doesn't mean a damn thing. We saw unmarked helicopters there too. Could be Uncle Sam is the one mutilating cattle. That UFO might have just been watching the idiots!"

"And I'm the Queen of Sheba," said Tom.

"Look, Tom, I was illuminated today by an intelligence far in advance of anything man can dream of. The space brothers love us, even though we bloody well don't deserve it. Their existence is no longer in question because I talked to them!"

"I believe you talked to something, Leo," said Tom. "But whatever it was, it's lying. You talk about facts. Well, your space brothers are trying to cover up the facts, and they've come up with a lulu of a story. Since Satan is the master of deception, I believe he's the only one who would even attempt a lie this big."

"You mean the guy in the red suit, with horns and a long pointed tail who carries a pitchfork and comes out on Halloween? asked Glidewell with a sarcastic tinge to his voice.

"Three nights ago I accepted Jesus Christ into my heart, Leo," said Tom. "And I feel myself changing on the inside. Jesus is real, Leo. He took my craving for alcohol away. I used to have to down those five or six drinks every day when I got home from work—and then there were the nights I got really wiped out, didn't know what I was doing half the time. But when I accepted the Lord a voice deep down inside said that I would never drink alcohol again. It was an ancient, powerful voice and I knew it was God talking to me. The craving for alcohol left me, Leo—completely. I threw all the booze away. No withdrawal—no second thoughts. Jesus delivered me from booze; he's alive and if we're born again he can help us. And if you're going to ignore the fact that the Devil is active on this planet . . . well, Jesus talked with the Devil in the wilderness of Israel and he is a real creature." Tom grabbed the paperbound Bible that lay before him and turned it up on end so Glidewell could see the cover. "The truth is in this book, Leo, and it says in here that Satan comes to murder, steal, and destroy. I tell you—I believe that's why the UFOs are really here, and I think the evidence points to UFOs being a direct manifestation of Satan and his fallen angels."

"That's absurd!" said Glidewell.

Tom tilted the glass of grape juice and took a long pull. He dabbed at his purple lips with his left forefinger before he continued. "Let me ask you this, Leo? What about the second coming of Christ—where do the brothers say the New Age fits in with Christ's return to Earth?"

There was a hard, steely look in Glidewell's eyes by now and it resembled that of an animal blocked off from its prey. "Christ is one of the space brothers," said Glidewell. "You should have remembered that from Desert Rock. I look at his earthly tenure as more of a symbol than anything else."

Tom shook his head negatively. "Jesus said if you didn't believe in him, at least believe in the miracles he did," said Tom.

"Can't you see it?" said Glidewell. "The space brothers have superior technology—that's what the Christ figure used to implement the miracles. Any of the space brothers can do what

He did—they're hundreds of thousands of years ahead of us."

"That's a lie of the Devil!" said Tom suddenly, automatically. There was anger in his voice now. "Which of the other UFO beings shed their blood on a cross to save man from eternal damnation, Leo? Maybe you better ask them that!"

Glidewell took a sip of the purple juice before he answered. "You're not being logical," he said, rubbing his chin arrogantly.

"About what?" queried Tom. "Jesus lived a sinless life and humans put him to death and he rose from the dead; it's all historical fact. He healed everyone that came for healing and he knew that demons were real and he cast them out of people and the people recovered. But in the last years of this age demonic beings are somehow able to materalize on Earth and pose as space creatures. That's the secret to the UFOs—I know that deep down inside me."

."Rubbish!" hooted Glidewell. "Even if there were demons, they can't materialize structured craft that radiate complex electromagnetic signals."

Tom drank the last of the grape juice in his glass and, as he was tasting it somewhere inside him, he peered at Glidewell carefully for the briefest of moments. He saw the darkened ridges under Glidewell's eyes and the wild, almost hypnotic look in his eyes—as if he thought the secrets of the cosmos were finally within his grasp. But, the other thing he could see in them now was a ravenous, lustful look, and he imagined Glidewell having visions of inventions and millions of dollars already dancing in his mind. Tom believed now that the eyes are the windows to the soul, and what he saw in Glidewell's gave him a dark feeling of foreboding.

"How do you know what demons can do?" Tom asked Glidewell very simply in a slow, calm voice. "Lucifer is an angelic being of a higher order. The Bible says he is the master of deception. He is the father of lies. How do you know he can't create the appearance of a space ship that emits anything he chooses? How do you know?"

"I had hoped you would at least have kept an open mind about this whole thing," said Glidewell as he got up from the chair. His face seemed gaunt and drawn. "If you're going to be a bloody fool about the greatest thing that has happened to man since our brothers from space first seeded this planet, if you refuse to accept the leap in evolution that is almost upon us, if you're going to be dogmatic about religion—then you will never see the truth."

"I'd like to pray with you, Leo," offered Tom. "I really would."

Glidewell looked at Tom for a long time before he spoke. "No, old chap. I think not."

"God help you," said Tom. Glidewell turned toward the door and started walking. Tom grabbed the Bible on the table and caught up with Glidewell. "I'd like for you to have this," said Tom, extending the book toward Glidewell. "The secrets of the universe that we're all looking for—they're in this book, Leo."

"No thanks; I've got one in my room," said Glidewell.

"Well, then, read it sometime, Leo—really," said Tom. "Give 'er a try."

"I shall consider it," replied Glidewell as he reached the door. Tom nodded silently and let him out. He laid the book down on the nightstand and undressed for bed. He crawled into bed, looked at the blue-glowing digits on the clock that displayed 2:01, and removed the Gideon Bible from the nightstand. The Second Chapter of Acts was the last thing he read before he went to sleep.

30

The Shadow of the Unseen

Ray Stone's stubby, blue-veined hand was sticking out of the doorway—at that angle just a hand and nothing else. It was the Friday afternoon once a year when Johnson Aircraft engineers found out their salary increases. The IBM clock on the slick gray post in the front of Tom Kruger's desk showed there was only 53 minutes left until the weekend began. As fate or design would have it, he was yet to find out about his raise. The increase this year would mean something special; and, for that reason, it would be unlike any of his previous yearly increases, even though inflation had slowed from triple digits to double.

Tom didn't like his job any more—he didn't like the pay, or the lack of semi-private offices, or the gamesmanship that led to promotions, or the excessive amount of mundane, repetitive paperwork. But he was willing to do what he was doing the rest of his life if he could definitely find out if this was where God wanted him to serve—if aerospace engineering was on the right path. When he had given his life to Christ on that hot August night he had vowed to serve Jesus. And he knew Christ had delivered him from the craving for alcohol and from the sins of his life. Tom figured he really did owe Jesus the rest of his life, and he was determined he was going to live up to the bargain.

For the past few nights Melissa and Tom had prayed on their knees in the trailer's kitchen for a sign as to whether Tom should stay at Johnson or resign and get into something else that God might have for him. They had read the Bible morning, noon, and night for the past few weeks, and it all came down to one thing they both prayed would be the sign. They had asked God to make the raise Tom would be getting in the next few minutes a definite sign so that he could choose to stay on the path he was on or split off in an unknown direction.

Tom knew that he had done a good job for the company the past year; he had played a role in solving the F-170 design problems, and he had been living out in the desert for over four months without even making one trip back to his home in Atlanta. So by all human expectations the raise held promise of being a good one. But Melissa and Tom both knew now that the Lord would speak through the raise, and if it was higher than Tom's wildest expectations, he would know that he should stay with the company. But if the raise were low, he would know to go. They knew this would be the sign simply because they had asked the Father in Heaven to make it the sign. With inflation at 32% a year, it would have seemed logical to act that same way even without the prayer. But humans were creatures of habit, and even in a world where technology flourished, engineering jobs were relatively scarce; most engineers, as the turn of the century approached, didn't give up a job unless they were forced to by the company.

Tom gazed at the door relentlessly. Stone's hand was still sticking out, but Tom knew that he would be the next one called into the room. Everyone else had already been. Finally Stone's hand came off the doorframe and, as the department head strode past him, Stone stepped out into the open doorway and made eye contact with Tom, motioning him into the room.

"Tom, I saved you till last. I guess you noticed," said Stone after they both sat down across from each other at the conference table.

"I kind of figured that out, Ray," said Tom.

"Tom, you've done good work on the F-170," said Stone. "I know you sure impressed the hell out of me. We sent a hellava good recommendation on your evaluation sheet back to your department head in Atlanta."

"Thanks," said Tom softly.

Stone puffed on his cigar a couple of time and looked down at a computer printout and then back through the swirling smoke at Tom. "And there's one thing I'm glad of with the raise they have listed here."

"What's that, Ray?" asked Tom.

"I'm glad I'm not your real boss," said Stone, more nervous than Tom had ever seen him. "Tom, we thought we had a misprint when we first saw the amount of your raise, so my department head called back to Atlanta. And we've confirmed the figure."

"Come on, Ray," urged Tom as Stone puffed the cigar until the fire at the end became almost as long as the rest of the cigar. "The suspense is killing me—spit it out."

Stone took the cigar out of his mouth and gave it a questioning look. "Tom, I don't know what happened, but your raise is six dollars."

Tom was surprised. He knew the raise would give him a definite answer, one way or another. But somehow it shocked him a little that the answer had been that definite. Melissa had found out about her raise at two fifteen and had called Tom with the news that they had given her an "average" raise of $125 a week. And that wouldn't even keep her close to the cost of living index—much less six dollars a week!

Tom couldn't contain himself, and there was a great sense of relief that bloomed inside him—like it was one of those perfect 72-degree, clear sunny days inside him or it was like the feeling you get when you are young and healthy and you walk out into a perfect day like that and feel joy just to be alive. He felt extremely light, as if he were floating on a cloud—all of this added up to make him laugh.

"There's somebody high in the organization in Atlanta who doesn't like you very much," reasoned Stone. "And I'd be quick about finding out who that sucker is if I were you; otherwise he's going to ruin you. Hell, the rest room swabbies will end up making more than you if he keeps his hand in your pie."

Tom smiled at Stone. "That's okay, Ray, really," said Tom. "Just one favor I wonder if you'd do for me?"

"Sure, Tom."

"Relay the message to Atlanta that two weeks from today is my last day," said Tom.

"You're serious?" asked Stone.

"Yes."

"But, are you sure you don't want to think it over—haste makes waste sometimes."

"No, Ray—I prayed about whether I should stay or go, and the Lord has just given me the answer," said Tom. "So it's not really a bad raise—it's the best one I've ever had!"

Tom got up and stuck up his right hand in a friendly wave as he turned to leave. Stone clamped the short stub of a cigar in his mouth and shook his head. "Well, good luck—hate to see you go," said Stone.

"Good luck to you, Ray."

That night Tom and Melissa celebrated their raises by meeting Melissa's uncle in Santa Barbara for dinner. A big golden moon had risen from the sea by the time they came out of the restaurant, and the three of them walked along the beach that ran between the road and the ocean. The sea was like a great silver platter and it lapped in at the land, surging with its husky sounds, and pungent with the smell of fish. There were little clouds in the sky over the mountains that were illuminated by the low golden moon, and they looked like immense tufts of luminescent wool, white as snow in the dark sky.

Tom commented again about the Johnson Aircraft pay raises, and a burst of laughter came out of Melissa, and they all caught it and laughed as they walked by the side of the ocean.

"You both seem pretty sure about quitting," the colonel said to them as he looked out over the ocean.

"We really prayed hard about it, Uncle Jim—it was a pretty big step," explained Melissa. "We let the raise be Tom's sign, like Gideon's fleece in the Old Testament, but I feel led to help in whatever the Lord tells us to do—so I had to quit too."

"Whatdya think's in store for you?" asked the colonel.

"I think the Lord is calling us to write a novel," said Tom. "We prayed about our mission with a group from church last Sunday evening and when we got home we turned on the TV and the Christian Broadcasting Network had a two-hour special about the need for people to write books with a spiritual prospective—something that would delve deep into good and evil."

Melissa added, "They prayed on the air that God would show certain people that writing was their mission. And Tom and I both sensed that writing was what we would work on. We really felt that the Lord was speaking to us."

"Well, let me just say good luck," said the colonel. "It's a little unconventional, but, hell—it sounds like a darn good cause in this day and age."

"Tom's going to try to rough out a novel about the UFOs and I'm going to edit the manuscript on the computer and write to agents and things like that," said Melissa.

"Tom, I guess you realize there's been a lot of sci-fi written about UFOs and space creatures," said the colonel.

Tom examined the waves rolling toward them in the darkness and watched them as they broke a short distance away. He nodded abstractedly at the colonel as he gazed intently at the white glowing surf gliding over the blackened waters. Then he answered after a long pause. "I think the Lord wants us to write something that would tell it like it is—you know, something about the hostility, maybe why they're really here."

"Does that include telling them about Project O?" asked the colonel.

"I guess that'd be the best way," explained Tom. "But I don't want to go back on my promise to you."

"Forget what I said about keeping quiet," said the colonel. "In fact, there's a few more things the people should probably know before it's too late."

Tom cocked his head to one side and eyed the colonel. "There's more?"

The colonel laughed and then spoke in a serious tone. "Well, if you're going to capture reality about the UFOs, I would say your story should include two or three key messages for sure."

"Lay it on us, Jim," said Tom.

"First, the evil forces in the story must be shown as capable of assuming various forms," said the colonel. "I don't think these things have one certain form they're locked into, but a lot of forms. Hell, maybe they can disguise themselves. Maybe they can make humans see anything they want them to see. If you can show that it might give somebody a hint as to the origins of these things."

"That sounds good," said Tom.

"And, secondly," said the colonel, "the UFO creatures should be depicted as being after one thing and one thing only."

"Is ¦ what I think it is?" Melissa asked her uncle.

The colonel smiled and nodded at her before he spoke. "Extraterrestrials have been depicted as coming to earth in quest of human bodies, dead and alive, human spinal cords and brains, earth's minerals, human flesh as a food source—all these motives have been shown. But the good Lord might just be giving you a crucial story to get out. You could be the ones who tell the people that the UFOs are really trying to capture their souls—the part of people that can live forever and the thing that's vastly more important than silver and gold, or entire planets, or human spinal cords, or anything we could ever imagine with our puny brains."

"That's powerful," said Tom. "But it's goin' to be hard to make it believable. Most people today only believe what they can see and touch—just the material world."

"That's where the third part comes in," said the colonel. "Your story must have a true-to-life spiritual thread running through it, even if people have lost the knowledge about what true life really involves—a battle between good and evil."

"That part sounds excellent," agreed Melissa.

The colonel winked at her and went on to explain. "So the last thing I can give you is something I haven't told you before—but maybe it's the most important."

Melissa put her arm around Tom's waist and they stood, the wind wafting their hair, facing the colonel at the edge of the sea, waiting for what they knew would be something good, something that might make a difference between a common story and an uncommon one—the outline of which seemed to be, even now, taking shape in Tom Kruger's mind.

The colonel began again, speaking slowly in a raspy voice. "Not too many years ago a branch of the NSA contracted with the top scientists in the free world to make a study of the possible origins of the UFOs. The group they selected was made up of the top minds on the face of the earth—not the pop scientists you see on television all the time. These people I'm talking about keep a low public profile. Their names are not very interesting—you probably wouldn't even recognize them. But they are the best scientific intellects of our generation, and what they concluded fits right into this whole thing.

"Quite a few years ago one of Einstein's famous formulas showed that any mass that attained the speed of light would become infinite. Thus it was generally accepted that there was a barrier that prevented anything from moving faster than the speed of light, just as it was thought in the nineteen forties that a barrier existed at the speed of sound."

"Sure," recalled Tom. "I remember the formula."

"Well," said the colonel, "it turns out that we know a lot more today than they did in Einstein's era. The idea of infinity and infinite mass are, after all, man-made concepts, and therefore are subject to revision. There are experiments that seem to confirm a world beyond the speed of light."

"I think even Einstein along with Rosen found that spacetime had to open up into a second universe when a huge star collapsed," said Tom.

"Really," said Melissa, smiling.

"Yes," answered Tom.

"Anyway, I'm going to give you my bootlegged copy of the secret report," said the colonel, "then you can read the latest for yourselves. What surprised most of the people that got to see this thing was the unlikely fact that these high-powered scientists were in total agreement over several startling things. They theorized that our universe is overlaid by at least one invisible parallel universe. The one we can see and measure operates on this side of the speed of light. And another, more powerful universe exists beyond the speed of light, where it is normally undetectable to our senses."

"I've heard something about this theory before," said Tom.

"Sounds reasonable—the basic ideas have been kicking around awhile," agreed the colonel. "Scientists knew fifteen or twenty years ago that our own universe behaves in a way that suggests the presence of a hellava lot more mass than it apparently contains."

"Far as I knew, they were still looking for about ninety percent of the physical matter—they don't know where it is!" Tom elaborated on the theme, waving a hand in front of him as if he were holding the thought and shaking it.

"They were looking," corrected the colonel. "If you recall, in the mid-eighties they detected powerful islands of gravity visually between earth and certain quasars, acting as giant lenses—splitting the quasars into two identical images. The top scientists, the ones without the secular humanism axe to grind, were puzzled that gravity sources of that size, closer than a quasar, could be completely non-luminous—unless, of course, these islands were huge universes on another invisible plane of existence such as the good book has told man about for centuries."

"Isn't it something how it was in there all the time," said Melissa.

"Right before their noses, Lissy," agreed the colonel. "So, anyway, a breakthrough was made about five years ago. An invisible shadow universe to our own was confirmed absolutely by the detection and measurement of gravitation waves in a secret experiment conducted in earth orbit. It confirmed not only distant other-dimensional universes, but parallel, unseen matter in and around the earth itself!"

"You're kidding," said Melissa. "And they kept something like that secret?"

"I'm sorry to say they did, Lissy," replied the colonel. "The people in power are running scared with this UFO thing and they don't want anybody to get a glimmer that millions of non-physical beings from a world of higher frequencies occupy the earth with us, and a lot of these dwellers are fairly nasty in their outlook."

"Since some of the dwellers are Satan's fallen angels," added Melissa.

"Exactly," replied the colonel. "Lord only knows who and what are down here with us. But, of course, the people who control the information flow don't see it as demonic or angelic at all—they don't see a possible polarization into good and evil. I'm afraid they're quite blind to the truth."

"How do the higher frequencies you mentioned fit in?" asked Tom.

"The report uses the frequency idea to expand on the 'superstring' theory quite a bit," said the colonel.

"Superstring?" asked Melissa.

Tom picked up the explanation. "The superstring theory states that subatomic particles don't exist as individual particles—they're really part of an extended object, which is called the superstring. We don't see the whole object or string because we are only tuned in to one segment at a time—the particles that go to make up our physical universe. Green and Anthony in 1985 suggested that a multitude of other previously unknown dimensions might exist. Anthony also pointed out that a subatomic particle string can be excited into other states just as a violin string can be vibrated in a series of harmonics." He looked sheepishly at the colonel after he had finished talking.

"This kid's got some kind of memory," said the colonel to Melissa, winking a dark eye. He hesitated a moment to examine the sky and then continued. "Basically, the whole idea is that the matter in the spiritual world beyond the speed of light is made up of the same subatomic particles as our own, but it's simply vibrating at much higher frequencies."

"So we're equipped to see only the particles vibrating at the lower frequencies," said Melissa.

"Exactly," said the colonel. "The secret report concludes that the UFOs are manifestations of life that exists in a parallel universe on the other side of the speed of light, and that life at the higher subatomic vibration rates is somehow capable of passing through the light barrier and existing or at least apparently existing at this lower frequency state." He ran the fingers of his right hand through his hair slowly and looked out to sea.

" 'Be not forgetful to entertain strangers; for thereby some have entertained angels unawares,' " quoted Melissa, her eyes beaming with a beautiful, faraway look.

"It's almost like there's gotta be a gate or something," reasoned Tom.

"Could be," said the colonel. "Tell you what—I'll slip you the report this evening when we go back to the ranch. If you meditate on it awhile, some fresh ideas might pop into your heads."

"Putting something like that in a story is going to be dynamite. Thanks, Uncle Jim," said Melissa.

"There's a lot more in the document besides the general parallel universe stuff," said the colonel. "For instance, five of the scientists postulate that the invisible mass in the shadow universe is concentrated in its own continuum inside or on the other side of huge black holes centered on our visible universe's galaxies. The rest of the brains thought black holes could only occur in free space. But either way if a black hole is in rotation, it can definitely act as a gateway or a bridge connecting an unlimited number of otherwise separate physical and nonphysical universes—they all agreed on that. And smaller parallel worlds might even exist in black holes inside stars such as our sun."

The wind murmured across the sea, and Tom could feel the air come in cool off the water. He blinked with the air in his eyes and tried to shape a question from what he knew: "So—lemme get this straight," he said, "these top minds are definitely saying that the spiritual world or the shadow universe, whatever we want to call it, exists right around us?"

"Yes, they definitely concurred on that," concluded the colonel. "And that could mean that miniature rotating black holes might reside inside planets like our own earth," he added.

"So the UFOs could easily come from inside the earth?" said Melissa.

"Quite likely—or a parallel dimension inside the earth, to put it more precisely. I think one of the scientists felt that the higher vibration world of what he called ultraterrestrials could extend to the same space where our atmosphere is located. These beings wouldn't necessarily need to center their lives in the same space we center ours—on the surface of the planet."

"Amazing," said Tom, scratching his head. "And publishable, I hope."

"Something just registered," said Melissa with sudden surprise. "You know, there's a perfect match for an earth-bound black hole in the Bible. I mean, I think it's been in the Bible all along!"

"That would add another piece to the puzzle," said Tom.

"Remember Revelation 20?" said Melissa excitedly. "It's in there!"

"Is that the part about the plagues?" offered the colonel weakly.

" 'And I saw an angel come down from heaven, having the key of the bottomless pit' . . . how's that strike you as a description of a black hole?" crowed Melissa, and then she went on, automatically, as if reading from a scroll that was unrolling magically in her mind. " 'And he laid hold on the dragon, that old serpent, which is the Devil and Satan, and bound him a thousand years. And cast him into the bottomless pit, and shut him up, and set a seal upon him, that he should deceive the nations no more, till the thousand years should be fulfilled: and after that he must be loosed a little season.' "

As the sea surged with a moaning roar and the bubbling white surf glided toward them in mindless motion, both men nodded like they had just seen something very esoteric and important. Beyond the shore the moon gave the sea a luminous path that stretched past the beds of kelp out to the sea's end, and they all watched the wind scatter the reflections of the moon into shimmering ripples of light on the moving water.

31

A Deadly Affair

It was Christmas Eve, 1999. On the Strip in Las Vegas the roulette wheels were turning and the prostitutes were on call. Outside, the night had settled like a black bell jar onto the neon oasis. Inside the casinos the blackjack tables were alive with the whispers of cards and the clicking sounds of plastic chips sliding together—dropping on expensive felt; the main showrooms were already filling with patrons who entered from wide, brightly lit hallways.

At about that same hour Leo Glidewell was eating his seventh cherry off a miniature sword he had fished out of a freshly made Manhattan. The lounge at Caesar's Palace was filled with customers, and a man in a red coat and pants was blowing a brass, buttoned horn, standing illuminated by artificial lights on a modest, elevated stage near the center of the room.

Glidewell examined the $50 bill after he slid it out of the pebble-grained, black leather wallet. He looked at the inscription IN GOD WE TRUST as if he were surprised by it—surprised that it was on there. Then he focused on the corner of the bill and nodded his approval to himself at selecting the proper denomination. "I don't trust anybody," he said when he handed the reddish-orange money to the waitress who had just stepped up with the next pair of drinks. The waitress's lips curled up at what he had said.

"I have to get change for this," she told him.

"What are you doing later?" Glidewell asked the waitress casually as he swirled the inside of his drink around with his forefinger. He had been tipping the girl with $5 bills all night.

"I don't get off till three," she told him. "How's the drink?"

"It would taste better if I were seated in a leather chair with a half-smoked pipe, surrounded by shelves of very old and rare books," answered Glidewell in an elaborate British accent. The young, dark-complexioned girl smiled at what he had said.

"Yeah—I know the feeling," she said. "I'm kind of fed up with this whole scene myself. I got a bum deal."

"Let me take you away from all this," said Glidewell in praticed, easy talk. "Rome, Paris, San Diego?" The girl's lip curled up the side of her mouth in a faint smile. She had a stocky build and wore a brief, mini-skirted costume, avocado green in color, with a plunging V-neckline in front. A shiny red Christmas tree ornament hung down in the bottom of the V from a long yellow chain. Her face was round and pleasant with dark eyes, which matched the color of her relatively short-cropped hair, and she looked to be in her mid-twenties.

"Well, I gotta get back to the bar. I'll bring your change. That bartender really burns me," she said. "I'm goin' quit this joint."

"Give 'em hell," said Glidewell. The girl turned and lazily walked back through the drab dim light toward the brighter, smoke-filled light that swirled at the other end of the room. Glidewell carefully watched her as she moved away, then, when she had stopped at another table, he downed a third of the whiskey in the short, fat hexagonal glass. His eyes focused on the distant bar and waitress as she stood with one hip lower than the other, getting his change and asking for drinks. He picked at a pack of filter cigarettes, fumbled one out of the package, and tapped it on the table. He lifted a metal lighter off the table and flicked a flame out, lighting the cigarette and drawing the smoke deeply into his lungs.

The horn player seemed to get worse the more he played, and some disorderly people beside Glidewell clapped when he announced his break. "Thank you for that applause, ladies and germs," the horn player said over the public address system in the lounge. "Don't look now, but we've been spiking your drinks with rocket fuel—see you on the moon." The musician's mouth flew open; his capped teeth flashed in the stage lights and his narrow head rocked back and forth on his neck as he laughed uproariously at what he had said.

Glidewell had almost sipped his way through another drink by the time the waitress came back to the table. He started to tell her to bring another pair of drinks when she said, "I showed them who they can treat like that. I showed them once and for all," she told Glidewell, wobbling on her feet almost imperceptibly.

"Good. That's telling them, my good woman," he said, and

laughed briskly. "Most bartenders are blithering idiots anyway."

"They're not goin' push me around no more. I quit 'em!"

"Come on. Sit down," offered Glidewell, slurring the S.

She sat down across from Glidewell and leaned her arms on the table. "I want to go dancing," she said. "Will you take me dancing?"

"Sure."

"I told them I quit and I'm goin' pick up my check on Monday. I want to go dancing.

"Anything you want, Ginger old sport," Glidewell said to her. "You going to change clothes or something?"

"No," she said. "I'm just going to get my coat."

"Capital idea," said Glidewell. "Shall we be off?" The girl looked at him, confused a little at what he had said.

"I'm not off," she said.

They both stood up uncertainly, and the girl stopped by the coat check room and retrieved a full length, light-colored fur, which she put on over her scanty clothing and wore against the cold wind that blew across the pavement outside the hotel.

Glidewell had them bring his car around and then he drove the girl to the Black Orchid lounge, where the parking valet had said a good band was playing. Inside, a dark-suited man escorted them to a corner table. The girl took off her shoes and fur coat and Glidewell danced to a couple of songs with her, accidentally stepping on her bare toes twice, and after that they walked back to the table. They sat and drank a few drinks and told dirty stories and, after almost an hour, they finished their drinks, paid the bill, and left. Glidewell got into his jet black Mercedes and, backing out of the parking lot slot at high speed, without looking, he rammed the back end of his car up onto the back end of a Chevrolet Corvette, making a loud, crunching noise.

He glanced back quickly as the girl yelled, "Hey—what the hell you doin'?" and saw the crushed fiberglass on the back end of the Corvette. He heard people running toward the parking lot so he extinguished all the external lights on the big Mercedes and wheeled the car as fast as he could onto the street. He accelerated rapidly and checked the rear-view mirror. There were people screaming at him, and a couple of men were running down the street after the Mercedes, but when he turned a corner they were all out of sight behind the next row of buildings he went past.

The girl's third-floor apartment was close to downtown. They got there at half past midnight. The first thing the girl did when they walked in was to open the window and bellow for her cat to come in. After a half a minute the cat jumped gingerly up on the sill of the window. He was a big Tom Cat, and the name she had given him was appropriate. Her apartment was shabbily furnished and dimly lighted. He went to the bathroom and after he walked out, leaving the sound of water churning, he asked: "What's all those syringes and stuff for in there?"

"Whatdya think? I'm a brain surgeon—I use 'em in my work." Glidewell gave her a wrinkled smile and walked in the kitchen where they got two partly frozen beers out of the pink refrigerator and the girl got a checkerboard out of a drawer and placed it down in the middle of the worn beige rug in the main room.

"I forgot how to play," said the girl.

"We'll play a practice game," said Glidewell. "You got any Debussy records?"

"Huh?"

The girl's eyes were distant and wide as she advanced the checkers across the board, trying to counter his moves. The game was rather loosely played as Glidewell cheated and she tried to catch him at it. And then they played another. In the second game Glidewell was moving the red pieces awkwardly with his right hand, which was propped up on his right elbow. His body was facing the girl's and his left hand began to caress her legs. When he leaned over to kiss the girl she backed away as soon as he touched her lips. "I wanna see your place," she snapped suddenly.

"Why, I'm just at a hotel." He tried to put her off.

"I wanna get outta here," she said. "Somebody could come looking for me—I don't want 'em to find me."

With that he got up, a little red in the face. "Let's go," he said. "But I'm counting on you."

"What are you, a mathematician?" she said, getting up from the floor.

"President of the flat earth society," he said. And they went out the door past the click of the light switch.

After the lovemaking and 111 minutes of sleep the liquor in his blood let him wake slowly. There was this most peculiar feeling when he came to, like heated electric air was all around him, and it was hard to breathe. Glidewell raised his head slightly off the pillow and peered straight ahead at the darkness in the hotel room. He felt a sudden shudder and his breath quickened as though he had been having a nightmare but couldn't remember it yet. Then he knew there wasn't any nightmare to remember—the reason he was breathing fast and hard was in the room with him now.

There was something or someone standing at the foot of his bed! Unbridled fear crouched in his mind ready to spring—it took all he had to resist the urge to run. The form at the foot of the bed was horribly misshapen, whatever it was, and he squinted his eyes in the darkness to try to make out just what it was in the shadowy light. At the same time this was happening a chill went up his spine as his mind silently screamed: It's in the room with me!

The first thing that Glidewell began to see faintly was a blood-red glistening, like eyes in the darkness, gloating down at him. He suddenly detested this hideous presence—this silent terror. He could feel beads of sweat ooze from his skin on his forehead and neck as he heard a sound like chuckling, filled with venom, come from the entity. He could smell a pungent stench waft toward him as if from an icy opened grave.

The longer he watched the shadowy image in dumb agony, the more he could make out what the apparition looked like. It seemed to be a stout, dark figure with a big muskmelonlike head, and this bloated head sat on its shoulders directly without benefit of a neck; He could almost make out a face in the dim light, but the lower body was darker than the surroundings, like it was covered with dark hair. He did glimpse a bulge of some sort where the stomach of the creature should have been when a faint ray of light from some passing traffic happened to slant through a crack in the window curtains. Then suddenly he saw the figure move and another chill shot up his back where his spine was. His strength seemed to have ebbed away. It was the most frightened he had ever been—and without wanting to he whispered, ''No.''

Just at that moment the woman beside Glidewell awoke with a start and, lifting suddenly from the bed, she let out a scream that pierced the air in the room. As the apelike form seemed to take a step toward her, she stiffened with fright for an instant, then sprang from the bed like a wild animal freed from a trap, and threw herself against the frame of the window. Glidewell leaped after her. He grabbed her, and she fought him like she was fighting for life itself. With clammy hands she scratched and clawed his skin, shaking screams out of her violently moving head in fitful bursts. By the time he had subdued her violent thrusts and the crying had started, Glidewell glanced at the foot of the bed. The Thing had disappeared. "Get me outta here," the girl pleaded through liquid snorts.

Glidewell hesitated a moment.

"Now!" Her shattering voice screamed, and then she broke out into a high-pitched, insane wail. Her eyes got wilder by the second, and she bared her teeth and then hollered in a voice tough as a man's, "If you don't get me outta here I'm goin' call a friend of mine and tell him you raped me. He kills people sometimes."

"What are you, crazy or something?"

"I mean it, buster." She got up and went for the telephone. "I'm callin' Charlie," she said, between hysterical, snorting sobs.

Glidewell grabbed her again as she started pressing the numbers on the keyboard. "Get your clothes on," he said. "I don't need all this."

Glidewell drove the Mercedes past the edge of the city, south along the straight black road. The clock on the dash read 4:08 when two distant lights like red taillights pricked the blackness in front of the Mercedes. He had eased the speed up to 90 by now, but whatever carried the taillights seemed to speed up and maintain the same gap between them.

Just as Glidewell had decided to open the Mercedes up a little more, the lights in front of him reversed with great suddenness. Like the glowing eyes of a gargoyle attached to something the size of a building, the lights accelerated and bore down on the Mercedes. In the twinkling of an eye the thing was almost on top of him. And when it was too late, when fear had already frozen his responses, he squinted his eyes as the huge, 100-foot object came upon him, glowing so intensely it seemed the air itself glowed red like fire. It was incredibly large, egg-shaped, with illuminated streamers dangling down below, and it was making a high-pitched, piercing whine as it streaked the final few hundred yards, fast as an artillery shell.

He hit the brakes. The last few feet away, the sound of it's coming was overpowering, shrieking at the night like a banshee. Just before it struck, in Glidewell's last instant of terror, the craft looked to him like an enormous, translucent jellyfish—some lighter-than-air horrible mutation of nature the scientists had missed all these years, hostile in its intent, rare in its appearance . . . somehow pulsating in the night like a red-flashing police car beacon . . . and then it was too late to think anymore. In the final fraction of a second all he saw was a blinding glare, and then the UFO impacted against the Mercedes with a loud, metallic noise, shattering the windshield and venting its fury against the roof-line—scraping and bending the roof as if it were cardboard.

The hurtling craft seemed to ricochet and rebound off the top of the skidding car. As the car veered violently across the highway the UFO angled up into a vertical climb and streaked out of sight, melting into the night in a few seconds. The Mercedes dug into the sand beside the road with a great deal of sound and fury, then rolled twice before it came to rest, a twisted, splintered wreck.

32

Notes from the Underground

When Tom Kruger strode through the door to Room 236 at the Las Vegas General Hospital, Glidewell's lawyer was already inside, impatiently waiting. The man who had invited him to this dismal room, using a bearlike telephone voice, seemed like he would have been older, more husky; but the young lawyer who rose now to greet him in the sunlit room was perfectly ordinary looking with an efficient-looking, dull face, beady eyes, and an absolutely average-sized body decked out in a French, pin-striped gray suit. "How do you do, Mr. Kruger," the man said blindly. "Sorry I couldn't give you many of the details on the phone. It was part of my job to be a little mysterious. Mr. Glidewell wanted it that way."

"Nice to meet you," said Tom. It seemed to him that he noticed a little discomfort showed on the lawyer's face now that he looked more closely—a little coldness behind the keen eyeballs. Tom turned away from the man and stepped over to the bed where Leo Glidewell lay unconscious. His head was swollen horribly—it looked like the top part of his head had puffed to nearly twice the size Tom remembered. "Is he . . . I mean, do they give him any chance?" asked Tom, glancing at Glidewell's motionless off-color face.

"I don't think the physicians hold out much hope for Mr. Glidewell," the lawyer offered. Tom had the definite impression that the lawyer felt ill at ease calling people *mister*.

"You said it was a hit and run?" queried Tom as he peered more carefully at the head of the pillow. *There's something gray they put up his nose,* he thought.

"They don't know who or what hit him, unfortunately," lamented the lawyer. "Hell, I wish we had a lead. No skid marks but the ones his Mercedes left when it left the highway. No witnesses. He had a woman with him, but she was killed instantly. It's a wonder Mr. Glidewell made it this far—fairly nasty collision—they found his teeth scattered all over the highway—been in a coma . . .''

Tom bent down closer to Glidewell's head. He knew what the gray was now. *Glidewell's brains are coming out his nose*; the thought sliced through his mind like a cold blade and stabbed him with a sickening feeling that seemed to plunge down to his throat. He bent his head, touched Glidewell's arm a moment, and moved his lips in a murmuring, barely audible prayer. The lawyer was silent as he watched, then bent over to retrieve a manila envelope from the chair by the window. He walked toward the bed and handed the envelope solemnly to Tom. ''My instructions were to get this envelope to you in case Mr. Glidewell died or became comatose,'' said the lawyer with dread in his voice. Then, a little brighter, ''He must have felt whatever's inside to be of utmost importance— that's all I know about it.''

Tom nodded as he took the envelope, caressing for a moment the hard ridges and symbols on an elaborate seal of red wax. It looked like something Glidewell would have done.

''Not much we can do in here, I'm afraid,'' said the lawyer. Tom looked at him without saying anything for a second, then let his gaze fall on a trapezoidal pattern the sun made on the corner of the room. They walked out of the room together. Outside the room the lawyer mumbled something like, ''Afraid I'll have to be off now—got a court case in San Diego this afternoon—twelve o'clock flight. Wish I could hit the casino tables a few more times, but that's life in the global village. Nice to meet you, Mr. Kruger and, oh, if whatever's in that envelope requires it, I'll be glad to help you.'' The lawyer fished in the handkerchief pocket of his suit coat a few seconds and brought out a gray business card. ''Here's my card.''

''Thanks,'' said Tom. ''Nice to have met you.'' The lawyer hurried off, and Tom headed for the visitors' waiting room, tearing into the envelope as he walked. He took a seat at the end of a row, farthest from the vibrating blare of the television set's speaker. Inside the envelope were only three sheets of paper, each with black, loosely scrawled writing on them.

He sunk his eyes immediately onto the first of the pages and began reading: ''Tom, I've got to get out of this UFO thing somehow. I believe now that I know too much for my own good.

I'm in over my head. This may sound pretty damn strange, but I found the base of the UFO types who are out to get us, or at least, one of their bases. I saw the whole thing. I mean, I went down inside this artificially constructed tunnel inside and underneath one of the mountains near the old prospector's place. He tipped me off after the last big California quake hit. By the way, I found out the prospector recently croaked—I couldn't find out the cause of death—I mean, natural or *otherwise*, heh, heh. When I saw him the last time he said his latest dog had been killed with a ray of some kind.

"Anyway, I was able to get down the tunnel undetected while the old man kept watch up above—he sure as hell wasn't going to be the one to go down into what looked like the strangest thing we had both ever seen before. I saw the underground mother ship or whatever you want to call it. The tunnel widened after a few hundred feet into a big, cavernlike opening. I think it was an ancient lava tube. There was a musty odor I could smell. Anyhow, the damn scout ships were parked in rows like planes on an aircraft carrier! I was there, Tom, only a couple hundred yards away—you've got to believe me. You're really the only one I trust anymore to tell this damn story to, and probably then, only if something happens to me.

"It may be that these creatures live down there—I still don't know the connection between them and the space brothers. But they are definitely the baddies—I'd stake my life on it. And I've come to the conclusion that these damn things under the earth are quite mad!

"As luck would have it, I caught a glimpse of a bunch of these UFO humanoids—or whatever they were—coming toward the edge of the tunnel where I was. I still don't know why they didn't get me. Somehow I made it out to tell the tale. Except, you see, I couldn't really spread the story around—*if you know what I mean and I know you do*! If I wanted to spend the rest of my days locked up in some camp or hospital ward somewhere I could have gone to the authorities, heh, heh. Our public servants who stand for truth (heh, heh), justice, and the American way.

"It was a real thrill departing the vicinity of the tunnel, by the way. The old-timer and I had just gotten back to the car when a black, completely unlit UFO floated out of the opening and followed us down the highway. I figured we were dead men, but what the hell do you think, some Navy jets roared into sight and the UFO did a one-eighty and got the hell out of there. So, damn it, Tom, the bastards are down there just as we suspected. And the SOBs keep their lights off when they don't want to be detected. And all the useful idiots they take for "rides" in the old UFO "up into outer space" probably get taken right down under the earth to the base I saw or maybe even other ones."

The ink changed then at the next paragraph from coal black to ballpoint blue. "I'm not sure what I saw down there was even objective reality anymore. When I was down there my mind was acting funny; weird and awful thoughts were popping into my head that made me want to do some awful things to other people. As I try to think back in my mind now and use all my psychic and not so psychic powers, it seems it could've all been some sort of super holography I saw, base and scout craft and all. But, of course, that would mean projectors.

"I have the definite impression from everything I know and have seen that they're stepping up their activities—maybe our technology's getting too damn close to theirs and they are ready to come to the surface en masse and slap us down or set up a dictatorship and rule mankind openly. I still think the advanced races from the other plantetary systems are out to help us—if they can.

"I had to jot this letter down in a hurry. I hope it makes sense. If I have time and guts, I'm going to add some more details to these sheets. If anything happens—I hope you figure out a way to tell the world before the powers that be can shut you up.

"Your friend, Leo Glidewell."

Tom was silent and very still a long while after he had read it. He just stared for a while at the writing on the last page, not seeing it. Then he shuffled the sheets back to their original order. He wondered for a minute if Glidewell had dreamed it all up; he tried to use what he knew already to reason the whole thing out, but then an irresistible thought took over all his efforts at logic: *Leo was either crazy by then or he really went down in the tunnel. Either way it wasn't pleasant. But why would he make something like this up?* And Tom felt sure then that Glidewell had really believed what he had written. And one other thought came to mind now as he keep turning over and looking at what he had just read in his brain: Glidewell had been scared stiff!

In the old days something like this would have made Tom want to find some strong drink and consume quite a lot of it in a short space of time. But now, instead, after what seemed a long time, while thoughts wove themselves through his mind, leaving strange and sinister threads, he knelt on the floor of the waiting room, bent his head toward the floor, and prayed to God for wisdom.

33

In the Wilderness

March 2, 2000, had been an unusually warm day after the last of a high desert winter. Books and papers were stacked and strewn all over the top of the desk Tom Kruger had set up in the living room at one end of the house trailer. As the day outside started to fade he sat in front of a big bay window, pushing a chrome ballpoint pen across a $3 blue-lined college notebook. He had on a white T-shirt with the Mickey Mouse cartoon character on the front side, and it was wet under the arms. Resting under the small desk, his thighs had khaki-tan shorts halfway down them and his feet were bare. There were beads of sweat dropping down occasionally off his forehead onto the paper he was writing on and sometimes it interrupted his writing when the pen would plunge into a wet spot on the paper. On the wall to the right of the desk was a calender picturing a man standing in blue water up to his knees, fishing. And beside that, a three-by-five card read: FOR GOD ALONE MY SOUL WAITS IN SILENCE.

He paused a moment and wiped the sweat from his brow with his forearm. Out the window he could see the small, familiar form of a distant Joshua tree, but the rest was desert—a semi-barren flatness that ran to the distant mountains. The only features that broke the monotony of the distant view were telephone poles that showed like toothpicks in the distance toward the railroad tracks and late at night he could hear the lonesome train whistle blow as it haunted the desert night. Then at other times in the night as he drifted off to sleep he would almost believe there were unseen beings whose voices urged him on in the wailing wind outside the trailer—who somehow sought to help. And when the wind was strong at night it lifted his spirit and that, along with reading the Bible, helped his mental stamina so he had kept on with the grind of writing. To him, writing was almost like pulling a never-ending supply of one's own teeth—one after another, day after day.

Fifteen months of writing beyond the edge of town and married life with Melissa's good cooking had put some weight on him, and he had a brown, heavy beard that gave his face an older, disciplined look. The novel they had been working on was nearly half finished and, during the past month, the right ideas were beginning to show up on the paper almost effortlessly—or at least that's how it seemed to him. The thought struck him that the final chapters would probably be better than the initial ones, but the whole story was blooming into a recognizable shape in his mind now and transforming itself into equivalent words at the end of his pen. He realized now that writing fiction had always been a desire of his heart. This story had come out from deep within him and, at times, he could feel the story wanting to get out like a burning fire shut up inside his bones; but when it hit the page it always lost something in that process, and brought with it unexpected imperfections. That's where Melissa's talent really showed. From a natural love of literature and the books in her family's store, she had developed a fine sense of the finished words novels were made of. She would take his raw words and build on them like hanging the layers on a skeleton to give it the structure that would let it live. Also she would check his grammar, starved from an engineering career, and finish off each chapter by letting the computer check the spelling. Like a fine craftsman she had molded and sculpted the chapters until they said the right things.

With all the unbelievable effort story writing was to them, Tom marveled to himself how they could be this close to being finished with a first novel. He didn't really know much about writing a novel—he had never tried anything remotely like it before. And there had been the winter months when the money in their bank account seemed to be dwindling with astonishing and fearful rapidity, and he had been tempted to go back to engineering for money. But the resumes he sent out had brought no responses.

The newspapers waxed at regular intervals about the nation-wide shortages of engineers, as always. But Tom continually observed the scarcity of engineering want-ads in the *Los Angeles Times* and the total lack of replies to letters and resumes he had sent around the country in resonse to the few ads he ferreted out. *It's like engineers are growing on trees*, he had thought in his darker moments—and: *It's like the U.S. is a mecca for engineers from every Tom*

Dick, and Harry of a country throughout the world. Melissa had offered to look for a job, but Tom didn't let her. She was the critical mass in the writing team, changing the scrawled writings into the typed finished drafts. If the story was going to be told in a publishable form, she was the one who would make it saleable.

They had gotten into the habit of praying every morning and, during the depressing desert winter, they read the Bible every day. In small increments their faith in the God of the Bible seemed to grow stronger and, with that, their confidence in a novel that they could only see in their minds steadied and stayed with them, and those things sustained them.

From the nearest bedroom he could hear the smooth, rapid clatter of the keyboard Melissa was using to edit and store the story on magnetic disk. Outside he could see the waning rays of the sun reflecting with golden glintings off the rotating windmill that generated electrical power for the trailer. Rays of light slanted through the window and illuminated the wall to his left like yellow brass. A glass of leftover Vernor's ginger ale sat on the small breakfast table in the kitchen behind him, and the sun through the window made the liquid sparkle like molten topaz.

Tom's tired eyes seemed to peer mesmerized into the desert dusk for a minute or two, then they squinted and looked down as the next few sentences for the novel did their dance and flowed through his mind. He flipped a page in the notebook quickly, making a loud flapping sound, bent down and began writing quickly: " 'The unidentified flying objects don't come from outer space,' said the colonel.

" 'Where then?' the other man asked.

" 'I'm afraid what controls the UFO manifestations is a race of beings hostile to man since the dark, dim past of this fallen planet,' said the colonel. 'And these other intelligences are out to deceive and eventually destroy all of mankind.'

" 'What intelligences?' asked the other man.

" 'It is none other than the fallen angels who rebelled against the God of the scriptures under the high command of Lucifer. And they're coming upon the earth now to deceive man and capture every human soul they can before the return of Christ. There's no absolute proof of this, of course, maybe there can never be proof—but there's a high probability.'

" 'The scriptures say a big lie would be perpetrated on the world in the last days,' said the girl. 'Matthew, that's where I think it talks about it. And it says the lie will be so believable that even the elect would be fooled if it were possible!'

" 'I think the big lie and the UFO extraterrestrials are one and the same, Angela,' said the colonel."

Melissa walked into the room while Tom was busy writing. "How's it coming, honey?" she asked him.

"It's just flowing," said Tom, smiling as he spoke. "I can't write it down fast enough. It's amazing!"

Melissa put a stack of freshly typed pages down in one of the few uncluttered spots on the desk. "Here's the short story," she said as he stretched his writing hand down toward the floor, almost writing on it with the tip of the pen. Then he scooted his chair out from the desk. "I put in all the final corrections," continued Melissa. "There shouldn't be any mistakes, but look it over."

Tom dropped his pen on the open notebook with a small thud. He patted his right knee as he looked up at her, and Melissa sat down on his legs. He gave her a kiss on the mouth.

"I love you, Tommy," she said to him.

"Me, too, Lissa," he said, examining the rare beauty of her face for a moment. Her eyes looked into his and shifted with a fresh happy look as she took in his face. They kissed again for a long time.

"You hungry?" asked Melissa after a moment.

"I'm starved!" he answered. "Where's the boy?"

"I thought he was in here with you," she said. She turned away from Tom, shielded her mouth with her right hand as if she were going to call out over a great distance, and yelled into the room she had just left, "Shadrach! Come on, boy, get in here!"

A Cairn terrier popped out of the doorway to the spare bedroom and trotted toward Melissa's voice. He had a heavy mottled coat of hair with brindle, brown, and black in it, and as he came into the kitchen, wagging his tail, the sun caught the darker whiskers that surrounded his mouth and they lit up a translucent red. The dog paused for an instant by the kitchen table to scoop up a bow tie-shaped piece of whitened rawhide and brought that over to the two of them at the desk. Tom reached down and patted him on the head. The dog backed away and growled, then shook the big rawhide toy violently from side to side until it flew out of his mouth, careened through the air, and slammed into the refrigerator. Melissa and Tom both laughed at that and she gave Tom a hug and kissed him.

"He's hinting at dinner," Tom said to Melissa, nodding toward the dog, who had pounced on the rawhide at the foot of the refrigerator.

"I can take a hint," said Melissa, rising from Tom's lap. "How 'bout chicken and rice with lima beans for the vegetable?"

"Sounds good," said Tom.

"I was asking Shadrach," joked Melissa. "Are you hungry too?"

Tom patted Melissa's back side as she stood there against his kneecaps with a smirk on her face. She smiled and walked on into the kitchen. He picked up the pages she had put on the desk and began to read them for the sixth or seventh time, it seemed. They had written it as a brief symbolic version of what the longer novel would be, and even though he had read it time after time, it always gave him pleasure to see the latest transformation from the roughly whittled sentences into a carved figure. *Melissa's better than Willa Cather*, he thought, beaming deep down inside. With his photographic recall of people and places and her way with words, they had a pretty potent literary team, he reflected. *Cather and Kodak*, he thought, and laughed out loud.

As he began to read this eighth version of a short, simple story, with its cold black type on the fine bond paper, a hope glimmered within him that their mission was a little closer to the fruit-bearing stage. And, if there were no more mistakes in this copy, he would drive to the Lancaster post office in the morning, make two Xerox copies, and send the original off to a science-fiction magazine in a 9-by-12 envelope with a self-addressed, postage-laden envelope inside, in case the editor wanted to send it back. And maybe he would even remember to pray before he dropped it in the slot.

34

The Men in Black

Two hours after supper, outside the trailer in the cool May darkness, three lights appeared above the distant horizon. The lights instantly began bobbing and swerving in the distance, changing from an in-line formation to a roughly triangular alignment that varied as one light would shoot away for a time, then return, and then another color would break formation to move away. The brightest of the lights was scarlet red, the second light was yellow, and the third was Kelly green. The trio looked in an odd way like traffic lights, somehow detached from their normal alignment and playing games in the sky.

Soon after the strange lights had appeared the Cairn terrier darted toward the screen door, pulling up short with his head and shoulders angled forward, letting out a flurry of barks. Tom Kruger dropped his notebook and pen and raised up out of the desk chair; his legs felt stiff and sore from a 12-hour day of writing on the final chapters of the science fiction novel. He snatched a searchlight from the bookcase, opened the screen door, and stepped out on the porch, the dog tagging behind.

"Whatdya see, Shad," he said to the dog who ignored him and continued barking fiercely, hanging his head and shoulders over the edge of the steps. Tom flicked on the light, then swung the beam slowly in an arc, covering the ground around the trailer. As he wheeled right he spotted the formation of lights cavorting in the southern sky. He flicked off the lantern a moment and peered in the darkness at the lights. Then for some reason he didn't understand he turned on the lantern and pointed it at the distant nocturnal lights.

As if by command the green globe of light instantaneously broke formation and darted out of the night at him. The dog snarled and backed up toward the door, then whirled until his nose touched the screen.

"It's just a light, Shad," said Tom, staring at the expanding UFO. The dog let out a whine and started clawing at the screen with one paw "Shad, quit that!" hollered Tom, who reached to open the screen and let the dog through.

He edged down the steps, watching the green orb accelerate like a fast jet, then pass directly over him just as he reached the ground, and it was so close he could feel heat coming from it. As the phenomenon went over he saw the light was attached to the front of a delta-wing structure and it was making a humming sound like a quiet refrigerator makes.

In seconds the strange object reversed course and then glided back over the trailer a few thousand feet further up in the air this time, until it swiftly gathered speed and rendezvoused with the other lights in the distance. There had been six or eight faint pinkish lights spaced along the trailing edge of the UFO and as it passed, he saw them dimly reflect off the surface, which had resembled blackish foam rubber, pitted and pocked. Another of the lights flew over a little higher this time, and a chill shot up his spine, making him say a prayer to the good Lord, his lips moving silently, and in a moment the apprehension he had felt vented from his mind.

Just as he thought about calling Melissa the three lights shot up in the sky until they were pin-head sized, then they were lost in the blackness between the stars in the upper reaches of the bowl of night. Tom stared absentmindedly at the spot in the darkness where they had vanished while the spring breeze hummed across the barren land. He broke the spell by checking familiar constellations, then climbed the steps and tramped back into the trailer. It had been a different type of UFO, he thought, as he felt his heart still beating a little faster. A *snare and delusion of Satan*, he thought in his mind as he made his way toward the steady clatter of the computer keyboard in the other room. *The whole display was a customized vision, intensely lighted, signifying nothing*, he assured himself. The UFO had presented all the appearance of a real physical craft but, for a moment in his mind, Tom debated with himself whether that was even true.

He went in the small bedroom and looked over Melissa's shoulder at the line on the black screen being filled with glowing yellow letters, then leaned to kiss her on the cheek. "You gonna quit soon?" he asked her.

She stopped her typing and arched her head back as he kissed her. "Yeah," she answered him. "I think I'll quit after a couple more pages. And after you sell this novel let's get a new desk and chair—my back's killing me."

"You got it, kiddo," he said. "Want some coffee?"

"No, hon, it'll just keep me up," she answered.

"Okay, I'm goin' to fix me some," he said, patting her on the shoulder.

"Did you see who's under the table here?" Melissa asked Tom. He angled his head to look and there the dog was, lying contentedly, licking the pad on his right paw.

"What'd you do to him out there?" asked Melissa.

"We saw a UFO," said Tom.

"You're fooling around with me now," she said.

"Nope, it was shaped like a bat—flew right over my head. Shadrach did his duty and tried to rip his way back through the screen door."

"And you just let me type away in here and miss all the action?" complained Melissa. There was classical music playing on the mini-disc player in the room, and Tom upped the volume on his voice a little to talk over a sudden surge in the loudness of the music.

"It's a wonder you can hear anything with this music going!"

"Isn't it marvy—this part is one of my favorites," said Melissa, waving her hands in precise, rhythmical motions as if she were directing an orchestra.

"What's the name of it?" asked Tom.

"Mahler's *Symphony Number One*," she replied.

"Not bad," he nodded, and stretched his lips in a smile.

"I love it," she said.

"Well, anyway, next time if the UFO lands or something, I'll bring the occupants straight in to see you," he said, and laughed as he left the room. In the kitchen he made a cup of instant coffee and sat down with it at the desk. He had just begun to work on the next to the last chapter when he heard a car coming slowly down the gravel driveway. After the sound of gravel stopped he heard car doors open and close and so he got up and went to the door.

Tom turned on the trailer's porch light and through the metal mesh he saw two men approach—a gray Lincoln was parked on the patch of white gravel behind them. The men had on dark suits and, in the car, he could see another man waited behind the wheel. The men who came toward him both had odd faces with peculiar, light hazel, oriental-looking eyes. One man looked to be barely five feet tall, and his height contrasted sharply with the second man's, who looked to be over six and a half feet tall. Tom swung open the screen door, went out on the porch, and pulled the main metal door closed behind him before he let the screen door close.

He came down the steps and the two men pulled up. "Hello," said Tom cautiously.

"Mr. Kruger, I presume," said the shorter of the two men, who looked like he was a brother to the other man.

"Yes." Tom gazed into the first man's fish-on-ice eyes. There was no emotion he could detect—only the dull gaze some animal eyes have.

"We understand you're a writer," said the thin, short man, arching his neck back a little arrogantly, showing odd wrinkles that seemed to encircle the man's neck.

"I'm going to have to ask for some identification," said Tom, "and I'd also like to know what you want."

The short man flashed a blue-gray plastic card at Tom quickly, as if it were a rare piece of literature that might be degraded by the presence of air. "I'm afraid I'm goin' to have to see that ID a little closer." A little smirk showed at both men's mouths as they ignored what Tom had said.

"Kruger, we wish to put your writing talents under exclusive contract with our organization," said the man unexpectedly.

"And just what organization is that?" asked Tom, flushing a little with sudden inexplicable warmth. "And besides—what do you know about my writing?"

The taller of the men pulled a packet of paper out of the inside of his coat. It was bent in half long ways, and he unfolded it and then held it up to Tom's face. Even at a distance in the dim porch light, Tom recognized it as a copy of the short story that two New York magazines had already rejected—the one he had called *The Theory*.

"How did you . . . ?" began Tom, his eyebrows lowered in disbelief.

"We have friends in high places," the short man said in a mysterious tone of voice. It sounded to Tom like the man had a foreign accent, but he couldn't quite place it.

"Well, whoever the hell you represent, tell them that whatever I write will be published through normal channels, the good Lord willing," said Tom sharply. "I don't intend to write limited editions!"

"You have more of these science *fictions* in the works, I take it?" The arrogant stranger rattled off the words with an odd inflection.

"That's confidential information!" hissed Tom curtly. He glared at the shorter man.

The tallest of the men pulled out another set of typewritten papers and handed it to the shorter man, who passed them in turn to Tom. He had never seen anything surprise him more than what they had given him. The stranger had handed him the first several chapters from his novel. Tom's face turned crimson with anger. He felt like he had been violated by something cruel and demented. "Where the hell did you get this?"

"Look, Kruger, we are not sentimentalists like you are, eh?" said the short, ugly man. He had a twisted, cruel mouth and it seemed to make his words come out cruelly. "The terrible shame is that the things you believe are incredibly stupid. This moronic junk will never be published—don't you even know that much?"

"We'll see about that," was all that Tom answered.

"With three hundred thousand you could reap a great deal of enjoyment," said the short man.

"If you're talking money, I'm not interested," said Tom. "It's only engraved paper."

"You don't understand," said the short man. "This type of writing can produce unpleasant occurrences for a multitude—it's this fiction of yours that torments people. I don't know why you have to lie like that." The tall man narrowed his glittering liquid eyes and glared at Tom.

"I think you're the liar," said Tom. As soon as he said it the tall man flipped the story pages on the ground and, simultaneous with that, the trailer door opened. Tom wheeled in time to see Melissa stick her head out. Shadrach began barking at the top of his lungs.

"Stay in there!" ordered Tom sharply. He held his hand up and waved her back. "Close the door and keep the dog in there—these people are just leaving."

"What do they want?" Melissa asked anyway.

"They're sellin' stuff—close the door!" shouted Tom. Melissa peered through the narrowing crack as she pulled it closed. Tom turned back toward the strangers. The tall man had a small device shaped like a five-cell flashlight with a conical head, and he was pointing it down at the pages, working a trigger. A stream of fire shot out of the tube and set the papers afire, and they blazed up for a moment, then were gone, the breeze floating black ash into the air.

"I suggest you people leave," said Tom angrily as the tall man withdrew the device.

"Are your other stories as filthy as that one?" asked the short man, looking down at the remaining ashes on the gravel, then looking back up at Tom with hard eyes.

"That's none of your business," said Tom. "I'm goin' in now. My writing's my business—you got that! Next story you see you'll have to pay retail." Tom's voice had come out like a roar. The veins in his neck stood out like thick lengths of spaghetti.

"If you continue writing lies, grave and unforeseen coincidences could befall your wife and even you, eh?" the tall, ugly man said. "There might be some misfortune in your future, eh?"

"If that's a threat let me just tell you that He who's in me is greater than he who's in the world," said Tom. "Now get off this property—I'm goin' in and call the cops right now!"

"God is a figment of your mind—you'll know that very soon, I'm sure, eh?" said the short man, sibilantly. The strangers stood there a moment, in awkward, aggressive poses, staring at him as he turned and climbed the stairs. He was reciting part of the 96th Psalm in a low voice as he went in through the door. "Heavenly father, thank you for giving your angels charge over us to keep us in all thy ways. A thousand shall fall at our left and ten thousand at our right but it shall not come nigh me." Melissa grabbed his hand tightly as he came through the door. They looked down at the two men who had turned and were walking back to the Lincoln, moving with an arrogant and methodical gait, and when they reached the car they split up and opened the rear doors on opposite sides of the car. They slid in, the engine started and the car was moving even as the doors were closing.

"Who were they?" asked Melissa.

"Some weird turkeys from parts unknown," he answered. "They're gone now."

"They sounded pretty hostile," said Melissa. "You know, to be 40 miles from nowhere, this place is getting pretty popular."

"A regular beehive of activity."

"Do you think they'll be back?" asked Melissa.

"I don't know," he said. "I think we need to pray and I'm not sure 'Now I lay me down to sleep . . . is gonna do it tonight."

"What's the matter?" asked Tom the next morning at breakfast.

She intensified the strange look she had given him. "You believe in angels?" she said casually.

"Well sure."

"I mean—really believe, deep down and all."

"I think I'm among the top angel believers—I'm real big on 'em."

"I'm glad, because one came to me last night in my sleep," said Melissa. On the plates in front of them lay brown-gold pieces of fried chicken, and Melissa had made biscuits from scratch and, with the biscuits, they had wild desert flower honey a neighbor had given them.

"Normally we humans know those as dreams. So, was it in living color?" said Tom between biscuits. The honey had a beautiful, dark amber color, and it tasted clean and sharp and sweet.

"An angel spoke to me last night, Tommy," said Melissa solemnly. "And I don't think it was a dream: it wasn't like any dream I've ever had before."

"The last time this happened there was a star in the east." He tried to make a joke.

"Tommy, the angel told me that we had to leave this place and go to my uncle's," she said with a seriousness in her voice he hadn't heard before.

"Why?" questioned Tom, buttering another biscuit. "I've got to reread the whole first draft—add some stuff, make some changes here and there. It should only take a few weeks. Then we can visit your uncle."

"Honey, you don't understand," said Melissa. "The angel instructed me to get us out this morning and not come back!"

Tom put the honeyed, buttered biscuit back on his plate and stuck his right thumb nail in a crevice between his lower front teeth. "Let me get this straight, Lissa," he said. "The angel in the dream said to abandon our abode here and leave all our stuff?"

"He really did," she said. "He was real as you sitting there, I swear—he was a big guy, you know, in white and all, and he said take the computer and your writings and one suitcase."

Tom squinted one eye down as he examined her face across the narrow expanse of gray and white patterned formica, and then took his hand from his mouth and gestured his palm, face-up, toward her. "So the angel's saying pack light like we're going to Europe or something."

"This isn't funny," she said quickly in a uncharacteristically high voice.

"Okay. Okay," he said. "Besides bein' big, what did this angel look like."

"Handsome—and he had the standard wings—he looked like angels look."

"Big?"

"Really huge, like a pro basketball center, only bigger—clothed in a white shiny robe," said Melissa. A trace of frustration at his disbelief had entered her voice. "I swear he was real, Tommy. He was realer than us sitting here now."

"Okay—let me ask you this: did he say why we have to leave?"

"Something's going to happen; he wouldn't tell me what," she answered.

Tom had started in on another biscuit and was rushing the eating of it. He started up talking again while he was still trying to swallow a big chunk. "You mean something's going to happen in addition to all the stuff that's been happening around here?"

"Yes!" said Melissa, her eyes shining. He examined the expression in her eyes carefully, as if to make one last search for signs of incipient insanity or brain damage. But her eyes were clear and bright, and she was behind them and they never could have been duplicated.

"Well," said Tom. "I'd sure like to pray on this one." With that he got up and walked around the small table, leaned over, and gave her a kiss on her neck below one ear. "You're sure it was an angel?" He reached down and took half a buttered biscuit off her plate and ate it.

"I know that I know he was real," she answered.

"Okay, okay, what can I say," he said. "I'm gonna need a sign—I mean this is hard to . . ."

They kneeled together on the kitchen linoleum and he began, "Heavenly father, we come to you in the name of Jesus," began Tom. "Give us wisdom, Lord, to know what to do—give us a confirming sign. Melissa's a good kid, but I'm havin' trouble believing it wasn't a dream. Show us the way. Amen."

"Amen," said Melissa.

Tom went to the coffee table and opened the scriptures to a random page that turned out to be Luke, Chapter 17, and the first verse he read was Number 29: " 'But the same day that Lot went out of Sodom it rained fire and brimstone from heaven, and destroyed them all,' " read Melissa from the book. " 'Even thus shall it be in the day when the Son of man is revealed. In that day, he which shall be upon the housetop, and his stuff in the house, let him not come down to take it away: and he that is in the field, let him likewise not return back. Remember Lot's wife. Whosoever shall seek to save his life shall lose it; and whosoever shall lose his life shall preserve it.' " Tom stared at the page.

"I'd say that means to go," he said after a moment.

"I'll call Uncle Jim," said Melissa. Tom nodded. She stepped to the phone and worked the sequence of buttons. Tom went into the other room to start packing.

"What'd he say?" asked Tom when he came back in the room.

"He said don't waste any time," she said.

"What—did he see the angel too?"

"Oh, Tommy, let's hurry," she cried, almost in tears now.

Tom looked at her and smiled. "Don't get melancholy on me," he said softly. He walked to the big bay window and looked out. "Come over here!" he shouted. Melissa came over and saw he was pointing out the window at a snow white turtle dove sitting on the clothesline. "Is that a California-type gull?" Tom asked her.

"No," she said. "We had them in Santa Barbara. Gull's legs are long with webbed feet on the end."

"Is it a pigeon?" he asked.

"No," she said slowly, as she squinted her eyes against the sun to see better. The bird looked to be perfectly white with black, obsidian eyes and a small black bill. It was turned toward the bay window, looking straight at Tom and Melissa, and it made a soft, rolling sound that came through the window. "Coo—curroo." The bird repeated the call over and over as they stood listening. Suddenly the bird flew up and pecked at the window while they stood motionless, astonished at what they were seeing. Then the dove flew off. Tom looked over at Melissa. "I got the computer ready to go. Let me eat two more biscuits and another pound of honey, then let's blow this joint!" And there was a peace in the room it seemed they could almost touch.

"I'll start packing the big suitcase," she said, turning quickly toward the other end of the trailer.

"That's the fastest I've seen you move since the day you dragged me down to look at wedding rings," he called after her scurrying, pretty form.

They pulled away from the trailer 20 minutes later. It was already hot in the desert, and the wind was blowing in spurts and kicking up dust. "I've never seen an all white dove in the desert before," he said. "Have you?"

"That had to be the confirming sign of what the angel told me," said Melissa. "And the Bible verse." Tom nodded as he eased the Oldsmobile's accelerator pedal down until the speedometer climbed to the orange 60 mark. Melissa sat close beside him and next to her the dog stood, lurching from the acceleration.

"I love you," she said to him.

"Me too you," he said back to her. She leaned over and kissed his cheek, and Shadrach put his paws on the dashboard and looked out the windshield at the road moving toward them, his tongue rippling in the hot air.

35

California Exodus

The three helicopters streamed out of the north an hour before the sun had completed its ascent of the eastern sky. Below and ahead of them, the white trailer glistened brightly in the sunlight. The three aerial machines had small bulbous noses in front, the round darkness of spinning rotors on top, and long tapering tails. They were soot black in color with gray-tinted glass windshields, which obscured the interiors, and they looked almost like huge multieyed insects, dangling strange, skidlike legs as they flew.

The center helicopter broke formation as they neared the Krugers' trailer, and swooped down at it in an arc. The drone of the lone copter's engine seemed to intensify, and the rotor blade popped and beat at the air as it dived. The helicopter's body appeared to be made of dark neoprene rubber and, as it flashed down toward the ground, no sunlight reflected off the craft. Its blackness contrasted starkly against the bright blue sky. Flames shot out the back of tubes on both sides of the helicopter's midsection and out of the front of the tubes a salvo of missiles, like aerial torpedoes, leaped forth in split-second succession.

The rockets swished down like comets, tails fiery, curving toward the ground, leaving plumes of gray smoke until they detonated against the trailer. A huge ball of fire and a reverberating boom burst out of the ground where the trailer had stood. There was smoke and forks of flame shooting out of the trailer's disintegrating form, and pieces of the trailer spun outward in all directions, littering the air with shredded debris.

The second helicopter had followed the first one in, and it launched a second salvo of missiles that impacted what remained of the trailer and exploded with air-splitting sound, smaller fireballs blooming and whirling around the main fireball. Even after the last of the structure had exploded with great fury, noise seemed to hover in the air for an instant and then died out across the barren land.

A great billowing column of expanding black and red fire ascended as the helicopters that had unleashed the exploding missiles climbed quickly to rejoin the other aircraft. The formation, once joined, made a banking arc in the air as it circled and turned northward. The V formation passed over the black smoke and small orange fires, then gathered speed and was lost to view. All that remained to show they had been there was the isolated patch of flaming ruins beside the gravel driveway, faintly crackling in the noonday sun.

"Come on in—rest your bones and have a spot of tea," said the colonel, ushering the Krugers into the red-tiled hallway, then kissing Melissa on the cheek.

Tom held the Cairn terrier on a leash and pulled him close when he looked like he was sniffing out a place to lift his leg. "Don't mind if we do, Jim," said Tom a little sheepishly.

"Wonderful," said the colonel cheerfully. "Now I want you both to tell me everything that's happened in the last few days."

"Do you mind putting us up for a couple of nights?" Melissa asked her uncle. "We're going to sell the trailer, I guess."

"Lissy, don't even ask," instructed the colonel. "Do you realize how much room I've got in this house? It seems pretty darn large—ever since Margie passed away."

"Well, we just probably need to stay a couple of days," said Tom.

"Fine, stay as long as you like, Tom," replied the colonel. "How about some lunch?"

The young couple smiled and nodded. Melissa put her left arm around Tom's waist and he slid his right arm over her shoulder as they followed the colonel into the kitchen. The smell of soup was in the air, and Tom could see a medium-sized steel pot steaming through the lid on the Jenn-Aire cooking stove in the center of the room.

They dined on tuna fish sandwiches Melissa had made and the lentil soup from the pot, and in the background there was a radio on, with slow music playing. Like a jolt from nowhere, the news of the destroyed trailer came on the 1:55 afternoon news broadcast. After they heard it the three of them sat there stunned for a moment, and tears welled up and came out of Melissa's eyes.

"They won't give up," said the colonel finally. "They probably had a monitoring device on your phone, and if they did they know where you are now."

"I shouldn't have called this morning," lamented Melissa.

"That's okay, Lissy," consoled the colonel. "I've still got a few aces up my sleeve."

"What's the next move?" questioned Tom.

"Well, assuming they didn't monitor Lissy's call this morning when the operatives find out they didn't get you they'll still make the connection with me and they'll show up here." The colonel lifted his cup and sipped the rose hips tea. The shiny white surface of the cup had large red letters on one side that read: AIM HIGH. The tea was red, a little lighter than the letters on the cup, and had a citrus smell that seemed to waft up out of the cup with the white vapor Tom could see drifting above the rim. The colonel rotated the cup in the palm of his hands as if warming them, and then sipped again at the edge of the cup. The other side of the cup had the silhouette of a blue jet plane on it, with words below: AIR FORCE—A GREAT WAY OF LIFE.

"I'm sorry for getting you in trouble," Tom told the colonel.

"It couldn't be helped," said the colonel. "The UFO disinformation campaign is apparently heating up—they must be worried. It's like sitting on a powder keg."

"How in the heck did they get hold of my writing?" asked Tom. "I only sent the short story to a couple of sci-fi mags—I sent several chapters of the novel to a literary agent in LA."

"The NSA has extensive contacts in all the major media—television, movies, newspapers, and book publishers," explained the colonel. "It was a longshot, but the wrong person must've seen your submittals. The contacts have standard procedures to be on the look out for certain key material—if the key stuff comes across their desk, they flag it and call a certain phone number. The NSA pays big money for information like that. It was my fault for not explaining things in more detail. But I honestly didn't anticipate they'd come down that hard that fast. They must be intensifying their efforts."

Tom nodded. "You still think we can get the novel published?" he asked the colonel.

"Yes, if you still want to chance it; but from this point you're going to have to move with extreme care," said the colonel

"You'll have to use a pseudonymn, of course. And I know a New York literary agent I think we can trust. Besides worrying about the novel, you'll have to establish another false identity merely to keep them from catching up with you. Work in the aerospace industry is definitely ruled out—they'd trace Tom or Melissa Kruger down as soon as you tried to activate your security clearance. So, you see, your old selves have to disappear from the face of the earth."

"And since we can't work in our field of endeavor, if we get to where we need some money, Tom's stories have to sell!" said Melissa.

"Unless you both want to work at the Burger Chef," said the colonel. "And I'm afraid that's out of the question simply because it's much more expensive to live under cover as compared to a normal existence. To protect your true identities you'll have to pay cash for everything—you'll have to avoid any background checks. And so will I."

"You think they'd bother you?" Tom asked the colonel.

"They will if they are allowed to," answered the colonel. "As you probably realize by now, they don't want the lid opened on this particular can of worms. Your writing is too close to the truth."

"Where do you think we ought to go?" Melissa asked the colonel. "I mean Australia or Brazil or someplace?"

"I don't think any of us should attempt to get out of the country—it's too risky now," reasoned the colonel. "We'll need to keep away from the west coast and from big cities—they're too controlled in this day and age. The best thing will be to live someplace outside a smaller city or town."

"What about driver's licenses and stuff like that?" questioned Tom.

"I'll get you all the false ID papers you need," the colonel assured them. "Throw whatever papers you have in your wallet away—it's no good, I'm afraid, except cash." He winked at Melissa, and the corners of his eyes crinkled down into long, happy lines. Melissa winked back at him and smiled. "Blasting your trailer was no accident!" continued the colonel. "If they ever track you down again they'll most likely do everything in their power to make certain they finish the job."

"They would have got us this time, but the Lord delivered us," said Melissa, and Tom nodded.

"I believe He did, Lissy," said the colonel. "But remember, just because we're Christians we don't have to check our brain at the door. Keep under cover. There have been people that knew too much about the UFOs before. One scientist several years back connected the demons of old and the UFOs of now and he began to get a little publicity.'' The colonel stopped talking abruptly and, lowering his gaze, he seemed to examine the pattern of the fake wood grain in the table for a moment.

"What happened?'' Tom asked him.

"Well, he had an unfortunate accident while he was on a trip with some government cronies,'' said the colonel. "He had to be dredged out of Kentucky Lake. While he was waterskiing he somehow got dumped in an isolated cove at the lake. There was a convenient nest of cottonmouth water moccasins right where the boat accidentally slowed down and dumped him. His body sustained over fifty bites. He died before the men in the boat got to him. It wasn't too long before his body was bloated like a balloon in Macy's Christmas parade.''

"That's non-habit-forming,'' said Tom.

"Intelligence people did that?'' questioned Melissa.

"I saw his file at headquarters—there were a lot of indications that it was a masterpiece of planning.''

Tom blinked his eyes a few times while thoughts coursed through his mind, framing the next question. "Jim—just for the sake of discussion, what if they *don't* come after us? What if they figure they've scared us out of this UFO thing by destroying the trailer?'' The dog drowned out the last part of what Tom had said with a bark as he stood by the bowl of tuna he was eating. He woofed down another bite, then lifted his broad-faced head and barked sharply again.

"Shadrach,'' said Tom automatically. "Hush up!''

The colonel got up from his chair, stepped over to a window on the left side of the room, and, as soon as he looked out he said in a controlled voice, "They're here already.'' Almost on top of that a beeping sound came out of the kitchen. "My driveway alarm,'' explained the colonel. Tom sprang out of his chair and ran to the window, the dog running with him, barking loudly, dancing and shifting on his paws, his nails clicking on the floor. There were beige automobiles coming up the driveway.

"Grab what you want to take and get the dog,'' shouted the colonel. "We better move it now!''

"I'll get the suitcase!" yelled Melissa. The colonel touched her on the arm.

"Lissy, let's get the hell out!" said the colonel. "You just get the dog. Tom, just take whatever you can bring in the kitchen in the next ten seconds!" Tom ran toward the guest bedroom, where they had put the scuffed, blue Samsonite suitcase. "Get your butt in gear; we've got less than thirty seconds. Let's go!" the colonel shouted after him.

Several seconds later Tom ran with the suitcase and the aluminum briefcase into the kitchen. At the door to the kitchen stairs the colonel had a brown suitcase in his hand and Melissa had Shadrach in her arms. The three of them raced down the wooden stairs, which groaned and squeaked under the weight of the hard, fast footsteps.

"Where the heck are we goin'?" Tom shouted down the stairs toward the descending colonel.

At the bottom of the stairs the colonel tossed an answer back over his shoulder as he dashed forward. "We've only got a few seconds—come as fast as you can!" The colonel crossed the length of the basement floor in a hurry and at the other end he halted at a darkened glass sliding door. He unlatched a small metal cover up on the wall, beside the glass door, and quickly flipped a bank of steel toggle switches that protruded from a recessed control panel. Lights illuminated on the other side of the glass door, and Tom could see a helicopter bathed in light, surrounded by a large hangarlike enclosure. Tom knew the glass door in front of them was a portal to the huge structure he had seen once, at the rear of the house.

Tom heard the doorbell upstairs ring through the basement floor, Shadrach barked, and Melissa grabbed his snout for a second and chastened him. "Shad—be quiet!" The colonel slid the door open; they followed him through the opening, and Tom could see the enclosure's ribbed metal roof already opening to the sky.

"A helicopter in your garage!" Tom shouted at the colonel, who opened the left-hand door for them to get in.

"Why not?" said the colonel as they stepped up into the big gray machine. The colonel scurried around the front of the machine and climbed into the right side of the cockpit. They fastened their safety harnesses and the colonel began hurriedly working controls on the panel in front of him.

"An old spy like me has to have a secret hobby," said the colonel as he started the engine. "It looks like it's going to save our hides on this particular occasion!"

"Where'd you get it?" said Tom loudly, over the noise of the engine.

"It's U.S. Marine war surplus—I picked it up through a buddy in the Pentagon!" The colonel's attention was fixed on the RPM gauge while he slowly rotated the throttle.

"Unbelievable!" shouted Tom over the loud, pistonlike whirling of the rotor. Tom was in the front left-hand seat, and Melissa was in back of them, struggling with the dog, who was trying to escape her grasp. Tom turned and shouted to her, "Some people have homemade wine in their basement, some have fallout shelters—your uncle had to have a helicopter!"

"Praise the Lord!" shouted Melissa as the colonel made a final scan of the instruments and rotated the throttle the final increment until the RPM was right. He worked the control stick to lift the helicopter off, and they flew up and out the front of the garage. The ground behind the house fell down away from them, and the craft picked up speed quickly as they skimmed over the line of trees that guarded the view of the lowlands that rimmed the coast. As they ascended they could see Santa Barbara, with its red roofs, lovely and serene, and beyond that, the dark blue of the Pacific.

The noise inside the helicopter was loud, and the colonel handed Tom a pair of earphones and when he put them on he heard an electronic version of the colonel's voice telling him to have Melissa grab headphones in the back and put them on. "We'll head toward Los Angeles and get lost in the ground clutter," said the colonel over the intercom after Melissa had the earphones in place. "Just in case they decide to vector in an intercept."

Tom looked at the colonel, who was grinning at him. "I'm sorry we got you in the middle of all this," Tom said to the colonel, forgetting the colonel couldn't hear him since he had the only microphone.

When the colonel saw Tom speaking he pointed to his left ear with one hand and shook his head negatively. Then he filled them in on the plans. "I've had a long-standing pact with a buddy in LA. He can fly us out. They'll be watching commercial transportation. You two want to know something?" And then, not waiting for an answer, "We left a lot behind. You won't be able to even get your money out of bank accounts—they'll put an immediate marker on the accounts. If you went in tomorrow to draw it all out you'd be told that they couldn't process it that day. They'd tell you their records were messed up and they'd ask you to come back, or they would offer to mail you a check if you would leave them your current address. Either way, the powers-that-be would be notified. After Margie went to be with the Lord I turned all my assets into gold, silver, and cash. There's enough there to give you a good start wherever you go."

As Tom gazed at the twinkling sea ahead of them he felt somehow like a surreal character in the dream of some giant being—fleeing on wings of steel from the cold, deadly terror that sought to overtake them.

36

When Strangers Last in the Barnyard Bloomed

The eighth month Kentucky night was filled with the sound of crickets rasping in hollow sounds across the fields that surrounded the house. Tom Kruger had become accustomed to working late into the evening on the screened porch that faced the barnyard and overlooked the panorama of bee pastures that sloped down beyond it. The porch was at the rear of a fine, well-built house that they had rented from a retired couple who had gone to live in a new condominium, some 20-odd miles away in Louisville. Melissa had shuffled and changed old sentences on a second-hand computer, and Tom had added thousands of new blue ballpoint words on the school-tablet pages by the light of a brass lamp that gave its light through a yellowed linen shade; and through the months they had polished the story as if it were a gemstone being rounded on one side and then the other until a symmetry came forth—until the pits were smoothed over.

As he thought pleasantly about the months spent in semi-seclusion the light from the lamp threw its familiar, dusky circle onto an old desk he used, beside a stuffed raccoon that perched, in perpetual vigilance, on a varnished tree limb. Tom and Melissa had struggled with the story, page after page, six days a week—revising, adding chapters until the whippoorwills would come out and sing their songs to the shining stars late at night.

Sometimes he would walk around the house after writing and look at the dark trees that ran up into the hills on one side of the house, or wander out by the barn and look at the way the unused pasture dropped away toward the pond. On serene summer nights the pond would lay like a darkened mirror, a stone's throw away among the tall growth that ran through the darkness to the edge of the Hosclaw Hills. On clear nights he would gaze up at the stars and planets and still be impressed by their splendid displays. There had been many nights when Melissa had already gone to sleep by the time Tom returned to the dimly lit bedroom, and Shadrach would be sleeping beside her on the bed, and Tom would have to escort the dog into the kitchen and coax him with a Milkbone into his own rumpled bedding.

In back of the house there was an oak tree of large diameter with huge triangular roots that radiated out from the base like miniature geological ridges. Tom had been attracted to it since the first day they moved there and, after many nights of noticing it while he wrote, the old tree got to be like a timeless and true friend. He had grown accustomed to quietly staring at the dark form of the tree whenever he hit a snag in the story, and sometimes he would come up to it and run his hand along the smooth, uneven bark. In the depths of those evenings it had seemed to take on a gnarled, mystical appearance, like that of magic trees in boyhood nursery rhymes. In those meditative moments, with the magical tree as a centerpiece, the whippoorwill night would fill him and recharge his mind, and the fresh air had been a tonic that would clarify what he was trying to say. And, after a while, the sentences he had been missing would begin to flow from the innermost part of his mind, and all he had had to do then was get back to his spot, beside the raccoon, and put them on paper.

But tonight the final draft of the novel was finished, and Melissa and Tom sat on the back porch steps talking quietly, the light that came from the screened-in porch reflecting in their eyes. At the moment Tom was sitting, silent, thinking the story they had just spent more than a year preparing wasn't really very good and would probably never be published. He had just finished reading the story front to back, and it was dull and corny now that he reflected on it with his mind. The words weren't right in a lot of spots and, of course, there was no easy way to fix it except throw it away and start on a complete rewrite.

"Can you believe we're finished?" said Melissa brightly.

"Well, we still have to touch it up here and there," said Tom. "You realize, we're not really writers. And, I tell you the truth—I don't think the story's too hot now that I think about it."

Melissa kissed him on the cheek. "I think the book's good," she assured him.

"Well, I guess we'll see how Masterson and Sweeney like the ending," said Tom, a trace of dejection in his voice.

"They'll like it," said Melissa brightly. "Besides, Uncle Jim probably wouldn't speak to John Sweeney again if he didn't sell it to some big publisher for us." Melissa laughed.

"We're pretty low on money—maybe I should get some permanent job someplace—you know," said Tom.

"The Lord will provide all our needs," said Melissa. Tom nodded.

Suddenly there was a swishing sound in the air, high, out beyond the barn to the east. They looked up and spotted a lighted object swooping down toward them at 45-degree angle from in back of the barn, which stood south of the house. The unknown light's descent was straight as a ruled line, coming in at the speed of a jet plane about to land, and a pencil-thin, luminous blue exhaust trailed behind it. The color of the UFO was scarlet, and it bathed the barn behind the house with a red light as it hesitated for a moment when it got within 100 yards of the ground, and then lowered behind the barn. They heard a sound when it went behind the barn like that of a big machine setting down on hard earth.

Shadrach barked at the UFO while it was in the air, and after it lowered behind the barn the dog leaped off the steps and charged toward it. "Come back here, noodle brain," screamed Melissa as she raised up off the step. The dog ignored her for a few stubborn seconds, then yelped a couple of times and bolted past her toward the screen door. The dog was whining pitifully by the time he reached the porch, and Tom let him in the door on his way in to get the flashlight. As soon as the dog cleared the door he fled for a spot underneath the tan wicker couch.

As Tom brought the black plastic flashlight down the steps he had a peculiar taste in his mouth, like the sensation one gets when a piece of aluminum foil touches a tooth filling. Melissa waited a few yards from the porch and started up with him as he came by.

"Why don't you stay back at the house, Lissa?" he told her.

"Not me, brother!" exclaimed Melissa. She hooked his left arm at the inside of the elbow and tagged along beside him. "I don't like to be alone when things we're writing about show up in our back yard."

It was a nearly starless night, and they crept slowly along the hard, shadowy ground with the small beam of light pointing the way. At first when they made their way around the edge of the barn they didn't see anything. As Tom swung the flashlight's beam along the long backside of the barn, starting close and then working it further out along the ground, the light picked up a dark, elliptical object resting just beyond the far side of the hayloft, where a grove of small apple trees began. The object was sitting on the small slope that led down from the barn. They could hear a faint noise coming from it like a muffled, secret hissing. He swung the light away from it for a instant, toward the foliage in the trees behind it, and the thing looked very black—darker than the shadows around it. Then he scanned back across it with the flashlight, and the light defined the shape of a football with sharply pointed ends.

Melissa and Tom stopped in their tracks, and he flashed the light along the upper surface of the object. There seemed to be a row of windows on the upper part that showed glasslike in the light and, surprised, Tom clicked off the flashlight. In the darkness now they could see a very dim, ghostly light flickering behind the windows—soft and milky white. The light seemed to throb with changing tints of bluish-green, like the movement of waves. The light from the windows wasn't strong enough to reflect onto the surface of the craft and illuminate the dark parts of the object. But as Tom's eyes began to adjust to the dim light he could see the bottom edge of the craft was illuminated with an extremely faint yellowish-orange phosphorescence, like someone had carefully painted the very edge with a dull phosphorescent paint.

"Let's go!" urged Melissa in a loud whisper. Just then a dark shapelessness seemed to move underneath the strange craft. All at once there seemed to be the semblance of eyes in the shadows.

"Wait, there's something happening below the thing," said Tom, switching the flashlight back on and pointing it underneath the object. The light met eight glassy eyes set in melonlike heads on top of four grotesque monsters. Melissa and Tom edged backward a couple of feet. The only sign of life on the creature's hideous faces was contained in the eyes, fixed on Tom and Melissa—dully glistening and moving in the flashlight beam like robotic sensors. The eyes were huge and dark, with no separate whites and pupils—almost like a transparent covering containing black liquid.

"If these turkeys ask for our story, tell 'em it's copyrighted." said Melissa in a low voice. As the last of her words came out a red glow suddenly radiated from the bottom of the craft and bathed the strange creatures with a ruddy light. The beings had thin, gray faces with pointed chins and thin slits where a mouth and nose should be. They began to walk toward the man and woman, and two of the creatures raised their arms toward the humans as they came on at them. It felt to Tom like death approaching, like it was all over.

"I don't think they care much about Library of Congress regulations." Tom threw the words over his right shoulder as he edged between her and the creatures.

"Jesus, help us," said Melissa in fast, sharply edged words as she took hold of the back of Tom's belt and began edging back.

"Thank you, Father, for giving your angels charge over us to keep us in all thy ways!" hollered Tom, glancing for a second up at the dark sky where no stars floated. A voice spoke suddenly in his mind, as if someone had installed an electronic speaker inside his head. "There's nothing up there but clouds, chump—why do you bother to call?" Then a thin beam of red light came out of a tube in the hand of the nearest creature, and struck Tom in the chest with a paralyzing electric jolt. The last thing he remembered was the intense numbing pain in his head, and then he lost consciousness. The horrible creatures moved like stalking beasts, with a gliding slowness, silent like dreams, toward Melissa, who was muttering prayers in a low voice.

At that same instant two giant men appeared out of thin air, near the barn, between Melissa and the grotesque beings. They had materalized from two tiny spiders of light that had woven expanding webs of luminosity in a coulomb of time until they stood facing the unknown horror, their backs to Melissa. She knew somehow, deep down inside, that the two were angels.

The four humanoids from the red-lighted craft continued forward stiffly in ominous silence toward the two angelic beings. As the two monsters in front pointed the ray tubes at the white-clad angels, one of the angels extended his hand toward the pot-bellied runts and rattled off a sequence of words in a strange language. Then the other angel raised his hands in the air as if he were a cowboy reaching for the sky, and he spoke words on top of those of the first angel. There was a streak of light like a tongue of fire that sprouted from the right palm of the tallest of the beings in white, and it spread into blazing branches and leaped for a micro-second across the short span of darkness, slicing through the creatures, erasing the hideous bodies, then erasing the UFO behind them in a silent flash. The four alien entities and the craft behind them had vanished—melting like vapors into the blackness of the night.

Tom regained consciousness just as the UFO and its creatures dematerialized, and he felt like something invisible flew by him in the dark. The two angels turned and stepped slowly toward where Melissa stood and silently observed Tom as he lifted himself off the ground. They were very tall, each appearing to be well over eight feet, almost nine. They had extremely broad shoulders, and their clothing was one piece, shining white, loose fitting, resembling clothing of ancient Israel. "What the heck happened?" Tom asked Melissa, his head still down. He hadn't yet noticed the two angelic beings who stood behind him, slightly to his left.

Melissa nodded past Tom, her eyes wide and smiling. "Tommy, I think you'd better take a look behind you," she said, extending her hand over his right shoulder.

Tom's head swiveled around to face where she pointed. The angels were only seven or eight feet away from him, and when he turned toward them the towering apparitions startled him like an electric bolt in his mind.

"Don't be afraid," said the tallest of the angels. The creature's voice was beautiful, very harmonious, almost songlike. Melissa started to kneel on the ground. "We thank you . . ." Melissa said to the angels.

"Don't do that," said the tallest angel. He motioned for her to stand up. "We're servants of God just as you are. Thank only the Father of lights—we deserve no special regard."

"Well, thanks for our Father of lights—something grotesque was happening," said Melissa.

"We can't remain with you for much of your time," said the shorter of the angels, smiling directly at Melissa. This one had a calm, peaceful voice, much deeper than the other's, and in the depths of the tone there seemed to be a great reservoir of strength. "We bring a message of good cheer. There are dark powers around you. But do not fear the Devil or his manifestations on the Earth. For even as the works of Satan increase in this final time before our Lord Jesus returns to earth, so the works of the children of God must increase. The gates of Hell shall not prevail against the children of the Father of lights. There is much to do before the final hour—and men's souls are in the balance between eternal life and destruction, between a Heavenly mansion and the fires of Hell.

"The Satanic battle of darkness and death against the children of light approaches its end," said the taller angel. "But do not fear—there is no power on earth or under the earth that can harm you while you are in Christ. Here is a message of truth: Just as demons of like personalities prefer to inhabit the same physical-locations on the earth, so the descriptions of the unknown aerial phenomena and their occupants change according to the locale and the nation where they are perceived. Landings such as the one you have just witnessed are the work of Satan and the demonic powers of this dark world. And the demons of this locality were responsible for what you saw tonight.

"After the war in the celestial realms, which ranged over the entire universe and enveloped what you know as other galaxies and the farthest shores in your heavens, Satan and the angels who fought against God were sent to a realm in the heavenlies that allows them access to earth. Dwellers on other worlds throughout the heavenlies were saved from further onslaughts by the dragon Satan and from influence by his wicked angels who had not kept their first estate. Judgment awaits them. What human philosophies have never seen is that the spiritual forces of evil in the heavenly realms, through their willful rebellion, have corrupted and brought death and decay to the earth as they have to other worlds of flesh and blood in the heavenlies. None of the universe was created that way.

"In the eons of time past the Father and Son had to deal with Satan, who had corrupted the heavenlies and earth. The Son was slain to purchase your liberty and that of many others. For the Father's loving kindness endures forever; he sees you through the blood of Christ and you are blessed. As in Romans 8:19, your present sufferings are nothing compared to the glory that will be revealed in you. Even the creation waits with eager longing for the sons of God to be revealed. All of this message should be discernable in the novel for the elect's sake."

The taller angel widened his mouth again as if to speak, but no sound came out. The shorter angel had opened his mouth in the meantime, and when he moved his lips he spoke. "There are also other Satanic forces from celestial spheres manifesting in your sky as strange sights in the last days before the Evil One is revealed—they are now being restrained from further interference with affairs in the earthly realm for a time, as that Man of Satan is also restrained until the Spirit of Christ is withdrawn."

"Verily, a great deception involving the UFOs will soon visit the Earth," continued the larger angel. "Satan and his allies will pose as physical beings who come from other star systems to deliver mankind and save the world. Using all counterfeit power and lying wonders, the Wicked One of Sin will deceive many. By these delusions that Man of Satan, that beast, will exalt himself and, at the appointed time, Satan will claim to be the God of the Universe."

"This is a personal message from the Most High," declared the shorter angel, his powerful face smiling and radiant with light. "What you have written will be accepted and published. Make the revisions that are needed to reveal what has been told to you this night and, with all diligence, make those changes needed by the publisher, except you must not remove the spiritual essence that lets Christ's light shine through, and do not add anything unclean to the story. Hold firm, and your story will be published in seven months, for the end of the age is at the door. The angels will make certain that you are given a sum of money in advance of publication sufficient to remove concerns you have had over what you shall eat and where you shall live, and the other things of your life. Do not go to the city for employment.

"Keep Proverbs 16:3 always in mind," said the other angel in a very soft voice. "You were walking in the light, but now you shall walk in a new and more powerful light, sayeth the Lord."

"We bid you everpresence," the angels said in harmonious, simultaneous voices that faded with the light of their presence like echoes into the air. The giant beings disappeared then as suddenly as they come. The darkness had swallowed them as suddenly as it had spewed them forth. Tom had glimpsed a bright streak of light in the corner of his left eye as they vanished—that was the only sign of their travel. After it was all over they both stared at the place where the two angels had been standing for the longest of moments and then they turned back on the path that led to the farmhouse.

"Thank you, Father," said Tom as they ambled up the narrow path. He found Melissa's hand and gave it a gentle squeeze. It was a miracle they had just seen, he thought. It was one of those things that happen from time to time in the battle between good and evil at the interface between this world and that bright and distant shore beyond this physical place. And some portion of humanity, small or large, has known about the interface and the other world throughout all the ages.

The entire event had been so bizarre that it already seemed like a dream recalled, but Tom would never forget the way their God had moved Heaven and Earth to protect them and relay a message of hope and truth from that normally invisible world of powerful beings. A kind of joy seemed to radiate from him, inside out, as he reflected on the startling incident, and he felt incredible peace come over him—the same kind he had felt the night he had been born again.

"As one of the top angel believers of all time, how 'bout them apples!" said Melissa in a smooth, soft voice. She looked at Tom and smiled.

"What a wonderful God we serve," said Tom without thinking.

As they walked past the corner of the barn the moon appeared through broken, variegated clouds on their right under the lowest limb on the big oak. A west wind had started to clear the sky, but the atmosphere in front of the moon still carried a thin layer of haze, and the milky light beamed through that, surrounding the moon with a rainbow ring, casting faint shadows of tree limbs on the ground, and the two of them walked through those gnarled, sinuous shadows and on, into the house.

37

Christmas

It was Christmas Eve, 2002. The yellow light inside the Medora Methodist Church gave it a warm, cozy pleasantness as crystalline, white-furred flakes of snow slanted down through the cold darkness outside the white window frames. Tom Kruger glanced out the frosty glass for a moment and watched the snow flurries swirl through the big outdoor floodlight's wide, slanting illumination. All the different snowflakes he had ever examined close up flashed through his mind for some strange reason just then—and he saw each of them take its turn in his mind, clear and detailed as he had seen them the first time.

As the internal images continued to dance in his mind he thought of the totality of the collection of snowflake patterns, beautiful and unique, as if they had been designed by a master artist, and no two of them had ever looked the same; taking all that into account made him feel small and respectful of the designer of both the internal sequencing patterns and the real, more distant snow swirling in the chill outside the windows. Melissa glanced over past him and smiled at the sight of the moving, glistening snow as they sang and harmonized their voices with those of the other people in the church. Melissa smiled at him as she sang and then turned back toward the front of the church, and her eyes looked sweet and beautiful, as if they were seeing deeply into a room of hidden treasures.

A peaceful, relaxed feeling came over Tom then, as he sang and let his eyes play over the front of the church, with its candlelit background of red poinsettias; his mind seemed to blend in with the golden light in front and the smell of hot wax and burning candles in the chapel, and there was a feeling of the room being very vast and old somehow. To the right of the pulpit there was a small stable, with statues of Mary and Joseph and the Christ Child on the floor. Around those figures there were bearded shepherds and wise men in fine ceramic clothes, and their animals gathered around them. Above the roof of the miniature stable, a 60-watt Star-of-Bethlehem brightly blazed, radiating its glow along five clear plastic points. The song ended, and the small choir opposite the nativity scene turned the pages on their sheets of music. A stout, bearded choir leader announced the next selection. "Please turn to hymn number sixty-five."

The congregation started the next song, and Melissa's eyes took on a bright, moist look; her face resembled a beautiful child's, as the words flowed from her lips:

"*Silent Night, holy night! All is calm, all is bright! Round yon virgin mother and child! Holy infant, so tender and mild. Sleep in heavenly p-eace, Sleep in heavenly peace.*

"*Silent night, holy night! Shepherds quake at the sight; Glories stream from heaven afar, Heav'nly host sing, Alleluia! Christ, the Savior, is bo-rn! Chr-ist the Savior, is born!*

"*Silent Night, holy night! Son of God, love's pure light. Radiant beams from your holy face, with the dawn of redeeming grace, Je-sus, Lord, at your bi-e-rth, Je-e-sus, Lord, at your birth.*"

After the service had ended they lowered their heads against the wind as they came down the steps from the church and then turning left away from the wind, they hurried quickly to the car. The white frame church and the white ground contrasted starkly against the close dark woods that encircled the church and slanted up the hill directly behind it. The snowfall was heavier by now, and Tom could smell the wet, crisp spruce and pine that loomed over them as they stumbled through the deep snow that spread its silence to soften their footsteps and dull the lively conversations and laughter that flowed out of the front door of the church as children dashed down the steps into the fresh snow, their eyes laughing and glistening in the floodlights that shone from the side of the church.

Tom drove to their farmhouse in the old car, slicing over the snowy road, skidding a little around the curves and on uphill runs, past the darkened woods on the sides of the road. As they made their way through the curves the snow flew at them from the starless black sky, glowing in the headlights like white velvet fireflies.

Once the car was stowed for the night in the old shed that served as a garage, and Melissa had struggled to unlock the door with a gloved hand, Tom made for the fireplace and started the log fire to add a radiant warmth to the rest of the long Christmas Eve. He turned on the string of miniature red lights that spiraled around the circumference of a thick-branched pine he had cut down and brought in from the woods. Then Melissa brought in the dinners of turkey and dressing from the kitchen, with their companions of vegetables and cooked cranberries, and set the plates on a low table so they could eat in front of the fire.

Tom turned on the television as she brought in the plates, and they first found out the president had been shot. A man had killed him while he walked through a kitchen at a hotel in Colorado. A foreign-looking man who couldn't speak English had thought the country better off without President McGuinness. There was no video tape on the killing, so NBC was running a picture of the assassin and the video tape of the president's speech, made to a woman's club before he had gone into the kitchen. O'Fallon had been sworn in as President. The President's death brought a great sadness to the Christmas Eve in that room, and so they turned off the TV and ate in quiet silence for a while.

There was a single Christmas package on the coffee table in front of the fire; they had saved it for when they finished dinner, and even in its cover of brown mailing paper it seemed to take away some of the loneliness in the room, just by sitting there. They talked for a moment after they had eaten, and they tried to relieve the loneliness by recalling past Christmases and the friends and family they had spent them with. That only made it worse since they knew they couldn't contact them or see them for a long while because of their undercover existence.

After they had worn out the stories they agreed to open the small, flat package that sat on the table in front of them. The package had a return address of: "C.C. Breyfogle, P.O. Box 977, Grand Rapids, Michigan," and they knew by the name it was from Melissa's uncle. Melissa went to the kitchen, fixed two eggnogs with floating, grated nutmeg, brought them in, and set them on the table in front of the red- and orange-tongued fire. Melissa tore off the brown wrapper and inside there was another red-and-green

Christmas wrapping over the package. "Uncle Jim used to give such nice presidents," she said in a rhapsodic voice as she admired the wrapping a moment. Tom sipped the egg nog. He could taste the nutmeg separately and smell the spice like aromatic perfume within the upper confines of his glass.

Melissa finally dug into the package carefully, trying to salvage the paper. Tom gave her an impatient look until she finally tore one end of the wrapping off. Inside there was an olive green book with gold and dark green decorations on its cover and down the slim spine. The title on the cover was *The First Christmas Tree*. Laid inside the front cover there was a note and a money order; she glanced at the amount on the money order, smiled sadly, then handed it with the book to Tom. With a brave voice, she proceeded to read the note aloud:

> Dear Melissa and Tom,
> All my love to you both during this Christmas season. I hope you get this in time for Christmas day. We had 31 inches of snow in Grand Rapids on the 10th of December—they call it "lake effect." Sure is a lot different than Santa Barbara.

Melissa's sad eyes looked inward as she seemed to recall something while she continued with the letter.

> I'm doin' fine otherwise. Working part-time at Kregel's Bookstore on Eastern Avenue in the used book department. All they sell are Christian books. I've always loved good books, so I feel right at home. I trust this Christmas finds you both well.
> I guess this 'change in lifestyle' is harder on you than me. By the way, Sweeney in New York said he definitely had a publisher lined up when the final draft of your novel is ready. We already have a set up (with Swiss bank accounts and all that) to keep your true identity and whereabouts a secret—although Sweeney realizes he's putting his agency and maybe even his neck on the line. If the book gets out, the inner layer of the government onion will try to get at you with renewed vigor, and they might just try to rough my New York friends up a bit to get past the

safeguards. It's a shame people don't even realize
that they're not really free anymore.

Anyway, I bought you a book from our stock at
the store. It's a nice first edition, published 1897,
written by a writer little known and long forgotten by
the 'contemporary world.' Consider it my Christmas
card to you. It's very important that you read pages
15-19 as soon as you get it. On those pages you'll find
what I would say to you if I could see you this
Christmas—only van Dyke says it better. Enclosed in
the front of the book is a money order—it's my
Christmas gift to you both. Hope to see you soon. Be
sure to write me at my new P.O. box—looks like I'll be
up here a while.

God bless you. Jim.

P.S.—After you've sampled van Dyke pages 15-19
I expect you both to attack the final draft of the book
with renewed vigor.

Melissa laid the note carefully on the table as if it were fragile
and precious, and picked up her neglected eggnog. While she
sipped at the glass of thick yellow liquid, Tom flipped to page 15 in
the book and began to read the first of the words off the fine,
decorated pages: " 'Then Winfried began to translate the parable
of the soldier into the realities of life.

" 'At every turn he knew how to flash a new light into the
picture out of his own experience. He spoke of the combat with
self, and of the wrestling with dark spirits in solitude. He spoke of
the demons that men had worshipped for centuries in the
wilderness, and whose malice they invoked against the stranger
who ventured into the gloomy forest. Gods, they called them, and
told strange tales of their dwelling among the impenetrable
branches of the oldest trees and in the caverns of the shaggy hills;
of their riding on the windhorses and hurling spears of lightning
against their foes. Gods they were not, but foul spirits of the air,
rulers of the darkness. Was there not glory and honor in fighting
with them, in daring their anger under the shield of faith, in putting
them to flight with the sword of truth? What better adventure
could a brave man ask than to go forth against them, and wrestle

with them, and conquer them?

" ' "Look you my friends," said Winfried, "how sweet and peaceful is this convent tonight, on the eve of the nativity of the Prince of Peace! It is a garden full of flowers in the heart of winter; a nest among the branches of a great tree shaken by the winds; a still haven on the edge of a tempestuous sea. And this is what religion means for those who are chosen and called to quietude and prayer and meditation.

" ' "But out yonder in this wide forest, who knows what storms are raving tonight in the hearts of men, though all the woods are still? Who knows what haunts of wrath and cruelty and fear are closed tonight against the advent of the Prince of Peace? And shall I tell you what religion means to those who are called and chosen to dare to fight, and to conquer the world of Christ? It means to launch out into the deep. It means to go against the strongholds of the adversary. It means to struggle to win an entrance for their Master everywhere. What helmet is strong enough for this strife save the helmet of salvation? What breastplate can guard a man against these fiery darts but the breastplate of righteousness? What shoes can stand the wear of these journeys but the preparation of the gospel of peace." ' "

" ' "Shoes?" ' he cried again, and laughed as if a sudden thought had struck him. He thrust out his foot, covered with a heavy cowhide boot, laced high on his leg with throngs of skin.

" ' "See here—how a fighting man of the cross is shod! I have seen the boots of the Bishop of Tours—white kid, broidered with silk; a day in the bogs would tear them to shreds. I have seen the sandals that the monks use on the highroads—yes, and worn them ten pairs of them have I worn out and thrown away in a single journey. Now I shoe my feet with the toughest hides, hard as iron no rock can cut them, no branches can tear them. Yet more than one pair of these have I outworn, and many more shall I outwear ere my journeys are ended. And I think, if God is gracious to me that I shall die wearing them. Better so than in a soft bed with silken coverings. The boots of a warrior, a hunter, a woods man—these are my preparation of the gospel of peace." '

" ' "Come, Gregor," ' he said, laying his brown hand on the youth's shoulder, " 'come, wear the forester's boots with me. This is the life to which we are called. Be strong in the Lord, a hunter of the demons, a subduer of the wilderness, a woodsman of the faith Come!" ' "

By the time Tom had finished Melissa was sobbing softly, tears streaming down her cheeks, reflecting the fire like silvery-orange Christmas-tree icicles. It was snowing harder by now, and the wind blew over the house and made a strange muffled sound ebb and flow from the fireplace, and the log fire danced.

38

The Storm

It was September, almost nine months later. The morning was cool
and treetops outside the farmhouse window shone with vivid
green in the yellow morning light. Occasionally the leaves would
flutter and rustle slightly as a breeze circulated among them and
the fresh clean air would come through the open window, bringing
the pleasant smell of the land into the room. The light dronings of
insects came from the line of trees behind the house, and there
were birds repeating their tender, melodious calls. There were
long shadows and the soft dew was still on the grass and a broad
patch of sunlight made some of the dew glow like tiny clear pearls.
Two squirrels with reddish-grey fur were chasing each other playfully in and out of rustling branches.

There was a shining, purplish-black bird, Tom and Melissa
could see, eating small red berries off one of the closer trees,
choosing very carefully, occasionally calling in a shrill, complex
warble. They had just finished a breakfast of fresh eggs from their
laying hens, whole wheat biscuits, and fried green and white
Mutsu apples. On the table beside Tom was one of the copies of
the second edition of their novel, which he was inscrib-
ing with a ball-point pen. As he was writing he thought about
the reviews he had seen, which had ripped into the book's
flaws and "sacharine style" like rats on a sweet, dead body. He
stopped writing for a few seconds and yawned loudly, stretching it
out, vibrating the air in the room with the sound.

"What was that?" exclaimed Melissa, pretending to be
startled.

"The cry of the wild seahorse," he said as he bent over the
front end paper and resumed the writing.

"You're silly," she informed him. "Seahorses are little tiny creatures.''

"They were a lot bigger in the old days," he told her.

Melissa shook her head. "Who's the famous author sending that one to?" she inquired.

"Your uncle," said Tom. "I think I'll just sign our pen name. He oughta love that."

"How about the other eleven copies?"

"I think I'll probably leave 'em on the shelf and stare at 'em awhile," he answered. "They look real nice, all stacked together."

"What did they say at the bookstore when you picked up all those copies?" said Melissa as she turned toward him. The apron she wore had SHEPARD OF THE HILLS in brown, glazed lettering across it.

"The special order clerk said it must be a good story," he said. "I said it wasn't bad and gave her a copy to keep for herself. She said she'd order some for general shelf stock. She was a nice kid." Melissa gave him an odd look, put the dry dish down, and wiped her hands on her apron as she walked up to him. He put the book with the shiny red and black dust jacket down and leaned back in his chair. She sat on his lap and gave him slap on the right arm. "Watch out," he warned. "That's my writing arm."

"How nice of a kid was she?" asked Melissa playfully.

"Oh, she was real young—just a child," he answered. Melissa hit him again.

"Not like your old wife, huh?"

"I love my old wife—I mean my spring chicken."

"I wonder why we haven't had any babies yet?" she asked seriously, out of thin air.

"We will—it just takes longer with some couples," he answered.

"You think we ought to go get checked by a doctor?"

"Do you?"

"No," she answered slowly, "if it's meant to be, I guess the Lord will bless us with one when the time's right," she said. He could see the down on her skin lit up from the morning light that came into the kitchen, and it made her face look very beautiful to him, and he kissed her gently on one side of her mouth where a rounded puff of her face protruded.

The sound of hard nails on linoleum interrupted the kiss. Shadrach had just cleaned up the chicken meat left over from the night before, and the dog swaggered, full-bellied, toward the kitchen table, licking his lips. He stood a moment looking up at his masters, then let out a deafening bark and sprang toward the living room, with a flurry of deep-throated barking as he scrambled to the front door, his legs darting out behind him as he ran. The next instant there was a knock at the living-room door. Melissa got up, stretching one side of her mouth with curiosity. Tom eased out of the chair and ambled through the dimmer living room to the front door. Melissa followed him, then bent down and scooped up the dog and, as he barked over her shoulder, took him into the kitchen.

A young steely-eyed man in a new tan uniform greeted Tom as he swung open the door. Parked in the driveway was a small gray van of a foreign make that had a logo on the side reading BULLITT COUNTY HEALTH DEPARTMENT. "Can I help you?" asked Tom.

"Possibly so," said the craggy-faced man. "We've had reports of a peculiar odor coming from this area."

Tom's eyebrows lifted. "Really? Well, I guess I don't know what that could be. We haven't noticed anything."

"Well, sir, we've gotten quite a few reports of something that stinks around here," said the uniformed man. Tom looked down and noticed the wide brown belt and, at the man's side, a revolver in a leather holster.

"What kind of odor?" questioned Tom.

"It's like there's something rotten around here—like rotten flesh." The man had an odd, penetrating light in his eyes, and it was uncomfortable for Tom to look at him for very long.

"I'm sorry, I don't think I can help you," said Tom.

"Do you and your wife both work?" asked the stranger. There was something Tom didn't like about the stranger's tone of voice.

"That's confidential information." The words blurted out of Tom's mouth almost automatically.

"I'm afraid we will have to take further steps to alleviate this problem of odor in your neighborhood," said the man in a strange, arrogant, civil-service voice. He seemed to glare at Tom for a second or two.

"Well, I'm sorry I don't know anything about an odor. I can't help you." Tom swung the door partially closed and cocked his head to keep the man in view. "Thanks anyway."

The man pursed up his lips, stared a moment, then turned and walked slowly away, casting examining looks on both sides of him as he returned to the health department van. Tom closed the door and watched the man's slow departure out the left front window through the transparent curtains.

"That was weird," Tom told Melissa in the kitchen.

"What?"

"This guy from the health department was out there saying people have reported some kind of odor in this area."

"An odor?"

"Like rotting flesh."

"That is weird," agreed Melissa.

A little later, after supper, Tom was sitting on the screened porch writing notes for his next book into a fresh, spiral-ringed notebook when he heard Melissa scream, "Tom." He sprang from the couch, scattering the notebook, and leaned into a run until he got to the kitchen. Melissa was sitting at the kitchen table holding a dish towel to her mouth.

"What's wrong?" Tom asked her.

She pulled the towel away, and he could see blood trickle out from under her upper lip. There was a partly eaten apple lying on the table, and the sight of a thick metal needle sticking out of the fruit's greenish-white flesh gave him a sick feeling.

Melissa grimaced, and little wrinkles formed above the bridge of her nose and at the corners of her eyes as he lifted and searched her upper lip until he found where the cut was.

"Is it bad?" she asked after he had let go of her lip.

"Not too bad," she replied. He led her into the bathroom, washed the wound, and dabbed iodine on it.

"Will it swell up, do you think?" she asked him as she gingerly dabbed at the lip with her forefinger.

"No, kiddo, I don't think so."

"I don't want to look like a Ubangi tribeswoman."

"Who would do something like this?"

"It's hard to know," said Melissa. "Jesus said that the love of many shall wax cold in the last days."

"It could be the pickers; it could be the shippers . . . or the people at the grocery," said Tom, angry at the thought.

"I feel sorry for them," said Melissa.

Tom nodded. "I guess you're right," he said without emotion. They went into the kitchen and took armfuls of fruit out of the refrigerator, and Tom took a butcher knife out of the drawer and cut open the apples one by one. When he found another needle embedded in the third apple he had tried he took all the fruit out of the refrigerator bin, dumped it in a black plastic bag, and carried it outside to the trash.

Melissa turned the television set on, and when Tom came back inside the weatherman was announcing that it had been a record year for tornados. "And unfortunately the conditions that cause these dangerous storms are again present in the Channel Three viewing area. We're hoping for some relief from this weather pattern soon," apologized the weatherman, "but, as for tonight, a tornado watch has been issued for practically all counties in Kentuckiana. As a matter of fact, tornado watches are in effect all over the midwest tonight. Considering the vicious storms we've encountered so far this year, be prepared to take cover in your basement or some other safe area."

"Do you think we oughta batten down the hatches?" Melissa asked Tom. He angled his head to one side and examined the sky outside the kitchen window.

"It's blowing around out there," he said. "The sky's kind of green."

The national news came on the television, and it had stories about the famine and diseases that were rampant around the world. There were stories about fighting, and a whole series of terrorist bombings in Europe, the Middle East, South America, and Africa. A scientist from Arizona gave a report on the unprecedented increase in sunspots; a telescopic photograph flicked on the screen that showed the surface of the sun, and it looked like a white pizza, half of it covered with fuzzy black mold. The scientist told the newsman that the heat the sun was putting out was still the same as before the mass of sunspots appeared, and he said there was nothing to worry about.

After the news ended they got out the black King James Bible, and Tom read aloud from that until the pouring onslaught of rain and the wind came. That night, as Melissa slept beside him in his red-and-black nightshirt, before he would awake the next morning to watch her as she slept—she would somehow look French to him in the early light—behind his closed eyelids, he dreamt they were resting by the sea: *The bubbling surf was sliding toward the shore silently. One bright point of beautiful light was suspended low and distant over the water. The sun was just edging above the end of the sea and the sky was tinged with red at the horizon. A short distance out from the line of sand, adjacent to the uncertain water, he could see a jagged rock that seemed to point a finger at the heavens. Around the rock a white bird was flying in intricate patterns, laughing noiselessly.*

39

The Briefing

The stars above, like cosmic sequins in an inky cloth sky, twinkled small and bright as the Earth plowed through space and the spin brought the Middle East toward another dawn. That tiny span of land on the worldscape known as Israel was barely halfway into the earth's moving shadow, but the underground military command center on the outskirts of Tel Aviv was already bristling with activity. The military cabinet was in session, and a table surrounded by people had already waited several minutes for the critical briefing by the commander of the Israeli Defense Force to begin. The main conference room was modern and austere—long and narrow with a low, well-lit ceiling. The walls of the room were made out of mortar and gray stone except at the end opposite the door, where there was a varnished red oak recess in the stone. From the pattern of natural grain that showed between the clutter of reports, briefing summaries, 8-by-10 aerial reconnaissance photographs, black ashtrays, leather briefcases, and half-empty styrofoam coffee cups, the table looked to be made of the same wood as the alcove at the end of the room.

The gray-haired Israeli commander entered from the single doorway that opened into the room and walked briskly to the far end. "Gentlemen, if I could have your attention," he said. Reports and photos went back on the table and, in a brief moment, the conversations ended and the eyes in the room fastened themselves onto the IDF commanding general. An Israeli soldier swung the conference room door closed from outside the room and the general extended a telescoped silver pointer and began the briefing. He was a handsome man with an angular, bony face, who looked like he was in his early fifties. He wore a tan uniform with large blue epaulets on the shoulders—the same as nine of the men who sat at the table before him. He had penetrating blue eyes with dark circles bold as greasepaint below them, and he stood calmly and very erect as he began the assessment by pointing with the silvery rod to the map on the wall.

"Gentlemen, as you are well aware, two IDF divisions are deployed in defensive posture on the Lebanon border and two face the Syrians on the Golan Heights. In the east we have three divisions. On the southern border we have three divisions positioned against the Egyptian buildup. At least three reserve divisions must be maintained in the event a breakthrough occurs.

"As outlined in previous briefings, approximately eighteen divisions of the Eastern Alliance have massed and deployed in forward positions to our north and east over the past week." The general swiveled the pointer toward red- and black-headed markers that clotted together outside the map's northern and eastern borders.

"In addition, approximately twenty-seven Iran-based Soviet divisions have been placed on active alert in the past forty-eight hours. American intelligence has informed us that the Soviets have launched two new reconnaissance satellites that will provide maximum coverage of the Middle East.

"Within the past few hours the Soviets have begun to move their entire middle-east force toward our northern and eastern perimeters in conjunction with eleven Arab divisions from the Eastern Alliance. From all the evidence at our disposal it appears that a massive combined Arab-Soviet ground offensive is in progress toward our eastern front with the probable eastern objectives of the high ground in Samaria, aiming for Jerusalem, with a simultaneous probe in the direction of Afula." The eyes in the room seemed to meet what he was saying with a haggard, almost casual resignation.

The gaunt officer swung the pointer up to north on the map. "Based on our radar bluffing systems and the pictures from the television drones, we anticipate extremely heavy, simultaneous attacks against the Northern objective of the Golan Heights with a probe from the Beka's Valley in Lebanon."

The general had an accent that made him sound almost German, and as he began again, his precise voice seemed to energize with a higher level of urgency. "With the size of the opposing forces, IDF HQ estimates that fighting a defensive containment war and then assembling reserve forces on the northern and eastern fronts would not be enough to counter the massive enemy forces involved, even without Egyptian involvement to the south.

"This takes into consideration our line of nuclear artillery units on the northern flank. The Soviets are well equipped with anti-radiation gear and the combined limits of size and number of the nuclear field shells we possess constrain the amount of damage we can inflict on the massive armies that we face, particularly on the northern flank. Our current estimates of the situation is that their second wave would have a good chance of getting through. Our chief military option at this point, discounting American involvement, would be to interdict the two main elements of Soviet and Arab forces while they are still well within Arab territory."

"How would you propose we do this, General?" asked the Israeli Minister of Defense, who sat near the left front edge of the table. He wore a long-sleeved white shirt, open at the neck. His voice was tough and had a weary edge to it.

"A nuclear strike force," replied the general.

"What justification do we have for a nuclear strike, General?" asked the minister, his eyes seeming to bore holes into the general's.

"The Soviet invasion force will be heavily defended by motorized anti-aircraft elements numbering upwards of twenty thousand as well as an Iran-based air detachment with approximately five hundred combat interceptors."

"First line?" the minister interrupted.

"Intelligence indicates a high preponderance of SU-27 Flankers, and we think some of the newer 31s," interrupted the head of the Israeli Air Force from halfway down the table. He had a short, bull-like neck and thick protruding lips that seemed to pout between his words. "We don't have much data on the 29s."

"Most of the Arab air forces were reduced to a minimum during IAF retaliation against their softening up raids in the past six days," continued the air force general. "Nevertheless, if we were to attack the Eastern Alliance and Soviet combined forces with fighter bombers into the teeth of extremely dense ground-to-air and air-to-air resistance, the enemy has the potential in numbers and quality to counter and overcome IAF forces, inflicting heavy damage and unprecedented losses to our aircraft and crews."

"With the combination of forces capable of moving against us," the commander took over from in front of the alcove, "and the possibility of second and third echelon follow-up by Soviet land and air forces, there is a high probability that our losses in conventional defense will be severe enough to leave our major population areas vulnerable to air, long-range artillery, and rocket attack.

"Given the classic Soviet blitzkrieg plan of attack, if we fail to destroy the superior numbers over Arab territory, Israeli cities could conceivably be penetrated by ground attack and our existence as a country could well be terminated."

"That last possibility is unacceptable, General," said the Minister of Defense. "What size nuclear force would you require?"

"One hundred forty first-line fighters minimum as cover and SAM supression—eight to ten jammers," answered the IAF general from his spot at the oak table. "We anticipate extremely dense mobile and fixed SAM and anti-aircraft guns in the area of the advancing troop concentrations. And, of course, we have to counter the large number of Soviet interceptors in order to protect a relatively small fighter-bomber force."

"What's the projected size of the bomber force?" the minister asked the air force general across the table.

"We would utilize approximately half of our seventy-two F-15E enhanced Eagle force," replied the IAF general. "Twelve armed with nuclear devices and another thirty armed with conventional bombs and air-to-ground missiles. The Eagle's are tailored for this particular mission."

"Are these numbers adequate to assure success?" asked the minister.

"I would like to use more defensive aircraft, but, with the required reserves and the minimal aircraft committed to the other fronts, a hundred forty to maybe one sixty is about the top figure of combat-ready fighter-bombers available for deployment against Soviet and Arab air and ground forces in the northern and eastern theaters.

"We conceivably could add a few F-16s to the bomber force, but we're limited by two basic constraints. First, we possess a limited number of nuclear bombs and, secondly, we must hold nearly half our nuclear strike force in reserve for Moscow and Leningrad if we should fail to halt the Soviet advance into our territory." The minister of defense nodded agreeably, knowingly.

"What size nuclear weapons?" asked a somber, intelligent-looking civilian halfway down the table.

"The majority of the weapons in our stockpile are ten to 40 kilotons each," replied the IAF general. "Each aircraft carries one. The F-15E Strike Eagle has been fitted specifically for this class of mission against a highly lethal, Soviet-style air defense environment. The advanced radar, weapons officer in the rear seat, and other crucial subsystems give the Eagle an excellent chance for survival in the extremely hostile environment we will be facing—that is to say, against an unprecedented combination of sophistication and numbers of in-place and mobile SAMs." As the Israeli Air Force general began again, he shifted in his seat a little, a shallow, brief smile on his lips, expanding and contracting in a peculiar way, then gradually fading. "The United States put the E in production primarily to counter the threat of a Soviet-Warsaw Pact attack at blitzkrieg force levels on western Europe. The survivability of this aircraft in the densely defended anti-aircraft situation during conventional or nuclear weapon delivery is excellent.

"There's a good possibility that at least two thirds of the nuclear strike force would get through to designated targets. Three ten-kiloton bombs on target would be enough to destroy the massed Soviet and Arab forces to the east. We need three more to effectively counter the numbers in the northern theater.

"In the initial sweep the IAF interceptors will have to engage and defeat the Soviet interceptor force to allow the bombers to come in and hit their targets. But we don't expect any problems with whatever they can throw at us from the air. The ground barrage will be the crucial difficulty, but, as we have stressed, the F-15E has been designed to operate in that high-risk environment. And if we effectively take out a high number of SAMs, we believe the chances of penetration are excellent."

"What's your window for the operation, General?" asked a borad-shouldered man to the right of the defense minister.

"To strike them well within Arab territory the outside limit on the strike is about six to eight hours," replied the IAF general.

The defense minister rotated his left wrist and eyed the dial on his steel watch. "It's two-forty A.M.—how soon can you launch the first sorties?"

"Two hours at the outside," replied the IAF general, his eyes keen and confident, his lips drawn back into a slight smile of anticipation.

"And there's no other way to assure defense of our borders?" the defense minister said to the commander, who had compressed the pointer and restowed it on the blackboard tray.

"Not in our judgment—not without the U.S. involvement." With that, the bone-thin commander took a seat in a chair at the head of the table.

The defense minister slowly turned his head left and looked inquiringly at the small-statured prime minister, who sat at the head of the table nearest the door, opposite the IDF commander and the colored map on the wooden wall. "Mr. Prime Minister, I consider the nuclear strike outlined by generals Yurowitz and Weindorf to be our only option at this time," he said simply.

The prime minister was silent, and his eyes had an inward stare for the moment while he seemed to weigh the mission's ramifications carefully in his mind. His thinning, white hair seemed to glisten slightly in the light that came from the ceiling-mounted illuminated plastic grids. For another minute he looked down at the table in front of him and seemed to examine the contours and ridges on his loosely clasped hands.

After a moment he looked up, tension showing on his face. "As you know, we have asked the United States for assistance to counter the soviet buildup. I've spoken to the American Ambassador and Secretary of State within the past few hours. He has promised support with all the material we need as quickly as we need it. Sixteen additional F-15Cs will be en route within twenty-four hours. The secretary neither offered American ground forces nor did we ask for them. He did mention that if Israel made a formal request for United States military intervention against a Soviet force, it would probably be blocked by the U.S. Congress. They evidently have that power in this day and age. He said there was no media support and no public support for commitment of U.S. troops. I thanked him for his support and promised to keep him informed of any significant events." The prime minister paused and sighed wearily. His eyes took on a bright, strangely bittersweet look.

"Yesterday we brought the anticipated Soviet intervention before the United Nations at ten A.M. New York time," continued the prime minister. "Of course, the Soviets claim they are engaged in a military exercise at the request of the Eastern Alliance. As you know, the vote in the General Assembly went against us. We were condemned by Communist countries in Africa and Central America for threatening the peace in the Middle East by our preemptive strike against Syria."

The prime minister shook his head slowly, affirmatively. "So, the world will not easily forgive our use of nuclear weapons. But, gentlemen, the world in this hour of history is blinded by the absolute evil of a godless, corrupt dictatorship that has poisoned the news organs of this world with its crude Pavlovian conditioning, drafted and broadcast from the inhuman abyss of the Kremlin. Historically, much of the world has stood against Israel as the majority of the UN now does. Israel will be condemned no matter what we do to protect the land that God gave our ancestors.

"Much of the world now stands by, in anticipation, as they watch the Soviets approach our border. As usual, the major news organs give the disinformation of the atheistic barbarians more credence than the truth. A military force that includes five hundred thousand Soviet troops, which exceeds the Communist military machine in Eastern Europe, now advances toward Israel from Jordan. The Soviets and Syrians even now are moving in from the north and northeast. Our population centers have already been attacked by the latest Arab air and missile offensive. And the world waits and happily gives us the privilege of making sure the peace-loving Soviets don't kill every one of our men, women, and children.

"Before man knew of such a thing as petroleum or the wealth of minerals on the African continent, I believe the Biblical prophets foretold that Soviets would come down from their kingdom to the north of Israel and invade our land one day. The prophets even foretold that the enemy would take the land of Iran first.

"Gentlemen, although most of the prophesies have come to pass, much of the world think of them as outdated and mythological. And so the world stands ready for the destruction of Israel—the Eastern Alliance's final solution." The prime minister's eyes blinked slowly, then he scanned the men around him, his gaze silently addressing each one for the briefest of moments. Then: "The Communists of the world talk of peace and smile their secret smiles while they await the news that the

Soviets have overrun the land bridge to Africa and killed us all. But the Book of Ekzekiel had something slightly different to say about the Russian invasion—God told him that the invading hordes would be destroyed by fire from heaven."

The prime minister lowered his head and paused for a moment. Darkly etched circles stood out underneath his heavy eyes. He raised his head, took a deep breath, and exhaled slowly. "We don't have much choice. I am certain that we must launch this attack. I am therefore approving the use of nuclear bombs up to ten kilotons for this operation. We will bring the Soviets fire from heaven. And, may God be with us."

40

The Israeli Attack

It was still early on October 19, 2003. The dawn was a few moments away over the eastern hills and the morning star was losing its brilliancy. The sun put a pink-orange edge on the eastern sky as it seemed to hesitate below the edge of the Negev desert while the first of the Israeli Air Force aircraft rolled from their protective hangers, which stood out in the dim light like triangular, long-sided tents—oddly rigid, closely spaced. At the three other Negev bases in the south and two northern bases, there were other planes coming to life. The gathering whine of jet engines suddenly interrupted the immense desert silence, and with the whines came a roar and then another until the noises built up to deafening crescendos as the planes rolled over the ramps and out onto the runways. Electrical cables snapped from connectors in the wheelwells as each aircraft pulled away from its parking slot and, in the low-intensity, artificial light, the cables looked like miniature steel-encased umbilical cords from giant, winged metallic beasts as they eased away from birth. The final takeoff and mission instructions had been revealed to each aircraft's pilot through the thin cables that were being left behind on the concrete parking ramps. Until the fighting began strict radio silence would be observed.

A trio of Grumman E2C airborne early warning aircraft, with their radar antennae mounted on their upper surfaces like the flattened caps of giant mushrooms, rolled out from separate hangars and lifted off the runway first. Then, after a moment, McDonnell F-15s and General Dynamics F-16s lined up in pairs on the main runway complex as the pilots went through final internal checks. The intense lights on their landing gear struts cut a path of light through the gray dawn, their red integral wing-tip lights flashing at steady intervals. The early morning air around the base roared and the desert vibrated in resonance with the powerful jet engines as the aircraft stood firm in staggered pairs, while the pilots tested their control surfaces and stoked the fire in the engines so that flames licked at the rear of the tubular exhausts.

By now others were already rolling down the runways with deafening roars coming out of the powerful Pratt and Whitney engines, as precise, controlled explosions lifted the planes gracefully up into the air to take their place in an aerial armada that would be Israel's best chance to stop the Soviet invasion and preserve the very existence of their country. The IAF warplanes took off in pairs at closely spaced intervals, borne on tubes of fire like winged chariots slicing up through the blue-black air. Thundering, sputtering roars permeated the desert around the IAF base and then the sky began to fill with roars like moving thunder as the procession of war planes climbed, and made wide sweeping turns until more of them took off. The aerial combat machines gathered in formations, high and low, and disappeared to the north and east, headed for the miles and miles of Soviet-Arab columns that were knifing toward Israel like giant juggernauts.

The air was already pinkish-beige where the distant mountains met the sky and small gray clouds were visible low above the horizon. Other F-15E aircraft lifted off the ground in precise tandem climbs and, pouring north a few minutes behind the interceptor and SAM suppression aircraft, the Strike Eagles formed in diamond-shaped formations as they sliced above the blurred wasteland of the desert, pilots wordless and tense in their cockpits. By the time the sky had filled with aircraft the gray clouds at the horizon had disappeared with the rising sun, melting into the deep blue of crystal-clear sky.

As the winged machines accelerated toward their appointed tasks and lead interceptors at 30,000 feet formed in tight-knit, six-plane diamond formations, their wing tips only yards apart, the planes in the rear positions rocking in the turbulent slip streams of the formation leaders. A pale orange band spread across the sky as the war planes streaked toward the north, and the pilots could see bluish-purple clouds float low in the orange sky like plateaus in some far-off aerial kingdom.

Above the first waves of fighter-bombers there were Wild Weasel aircraft with complex radar countermeasure electronics on board that would be used to disrupt Soviet air-to-air and surface-to-air radar. They had climbed to 50,000 feet, using full afterburners from the runway straight up to mission altitude, and right behind them F-16s flew at 40,000 feet in groups of four, some armed with missiles that would home in on enemy radar transmitters and destroy the central nervous systems of the surface-to-air missiles; others were armed with 500-pound iron bombs that would be used to finish the enemy SAMs off. After that, came more F-15C interceptors in precise escort formations—in groups of six, 30,000 feet above the F-15E fighter-bombers, which trailed in slow pursuit 1000 feet above the deck.

Even more aircraft streaked through the sky behind this first wave of aircraft, formations of F-15Cs, F-16s, and Lavis at 30,000 and 10,000 feet, three miles left and right of the main attack formation. Behind the armada the big propeller-driven E2C Hawkeyes flew in gradual circles, standing off from the battle zone, already plotting data from radar bluffing drones, ready to coordinate the air and ground attacks. Just a moment before on the rows of internal radar screens they had picked up the first wave of Soviet MIGs taking off from their Arab bases to meet the approaching IAF forces. There were already over 100 MIGs in the air.

The formations of IAF attack aircraft had reached speeds approaching MACH-0.9 as they flew together in 2500 cubic miles of sky toward the advancing blitzkrieg of men and machines. In 18 or 19 minutes, after engaging Soviet fighter planes, they hoped to be over the battle triangle in the air above the far Jordanian countryside, and below would be the advancing Soviet and Arab columns. At this same moment a slightly larger northern armada of Israeli war planes were just lifting off from IAF bases outside of Tel Aviv and in a half hour they planned to be slicing into the skies above the first wave of Soviet and Arab forces moving through Syria toward the Golan Heights. But first they would have to fight their way through several elite wings of the Soviet Air Force.

A few minutes later the IAF eastern aerial armada streaked over the ancient ruins on the hill of Masada. From above F-15Es presented a stark contrast to the ancient battlegrounds as the six jets knifed in diamond formation at low level across the dawn-lighted landscape, the white-circled blue Star of Davids visible on each wing, their sleek canopies dark in the low sun like the eyes of giant insects. The citadel of Masada had fallen to the Roman army in A.D. 73, and all modern Israeli military men and women swore oaths that this hilltop, with its steep, clifflike sides, would never fall again.

As the next formations of F-15Es flew over the Masada ruins the sleek, daggerlike tips of missiles protruded from the front of the wide, swept wings and seemed to almost point along the walls where the ancient buildings had stood, and almost appeared to trace the ghostly lines that showed from the air where so many human feet had trodden and left their collective image in the ground. And as the formation of bombers cleared the ruins one could see slung below every third Strike Eagle the big gray nuclear bombs tethered like precious cargo.

As tight formations of war planes successively crossed the sky above canyons that etched the sides of the Masada hillside and across the snaky, jagged road that ran up to the ancient crypt, the Dead Sea lay seconds ahead. A split-second after the first Israeli jets had crossed the Dead Sea coded messages were sent out from the early warning Hawkeye aircraft—a large group of bogeys with radar signatures of Russian SU-27s and MIG-29s were headed directly at the Israeli attack force, closing fast from 200 miles away. The Hawkeye would vector in the various IAF interceptors against the large number of planes, and the out-numbered Israeli pilots would divide the Russian bogeys like wolves splitting a herd of doomed animals between them.

When the first of Jordan's surface-to-air missile sites came within range the Israeli F-16s began swooping down and releasing their laser-guided missiles, which locked in the enemy radar beams and rocketed down from the skies until they exploded inside the Soviet radar and guidance centers. More Israeli aircraft took their turn and flashed down, dropping 500-pound iron bombs onto the brain-dead missile batteries. At the same time other Lavis and F-16s were diving at the anti-aircraft guns that blazed away at the Israeli warplanes. All along the battle zone the laser-guided projectiles would slant down time after time, flash into the Soviet armored guns, and detonate with a fury.

Lighted flares and metallic chaff like aluminum confetti were popping out of other Israeli jets above the battleground as they circled over. Through the heavy bombardment, the IAF ground attack war planes dodged and weaved, and now and then the enemy fire would hit an IAF airplane and it would blossom with smoke and fire and plummet from the sky. Sometimes canopies would come off the planes, and IAF pilots would rocket out of disabled planes, and chutes would blossom in the midst of the flak-darkened sky—sometimes the jets would disintegrate or the canopies would stay on and the aerial machines would take the pilots to a sandy grave.

Even as the F-16s and Israeli Lavis cleared the ground SAM sites and AA gun batteries the Soviet fighters were already in range of the Israeli interceptors and the F-15s and F-16s suddenly dashed with afterburner power to meet the oncoming force, splitting the brisk autumn air with volcanic roars. After a half-minute of acceleration the lead Israeli interceptors slowed and, locking onto the first of the Soviet jets with radar, began firing the medium range AIM-7 Sparrow missiles. The initial covey of 12-foot, 500-pound projectiles fell short, but a few seconds later the first of the MIGs burst into a fireball, then another one, and the Soviet war planes began falling out of the sky.

Almost immediately the MIGs on both flanks of the main Soviet formation altered their courses into wide left then right turns. The lead MIGs, who came straight on, went into dives at almost the same time. As they did that lead Israeli jets began curving left and right into the flanking MIGs, and lower-altitude F-16s angled up and came at the diving enemy combat machines, head on at combined speeds of more than 1200 miles per hour. As the first wave of Soviet interceptors closed, they fired cannons at the turning and diving IAF jets; missing, the MIGs flashed under the now hard-turning F-15s and F-16s.

As the opposing aerial formations flashed by each other 1000 feet or so wingtip to wingtip, the first of the MIGs rolled into climbing left and right turns toward the rear of the second wave of IAF interceptors. The lead IAF jets pursued them, turning hard to get inside their turns, until the first of the F-16s fell in behind a MIG-29 as it straightened out on the tail of an F-15C. In an instant the F-16 pilot launched a Sidewinder missile that flew up the MIG's tailpipe and exploded; then another sharp-turning F-16 positioned and fired—another MIG came apart in the air. One of the MIG-31s fired off two Atolls, one of which struck an F-15C and blew out the left side of the fuselage, and the plane burst into gray and red fire and hurtled down through the air. At that the rest of the lead MIGs took evasives toward the desert floor below, and Israeli jets dived to follow.

The next wave of MIGs were coming in now and, using the first radio commands of the battle, Israeli interceptors broke hard away from each other, left and right, high and low, all in split-second synchronization. When the Soviet interceptors turned at the breaking IAF jets the supporting IAF wingmen turned into the pursing MIGs. Other maneuvering F-15s and 16s reversed their turns back into bandit MIGs. As MIGs flashed toward IAF jets, cannons blazing, the Israelis rolled to give the jets a knife-edge side profile and, seconds later, supporting IAF interceptors fired their M61 Gatling guns at the exposed MIGs, spitting out 100-round-a-second bursts of high-explosive incendiary bullets. Several Soviet and IAF interceptors took hits and littered the air with debris as they flared up with bright glares, broke apart, and tumbled out of the sky.

As that battle continued, other formations of F-15Cs and F-16s in the north streaked in position to engage the wave of Soviet targets that hurtled toward Israel from Syria. The young flight leader of the lead formation of F-15Cs, at the bottom of a vertical V formation, now spread from its radar-deceptive tight diamond, called the central aerial command post, "Blue Fox to Bullseye. We have acquired multiple targets—240 degrees at seventy, MACH 1.8, positive ID of Red force baker."

"Roger, Blue Fox," radioed the command post. "Come up Blue Wolf and Blue Tiger—ten thousand above Blue Fox. Blue Lion, turn right to two-hundred-fifty, descend four thousand."

"Roger, Bullseye," radioed F-15C group leaders in precise, hard voices.

"Go to AB," radioed central command.

"Roger," came the responses.

The six F-15Cs in the lead and six trailing F-15Cs engaged afterburners, and flames sprouted out of the big Pratt and Whitney exhausts, hurling the war planes forward at an incredible rate toward the enemy formations. The F-15s began picking out their Soviets MIGs on the Hughes radar sets and, as they streaked toward their prey, the needles on the Airspeed-MACH indicators inside the various cockpits rotated past MACH 1.0 and began inching around the dials.

F-15C pilots used their computer-controlled radar lock-on modes to track the Soviet war planes as the enemy hurtled toward them and the F-16 SAM jets, below and behind them. In each plane the heads-up display loomed above the instrument panel like a ringed outcropping of polished crystal upon which various brightly colored holographic symbols flickered and moved and etched their marks onto the backdrop of sky in front of the pilot.

Using these glass portals, each Israeli pilot lined up selected Russian MIGs for the kill. The pilots bracketed the proper enemy radar blips by engaging the target designator switches on the aircraft control stick, and watched the bracket adhere to one of the blue-green rectangles on the optics in front of them. With training and constant practice behind them the operation of the electronic target acquisition and weapons delivery controls were like a very expensive computer video game—with the exception that a major mistake left little room for a second chance.

"AIM-7 locked—bogey in range," radioed Blue Fox Two. The pilot inside the cockpit of Blue Fox Two triggered the weapon release button on his control stick as he moved the stick to the right. He watched the Steering-Error-Circle on the Heads-Up display at the top of the instrument panel. Amber gold numbers were pulsating and changing on the HUD, showing speeds and altitudes, bearings, and steering data as required to keep the missile on track. Giving the air-to-air missile a continuous radar reflection to home in on, the pilot continued to steer the F-15C Eagle toward the Soviet MIG-29 as the enemy plane tried to evade the approaching missile in a tight, left-banking dive. Electronic circuits inside the streaking AIM-7 Sparrow altered course to keep a track on the radar beam reflected from the Soviet interceptor until the missile impacted just above the root of the MIG's wing on the left side. The first of the Soviet MIGs was destroyed by a shattering explosion, and the pieces of the plane billowed into a fireball and plunged toward the ground below.

Within seconds air-to-air missiles launched from Israeli Air Force Eagles began to detonate on target and bring more Soviet planes out of the sky. MIGs shot past the second wave of F-15s at 2000 to 3000 mile-an-hour closing rates, and the Israeli pilots could see their cannons blazing. After they passed by the Russian pilots put their aircraft in sharp, winding turns, trying to get the tails of Israeli jets at the back of the formation. The Israeli interceptors slowed to corner velocity and maneuvered toward the Soviet war planes. The MIG pilots fired heat-seeker missiles at the Israeli F-15Cs as they positioned on their tails and fired cannons in close, and cannon fire hit one of the F-15s. The canopy came off and the pilot ejected as the plane spun in a lazy, smoking spiral toward the ground.

The lead group of IAF jets banked hard on the edge of maneuverability and evaded Russian projectiles and a second group of F-15s flashed in position behind the MIGs, from almost out of nowhere it seemed, and started firing away with the M61 Gatling guns and the Sidewinders, knocking the twisting, banking Soviet machines out of the sky, one after the other.

"Blue Fox one to Bullseye," radioed the flight leader of the second group of F-15s. "I just got two more kills on MIG-29s. Just two pieces of cake. The Soviets are probably better at going after airliners. Just a touch slovenly against MIG killers, Incorporated."

And all over the skies planes from the U.S.S.R. began exploding, and Sidewinder air-to-air missiles flew up multitudes of MIG engine exhaust pipes, turning the planes into fire and heated metal, and some of the MIGs lost wings and tail sections to the big Gatling gun projectiles and plunged from the Syrian skies, trailing flames.

Over half the initial wave of MIGs were destroyed before the Soviet pilots even knew they were under attack. Israeli pilots utilized telescopic optical video units to record some of the kills on video tape. The system was connected by F-15 airborne computers to the radar target tracking system, and the Israeli pilots could see the red stars on the sides of the MIGs in a four-inch screen before the MIG pilots could even spot a speck of an F-15.

Two of the first Soviet MIGs that pierced the escort screen were pursued by Colonel Ariel Haiva in an F-15 that had Hebrew letters painted on the left side of the nose that, translated in English, read *Cyclone*. Above the Hebrew letters were seven red, white, and blue bull's-eyes, signifying confirmed kills of Syrian Air Force MIGs. The slightly built Israeli colonel flicked at push buttons on the central computer and then concentrated on the Heads-Up display, which stared at him from atop the instrument panel like a giant ground-glass crystal ball. Scintillating colored dots and moving symbols flickered on the crystal display.

The nearest of the MIGs was within three-and-a-half nautical miles and was heading straight at the lead formation of F-15E fighter-bombers, which were 20,000-odd feet below. "Bandit MIG-27 dead ahead, going right to left. About one-one-three-zero. I'm inside R-max," radioed Colonel Haiva to the flight leader.

"Roger, Blue Lion Three," replied the flight leader from his F-15C one mile to the rear and slightly above Colonel Haiva's

F-15C. "I'm checking your six, Cyclone. Go for it!"

"Bandit MIG in hard left climb," radioed Colonel Haiva. The IAF combat pilot flipped the air combat machine into a left bank, and the maneuver hit him like a car striking the side of the F-15 at 40 miles an hour. "He's coming way high. I just pulled 9 gs and got inside that sonofabitch."

"Roger, Blue Lion Three," radioed the flight leader.

Colonel Haiva pushed the stick to the left in order to center the HUD steering dot onto the targeted MIG-31. A computer-generated circular image surrounded the MIG dot on the big glass display in front of him, the image expanded suddenly, and Colonel Haiva depressed the LAUNCH button on the underside of the grip stick to fire the AIM-119 Sidewinder missile. "Fox five," radioed Colonel Haiva. The missile sprouted flame, left the F-15C behind, arched upward in a tight turn, and headed straight at the maneuvering MIG-31. The missile overtook the MIG and flew up the left-hand tailpipe. The MIG disintegrated into a bright orange ball of fire and debris. "Bandit destroyed," radioed Colonel Haiva.

"Roger, Blue Lion Three, come left to 190," replied the flight leader. "You've got a bandit at five."

"Roger Blue Lion One," answered Colonel Haiva. He moved the control stick over toward his left thigh, and the Eagle banked sharply, down and to the left. Almost immediately he bracketed another MIG-31 while it maneuvered on the tail of a low-flying F-15E, and the MIG launched several air-to-air missiles at the F-15E fighter-bomber. The targeted Israeli jet manuevered violently, pulled up sharply in a climb, and evaded the Russian missiles.

The Soviet MIG-31 stayed on the tail of the F-15E as both pilots drove their aircraft up into the vertical. Colonel Haiva selected afterburner power, pulled back on the stick, and felt the familiar tingling in his fingertips as the seat of the airplane crushed the nerves in his back and tried to come through him. In another split second he banked to get behind the MIG-31. The sun and shadows constantly played over his helmeted face as he banked, rolled, and turned on the knife-edge of the limits of the F-15 and himself to try to come in behind the Soviet plane for another kill. In the next right-hand turn he almost blacked out, but in the next instant he eased up on the stick and when the nose came out of the sun he found the MIG's tail directly in front of him. As soon as the HUD circle came on, Colonel Haiva punched off two Sidewinder missiles at the Russian MIG below him, five seconds apart. As the first one fired, he radioed to the F-15E below him, "Fox five! Fox five!" The F-15E in front of the enemy MIG immediately cut its afterburners and banked to point the hot exhausts away from the heat-seeking missiles his IAF colleague had just fired.

The first missile struck the MIG, and a white plume of smoke came out of the side of the enemy plane. The MIG's canopy came off, and then the second Sidewinder struck the diving plane near the right engine, and parts of the MIG came off in a shower of metal. The Russian machine burst into flames. The MIG's nose angled downward, and it looked like a falling metal torch.

Pairs of Soviet and Israeli planes flew against each other in 700 square miles of sky, and beyond them came the advancing Soviet-Syrian blitzkrieg. It was electric between the cockpits of the Israeli interceptors after the first several kills. The excited radio exchanges told the IAF pilots they had a good engagement going and the enemy air force was being massacred. So they flew the planes at the edge of human-machine capabilities and twisted and banked in the bright air while winged fireballs sprouted and lit up the sky around them and debris rained down on the barren ground below. Occasionally an Israeli plane would explode and fall, but most of the shredded and convoluted pieces that came out of the sky had been attached to Soviet warplanes. Out-numbered, the Israeli pilots, with only their machines and what they could do with them between themselves and eternity, fought with extraordinary agility and harmony to kill the enemy and knock his machines from the desert air.

41

The Intervention

From the aerial command posts circling above the crossroads to three continents, inside the three E-2C Hawkeye aircraft, the coded message went out to the Israeli Air Force nuclear attack aircraft over Syria and Jordan: ''MIG Killers, Incorporated, confirms that Condo Able and Baker cold water faucets are go; Repeating—Phase 1 of Operation Garden Spot is complete. Commence Operation Abarim. Commence Operation Abarim.''

Major Levi checked the F-15's radar display while, with practiced, easy motions, he maintained the altitude at 150 feet as the war plane hurtled over the face of the land. With the Soviet SAM missile sites neutralized, the low flying was almost a pleasurable interlude until he started to sweat. But the day's work would be worth it if the Soviet military machine in Syria got its comeuppance.

When the command came through to begin the nuclear bomb run without hesitation he pulled the stick back, pushed the throttles into the afterburner position, and the F-15 bolted into a steep climb toward the top of the sky. He wanted to get some-where in a hurry and he treated the aircraft as merely an extension of his subconscious mind.

Major Levi's bomber was the lead aircraft in the first group of F-15Es and, as it flashed upward through the brilliant blue morning sky, the sunlight glinted off the gray-blue underside and the center-mounted nuclear bomb constrasted starkly, dark gray and bulbous like a strange, metallic parasite.

A half minute later the pilot leveled the F-15E off at 3000 feet. Captain Eshman, the Weapons Officer in the rear seat, saw the image of the main Soviet force displayed on the video screens in front of him. He selected a segment, then entered data into a keyboard on the computer front panel that his right knee rested against. In a few seconds all critical data on the enemy had been stored in the F-15E weapons release computer and, as the red SAM launch warning lights illuminated in the cockpit and the artificial computer voice uttered "Warning missile launch," Captain Eshman yelled into the cockpit intercom, "I've got the target data—go for the evasive!"

The pilot nosed the F-15 down and banked left to avoid a surface-to-air missile that had just appeared from the east like a thin, pointed telephone pole and flew in a curved path toward the IAF fighter. He rotated a switch and flipped a toggle switch that would cause metallic, radar-fooling chaff to be ejected in a continuous pattern into the air. At 500 feet altitude, the pilot pulled out of the dive, rotated the plane on its side with the right wingtip pointed at the ground, and the ten-foot missile flashed by the F-15E 300 yards to their right. To his immediate right, below them, the forbidding desert landscape raced by, and as he hesitated a few seconds before bringing the F-15 back to normal flight attitude, it seemed to him exceedingly strange that humans would want to fight over such a piece of land.

"T1 delivery status?" Major Levi asked Captain Eshman over the intercom.

"Go," replied the officer from the rear seat.

"Roger," said the pilot. It would be less than a minute now before he would begin the sequence that he had often practiced over the Negev and, if it were successful, the first nuclear bomb would be dropped on a target in anger since the Americans did it in World War II. And if the two men failed to complete the nuclear toss, there were other F-15Es in second and third waves that were only minutes away.

Major Levi adjusted the plane's speed and entered data into the central computer, using the keyboard on his right side. Far above him, to the east, a mysterious silvery cylinder suddenly appeared as if out of nowhere. The wingless, silver object hurtled down from the heights until Major Levi caught sight of it descending several miles ahead of him, coming down over the Soviet-Arab invasion force whose machines were dark, serpentine fingers following the contours of the still distant landscape.

"Garden Spot One to Bull's-eye," radioed Major Levi to IAF aerial command in one of the E-2Cs. "We have a large unidentified bogey at twelve o'clock, descending at high speed, vertically;

bearing two-six-five at thirty. It doesn't appear to be of Soviet manufacture. The bogey appears to be an extremely large metallic cylinder—we've got a half-inch blip on our scope up here!''

"We copy Garden Spot One," radioed the distant command post. "We just got the track on it—the bogey appears to be moving in excess of twenty-five kilos. Wait! It just stopped at sixteen thousand feet. It appears to be hovering!''

"Well, whatever the hell it is, get us some escort," radioed Major Levi as he looked out at the distant silvery structure, motionless and high above him to his left.

"Roger, Garden Spot One," replied the command post. "Blue Wolf One—this is Bull's-eye. Turn to two-two-zero, descend to twenty thousand. We have unknown bogey in the vicinity of Garden Spot One. Call us when you can identify."

"Roger, Bull's-eye," the Blue Wolf flight leader radioed back, then snapped his F-15C into a quick left-banking descent toward the Garden Spot One's position.

The huge metallic cylinder hovered ominously in the middle of the sky above the Soviet invasion force for the moment, the sun glinting off its mammoth curved surfaces. The unknown aerial machine appeared to be made of sections, like a tall stack of 100-foot silver dollars. Suddenly the sections on the unknown craft split apart, and separate disk-shaped craft emerged from the stack and scattered, flying off in different directions toward various points on the compass.

"Garden Spot One to Bull's-eye!" the excited voice of Major Levi crackled on the assigned radio command channel. "The unknown bogey just split into twelve to fourteen unidentified objects! These disk-shaped machines came apart out of the cylinder like bats out of hell. One of the bogeys is on an intercept to our position. The other targets are flying on various divergent headings."

"Roger Garden Spot One—we've got Blue Wolf on the way. ETA of thirty seconds."

"Roger," answered Major Levi. "We're starting our run." Levi aimed the F-15 Strike Eagle toward the vertical once more and clicked the throttles to the afterburner stops. Yellow-orange, translucent fire extended out the rear of the F-15E's twin tail pipes as the plane gathered speed and climbed effortlessly toward the top of the sky.

"Blue Wolf One to Garden Spot One," radioed the lead pilot

as his interceptor dived toward the flying disk that streaked toward Colonel Levi's bomber. "We're on an intercept of your bogey. We're coming in from your right and we'll be coming close to your course—hold steady . . . till . . . back . . . you." The communication from the Blue Wolf flight leader became garbled and then broke off abruptly. Major Levi worked the comm panel to get the Blue Wolf flight back on the radio, and then he tried the Bull's-eye aerial command post, but there was only loud, pulsating static on every channel he tried.

"Garden Spot to Blue Wolf, come in," he repeated twice, and the response was only static. "Garden Spot One to Bull's-eye. Do you read me?" Same electronic noise hissed out an answer. Levi adjusted the UHF/VHF controls and increased the volume to the 90% detente on his communication gear and tried again. "Garden Spot One to Bull's-eye, come in." The sophisticated radio equipment in the F-15E would give him only electronically amplified hiss in return.

The pilot in the Blue Wolf One F-15C streaked down past Major Levi's climbing F-15E until the pilot of Blue Wolf locked his weapons control system on the flying disk's radar image and then readied a Sparrow missile for launch on the Armament Control Panel, which was lit up like a Christmas tree left of the main instruments. He watched the cathode-ray image of the flying disk straighten out on the radar screen, then checked the bogey on the Heads-Up display. The target was inside the dotted circle and the cross-hairs were almost lined up. He readied his finger on the stick grip button that would send the missile screaming toward the unknown craft.

Suddenly, all the lights on the Armament Panel went out. "Blue Fox One to Bull's-eye," radioed the pilot in a worried, frustrated voice. "My Armament Control Panel's dead. My central computer's going wild!" The symbols and numbers on the HUD's image-combining glass in front of him flickered and changed into meaningless random symbology and numbers.

No response came back from the command post. The flying disk that had been headed for the climbing F-15E bomber suddenly changed its course and came straight at Blue Wolf One now. As the Blue Wolf One pilot searched his erratic instruments, unlighted displays, and gauges for some sign of the trouble, the dark blue-green of his radar screen changed to a burst of bright white and the moving dots and symbols disappeared from the screen. "My radar's being jammed!" shouted the pilot into his jammed microphone. "Come in, Bull's-eye. Do you read me? I'm breaking right, gang—whoever's still in the air." With that, the Israeli pilot flipped the F-15 control stick hard to the right. The aircraft responded with a hard jerk, rolling clockwise and then falling away sideways in the air.

At that same instant a bluish-silver sphere ejected from the disk-shaped machine, and the sphere zoomed up at a slight angle toward the fleeing Blue Wolf One F-15C. The pilot spotted the spherical missile and the IAF Eagle, in a full evasive, went into a spiraling roll, twisting and flashing in the sun at one, then two, then two-and-a-half revolutions per second.

The projectile from the UFO tracked the streaking plane, and it was only a matter of seconds until the device overtook the F-15 like a shooting star, and when it neared the diving Israeli aircraft the mysterious sphere veered at a right angle into it and entered the rectangular engine air inlet on the interceptor's right side. The F-15 disintegrated immediately in a quick, bright fireball that thudded against the desert air. Hundreds of remnants of the IAF plane careened outward from the expanding ball of fire and the flaming debris rained down from the sky.

Meanwhile, Major Levi had the F-15E past 25,000 feet, heading for 30,000. "Arm for strike," Major Levi informed Captain Eshman.

Captain Eshman flipped and reflipped switches on the fighter-bomber's Armament Control Panel. "The ACP appears to be malfunctioning," said Eshman. "I've lost every light on it!"

"Well, recycle it," yelled Levi. "Start from square one." The pilot eased the F-15E out of the climb at 29,500 feet. As he brought the nose of the F-15 Eagle down one of the UFOs, like a big metallic discus, loomed the size of a house dead ahead, through the front canopy, and Levi shouted into the intercom. "I've got a bogey on a collision course, I'm breaking left—now!" The big F-15 responded sharply to the pilot's quick, darting thrust at the control stick. As the Strike Eagle fell away to the left, the flying disk slashed by 100-odd yards to the right side of the Israeli jet.

"How's the ACP?" Levi asked Eshman in the back seat.

"Dead," answered Eshman.

"Can you go to manual release mode?" inquired Levi of his back-seat officer.

"Some of my data's pretty scrambled back here," replied Eshman over the intercom. "The weapon release computer's out to lunch, but I'm assuming we are go for a manual delivery."

"Roger," said Levi. "Okay, we're ready for final approach at your mark," Levi told Captain Eshman. They were at 14,000 feet by now, and Major Levi waited for Eshman's response. To the right, ahead and below, the massive Soviet military force was inching across the land in long, curving columns of machines and men. To the left of the diving Strike Eagle the silver flying disk flew past them, accelerating ahead of them on the same heading. The unknown machine glowed with an extremely faint greenish light that was visible at its close approach. The craft was slightly convex on top, with a thick rim that appeared to be eight or ten feet high. It seemed strange and forbidding, like the very edge of the human imagination. The pilot of the F-15E banked right toward the Soviet land armada.

"Counting down for final approach," shouted Captain Eshman over the intercom from the back of the cockpit. "Mark—nine, eight, seven, six, five, four, three, two, one."

Major Levi didn't wait for zero before he angled the F-15E up into another steep climb. The unknown silver craft flew out in front of them a few miles and then seemed to slow. "Give me a count for weapon delivery," said Levi to Eshman as the altimeter swung past 32,000.

"This data's approximate," shouted Eshman. "My computer's going wild. Okay, bleed your speed off to MACH-0.5."

The pilot kicked in the air brake and changed the climb angle slightly to drain speed from the aircraft. The flying disk edged in front of them, shining like a molten brass discus in the sun. Then a small silver sphere came out of the unknown machine and, simultaneously, Captain Eshman began the countdown: "Mark, nineteen, eighteen, seventeen . . ."

The flying disk picked up speed suddenly and slanted down toward a pair of Israeli Air Force interceptors that were flying wingtip to wingtip, climbing toward the unknown craft. Eshman continued the count in a monotone. "Eleven, ten, nine, eight . . ."

The silver sphere circled lazily toward the F-15E and, as the Strike Eagle neared the release point 15,000 feet over the Soviet troops below, Levi didn't even notice the device approach from 8 o'clock high. The strange sphere sped on into the F-15E and penetrated the plane's right air intake, turning the Eagle into an instant red-and-white glare. The explosion ripped the high thin air with a shattering boom. An orange and black fireball bloomed where the F-15E had been, and the debris slanted down from the sky, impacting the barren landscape below. A nebulosity of gray-black smoke clustered for an instant where the F-15E had been, but it began to dissipate quickly from the strength of the high altitude winds.

The Garden Spot Two F-15E followed the first F-15E's flight profile, and the crew went through the sequence needed to drop the atomic bomb as the first crew had done. They proceeded to enter the final bombing climb high above the Soviet columns of motorized tanks and troops and other armored vehicles that crawled along the land like a plague of strange insects, moving forms and shapes as far as the eye could see on the barren land far below.

With 30 seconds to go the pilot of the second bomber flipped the fighter into a series of turns at the edge of the g-limits to evade a Soviet surface-to-air missile. After the SAM slithered by and curved away the pilot and weapons officer maneuvered back into the final approach and the pilot pushed the F-15E toward the nuclear bomb's release point at the end of a climbing turn. "Five, four, three, two, one, bombs away," said the weapons officer from the rear seat as he depressed a toggle switch.

The pilot put the F-15E into an upside-down loop for an moment of afterburner thrust, then rolled the big jet to an upright attitude, and the F-15E accelerated away from the drop zone in a high-speed dive. "I have no confirmation of weapon release," said the officer in the rear seat. "I think it's still on the rack, Major."

"What in the hell's goin' on?" replied the pilot over the intercom.

"Something or somebody's jamming our weapons delivery system," shouted the back-seater.

"How about taking this big gray bird all the way into the target, Captain—are you game?" said the pilot.

"It's a no-go, Major," replied the weapons officer. "I'd personally take this bomb into ground zero with a fork lift if it would detonate. But the Armament Panel's dead. We can't arm the bomb. And it won't detonate if we can't pull the pins with the right electronic signal—isn't that right?"

"Roger," said the pilot. "I assume those unidentified bogeys are playing hell with our electronics—that's a possible for the lost radio too. I can't get through to Bull's-eye. Let's regroup and call it a day."

"Roger."

Just as the Garden Spot Two F-15E turned back for Israel the pilot could see the flashes below him of two more disintigrating Israeli interceptors. The next few minutes saw the flying disks and Israeli jets fight numerous battles over the skies of Syria and Jordan. In a few moments of time those skies were filled with dying Israeli aircraft.

After the last of the Israeli nuclear-armed war planes had been destroyed, the unidentified disk-shaped machines rendezvoused at a high altitude, flying in from all directions. The strange machines aligned themselves in an in-line formation, and the line of bronze disks began to ascend to a higher altitude. The formation resembled a gargantuan chain moving up through the sky, its solid metallic links flashing and glittering in the sunlight.

The UFOs accelerated as they climbed, passed the speed of light, and dematerialized, and when the last of the craft dematerialized it looked like this in slow motion: fully solid, accelerating at a fantastic rate, then suddenly opaque. Then, moving a short distance, the opaqueness faded, them moving a shorter distance it edged into translucence, and the blue of the sky showed faintly through, then a slightly shorter distance later the blue sky showed clearly through it, then another few thousand feet and the UFO image was dim and ghostlike, then in another few feet of space it was gone. And, moving from this space-time dimension to the other dimension beyond, through that nameless black corridor, they rematerialized in that other world hidden in the lowest parts of the earth, lying at the inner edge of the Black Hole that swirled with the center of the earth.

In the secret chambers in that alien dimension, which permeates the hidden layers far below the earth's crust, the other intelligences that influence the affairs of men on earth waited anxiously, for their time to increase their grip on earth was soon approaching. Through successive Ages, from this bottomless pit on the other side of the speed of light, powerful beings led by Satan had made their ways and their personalities known through those who dwelt on the surface of the planet.

After the Christ had come to earth and paid the ransom for sin these ultraterrestrials had intensified their delusions and influence from the gate of the bottomless pit and inundated the world with all manner of lies to prevent humans from understanding the mission Jesus had completed. They had led many away from the truth about the Son of God's mission and devised many schemes to prevent humans from accepting Christ's gift of eternal life in the Father's many mansions. The messengers of deception had projected evil forth into the earth's space-time continuum in their labors to deceive many and thus keep them on a path to a fire-laked world.

They had influenced and given power and position to certain leaders and movements at certain historical moments, and great wars and tyrannies had been the result. But much of what they wanted to accomplish had been restrained by God's angels and those who testified truly of Christ. The time was nearly at hand when this restraint would be lifted and Satan's greatest lying scheme would be manifested full scale on the earth. The earth would be delivered to Satan and to whom he would give it. And the night would come.

42

The Invasion

"Lunch is ready," hollered Melissa. Outside the black-framed screen door, stretched between the big oak and a sugar maple tree, Tom Kruger lay on a thick-rope hammock. He resisted her calling him a moment to continue gazing at the brilliant azure blue sky that showed between the maple's yellow-green leaves. The leaves gently circulated with the breeze and the colors changed and fluttered in rhythmic patterns that fascinated him. His head lay at the oak tree end of the hammock, and as he sighted along one of the fat limbs that angled out from the trunk of the tree he felt a pang of hunger in the pit of his stomach.

The surge of hunger made him swing his body over the side of the rope platform, interrupting the spell of the 72-degree October afternoon. As he walked toward the house, his stomach suddenly felt like there was a vacuum in it—like the inside of an evacuated Bell Jar. He saw a Monarch butterfly winging its way, veering and fluttering above the gravel driveway that ran around the left side of the house between two rows of honeysuckle bushes. He slowed and instinctively looked for signs of other Monarchs when the thought struck him that it was the season for the orange and black insects to be gathering before they took the annual journey south.

"Nature abhors a vacuum," said Tom as he rushed through the kitchen doorway, patting his stomach with his right hand as if it were a bongo drum. His stomach had made a sound like a barely ripened watermelon. He glanced toward the white enamel stove and sniffed at the air. "What's cookin'?"

"A rice dish," said Melissa, facing the stove in blue jeans and purple top, with an unbleached muslin apron tied at the waist. In front of her on the burner of the stove a white vapor jetted from one side of a large, stainless-steel, covered pot.

"Is there any meat in it?" he asked her.

"Some chicken sprinkled here and there," she told him as he came close and hugged her from behind.

"Great," he said, and kissed her on the nape of the neck. "I gotta wash up." He walked away toward the bathroom in the hall.

"It's ready when you're ready," offered Melissa.

"I'm ready!"

"I'll dish it up."

"Super," he said as he entered the bathroom. And then, sticking his neck back out the door, he said: "Turn on the TV, will you, Lissa?"

"Can't you wait till after we eat?" questioned Melissa.

"I want to see if there's any news on—there's a lot of stuff happening," he reasoned.

"Want to get the blood pressure going, huh?" she teased.

"High blood pressure's better than no pressure at all," he retorted.

"Okay, you win," she said, moving over to the television set atop a white-painted chest of drawers, pressing a small button on the right side of the gray screen. An automobile commercial flashed on the screen and a deep voice blared out with great authority through the perforated holes in the front of the cabinet. Melissa rotated the volume control to turn off the sound.

Tom offered the evening prayer after they had sat down to eat: "Thank you Father for these blessings from your gracious bounty through Jesus Christ our Lord and Savior. Amen."

"Amen," said Melissa. Then she got back up and rotated the small plastic knob on the television to let sound come through the black plastic grill. A slim man with thick black hair who appeared to be in his late forties was sitting at a desk giving the national afternoon news report. His hair appeared 20 years younger than his face, which had puffy circles under the eyes.

"And some observers say that the federal emergency programs instituted thus far simply are too little too late. For more on that we go now to the west coast."

A woman's face came onto the screen next. "Tim, I'm standing in a devastated area of San Francisco that was once known as Chinatown. The series of killer quakes that leveled this city and gave part of the downtown district back to the ocean has left this section of town looking like a bombed-out city. For the thousands of Americans who lost friends and relatives here and elsewhere in

California, this scene is a grim reminder of the devastation that has repeatedly struck California over the past eighteen months." The screen changed to reveal a quick, panoramic view of a partially destroyed city block. Then the annoucer's head reappeared. "And scientists with the U.S. Geological Survey say it can happen again—here or at other locations in the U.S. where major fault lines lay beneath the earth. Not much consolation for people who are already hurting here in California."

The reporter's voice droned on in a taunting, intellectual tone. "And, for the homeless who survived the August earthquake here in Chinatown, it remains a struggle for survival. Federal aid has been limited to ten thousand dollars a month for a family of four and, with the limited housing available, some say that is not enough. The Washington Administration says that federal money under the earthquake insurance program has already been allocated for this area, but that a combination of government red tape, bad weather, and private contractor abuse has resulted in little or nothing to show for the billions already spent. Some contractors have reportedly received large amounts of federal rebuilding funds and have left the country without even ordering supplies. Families who have stayed on the land of their mothers and fathers, like the Chu family, may simply have to leave this area where their roots are. And that is something that most prefer not to even think about."

A solemn Chinaman's face appeared on the screen next. He was young, with bright eyes. He stood in front of a large brown tent with sides that flapped in the breeze. "We've lived in this tent since we lost our place," said Mr. Chu. "The government agency people have promised us trailers, but nobody we know has ever got one. Our five kids have been sick ever since we been living in the tent. We signed for a contractor to build a house, but we haven't been able to reach him." The man's eyes teared up, and his voice broke up into sobs as he said, "My wife and kids don't want to leave, but there's no schools, there's no jobs—the government's not doin' nothin'." The Chinaman was silent for a moment, choked with emotion, his black eyes staring at the television screen.

"I think I'd move." Tom said to the television screen.

"We did!" said Melissa, then flashed a crooked smile. Tom nodded abstractedly.

Suddenly the picture of the sobbing Chinaman went black and

stayed black for a sliver of a moment. A seven-and-a-half-inch CBS Eye flashed onto the thirteen-inch screen and stared at them for a moment. Below the eye, in white letters, CBS NEWS SPECIAL BULLETIN glowed.

The picture of the national news anchorman illuminated the screen again. "This is Ted Kupchek in New York. I have just been handed this bulletin from our middle-eastern office in Tel Aviv." Melissa and Tom watched the small flat screen like two people with their minds in suspended animation. The announcer read from the sheet of paper he held stiffly in his hands. "At six-thirteen P.M. eastern standard time, a united Arab force in conjunction with a contingent of Soviet forces crossed into Israeli territory. Early reports indicate heavy fighting between the Arab alliance and Israeli defense forces. The invading force is reported to be very large and includes paratroopers from South Yemen, Palestinian freedom fighters from the north, and elements from Syrian, Iranian, Jordanian, and Libyan armies." As they listened raptly to the words the man was saying there seemed to be a great quietness between every word.

"Early communiques are sketchy, and we've momentarily lost contact with our satellite linkup to Israel," the newmans continued. "But estimates are that the first wave of the Arab liberation force exceeds one and a half million troops. However, we do have Mark Hussman live from Damacus, Syria. Come in, Mark."

"Do you realize that we're watching prophecy fulfilled right in our kitchen!" said Melissa.

"It's amazing," said Tom. "The Lord's coming soon—do you feel it?"

"I really do," agreed Melissa.

"Thank you, Ted," said yet another face on the TV screen. "The Syrian government is pretty closed-mouth about this whole military operation so far. But one thing they have said is that any military action that they may be engaged in is only in response to repeated Israeli military raids on arab civilian populations, their own as well as the recent destruction of the latest Iraqi attempt at construction of a nuclear reactor. The Israelis killed several Soviet civilians in that raid and so it's not surprising that the Soviets have finally joined the Arabs on the battlefield against the Jewish state.

"Since the Syrians don't actually recognize the existence of such an entity as the State of Israel, this military mission into Israeli territory is being called here a war of liberation. And the Syrians say the purpose of any troop movements is to regain land that belongs to the Arabs, and that serves to represent the Palestinian interests as well. As for the people in the streets—they seem proud that the big battle is underway and confident of the outcome of the war. That's all from here, Ted—this is Mark Hussman reporting from Damascus."

The anchorman came back on. "Thanks for that live report, Mark. Now we're going to go to the local stations for a commercial spot, but then we're going to come back to you in order to update this dramatic story. We will be on the air here as long as necessary to bring you the developments in the Middle East. We will also be going to reporters in the major capitals of the world to get reaction there. We are attempting to set up a live interview at the State Department at this moment." The announcer paused for a moment. "I've just been informed that the Israeli government has invited war correspondents into one of the major battle zones, and our camera teams are on their way to the scene. As soon as our camera teams can move from Tel Aviv to Tiberias, and when the satellite link is restored, we should be able to bring you live pictures of what is happening over there. More on that exciting development when we come back."

The screen flashed and changed to a picture of a giant glass of beer with intricate formations of bubbles moving through it, rising. The glass of beer began shrinking as people sang and a streaming waterfall of water came into view behind the glass and mountains behind that, and a loud happy song came out of the black plastic grill on the television. Water flowed down in a stream on the television, but the stream made no sound. Instead, a bold voice full of emotion repeated the name of the beer like an oracle from on high.

At 1:40 the next afternoon the first live television pictures started coming in from the Israeli war zone. As far as the eye could see Soviet machines of war rolled across Syria, streaming into the Golen Heights region toward the valley east of the Sea of Gallilee. From the town of Tiberias the whole world watched as the Soviet and Arab armies rolled with a grinding roar across the Golan Heights, destroying Israeli defensive positions as they went.

Occasionally sleek, twin-engined Israeli Air Force fighter-bombers screamed low over the advancing columns of sand-colored armored vehicles, and the planes that made it through the

barrages of anti-aircraft gunfire and missiles loosed their missiles
and bomb loads onto their military targets. Soviet mobile missile
launchers separated themselves from the moving columns and sat
stationary with their rockets angled up toward the sky like bloated
metal javelins. As Israeli planes streaked overhead in dodging,
knifing runs over the targets, enemy surface-to-air missiles would
launch from the rear of the war machines and rocket with a hiss up
through the sky, occasionally knocking an Israeli plane out of the
air with sharp thudding explosions and bright flashes of light. The
Israeli planes came at the enemy armies wave after wave. The air
began to fill with grayish-black bursts of flak, and some of the low-
level Israeli bombers took hits. A white puff of smoke would
appear on the body of a plane and then those planes would glide
into the ground like exploding meteorites. Plumes of smoke rose
from immobile and twisted Soviet war machines where bombs of
air-to-ground missiles had struck them, and all along the desolate
battleground explosions ripped the air.

The past several days had seen temperatures in excess of 95
degrees throughout Israel, and on this clear blue and tan day, with
the giant sand-colored, camouflaged machines and hordes of
soldiers moving through it, the temperature would probably reach
100 before noon.

As the first wave of the Soviet war machines came surging
across the wind-blown and battered terrain on the slopes of the
Golan Heights, Israeli artillery erupted with blistering barrages of
shells directed at the approaching armies. The thousands of Soviet
tanks ground forward with terrifying precision, rolling and bucking,
and their tracks crunched across the volcanic terrain with its
scrubby, dry vegetation. Behind them thousands of Soviet armed
personnel carriers stretched out like dark moving rivers, farther
than the eye could see.

The high plain atop the Golan Heights was dotted with
remnants of Israeli and Soviet war machinery—scattered and
twisted fragments of MIGs and F-15s, Flankers, F-4s, F-16s, and
Lavis; and burned and battered hulks of trucks, tanks, and other
surface vehicles; and there were the shredded remains of surface-
to-air missiles and launchers. Bodies of soldiers lay everywhere,
and you could hear the charred and bloated bodies popping in the
hot sun. Occasionally new vehicles would burst into flames from a
blast of explosives, and black smoke issued into the bright blue
sky from wounded war machines.

The distant rumble of gunfire carried across the Sea of Galilee, where 2000 years before Jesus of Nazareth had walked on the water to the town of Tiberias, where the camera crews of the world's electronic media were already filming the smoke and fire rising from the distant heights above them. As occasional aircraft from the battered, rationed fleet of IAF jets continued to roar low over the advancing army the Soviet anti-aircraft missiles left tenuous trails in the air like giant, standing cobras.

The first wave of the Soviet tanks appeared as if it would reach the Gamla Rise near the southern slopes of the Golan Heights within minutes. Ahead of the Soviet men and machines on the approaches from the Golan Heights to the Jordan Valley, there lay in wait the next blocking layer of Israeli defense emplacements, including nuclear military pieces. But if the invaders could break through those Israeli defenses, down the slope to Ein Gev on the shores of the Sea of Galilee, they would be into the agricultural land of Galilee, and it would be very hard to stop them after that. Nevertheless, ordinary people from around the world who had tuned into the live coverage didn't really know that, since the reporters didn't tell them.

A formation of 12 unidentified flying objects came into view then, arranged in a V like a flock of Canadian geese. Each of the craft was metallic, the color of brass, the shape of two soup bowls, rim to rim. As the formation slanted down from a great height, Israeli surface-to-air missiles rocketed off and streaked up past the UFOs harmlessly. The strange aerial armada continued down, slowing as it approached the battle line near the Golan Heights. Several of the UFOs broke formation, sliding back and forth over each other and oscillating side to side in a peculiar wobbling motion as they spun. Israeli missiles continued to swish past the UFOs, and the IDF anti-aircraft guns were spreading black flak into the air.

The UFOs separated and spread out into two intersecting lines in the air, less than 2000 feet above the battlefield. As the unknown craft hovered solitary purple rays of light shot out from the Saturn-shaped machines and pinpointlike beams struck Israeli nuclear artillery emplacements and set equipment and its operators ablaze. The Israeli troops collapsed where they crouched beside the heavy guns, as if they were merely dolls made out of cheap plastic that someone had stuck in a 3000-degree blast furnace. Their intense, brief screams turned into gurgling madness within an instant as the flesh under their clothes melted.

Blood and foaming gore ran out of the bottoms of the un-moving pants legs, and the heads and hands were not burned. The grotesquely maimed and contorted shells of bodies covered the ground along with the bubbling blood and slime left over from their insides. And the eyes in their heads looked like those of fish fried in a skillet. After the narrow violet beams had played back and forth over the Israeli army emplacements like searchlights sweeping a night sky, the UFOs suddenly shot straight up in the sky. A microsecond later, they were gone.

As if ordained by a precise and powerful intelligence, at the very moment when the first pair of Soviet T-92 tanks appeared across the Gamla Rise, something else out of the ordinary began to happen.

43

The Bolides

The first sign the world was given that something extraordinary was happening in the Middle East was a tremendous earthquake that struck Israel at 12:03 in the afternoon, Tel Aviv time. Walls inside cities all across the small country came down, and there were great chasms that opened in the ground all along the northern half of the country. The shock and vibration shattered human constructions, and people were knocked to the ground. The mountains moved, and stone cliffs avalanched to the lesser heights.

On the bramble-covered Golan Heights the intensity of the quake was incredibly severe, like a dog shaking a rat, and the ground seemed to roll like waves of the open sea. From beneath the earth there came a great roaring. Columns of the invading armies ground to a sudden halt while the earth shook and trembled and the foundations of the hills shifted. In little more than half a minute the quake subsided; almost immediately the Soviet armor started rolling again, proceeding toward Israel via their sinuous routes.

The weapons spouted fire in unrelenting streams as the armies sped across the barren outline of the land, and IAF jets continued with their sorties into the teeth of the juggernaut, diving and bombing and banking swiftly, some flashing into flames or disintegrating in the air from enemy fire. There were great columns of smoke from the weapons firing, and out of the smoke the vehicles kept coming like armored, antennaed giant creatures on the earth. In the air Soviet helicopters flew like huge winged tanks and launched missiles that sprouted from trails of orange fire and then swished down faster than the eye could follow onto Israeli defensive positions.

The first Soviet armored division poured from the Bek'a Valley across the northern Israeli border at 12:14 in the heat of the afternoon. It was 12:21 before the bolides came. Above the thundering, grinding roar of the armored columns and marching hordes that covered the country north and east of Israel like a storm cloud, an unusual sound suddenly came from the sky, like the wind playing in telephone lines—like angry bees swarming. Then a score of bolides appeared high in the hazy sky, each huge and brilliant as the sun, slanting earthward. To the north people in Tiberias began pointing and murmuring at what they saw streaking the battle zone on the Golan Heights.

As the gigantic meteors glided earthward in long, sloping paths, leaving trails of smoke and dust behind them in the dull blue air, great sounds like cannon fire preceded them from the vaunt of sky. In near and remote awe a myriad of witnesses on the Asian mainland and in the Middle East, along with an amazed global television audience, watched as the flaming bolides exploded low in the atmosphere, and huge flaming fireballs and molten sulfuric lava streamed down from the heavens upon the Soviet-Arab invasion forces, carrying with them a deafening roar. The sky seemed to almost fill up with fire, and it was spewing out onto the armies below.

Then more bolides appeared like huge mountains in the upper air and rampaged down through the gravitational circuit. The breadth of the skies above the invading Soviet and allied Arab armies seemed to glow like electrified gas in a tube. Fire and brimstone thundered down from the sky relentlessly. The aerial blast that followed the low-altitude bolide explosions blew armored vehicles and helicopters to pieces and hurled debris and rock and dust into the air. Hurricane-force winds followed the aerial explosions and expended their fury back toward the teeming invasion forces. All along the breadth and length of the first two Soviet divisions, whose columns had poured like great snaked creatures into the Golan Heights, troops burned to instant crispness, like insects in a forest fire, as coals of fire and flaming substance the consistency of jelly rained down on them in massive, lethal concentrations.

The display was widespread along the Israeli border and extended into large areas of the Soviet Union and mainland China. It lasted 118 minutes over the hills and mountains at the boundaries to Israel, and the lives of hundreds of thousands of the gray- and green-clad invaders ended in that short time. Above the invading army's battle zone the sky darkened half as black as night at just past three P.M., and the raging fires faintly illuminated the debris-laden sky with variegated patches of flickering light.

Fires started all across the Golan Heights and beyond as Arab and Soviet soldiers continued to pour out of their machines, stumbling, gasping for breath, and beating at the fiery air with their arms. Some of the soldiers bleated out the sounds of dying and destruction with blood-curdling screams. Some staggered and cried like trapped animals as flames engulfed them. Tank men came staggering out of the surviving armored war machines and began sprawling onto the volcanic ground—some overcome instantly by the heat from molten lava and flames, some still moving on all fours, clawing at the earth with death and horror in their eyes as they charred where they kneeled on the fire-covered ground.

The rocky land began filling up with death, littering the ground with charred black faces in smoldering uniforms that burned and mixed their ashes with the black sticky remnants of flesh. Hordes of soldiers disembarked armored personnel carriers, and some of them cracked off small arms fire as they tried to walk through the sheets of fire and then fell to the ground with agonizing screams that went on until their vocal chords withered and turned to black, leathery sinew. The fires and molten brimstone from the sky incinerated flesh and blood and hair and eyes and the bones and teeth would remain upon the ground. Eventually the fiery rain from the air made the landscape turn gray and black with bodies and machines.

Firelike storms began to rage across the invasion zone as fuel ignited and fountains of flame sprouted here and there. Heaps of ashes that had been men lay for tens of miles along the invasion route on the northern and eastern borders in the highlands of Israel. Intense winds sprouted and blew across Tiberias, bending trees and bushes over toward confluence with the ground. Concussions of war machines dotted the Israeli hills, and searing heat enveloped the miles and miles of invading armies. Sheets of liquid fire rolled across the invasion route like napalm. And as the firestorm intensified the scorching, intense wind carried dust from the incinerated bodies across the land, and it settled in crevices of buildings and in windowsills and along the streets of Tiberias. A strange smell enveloped the city like a dry pungent gas, and after a while everywhere the smell was like being inside the smokestack of a crematorium.

As it happened, the ones who were burned alive were the lucky ones. The intense heat had released the biological weapons from their shells prematurely and the wind caused by the bolide concussions in the air had carried the hybrid, heat-resistant bacteria all across the hundreds of square miles of Soviet and Arab troops before they could don protective clothing. The vast majority of troops in the second wave of invaders that had escaped the heavenly fire were enshrouded with drifting clouds of their own deadly diseases and became infected. With agonizing slowness the germs did their terrible, inevitable work downwind. Some of the diseased invading Arabs and Soviets used the last moments of life to fire projectiles from surviving weaponry at one another, and many died like mad dogs, killing fellow invaders as they themselves dropped.

A short while after five-thirty the dust in the air precipitated torrential rains. The rains cascaded down onto the borderlands and along the mountainsides. Rivers of water formed quickly into sinuous, snakelike meanderings across the barren landscape as the rain came down as it had never done before in that land. The remaining fires were obliterated from the battle zone, and men who were still alive in the path of the water were washed along with already dead corpses and ashes of corpses. And the water ran fast and opaque with mud and debris and human remains and dying bodies.

From the amphitheater of the Israeli lowlands near the Sea of Galilee retreating Israeli citizens stopped and watched the incredible, distant spectacle played out upon the ancient rise of mountains. And camera crews from major news services around the world recorded the destruction of the advancing Soviet and Syrian military machines from the area around Tiberias. Microwave antennae relayed the video pictures, and the whole event was broadcast to the world like a short, macabre science fiction play, feeding through small satellites that circled in precise orbits above the terrestrial sphere. Never in the history of human affairs had an army been so totally routed.

For more than 600,000 Soviet and Arab invaders who died on the hills and mountains inside Israel and, back from there, where they encompassed its borders, it was a fearful day of surprise and horror and agony before they crossed the threshold between life and death. And it would be seven months before Israel could locate the lion's share of the bodies on the sulphur-covered land and bury the masses of dead in a valley called Abarim, east of the Dead Sea. They would rename the land there and call it the Valley of the Russian Mob.

At the same time, over the populated parts of the Soviet Union, the fire and brimstone had also poured down from the sky like a small planet falling. Great cities in Russia and China had started to blaze with fires of apparent meteoric origin, and the humans and their habitations in those areas had suffered terrible destruction. On the edge of the great bolide explosions Israel and several Arab countries in the region had been spared from the rain of death from the skies. Before the continuous reporting of the events ended 20 hours later the news establishment anchormen had darkly etched circles like the canals of Mars beneath their eyes.

In the incredible magic of that moment before the world turned dark one could almost see that straight line through time between the prophetic wonders and the coming of the beasts that would rule earth with power from that dark invisible world; and all the barriers between what was real and what was not were about to come down.

44

Lo!

It was just the past the hour that separates one day from another, when the stars silently blaze. The darkly colored vehicles moved like a slow, secret caravan along the narrow country road until they came within a few hundred yards of the isolated farmhouse. Like a precise, many faceted machine, the cars cut their engines and rolled into the weeds at the side of the narrow road until they came to a halt in a line behind the thick growth that ran between the large front yard that sloped away from the farmhouse and a curve in the asphalt road. NSA intelligence men inside the cars, as if by silent command, paused and watched.

The lead car was a Lincoln, with a band of electronic panels above the inside of the windshield like that of a rich Arab. The man who rode in the passenger front seat spoke quietly into a microphone that hung like a viper's head from the end of a thick black cord sheathed with an armorlike, metallic covering. Up and down the line of automobiles, drably clad men readied tranquilizer guns and other electronic stun weapons.

Tom and Melissa left the remains of a burning log in the fireplace, came through the front door of the farmhouse, down the five steps that led from the small porch, and began strolling toward the barnyard. Melissa tilted her head back a moment and took in the glory of the stars. Tom could smell the smoke still in the air from the autumn burnings intermingled with the smoke from the fireplace that drifted up from the white stone chimney. There was a musty scent that seemed to come from the woods beside the barn, and the odors wafted around them and seemed to hover in the fresh, cool air of autumn as they walked hand in hand. There were fluffy white clouds that were roaming quickly through the sky, covering and uncovering star eyes. Melissa watched them scud like ghostly riders for a moment until, suddenly, the clouds seem to halt their heavenly driftings and the night became quiet all around them.

"Do you notice it?" Melissa asked Tom.

"It's quiet all of a sudden," answered Tom. "Really quiet."

"Listen," whispered Melissa. They stopped a moment and listened. "It's like the earth is holding its breath, listening the same as we are—waiting." Melissa took in a long pull of breath. With the treetops stilled and the clouds motionless now, the scene around them resembled a life-size panting of a dark, frozen landscape everywhere they looked. Tom glanced back up at the heavens and saw that the stars weren't glistening anymore, but, instead, the black invisibility of space was sprinkled with pinpoints of light that showed eerie, steady glows like burning grains of sand inset in the black bowl of night.

Like a flickering in the corner of his eye Tom glimpsed strange lights above the closest hill, unpopulated except for an old grave-yard. He turned to get a better look at the glowing and saw a multitude of light-enveloped forms rising off the tree-enshrouded heights. The southern sky right above the camelback of the hillside was thickly peppered with sparkling, oblong forms. It was like a great awesome swarm of dazzling, oddly shaped UFOs ascending slowly and steadily into the sky. He looked over at Melissa—she was watching the phenomenon by now—and then he was jerked off the ground.

Tom saw Melissa rising up beside him, her eyes big as quarters, and like heat lightning in slow motion the sky lightened a shade. Then the sky seemed to glow and the glow brightened until the whole sky lit up, blue-violet at first, then the shade lightened to dark scarlet red . . . and lightened. And the tufts of clouds looked like illuminated scarlet waves moving on the ocean, endlessly rocking. In one brief dance the treetops surged and rustled their parched autumn leaves, and then stopped and seemed to freeze once more. All the while, the color of the heavens changed and became brighter, lighter in hue.

Suddenly Melissa and Tom were enveloped in honeyed light as they floated upward through the air, drifting over motionless treetops, and Tom looked down on the smoke coming from the chimney top on the house; it was frozen in a curling stream below them as they glided over the housetop like monstrous birds. There was a sensation Tom had that an incredibly powerful wind had blown them off their feet and was blowing them higher into the air and the higher they got, the harder it blew, pushing them gently upward in a golden, protective cocoon of light. They heard a sound like a trumpet blowing in the sky, sharply and sweetly, and then a shout of ''come hither'' rang out above them. It seemed to reverberate through the night air like the sound of a multitude of woodland streams, amplified and intermingled together. There was a yellow luminescence around them, clinging to them like 24-karat transparent shadows as they lifted up toward the strange, rose-colored clouds.

It had all occurred without warning. One minute they had been standing there looking around them, then they saw some forms lift off the hillside, and the next thing they knew this glow, like that of the Milky Way, was all around them, and they were floating upward toward an unearthly, illuminated night sky. As Tom looked down he could see the frozen landscape shrink below them and the clumps of treetops move swiftly under his dangling feet, their red and gold leaves radiant and pretty in the gradually increasing light. When they were almost to the base of the clouds he saw a night bird, to his left, perfectly motionless in flight. He pointed it out to Melissa, and they smiled as they floated up past the bird, its wings stiffly extended, its shiny eyes dark and motionless like black beads.

Tom knew that the flow of time had somehow ceased to exist, as if they were being rapidly accelerated to the speed of light and the sensors of the mind were inoperative in this rarified region, and so the mind had frozen the inputs from the ordinary—from everything they knew—yet that couldn't be. He saw Melissa with real-time movements beside him, and he knew they were moving relative to everything around them. His attention went back to the vault of sky above them; he could see a cloud of brilliant golden light among the other clouds, and beams of golden light suddenly came forth out of the one cloud and radiated forth, lighting the sky bright as day in all directions. He could feel his body being drawn upward through the night air, precisely along one of the intense beams of light that shone from the sky. A voice deep and powerful called out sharp, cutting words in an unknown language and, after that, a great horn sounded, and a multitude of voices began to sing in the air above them. There were no words in any language they had ever heard before, but it was a blending of quite lovely music and a singing in perfect harmony—beautiful and unearthly.

And they suddenly knew it was Jesus in the cloud with a golden glow around him and his power and the glory that resurrected him was making the night light up as bright as day. Tom could see other luminescent people being drawn upward through the sky around them, as if swimming through the air along myriads of golden rays of light that radiated from the Son of God straight above them. Tears gushed from their eyes then like fountains, and ran down their faces in great streams, and they sobbed, making crying sounds with their throats. The clouds around them were like waves of amber-gold grain, glowing, flowing back and forth in unison as if the wind that pushed their bodies up was blowing the clouds in syncopation, backward and forward through the bright blue sky.

The most amazing thing happened next. The bodies that Melissa and Tom had were swallowed up into nothingness as they floated upward, and the tears were suddenly gone from their faces and their crying had stopped. New bodies had appeared around them instantly, and Tom knew when it happened because the new body felt so painless and powerful—perfect, as if the old one had been merely a used-up shell like that which a cicada leaves behind at a preordained time in its life. And as if they were seeing with different eyes, they could see giant angels mixed with the people in the air and on each side of them there was an angel, and when Tom saw their faces he recognized them. Above them now they saw Jesus in the middle of the golden glow, and his beauty and the utter love that flowed from him was beyond human description except to say it was glory. He shone with a light that was so intense, they had been blinded from seeing him before, in the old body. But now, with new eyes, they could see his hair luminescent, white as snow-colored wool; fire like flames seemed to come from his eyes, yet they were peaceful, captivating as magnets; his skin shone like burnished brass and its radiance was beautiful beyond anything they ever could have imagined.

There was something heavy and fast, like invisible rivers of living water that seemed to be flowing through Jesus toward them and on into them, and it made Tom recall that exact moment at the Lancaster Church on the Rock when he had accepted Christ the best way he knew how—he had put his whole heart into it. Into his mind, now, flashed that first scripture he had read back at his motel room, as a two-hour-old Christian on a joyful evening months ago. "For you yourselves know full well that the day of the Lord will come just like a thief in the night. While they are saying, 'Peace and safety!' then destruction will come upon them suddenly like birth pangs upon a woman with child; and they shall not escape. But you, brethren, are not in darkness, that the day should overtake you like a thief; for you are sons of light and sons of day. We are not of night nor of darkness; so then let us not sleep as others do, but let us be alert and sober. For those who sleep do their sleeping at night, and those who get drunk, get drunk at night. But since we are of the day, let us be sober, having put on the breastplate of faith and love, and as a helmet, the hope of salvation. For God has not destined us for wrath, but for obtaining salvation through our Lord Jesus Christ, who died for us, that whether we are awake or asleep, we may live together with him."

As Melissa's and his own light-covered forms neared the radiance of Christ, Tom stretched out his arms upward, and he could see his own glow extending 16 or 18 inches away from the skin on his arms in all directions, like twin tunnels of light above him. Deep down inside, he knew this whole encounter could be explained scientifically; there were laws he could almost see in his mind, but what people called science on earth could never have come close. His mind strayed from the laws of this new realm, the color of the glow around him fascinated him so—it was an unearthly rose-colored shade of blue—beautiful and peaceful to look at. As he looked over at Melissa, gliding beside him through the day-lit air, she looked more beautiful than before, and fresh with the same glow he had around her, and she smiled at him with a smile just like she always smiled.

There were, at the same time, more and more luminous people and angelic beings in the air all around them, and the world on the ground was moving again far away, but they could somehow see it up close. They could see people running crazily, in panic, below, their mouths agape with fear, their eyes glazed and frozen with terror at what was happening in the sky. They could see farmers and wives and children and strange men in dark clothing running and stumbling across the ground outside the houses on both sides of the Hosclaw ridge of hills. Some of the people on the ground ran while their heads spastically swiveled, flailing their arms at the air. They seemed to shake from the inside out, like frightened animals, their mouths in all stages of contortions. And Tom could see the small old graveyard behind their rented farmhouse, and most of the graves were unearthed and had given up their dead. The clouds around about them were golden now and in a beautiful continuous pattern throughout the sky like luminous fish scales, and it was very lovely to see.

Melissa began singing, and Tom joined in, as they entered the glowing, golden cloud where Christ was, and their voices blended with the celestial melody that seemed to come from far above them, at the outer reaches of the sky. Before light had glistened across these same heavens, before the oceans had splashed across their rocky basins, it had been foreordained from the foundation of the world that Jesus would come on a night such as this for those who believed in him—those sleeping in death and those who would never die. And in no time they and all who were with them left behind the Milky Way, swirling through the earth's night sky like brightly lighted diamonds and dust of diamonds.

They were brought to an extraordinarily large, beautiful meadow next. The landscape around them was brightly illuminated with a clean white light, and the sky was brilliant, unearthly blue, but the strangest thing: there was no sun in the sky. They had been brought with many others to a place so immense that they were alone with each other. They could feel others' souls in the distance beyond the powers of sight. Around them were small low hills, curved like giant tortoiseshells. There were animals, multicolored foliage, and heavily fruited trees everywhere they could see around them. Melissa had always loved violets, and after they had started walking, when they came upon some patches of the velvety purple flower, she started to bend to pick some and instantly a bouquet was in her hand. Tom started to think, *How did that happen?*, but before the question was fully formed, the answer came into his mind: "Here, the thought is the deed."

Where are we? Tom started to think.

"At a place I have prepared for you," came the premature answer from a voice that they knew. "Rest a while and then we shall feast. Even in your immortal body you can eat to the glory of God. And after we take meat and bread and you are filled we will rest for a time, and then prepare to defeat the forces of the Enemy."

"Where, Lord?" asked Melissa aloud.

Before she had finished the words the mind of Christ answered, "On earth, at the battle Armageddon, my sister."

Melissa and Tom strolled peacefully, their bodies giving off a faint white radiance even in the bright shadowless light. And while they walked lightly across the land they came to places where they saw people they knew and whom they hadn't seen for a very long time. The next thing they knew, Shadrach sprinted up to them from behind a grove of elms. His dark coat glistened in the light, and some of it had turned gray on his face, above the eyes and on his chin, and it made him look a little older. His tail wagged furiously and he licked at their hands as they bent to pet and kiss him. After that Melissa walked on the tops of the trees as she had always wanted to.

45

A Prophecy of Peace

The television announcer with the booze-swollen nose sat in the air-conditioned studio calmly looking at a six-foot television screen on the wall behind him. The big networks had all brought the old pros out of retirement, from their east coast estates, to contribute their analyses of the momentous events the world was witnessing, and this retired editor of the airways had wild brows slanted over his eyes thick as brushes. Underneath the light blue eyes big oval folds of flesh stood out. The man had on a navy sport coat, white shirt, and a $175 yellow silk tie. Hidden under the announcer's table he had on Levi blue jeans, Polo socks, and yacht shoes. In back of him there were the head and shoulders of another reporter hulking on the screen, and he was speaking into a microphone that he held like an ice cream cone. In a facility not far away, near Alexandria, Virginia, people from a super-secret agency were watching the proceedings on a set of 42-inch monitors.

"Don, the atmosphere here at the United Nations is charged with anticipatory excitement," said the reporter from the U.N. media room. He had a handsome, dark complexion. "There is—well, there's kind of an electricity in the air about the upcoming speech by President O'Fallon."

"Any ideas as to what the speech will be about, Joe—I understand there's been a lot of secrecy at this point," said the studio announcer, shifting in his chair a little and laying his shoulders back.

"The delegates are expectant and the rumors are that the speech will be dynamite," replied the other reporter. Behind him the seats were full of people from around the globe. "There has been no preview of what the president's speech will be about, but all indications are, from long-time observers on the scene, that it will deal extensively with the recent extraordinary events in the Middle East."

"Well, President O'Fallon has certainly been the most popular American president in history," commented the anchorman. On the TV screen in the media room at the secret Alien Reconnaissance Organization's headquarters, the white makeup showed underneath his eyes, and the purple arcs underneath that.

"I wish they'd get on with it or give us some good old entertainment on the Tee-Vee," said the heavy-set, thick-faced woman who sat beside the chief shift monitor at the ARO network communications panel. Her thick, black false eyelashes and caked, cobalt blue eye shadow made her eyelids resemble the bloom on some exotic, other-worldly flower. "It's been solid news on all the stations for two days. All they do is yak, yak, yak!"

"Shut up a minute," the chief monitor told her. "We've got a job to do here in case you're not aware of that fact!"

On the screen now there flashed the picture of the podium, surrounded by modern walls and expensive, commodious spaces. A man was approaching the speaking platform from his seat a short distance away. "And now, ladies and gentlemen," announced the anchorman, "from the United Nations, we are joining—live—the introductions of the President of the United States. Coming to the podium now is Dr. David Bennington, Secretary General of the United Nations."

"Members of the General Assembly," said the white-haired secretary, "today, at this time of apprehension and trouble for all nations, while our hearts and minds search for answers to truly extraordinary questions, I have the honor and great pleasure to present the President of the United States." The applause broke out and filled the room as the popular president strode forward. When he reached the podium the president gave the other man a broad smile that showed a lot of teeth, and the two men shook hands, the president clasping the Secretary General's hand with both of his own.

"Mister Secretary General, delegates to the General Assembly, and members of the world who are tuned in via satellite," the president began in his smooth, well-modulated voice. "Today, in the midst of terrible tragedies and unexplained occurrences that beset our planet, I bring you glad tidings." Once more uncertain applause rained out from the assembly that was spread out in a great semi-circle around the speaking platform.

"I should preface my remarks here today by asking you to not be alarmed by what I will tell you. Humanity and the institutions and governments of the world have made great progress over the centuries only to witness terrible events that thwart our evolution. We have just seen such events taking place in the Middle East over the past several days. At this critical hour our fervent hope and prayer has been that a miracle would come to take away this nuclear terror that faces us all—the threat of an all-out nuclear exchange that could lead to extermination of mankind. So, my fellow people of the world, in that context I come before you this day to bring you a great and important message concerning a miracle that has already taken place—a message from our friends on other worlds."

President O'Fallon blinked and paused as the crowd stirred and mumbled at what he had said. "I have been asked by beings from other planets to be a spokesman for them this day," said the president. Pandemonium broke out in the room then. Some of the reporters shot up from their chairs and hurried out.

After the noise and commotion had died down the president continued. "There are several events of the past several days that our friends from other worlds want to explain in order that humanity might understand what has indeed already occurred at this turning point in the destiny of the world. Then I have been asked to reveal a program and its curator, whereby peace will finally come to our beleaguered planet." Sporadic applause came from the uncertain gathering before him. "This plan suggested by our brothers from other worlds will allow citizens of earth to finally live out their lives in peace under a one-world system of government. One that will ensure brotherhood instead of our archaic system of artificial borders and monetary currencies." Applause again.

"Let me just tell you what I currently know about the intelligences who operate what most of the world has popularly called unidentified flying objects in the atmosphere of our planet. The earth has been under observation by advanced beings from several planets in our galaxy for approximately six decades. This series of observations was undertaken when automatic monitoring devices stationed in this solar system detected atomic explosions on the planet Earth.

"The advanced races of intelligent beings who inhabit neighboring worlds are united in an intergalactic council that peacefully monitors and even aids in the development of worlds that have problems during their evolutionary cycles. This federation of advanced planets controls the regions across our own Milky Way and into the six neighboring galaxies. This same intergalactic federation seeded this planet with life many millions of years ago. As part of the ongoing process they have monitored the evolving Earth from time to time throughout our history. Now, in this generation of Earth's advanced technological society, but primitive sociology, man threatens the extinction of this planet as well as possible destruction of the entire solar system."

The president paused, took a drink from a small water glass, and set it back down on the podium. The delegates stirred with low chatter for a moment, and it was picked up on the big NSA screen as an oscillating buzzing, as if a hornet's nest had been placed next to a distant live microphone.

Then he went on. "Since that fateful day when the United States exploded the first man-made nuclear device in our New Mexico desert, the intergalactic federation has intensively monitored the entire earth. All atomic research, production, and storage facilities have been constantly under surveillance since 1945. All other aspects of the world society were monitored, carefully analyzed, and the information was revised as necessary to develop a program for rescuing this planet and all the life upon it when the appropriate moment presented itself. Our neighbors from space prepared to intervene if necessary.

"When man's first primitive satellites were launched into orbit around this globe the intergalactic federation increased the level of surveillance. Two days ago the intergalactic federation agreed to intervene in the Earth's evolution due to the planned Israeli use of nuclear weapons against the Eastern Alliance expeditionary forces.

"Although, this information has been kept secret until this moment I must tell you now that elements of the Israeli Air Force nuclear strike force was prevented from delivering armed nuclear devices on Arab and Soviet targets that would have led to a probable Soviet nuclear counter-strike against Israel. This, in turn, would have most likely resulted in an escalation with a resulting American-Soviet nuclear exchange, since the United States has a

current agreement whereby a nuclear strike on Israeli territory is
considered to be a strike on our own territory. Unfortunately, to
preclude the use of atomic devices, many of the Israeli aircraft and
their pilots had to be terminated.

"As the Eastern Alliance advanced on Israeli territory to do
battle with conventional forces, it appears that the forces of nature
have intervened in the situation, and the latest reports we have
from the Middle East indicate that a large part of the invading
forces have suffered losses at the hands of an overwhemingly
devastating event that struck that region two days ago. Areas
across the land mass of the Soviet Union have also suffered great
damage and loss of life from what is thought to have been a
cometary collision, as you all know.

"And, now, as to the most recent tragic and unexplained
worldwide event, which occurred at approximately eleven o'clock
P.M. Washington time two evenings ago, I can only now relay the
message I bring from our space brothers of the intergalactic
council to the friends, relations, and loved ones of the hundreds of
millions of peoples who were taken. The people who so suddenly
departed this world were chosen to be taken away utilizing
advanced teleportation devices operated by forces of the intergalactic federation. These people are even now being settled in
relocation centers on another planet within the Milky Way galactic
system. Their departure at this time was deemed by the higher
powers in this region of the universe to be absolutely essential so
that earth can evolve to a new and higher level of peace and
prosperity.

"Now, I realize at this moment, because of what I have said
here today, the entire world is posing many questions. I shall keep
you abreast of any further communications I receive from the
intergalactic federation in the immediate days that lay before us.
Even as I speak to you peacekeeping ships from the intergalactic
federation under orders from the council are monitoring the
hostilities that still exist, and they stand ready to neutralize the use
of any nuclear weapon. The advanced intelligences in the galaxy
will not allow the use of such weapons on the earth since grave
consequences will result whenever a sufficient number of atomic
weapons are detonated. The intergalactic federation has
attempted to warn man of this. But intervention was at last
necessary. And, now, finally mankind must put nuclear weapons
behind him as a relic of a warlike and checkered past." The

president smiled at the applause this time.

"The first step of a truly lasting peace I announce today as President of the United States. In conjunction with all members of the North Atlantic Treaty Organization, who have a vital interest in the Middle East, we will be signing a pact with Israel that any nation that invades her sovereign territory will be attacked by the combined force of the Western Alliance of nations. In addition, we will be meeting with the Soviets and the Eastern Alliance in negotiations to bring us finally together in all ways as brothers of one world. With the help of the intergalactic federation, we expect to be successful in these negotiations.

"And now, I will introduce to you the new leader of the Western Alliance, who has been appointed by the brothers of the intergalactic federation to carry out the programs that I have outlined and that will ensure the survival of our races on Earth with limited intervention on the part of the federation itself. The intergalactic federation has charged the man you are about to meet with the responsibility to accomplish the changes I've touched on today. It is planned that he will also rule the Eastern Alliance. Because the intergalactic federation believes that the leaders of the world could never agree on one man to relinquish power to, the federation of our friends from the other worlds have made what they hope to be a fair selection of the gentleman who will become the chief administrator of the world government once the mechanics of that government can be put into operation. And because there will be some hesitation and doubt among the nations, the intergalactic federation wants to assure you that it stands fully ready to act as a last resort against any force or nation that would oppose the steps I've outlined here. To demonstrate to the world that the intergalactic federation has the technology and will to use that technology to enforce the peace, all major sources of power in the world will be interrupted for forty-eight hours beginning this evening at six o'clock P.M. U.S. Eastern Standard time. All electrical power installations that are required to maintain emergency or critical operations in the world society, such as those inherent in medical buildings or essential water supply power will not be affected. But all other electrical and battery-powered installations will be affected. The automotive traffic of the world will generally come to a halt with the exception of vehicles powered by diesel engines and emergency vehicles. Air and ground transportation systems should therefore phase out of scheduled operation, beginning immediately until further notice. I must emphasize that there is no cause for alarm since I have been assured that individual spacecraft operating at this very moment in our atmosphere are prepared to come to the aid of anyone who may need assistance. These people from other planets wish to emphasize that the power drainage is necessary to give man on Earth a sign that what we have announced before the world today is true, for there may be powerful forces and national leaders who will attempt to lead you astray and inform you that what I have told you here today is false. But I assure you that what I have told you is true and therefore, let the world rejoice for the threat of nuclear war is finally ended and a true and lasting peace has come to Earth. And with it our heavenly friends will share their wondrous technology so that one day soon it might truly be said of the Earth—lo, they have no more war, or sickness, or hunger, or oppression. And on that fine day the love on Earth will shine forth like the light from the Sun. Now, let me present to you the man chosen by our brothers from space to carry the tremendous responsibilities necessary to achieve one United Nations government, under guidance of the leaders on high—Mr. Michael Quanta."

The president nodded as the people in front of the podium stood and applauded. *Soon, you will bring down fire from heaven in the sight of all,* a familiar voice in his head said. O'Fallon felt an amazing exhilaration, a feeling of pleasure at what the voice had said, as he stepped aside and shook hands with the dark, handsome giant of a man who had come up to the podium from the first row. Quanta appeared almost seven feet in height, thin and wiry, very elegant in the way he walked and stood. They linked hands and raised them to the crowd as the applause reached a crescendo.

The president turned then, gathered the speech papers from the slanted surface, smiled warmly, waved his right hand, and then walked quickly with the Secret Service men to the exit. Then he was gone, and the people of the world remained and applauded, for they had never heard anything in the world like what he had said today. Beyond all doubt it would certainly be a moment long remembered by the peoples of the Earth. And they felt a sudden surge of anticipation at what the man who stood at the podium would tell them.

46

Son of the Morning

Outside the U.N. the sun was setting at the bottom of a copper sky, and it gave New York a surrealistic, sullen cast; inside the general assembly room an exceedingly tall, darkly handsome man began his address: "Fellow citizens of the world, I come to you today as an elder brother would after a terrible tragedy—to lay out a plan of acceptable action, a course to be steered in the hopeful days ahead—so that all will be well with our world once again." Quanta's words flowed with powerful feeling from a handsome, fiercely determined face. He paused for a moment as if to gather is exact thoughts, and he flashed a wide smile. The main assembly seated before him with its sea of gray and black suits stared in fascination at the speaker from various pink-, brown-, and yellow-hued faces. The outstanding characteristic of Quanta's smile, and the thing one would be prone to remember for a very long time, were the teeth—his ivory white teeth—the way they took over his mouth and hung in the air like those of a great carnivorous fish suddenly surfacing from the sea.

"My father is the ruler of the intergalactic federation that President O'Fallon has told you about today. The federation governs seven of the local galaxies, which each contain billions of stars and even a greater number of planets. A portion of the planets are inhabited. From upwards of 600 planets that make up the federation ten have been assigned to monitor and provide guidance during Earth's transition to federation levels of conduct. My mother is a native of San Francisco. Even though I have a different father, I am just a normal man like any other man on Earth, with the exception that I have been given special powers that will help me carry out my mission. Incidentally, to alleviate the possible fear that I have an exceedingly strange heritage, I might add that interbreeding among planetary races is common throughout the galaxies and was common in mankind's early history on Earth. In my particular case the intergalactic council thought it necessary that my father be one of them so that I would be suitable for the mission I now embark on." Quanta paused a moment and flashed a toothy smile that seemed to freeze on his lips while his dark, shining eyes panned the crowd.

"Now I must tell you of a truth that will be hard to accept for some, but that is commonly known throughout the local galaxies. In the most ancient of days the intergalactic council first authorized seeding of this world with the genetic code that rooted and evolved into the peoples and animals on this great planet." After Quanta told them that he was silent a moment. His eyes coolly regarded the crowd while it murmured like buzzing insects. Then he went on. "Humans were, of course, monitored from time to time throughout the years. When mankind on earth developed atomic weapons the intergalactic council, which rules the galactic federation, developed a plan to save mankind and the ecosphere of Earth itself. I stand before you today as part of that plan. I have been prepared since I was very young to perform the tasks we need to implement in our evolution to peace and a One-World Order of United Nations." Quanta's voice was deep and incredibly rich, as if a great cello had been given the power of speech in a world of violins. It was as if what he said mesmerized them all, through translations, in any tongue.

"Today, I announce to all the peoples of earth that a new world order has come to you—and because of it there will finally be a lasting peace on our planet. A great deal of wisdom from the advanced planets of this and other galaxies will be given to us on earth. Ninety-nine percent of the planets that whirl around the stars you see in the sky at night have no war or disease—no profiteering at the expense of others. Long ago on other worlds false money systems, prideful false religions, and harmful genetic and environmental elements that lead to war have been eliminated. In the immediate future we will be taking steps to abolish the wealthy class, who grotesquely use the talents and labor of others to accumulate their fortunes. We plan to bring a utopia to all nations—not just the Communist or capitalistic peoples, but rather all nations. All systems will become one system handed down from those who have watched over us for thousands of years. The new order is not political. Our space brothers, under command of my father, in a galaxy far from here, will provide justice for all, based on galactic laws that have evolved throughout hundreds of civilizations in the heavens far above you. It is more religion than government.

"Two nights ago, as the American president has mentioned, the earth entered a new age. Powerful energy fields transmitted by intergalactic devices in earth orbit were utilized in tele-porting—which is an advanced form of transportation—ah, tele-porting off the Earth all humans who were not prepared for the new age. Just to go into the technology of that a little, I can tell you that part of the monitoring program that our intergalactic brothers performed was the measurement of vibration energy levels and patterns for the individual life forces of every man, woman, and child on the face of this planet. As incredible as that sounds, with the technology at the disposal of the council, it is actually relatively simple.

"That portion of humanity who, by reason of improper parameters in their life-force readings, were not adaptable to the new world order that is even now coming to the earth, had to be relocated for humane reasons. The new age would have quite literally destroyed these people so they were mercifully taken away. Many of these appeared on the outside to be wonderful companions to loved ones, but their innermost vibrations would never have been able to attune to the true world of light and love that is about to blossom on the earth like a great springtime in cosmic evolution. It's a difficult concept, I know, but just think of the new one-world order as you would a great crystal vibrating at a high frequency that induces the same frequency in all organic matter around it. That is perhaps as close as I can come to explaining what the universal principle of light and love is all about." Quanta stopped a minute and surveyed the crowd, seemingly gauging the effect of his words.

Then, smiling as if he had told himself a joke, he continued lightheartedly. "You will notice very shortly that people's bodies will start to live longer on a peaceful earth—that is only one benefit of this new peace and love the world will see. You see, disease and wearing out of your bodies is not necessary—it is only a consequence of not having true light and love. And so, this great exodus was the first step necessary before peace on Earth could be ushered in. These people who were removed were not taken in vain. Do not mourn their loss, for it was necessary to ensure the survival of Earth itself and all the living things on it." Quanta extended his long arms to the front of the podium as he seemed engrossed with a new line of thinking for a moment.

"The intergalactic federation of planets wishes to tell you that a fair system of exchange must be instituted on the Earth. The peoples of the world at the present time must purchase what they need with United States dollars or gold. The use of one money over the other will always threaten the peace. Money leads to many evils. Therefore, a consistent worldwide monetary system must be implemented. Briefly, I might tell you that all present forms of currencies that cause profiteering and greed will be abolished. In their place will be world credit vouchers, as is practiced on all the civilized worlds in this galaxy. There will be no more concern about theft of money or credit cards, for we will implement a system where an invisible mark will enable you to transact all required business more conveniently than in the past. The justice and arbitration of disputes under the new government will be provided based on laws that have evolved throughout hundreds of planetary civilizations. I have prepared a request that committees of the United Nations take up these issues and present a workable plan to implement the demonetization of our system of buying and selling.

"In addition, the intergalactic federation considers the present diverse religious factions in this world to be much of the cause for friction in our society. Some of the more radical elements of so-called Christian faiths and other sects and various belief systems were teleported to the planet Caldoen with those peoples who, tragically, were not prepared for the peace and tranquility of a new world order." He paused to bask in a round of more vigorous applause that came from what appeared to be an astonished, captivated crowd.

"Thank you. Thank you," he said, bowing his head humbly. "Now I don't want to make this an overly long presentation today, for there is much we all need to accomplish. The federation has finally made itself known so that earth can enter a golden era—one far removed from anything ever imagined by man. The utopia dreamed of by great thinkers in the past is finally at hand. Every citizen of the new world government can count these days as days of salvation in the midst of dread. And we need the support of every citizen of Earth to make this government work—I am counting on that support.

"Everyone will receive a document that will outline the plan for the new United Nations government, and you will be asked to pledge your support to our common cause." Even the hardest faces in the audience seemed to have changed by now—transformed almost magically with faint, Mona Lisa smiles hovering on most of the lips of people who maintained cool, dispassionate eyes.

"The new United Nations of Earth with prevent all war with the aid of member civilizations of the intergalactic federation. Mankind's puny earth weapons are no match for the weapons at the disposal of the federation, who have intervened to prevent Israel's use of atomic bombs. In fairness to the nation of Israel, the new world government's first official act will be to sign a protection treaty with them so that we can assure their safety.

"Any nation that attempts to come against Israel or any other nation on the face of the Earth will suffer severe losses from the intergalactic federation forces that stand ready just outside the atmosphere of Earth. In fairness to Russia, whose homeland and expeditionary forces were struck by massive meteoric outbursts, we will all have to collectively restore their dignity and come to their rescue. Everything conceivable will be instituted to bring the people of Russia back to their feet again.

"As the American president mentioned, the demonstration of the seriousness of the resolve of the intergalactic federation to establish a one-world ruling system on Earth will commence within the hour. All unnecessary power will be prevented from being utilized for exactly 48 hours. I was given the talent and capabilities to perform the appointed task of establishing a one-world peace and administering a central planetary ruling system that will remove all friction-causing barriers—but I need each person's help who can hear me today.

"And now I must end the presentation and begin the work at hand because there is much to be done. My father and the council of brothers who administer the local galactic systems have given me a final message to bring to you at this dawn of a new civilization. In their long-delayed intervention they desire nothing but that the Earth eventually bloom forth and produce the fruits of peace, love, and the joy of life lived without fear and disease and death to overtake you. Thank you in advance for your help." The charismatic Quanta waved and left the podium. He walked past a sea of faces that had risen and started surging forward like iron fillings in close proximity to a magnet. He shook some of the friendly hands that extended along his path until he was almost midway between the platform and the exit.

Just at that spot two men with security badges pulled sawed-off shotguns from under expensive black suit coats and, before the real UN security men could stop them, the men fired orange-yellow blasts into Quanta at point-blank range. Both halves of Michael Quanta's head disintegrated and flew off in bloody streaming masses; he slumped down at the feet of the scuffling security guards as they ran up and subdued the strange men in black who stood staring at what they had just done like hypnotised, radio-controlled man-machine hybrids waiting for further orders on a non-existent carrier signal.

Television cameramen ran up with their compact video cameras jogging on their shoulders and scrambled to get the best angle, like jockeys in a 29-horse Kentucky Derby—pointing their glass-embedded tubes toward the vicinity of the fallen figure of a man as he bled in warm red spurts from where his head had been. A camera crew had staked out the best spot, between two security men, close to the spurting neck, and was first to zoom in on the dead Quanta for the live world television audience to see. When Quanta's head reformed from a horrible blood-infested, pinkish stub to a hazy ghostly image and then to solid flesh and hair, and, in a few short seconds, his teeth showed pearly white as he grimaced a little and raised a handsome head that hadn't been there seconds before.

Everything about Quanta's face was just as it had been before the horrifying, brain-searing shots had rocked the chamber. The video machine had captured it, and the whole world had a record of the most amazing thing that had ever been recorded on tape. After the 48 hours had passed, after that Great Blackout was ended, the peoples of the world who could get to a TV receiver would see the replay of the miracle occurring over and over, and a fearful wonder would seep into their minds. Later, in classic under-statement, the electronic and print media would boldly proclaim Michael Quanta as the most charismatic leader on the world scene in recent memory.

Less than an hour had passed on Earth. Beyond the confines of time the King of Demons rested in the netherworld known from ages past as Hades. In that region of nightmare images the Angel of the Abyss and his legion of demons laughed harshly as they saw the humans on the surface scurry wildly to brace for the Great Blackout. In that colorless world beyond a gate between time and eternity, in a realm that occultists and spiritualists had contacted over the centuries of earth time, a powerful ancient creature smiled a hideous crooked smile, showing teeth like the edge of a saw, and gloated over the extremes with which the world had greeted his son. The light in the strange chamber where Satan sat was like an almost extinguished twilight, filled with gloom, the dim light fluctuating almost unnoticeably between degrees of dimness. It was like a shadow world, teeming with nauseous hot vapors.

In that misty darkness shadowy outlines of images moved, and there were sounds like mechanized whirrings and hideous mocking voices speaking in guttural, throaty chantings of unknown words. It was a very real world, outside the electromagnetic spectrum of man and his instruments, inside a whirling vortex where an incredibly hideous and malevolent spirit land lurked beyond the speed of light.

The smoky chambers were alive with shadowy semblances of demons who were in the process of dematerializing, then reforming as the lying wonders known as UFOs in the atmosphere of the earth. A host of demonic UFOs, appearing metallic and tremendous in size, would shortly be over all the critical points in the world's power grids. In the hidden darkness, others of the fallen creatures, with strange, malformed images like imitations of withered and ugly human bodies, were manipulating ancient instruments with rapid, insectlike movements as far as the eye could see throughout an extended shadowy maze of tunnels that seemed to go on forever. Some of them, when the strange illumination reached its maximum, were barely visible, and their images showed huge, with black goggle eyes on their heads and sharp-pointed, catlike ears that quivered as they worked.

Seated on a flat projection that dully blended in with the omnipresent shadows, the Prince of Darkness watched the surface of Earth on a small oval screen enclosed in a structure exactly like one of those internally scenic easter eggs, ashlike in its colored grayness outside—its oval end port flickering with colored lights from inside. Scenes on the planet's night side flashed before the creature's strange eyes as he watched dazzling demon images hover over electric power grids, and he saw other glowing entities emerge over cities and towns to stop the flow of traffic. Legions of evil imps stood by to materialize as UFOs wherever energy was detected and, when that happened, fiery globes of lights would dart toward the energy source and disrupt whatever would attempt to move.

Satan's armored face seemed almost petrified, illuminated by a flickering glow. In his present form the creature appeared to be a giant serpent like the dragons of old. Just in front of the dim screen his goatlike head suddenly moved to and fro like a serpent at the end of an extended neck, thick and eel-like in its lengthy, curved appearance. The neck ran down to a huge body, and a tail twisted out beneath that, extending 20 feet or more. The tail was looped back on itself, and it was tipped with a triple lobe like a shark-finned arrowhead. Satan's knobby body showed red-black in the dull, shadowy light, and it had a texture like the scales of a fish. Running up along his spiny back was a zigzag of humps. Attached to that was the slender neck that ended at the head in a crest like a lion's mane except it appeared to be made of spines instead of hair.

The eyes of the creature were rather large, elongated around the side of his head, red with yellow pupils; they carried in them the exact expression of a dead animal whose eyes are frozen in the last look it ever took. Sprouting from amid spines on top of his head were two fat, rounded horns, the shape of miniature ICBM nose cones, whitish in color.

The crystalline egg-shaped screen's lighting played over Satan's ravenous, deeply etched contours as he watched the colored lights of Earth's night side blink out. In the dim light his face was a deep red in color with armored, furrowed skin like that of an alligator's. For a moment, he held open his cruel-looking mouth and gazed as if petrified, his pointed tongue perfectly still, suspended behind the rows of teeth. The huge creature seemed to inhale as he watched the colorless gloom take over man's habitations on the dark side of the planet's surface.

An unsurpassed madness was about to engulf the earth; those who had refused to accept the Redeemer—Jesus of Nazareth—were about to become enmeshed in the worst tribulation the world would ever see. And after that much of mankind would be reduced to a vast sea filled with tortured immortal beings immersed in primordial fire that would burn for a very long time. The Devil would be defeated by the King of Kings and after 1000 more years those who hate the light will be cast into outer darkness—at the edge of the Universe where the furnace of the first instant of time meets the lightlessness of utter nothingness. And that region would be inhabited by weeping and wailing and gnashing of teeth, and the smoke of their torment will spew forth after that continuously throughout the ages.

The anti-Christ would usher in the dictatorial mandates clothed in silken words those earthlings loved words so. Like fine actors on a great stage, all the kings of earth would take their marks and utter the proper lines as if Satan had said them himself. Like malignant horns of terror, his secret rule and unrelenting hate would systematically gore humanity, far and wide, over the entire face of the earth. In a few Earth years would come the great disillusionment. And there was absolutely no power on earth that could stop him.

Over the centuries since the first flood that destroyed dinosaurs and the flesh of the Satanic forces and all other life on the surface of the planet, from this world at the interface between physical and spiritual universes, these eternal spiritual personalities had projected terror onto the surface of earth. The battle had been fought over human souls for more than 6000 years, and it was almost over. After the sacrifice of the Lamb of God, these bodiless, other intelligences had concentrated on keeping man from the truth of the Cross and had battled God's servants in Christ, using powerful minds from their secret world. But, for 2000 years they had been restrained from all they would shortly do—now the restraint had been lifted.

The Master of Deception sat, pondering these things. Behind him, like a strange giant outcropping of black shining rock, a pointed pillar jutted, thronelike, and behind that the creature's thick tail constantly shifted, scraping the ground, making a sound like sandpaper moving across granite.

And then the ancient thoughts came to the Son of the Morning's heart once more: *I will ascend to heaven; above the stars of God. I will set my throne on high; I will sit on the mount of assembly in the far North; I will ascend above the heights of the clouds. I will make myself like the Most High.*

To a great many people on earth in the last skeptical years of the twentieth century, an invisible world battling for human destinies was beyond comprehension. The existence of Other intelligences outside the confines of the physical universe was unthinkable to many modern teachings, and even a subject for intellectual ridicule and physical punishment at the turn of the century. With infinite arrogance and cold calculation, the most modern of men and women ranged to and fro over the earth, seeking pleasure, and knowledge abounded. They knew so much and yet none of it was truth.

Even after the Great Disappearance, the pitiful intelligence inside billions of human minds failed to grasp the meanings in the Bible and in nearly forgotten legends: That a parallel world, populated by powerful disembodied beings existed in the earth and in the blackness of space near the earth, and that the hidden evil ones populating these domains regarded the surface world and all those on it with a hideous, cunning hatred.

Like a certain tick in some divine clockwork, the short season alloted to the Wicked One for the incarnation of his son had come and the power of darkness was upon the earth. And even now, as the remote gleams of fire in the sky appeared to increase their brilliancy and shine full force upon the ground over the night-girdled half of the world, the greatest of Satan's diabolical plans was being carried forward by the Powers of Darkness. An unimaginable enchantment was being brought against the earth, so that many in that vast herd of mankind, who had remained because they had refused to accept the truth and protection of the blood of Christ, would continue to believe a Lie and suffer eternal damnation.

And in the pit, Satan dreamed of all the souls he and his dark legions of evil creatures would take with them for the rest of eternity to the realm of the hot, blue-flamed lake, where there would be torture of unquenchable burning and sounds of unspeakable horror wrapped in soundless night.